ELLA

A Novel

DIANE RICHARDS

AMISTAD

An Imprint of HarperCollins*Publishers*

ELLA. Copyright © 2024 by Diane Richards. All rights reserved. Printed in the United States of America. No part of this book may be used or reproduced in any manner whatsoever without written permission except in the case of brief quotations embodied in critical articles and reviews. For information, address Harper-Collins Publishers, 195 Broadway, New York, NY 10007.

HarperCollins books may be purchased for educational, business, or sales promotional use. For information, please email the Special Markets Department at SPsales@harpercollins.com.

FIRST EDITION

Designed by Janet Evans-Scanlon
Title page art by Alex/stock.adobe.com
Part opener art © tannujannu/stock.adobe.com and by Alex/stock.adobe.com

Library of Congress Cataloging-in-Publication Data has been applied for.

ISBN 978-0-06-333865-4

24 25 26 27 28 LBC 5 4 3 2 1

To my beloved father,
Bruce Walton Richardson

"Just don't give up trying to do what you really want to do.
Where there is love and inspiration, I don't think you can go wrong."
Ella Fitzgerald

ELLA

Prologue

Ella Fitzgerald's sweating hands were icy, and perspiration kept breaking out on her forehead. She tried to dab at the sweat with a handkerchief, smearing her makeup, which left brown streaks on the white linen.

She felt her throat constricting, and now she was terrified that she wouldn't be able to open her mouth to sing.

She'd agreed to appear on *Toast of the Town*, a brand-new show hosted by an awkward young man named Edward Sullivan, on a tiny moving picture screen called "television."

She'd never done anything like this before.

It was a time of hope and possibility. None of them—neither Ella, nor Ed, nor television itself—had grown into what they would soon become. They all had a sense that something more, something bigger, was on the horizon, and they just had to figure out how to reach it.

But it was also a time of terror.

Ella would be performing in front of an all-white audience, and it would be live.

"But you always sing for a live audience," her manager, Norman Granz, reminded her, but this time was different. This wasn't just a stage show or a club where she could read her audience and connect with them—throw her head back, snap her fingers, and bop—see the audience swaying in their seats or dancing in the aisles.

Today she'd be performing in a studio, staged and static, and she would become a moving picture that would appear on thousands of television sets all across America; and once it was done and broadcast over the airways, it could never be undone.

Perhaps this audience wouldn't like the way she looked or sounded. She remembered what happened with Jackie Robinson. He'd broken the "color line" playing with the Brooklyn Dodgers and he and his family had been cursed and shoved at the games. Would this happen to her? She would be mortified. She would sink through the floorboards. She prayed there would be just one colored person out there in the dark. Then she could just focus on him. People often talked about the racism in the South but she knew all too well that there was a Jim Crow North that wanted nothing to do with the likes of her.

"Stop worrying," Norman kept telling her. She didn't know where he was now. Maybe he'd gone to get coffee or maybe to the bathroom. Right now she was all alone. There'd been a technician in the room a moment before, and the makeup woman who had turned up with makeup too light for her, but they were gone now. "It's going to be great. You'll see," Norman had said. But that's how he was, always an optimist. And even though he championed Negro artists, he was still white. He couldn't understand.

She smoothed her dress, bought yesterday, black satin from Saks Fifth Avenue.

She nearly fainted when she saw a slight smear of makeup on the fabric. She brushed at it with her handkerchief, and luckily it disappeared. This was a beautiful designer dress, tailored for her just that morning; and she had pearls around her neck and crystal earrings dangling from her ears. She'd made it to the big time. She had nothing to be afraid of. This was what she'd wanted all her life—to be treated like she was worthy of the best and to feel like she deserved it. This was what her mother had dreamed of for her. *Oh Mama,* she thought, *I sure wish you could see your little girl now.*

She'd gone into Saks and just inside the door she'd been stopped by the doorman and asked if she knew where she was. But Norman had made it right and she was wearing that dress right now. She swung her head to feel the earrings touch the sides of her neck.

Thinking about her mother made her also think about last night, lying on the pristine white sheets of the Waldorf Astoria. "I'm going to put you up in the Presidential Suite," Norman had said. "You're a princess. You deserve this. You deserve all the best things in life." The suite had been enormous, the French provincial furniture daunting and luxurious, but the memory that stuck with Ella now—the memory that circled around her like an agitated bird—was the smell of those bedsheets, fresh and full of sunshine. How had the hotel made sheets smell like sunshine? Ella had washed enough sheets, and she'd never heard of this before.

She wished she could tell her mother.

But she couldn't.

Instead she sat on a surprisingly hard vinyl chair in the greenroom of *Toast of the Town*, about to be broadcast live into thousands of homes, mostly white, and she could hear Ed Sullivan talking to the crowd, and her mother would know nothing of this.

Then Norman came back, self-assured and handsome, with his lantern jaw and impossible grin. And white. And carrying a teacup for her. She hadn't even asked, but he'd known anyway that she'd want it. "Here ya go, sweetheart," he said, and she thanked him, took the cup gratefully. Black tea with lemon. She began warming up her voice, sipping on the tea.

"You're gonna be great," he was saying, and then saying other things but she wasn't listening. She wished she'd had her nails done. The crowd wouldn't notice. But they would notice if she was frightened or nervous or vulnerable.

The past years of touring had taught her how to just stare above the heads of the crowd if she doubted herself. And she was going to look for that one colored person if she got scared.

The crowd roared a response to something Ed Sullivan said, and her throat closed up. She knew she'd forget the words. She knew the white people would laugh at her. "This ain't nothing," she told herself, thinking back, as she often did, to her very first performance, years ago now, at the Apollo Theater. "If you can survive contrary colored folks, you can do anything." She shook her head. "Now go head on. You been through a lot worse than this, girl."

This was true. She had been through a lot worse.

But, right then, it was as if she could draw a line, plot a chart, connect the misery from those terrible days after what happened to her mother right through those terrible years before the Apollo. The path would lead her here, to this moment. To this high cliff she now stood upon.

She would have to take the next step, march off the cliff's edge, and hope that the clouds below would be enough to hold her up.

Or perhaps they wouldn't.

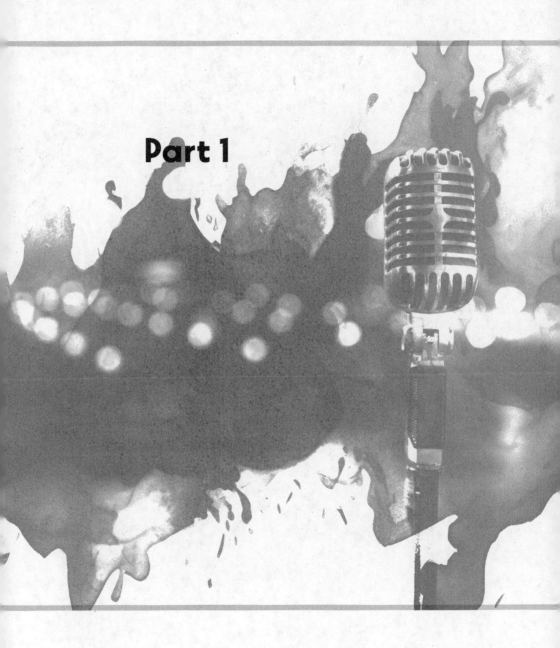

Part 1

1

The Last Glimpse

Tempie, Yonkers, January 14, 1932

Ella was in the living room when her mother Tempie got home. Connee Boswell's "Concentratin' (on You)" was blaring from the phonograph, the melody effervescent, making Ella's fingers twitch even before she'd started dancing. Ella was showing her sister Frannie a fun Charleston step when her mother hauled in two stuffed gray laundry sacks, their ends bunched tight with twine.

"You two have a good day?" her mother asked, rubbing where the string had bitten into her palms. Frannie vaulted to the doorway to give their mother a hug, and Tempie bent over her for a moment, rubbing Frannie's back.

Ella, always more reserved, hung back. "It was okay," she said.

"Just okay?"

Ella shrugged. "Yeah. Just okay." She was swaying to the music. She couldn't get enough of music; she wanted to devour it. She loved the boneless feeling the bass gave her, how she could lose herself, physically, inside it. Sometimes she didn't even realize she was tapping her feet or hands to the rhythm, or rocking slightly, side to side, in time with the beat.

"I'm not raising you girls right. When you see your mama come in the door, you stop dancing and come and help her." Tempie gestured at Ella. "Turn off that music and take these bags."

Ella turned off the phonograph and dragged the laundry sacks across the floor toward the kitchen.

"Pick those up. Don't let them drag," Tempie said.

Ella lifted them only slightly, straining under the weight.

"Did either of you start dinner?" Tempie often asked this, but neither Ella nor Frannie were good cooks. Both girls shook their heads.

Ella dropped the bags by the fire escape. Her mother was opening the icebox, pulling out potatoes, ham hocks, and collard greens. Ella edged around her, heading back to the phonograph.

"You can help me make dinner," Tempie said.

Ella glared at her. "Can we just finish the record?"

"Connee Boswell won't put food on this table."

"But you love listening to Connee Boswell." Nothing could be that wrong in the world, Ella felt, as long as they had music and dancing.

"Frannie, go in your room. I need to talk with your sister."

Frannie pouted and stomped off.

"And close the door," Tempie called after her. Then to Ella, "Come in here and sit down so we can talk proper."

She stood at the sink washing potatoes, then put them in a bowl, and sat down at the table with a knife to peel them. Her shoulders slumped; the edge of the kitchen table bit into her forearms as she leaned over the bowl. The light from the fire escape gleamed off the back of her head, and she suddenly seemed older, more exhausted than Ella remembered. But then she straightened, pointed for Ella to sit across from her, handed her a peeling knife. "I want to look you dead in the eyes. I will only say this once, and I don't want no back lip."

Ella sat down, her toes still keeping time to the big band swing in her head. Charles would love this step. She moved her hips from side to side in the chair.

"Stop that damn wiggling." Tempie passed her a potato. Her mother often sounded harried and put-upon, always exhausted, so Ella was used to this tone, used to "serious talks." *You need to help out more around the house. You need to mind Frannie for me.* Ella did her best, but she also wanted to dance—she was good at it. Sometimes she only felt alive when she was buried in the music, her whole body pulsing with the bass and the trumpets and the lyrics.

"You act like you don't understand how hard it is to put food on the table," her mother said.

"I help," Ella said, knife digging into her potato. After all, she gave her mother the seventy-five cents she earned weekly with Charles.

"I know you do," Tempie said. She put one damp hand over Ella's. A potato peel curled on her wrist. "But we need steady money. They're raising the rent again and things are gonna get worse."

"What's Joe doing?"

"You mean your father? He does what he can." But she didn't meet Ella's eyes. Joe Da Silva, her mother's husband, performed odd jobs around the neighborhood, acting as a part-time chauffeur in the winter and digging ditches in the summer. Other times he swept up and cleaned in a local welding shop, or in other local businesses, but his work was irregular. Ella didn't know where he went when he didn't work, but today he wasn't home.

Later, Ella wondered if her mother had been embarrassed—both for herself and for Joe. Tempie never admitted it, but she'd been the provider all along.

Tempie said, "We need to keep a roof over our heads and food on the table. You need to help out more."

"I can dance more," she said. "I could maybe go on Thursdays, too. And both weekend nights."

"You're not going to dance for a while. You're going to work with me."

"I—" Ella started, but her mother talked over her.

"I got you a steady job for after school and on the weekends. This is a good opportunity for you. I had to talk to a lot of people and call in favors to make it happen."

"But—"

"I need you to do this," Tempie said, forcing Ella to meet her eyes. "It means regular weekly money. More than you can make dancing." Tempie sat back a moment. "I have always supported you and your dreams of dancing, but you need to have something else going for you. Get some skills you can use if all that shuffling don't work out."

Ella found herself on her feet, eyes stinging. The potato sat brown and half-peeled in her bowl. "Me and Charles just entered the Lindy Hop contest over at the Troubadour. We paid for it. Twenty-five cents each. If we win, I'll make us money. A lot of money."

"It won't be enough, and we can't count on it. Sit down." Tempie gestured with her knife to the seat. "I told you I didn't want no back lip. You act like a wild pig running up and down this house every time I ask you to do something."

"But you promised me that I could dance!" For years, ever since she was small, her mother would whisper to her, "You can be anything you want to be. You want to be a dancer? Then dance. The world can be what you make of it." Now a life of scrubbing laundry like her mother unfolded before Ella, and that was no life she wanted to live.

"I know, baby," her mother said. She'd peeled five potatoes to Ella's one. "It's just that things have gone from bad to worse this time. You need to help."

Ella didn't understand. She could make much more money dancing than she could scrubbing some white man's undershorts. And what was Joe doing anyway? Shouldn't he be earning the money? "You promised," she said, and her voice came out as a shriek. "You promised I could dance! What about all your promises about 'never quitting'?"

Last year Tempie had given Ella a poem that she'd copied in red ink on a piece of lined paper. "Keep Going," it was titled, and it ended with the line, "You mustn't quit."

"Sometimes things ain't so easy," Tempie said. "I'm not saying you won't dance no more. Just that right now I need you to bring in steady money. Steadier money than your dancing can bring in."

"But I have to keep learning new steps!" Ella said. "There's always new steps and the good dancers know all of them! If I don't keep dancing I'll get behind and never catch up! Never!"

"Sit down," her mother said, slapping the flat of her hand on the table. "No back talk. Folks being put out they homes. Fighting in the streets for jobs. I need you to help your mama. I fought to get this job for you. Don't let me down. Please."

If only. Later, forever after, her mother's words would ring in her memory. That "please" would echo in her memory, and take on a gravity like another sun, pulling the tides loose from their shores. But right then, Ella twisted her face and huffed, "I ain't taking no job in the laundry. I'm gonna dance."

"You gonna help your mama." Tempie's words were precise, clipped, thin as the potato peels. "From now on you will go to school and after school you will work in the laundry with me. We have to survive. We can't rely on soup lines. There ain't nobody but us." She rubbed her eyes, weary. So weary, Ella would think later. All these signs, all these portents, and Ella didn't have the eyes to see.

Her mother sighed. "You're my pride and joy, Ella. Please do this for me."

But Ella couldn't hear her words. "I won't," she said again.

This woman, darker than most other mothers, had embarrassed her at school when she'd appeared outside her classroom dressed like help, carrying an umbrella for Ella because it was pouring outside. This woman had told her to dance for a better life, had promised that Ella wouldn't have to live like a domestic, a maid, a laundress, had filled Ella's head with dreams that she could rise above the squalor in Yonkers, had bought her music and a phonograph, had beamed when Ella had danced, had applauded when Ella sang.

All of it was a lie.

"I ain't gonna be like you," Ella screamed. "I ain't gonna do laundry for a living! That ain't gonna be me!"

"So you raising your voice now." Tempie pulled out her leather belt, bunched it in two. "Your Aunt Virginia told me I was going too easy on you. She was right. You need to think about someone other than yourself."

Ella backed away toward the living room.

"Where you going?" Tempie stood, too, dropping the potato and the knife with a clang in the bowl. "Get over here."

"You're just a—" Ella struggled to find a word—"just a—a no-body. Working in white women's basements. Cleaning their clothes. I want—"

In a movement swifter than Ella had anticipated, her mother snatched her arm, holding her fast. The belt whistled through the air, and walloped loud and sharp, as Tempie lashed it hard against her legs.

At first Ella couldn't feel the physical pain, so deep was her outrage and fury. She stared at her mother with all the hatred she could muster, willing with all her might that her stare would kill her mother right there before her eyes. The more she stood, refusing to cry, the harder her mother whipped her: three, four, five blows.

"You dare to 'spute my word." Now Tempie swung the belt over her head, lashed Ella's arms and back.

Ella was rigid, determined to withstand this. She had a volcano sizzling within her for what she wanted to be: a dancer, free to be anything other than what her mother was. She would not cry. She would not flinch.

Finally, Tempie put down her belt. She had tears on her cheeks, or perhaps it was sweat. She levered herself back into her chair, her fingers whitening as she gripped the edge of the table. Ella tried to imagine all the hateful things she could call her mother but instead she thought, over and over: *I wish you were dead.*

"This will be your last week dancing," her mother said. "You'll start at the laundry with me on Monday."

Ella didn't answer.

She didn't look at Tempie as she marched out of the room and into the tiny bedroom she'd shared with Frannie. Didn't speak to Frannie, either, who was staring over at her with eyes wide. Ella lay fully clothed on their bed, covered herself in the thin blanket as if to shut out the world, and shoved her rage and sorrow into a vault, a tight safe. She refused dinner, lay in bed without coming to the table or acknowledging her mother or stepfather, when he got home. When Frannie tried to speak to her, she turned her face to the wall.

She'd never forgive her mother, she vowed.

Never ever.

The next morning, from her bedroom, Ella heard her mother singing "Down Hearted Blues," her favorite Bessie Smith tune.

Ella was late for school—her mother had woken her as usual, but Ella refused to budge even when her sister Frannie had grumbled out of their shared bed, packed up her books, and headed out for breakfast. Still Ella lay there, listening, despite herself, to her mother singing—singing!—from the kitchen.

> *It may be a week*
> *It may be a month or two*
> *But the day you quit me, honey*
> *It's comin' home to you*

As usual, the relentless stench of soaking laundry, acrid with grated lye, soap, and bleach, surged into the rest of the apartment. But the stink wasn't the issue. Ella was used to that. The issue was her mother: Ella hated her, hated how she looked, hands red and face squeezed tight over those pots on the stove, hated the memory of the beating she'd taken and could still feel all over her body.

She knew her best friend Charles would be waiting for her to walk to school, and it was cold outside, so Ella finally shifted on the mattress, her back and shoulders stinging from last night's belt. When she uncurled from the bed, her calves throbbed with each step. Gingerly Ella slid into her school clothes. Tempie's singing rang through the apartment. It was melodic, Ella allowed. Few people heard Tempie's voice, locked up as it was in the kitchen with the laundry and the boiled potatoes. Served her right, Ella thought. Her mother deserved to be trapped in her dead-end world. Ella wanted something better. She'd head out for school right now, without even saying good morning to her. She knew that would hurt her mother, and right now she wanted revenge.

Ella took three steps toward the door, passing the Christmas tree that was shedding a carpet of brown needles across a corner of the living room. She'd almost reached it when her mother called out, "Ella, is that you?"

She could refuse to answer, just open the door and disappear, but instead she said, "I'm gon' be late."

"You get in here," her mother said. "If you got up when I called, you'd have plenty of time. You make *me* late."

There was no escape. "But I'm gon' be late—"

"Stop this nonsense. I need more lye. It's in the bag by the back door."

Frannie was in the living room—she'd already eaten and could easily have gotten whatever her mother needed, but no, Ella had to do it. As usual. In the meantime Frannie was making a big show of wrapping her textbooks in one of Joe's leather book straps that he'd made during his stint working at a tannery. Frannie didn't offer to get the lye, even though she was right there.

So Ella headed back to the tiny kitchen. The humidity smacked her as soon as she slipped through the doorway. Now her combed hair would nap up. The kitchen was little more than a bump-out extension of the living room: one wall of cabinets, with a sink and small stove on one side, and on the other a small table that barely fit the four of them.

As Ella had envisioned, her mother was bent over the washtub next to the sink, raking the sheets over the washboard. On the stove, cast-iron cauldrons of water bubbled and rattled like living things, desperate to escape.

If only. These two words would haunt Ella for years, would send her bolting from sleep, breath locked in her throat; would tap her shoulder almost companionably, and then throttle her when she turned to look. If only she'd knelt down next to her mother, dunked her hands, too, in that scorching water. *Here, Mama,* she could have said, *Let me do it for you. You sit back now and rest a minute.* There were hundreds, thousands, of words that Ella might have said that morning—that she imagined, later, she'd said. If only she'd said them. If only she'd acted differently.

Instead she said nothing, last night's bruises burning where her blouse rubbed them. She was still so angry that she had decided to forgo breakfast, but now she could smell the richness of her mother's just-baked cornbread hovering above the laundry smells. She reconsidered. Maybe just a small piece. She veered around the washtub and over to the back door that led to the fire escape. The container of Red Devil Lye lay on its side, some of the white powder spilling onto the laundry sack. The horned, grinning demon on the cover seemed to wink at her as she picked it up.

When she handed the lye to her mother, Tempie grimaced as she straightened, wincing with a grunt. She was tall, broad-shouldered, with dark amber skin, and a low, ringing laugh on the rare occasions that Ella heard it. Above high cheekbones, her eyes looked exhausted.

A few years back her mother had gotten into a car accident, and although she seemed fine, she often said that her back ached, or her ribs, or sometimes her hips. She had trouble standing sometimes. Maybe, Ella thought, her back was troubling her today.

Despite yesterday, Ella found herself saying, "Mama, you alright?" The soap fumes, bubbling up on the stove, sucked up the air.

"Of course I'm alright," her mother said, pressing the small of her back and then bending back over the washtub, sprinkling in the lye. "Why you ask me that? What you gon' do if I'm not alright?"

Ella never forgot those words, but in that moment she regretted that she'd asked.

She slid over to the counter, toward the cornbread covered with a dish towel, and cut a larger piece than she'd originally intended, pulled it from the pan. It was golden, deliciously warm.

"You remember what we talked about?" her mother said. "You be back by four today."

Her mother didn't have to say it again, didn't have to gouge the wound even deeper. "I know," Ella said. She cut a second, even bigger, piece of cornbread while her mother wasn't looking.

"I don't want to be chasing you all over the streets tonight."

Tonight would be one of the last nights that she and Charles would perform dance routines in local Yonkers clubs: seventy-five cents each to entertain the crowd. Ella lived for dancing, and this was good money for a fifteen-year-old. But apparently not good enough for her mother.

"Fine," Ella said, flouncing out of the kitchen.

"Make sure you put on your winter boots and wrap up," her mother called after her. "Put on that wooly hat your daddy bought you. Frannie, you bundled up good?"

"You know I don't like that hat," Ella said; and her sister, who'd been lurking by the door waiting for Ella, yelled out, "Yep, I'm wearing my gloves, too."

"Glad one of you has sense," Tempie said. "That's how you catch cold. Trying to be cute with your head uncovered and your legs showing."

"Okay," Ella said.

"Bye, Mama," Frannie called out. "Love you!"

"See you later," Ella said. She grabbed her wooly hat from the wall hook and jammed it on her head. She would stuff it in her pocket as soon as she turned the street corner.

Afterward she was glad that she'd taken it, glad that she followed the last request her mother ever made of her. If only she'd said "I love you," the way that Frannie had done. But she didn't. Instead she closed the door behind her, never knowing if her mother answered; or what she had said if she did. Forever after, she imagined turning back into that hellish cavern of a kitchen, hugging her mother tight around the waist; imagined hearing her mother's "Love you" float out into the winter morning like a benediction. *If only.*

She opened the door to the bitter January sunlight, turning briefly to look behind.

And that was her last glimpse of Tempie alive—bent over a hot wash basin, arms submerged.

Outside, the few inches of snow had melted into a dirty scum. Sure enough, Charles Gulliver was waiting for her on the sidewalk. She could tell he'd been there for a while.

Ella couldn't tell him about the beating, about what her mother had said last night. She couldn't bear to speak the words, as if saying them out loud would make them truer.

Frannie ran ahead, met up with her best friend Maisie. Charles chattered on about dance practice, about the Troubadour that weekend, and would they be able to practice tomorrow all day. Ella trudged silently along next to him, kicking at frozen slush balls, not wanting him to know that her dancing days were over.

2

The Bitterness of Lic-O-Rice

January 15, 1932

Ella didn't like math much, but was good at it, so she knew she didn't really have to pay attention. Instead she tapped her feet beneath her desk in geometry class, imagining the routines that she and Charles would practice after school. They were focusing on the Lindy Hop's "Chase into the Tandem." The last time they'd performed, she'd fumbled the timing. They'd drill down the steps this afternoon at his house, until she had to be back home for dinner.

She dreaded telling Charles that he would be losing his dance partner—kept hoping that if she ignored thinking about last night, about her fate at the laundry, it would just go away.

She'd lose Charles, too. She just knew it. When Charles looked down at her, he made her feel beautiful and feminine. He was growing tall and broad-shouldered, and every once in a while would look at her a little differently: a leaning-in, a softening around his jaw, that made her feel special. She'd imagined that one day they could be a famous dance couple, in love on and off the dance floor. Now she wouldn't even see him regularly.

Only last week he'd held her hand as they'd walked past a group of girls in the hall, and Myra Johnson had stared at her extra long, as if she hadn't known who Ella was before then. Myra always wore her skirt a little too high and would sidle up to boys and bat her eyes in a way that Ella thought looked silly. The boys seemed to like it, though, and were always hovering around her, laughing at whatever she said. Myra, blank faced, glared at Ella as Charles held her hand and talked to her about the weekend, and Ella wasn't paying attention to Charles, she was feeling the pressure of Myra's stare and enjoying it immensely. It was about time Ella had a boyfriend. Charles had never tried to kiss her but maybe sometime he might try.

Now he'd be looking for a new dance partner. Myra Johnson, or Kelly Hayes. Ella thought that both girls were prettier than she was, with lighter skin and longer hair. They seemed to glide when they walked, as if on casters. Ella struggled to walk without feeling gawky.

She never felt gawky dancing in Charles's arms, though. When she was dancing, she felt like she belonged. And there was that syncopated twist that she wanted to get right tonight. She knew if she kept a little more tension in her elbow and pushed back into her left foot that she—

"Ella?" She didn't immediately hear Mrs. Beckley call her name. Her feet were shuffling under her desk, trying to get the step right. Was it toe-ball-heel, or ball-toe-heel? "Ella."

She looked up. Mrs. Beckley—the whole class—was watching her. Mrs. Pierce, the secretary from the office, had come in and was staring at her, too. Their eyes on her were like feathers, wispy and faintly prickling.

"You need to go to the front office," Mrs. Beckley said. "Get your things."

Fear slithered in like cold, so faint she didn't feel it immediately, only gradually becoming aware that it was wrapping itself around her. She barely remembered grabbing her geometry book, following Mrs. Pierce's wide derriere out of the room and down the hall to where a man in a uniform waited for her.

A policeman. Now her fear was an ice pick, its chill stabbing into her; she was trembling. Mrs. Pierce was saying, "This is Officer Rocco. You need to go with him." She helped Ella on with her coat, her gloves, her wooly hat. Ella couldn't ask what had happened.

The officer was in his mid-thirties, with a mustache and big teeth. He seemed uncomfortable. "Please come with me. We're going to see your father," he said, and then, "You want a Life Saver?" He held out a silver roll of them. The top flavor was Lic-O-Rice.

Ever after, she hated the taste of licorice.

Officer Rocco offered her his hand. And even though she was fifteen and not a child anymore, she took it. His hand was warm and comforting.

"We're going to get your sister," he said after they were outside. Frannie was at the middle school down the street.

Finally, Ella found her voice. "What happened?"

"We're going to your father," he repeated, not answering the question. They descended the stairs and turned left, trudging through puddles of slush.

The licorice's sickly sweetness flooded her mouth like bile.

"What's going on?" she asked again. Her fear was everywhere now, she was breathing it in with the cold rawness of the slush and the winter afternoon.

Officer Rocco didn't respond, seemingly intent on keeping his leather shoes dry. In a few moments they were at Frannie's school. Inside, Ella huddled against the wall as the policeman went into the office, closing the door behind him. She snuck over, put her cheek on the smooth cool wood, listening, but could only hear the murmur of their voices.

Moments later the door opened and she snatched herself back. A secretary slipped up the corridor, returning a few minutes later with Frannie.

Ella's sister was slightly plumper than Ella; she usually sported a wide grin and loved to stick her tongue out at adults when they weren't looking. Now she seemed as frightened as Ella felt.

"Why are we here?" she asked Ella.

Officer Rocco answered instead, "I'm taking you to your father."

"That's all he'd tell me," Ella muttered to her. She grabbed Frannie's hand, who squeezed twice. Ella squeezed back. She was still terrified, but now with Frannie here she found the courage to announce, "My daddy's at work. He don't get off till five-thirty." Joe wasn't her real father, but everyone called him her daddy.

Officer Rocco just said, "Come along, girls" again, and they were outside, and the cold January sun was glaring.

None of them found more words. The Life Saver had dissolved, and the aftertaste lingered, pungent on Ella's tongue. Frannie clutched her hand, and even though they both were wearing gloves, their grip was so tight that the knuckles of their fingers ground painfully together. The sound of their feet on the melting snow took on a hypnotic quality, the repetitive rhythm of a snare drum.

Ella thought of possibilities, trying to figure out what was going on. Had there been an accident? Had the apartment caught fire? Had

Ella done something wrong and the school had found out—if so, what could it be? She played hooky a lot but they didn't call a policeman for that, did they? Why were they going to her father and not her mother? Her mind spun.

He led them up School Street and then beyond their apartment building without stopping. "Wait," Ella said, "this is where we live."

The sun had disappeared into the clouds. The tired brick buildings were bleak and ominous.

"I'm actually taking you to—" he reached into a pocket, pulled out a small notepad—"to Irene Gulliver's. You know Mrs. Gulliver, right?"

"Yes, of course," Ella said. "She's my friend Charles's mother." Ella was entirely confused. She'd left Charles back in the geometry classroom. She couldn't understand why they were going to his mother's house without him. There must be some mistake. Perhaps they meant to get Charles instead of Ella and Frannie. She wanted to ask but thought that Officer Rocco would think she was ignorant, so she held her tongue.

The brief trek next door to the Gullivers' seemed endless. Again, they didn't speak. Ella wasn't sure what to say.

"We'll be there in a bit, girls," the policeman said, as if they didn't know where they were. He hit the buzzer and the door opened immediately, without Mrs. Gulliver saying, "Who's there?" over the intercom like she usually did. As if she'd known who'd be buzzing.

As they came off the elevator, she stood waiting for them in the open doorway, tall and strong, with a scarf over her hair. "Come in, girls, come in," she said. "I made you bread pudding."

"He said he's taking me to my father," Ella said. "Where's Mama?"

Mrs. Gulliver looked at Officer Rocco. Ella desperately wanted to know and never wanted to find out what that look meant. She felt lightheaded, clutched Frannie's hand even tighter. "When will my father be here?" she tried again.

"I want my mama," Frannie said.

Mrs. Gulliver said. "Come on in, girls. I know you both must be hungry."

They said goodbye to Officer Rocco and trooped in. Without Charles or his sister Annette—they both were still at school, of course—the apartment seemed too silent. Pictures of Jesus, palms up and bleeding, stared mournfully down at her. Tiny Victorian figurines whirled on shelves. The white couch was carefully covered with plastic. Ella knew better than to sit on it. She headed to the small linoleum table in the kitchen, where she and Charles often did homework. Sometimes they sat in the living room because the space there was bigger and they could move the armchair out of the way and "take a break"—Charles's words—to practice dance steps when they were tired of homework. Ella didn't feel like dancing. Her legs were shaking and she felt like she was going to be sick.

Mrs. Gulliver set a bowl of bread pudding in front of each of them. Eating came easily to Ella; she ate when she was nervous, anxious, upset, bored. She'd heard of people losing their appetites, but that had never happened to her, and it certainly didn't happen now. The light reflected solemnly off the pudding's surface, and she dug in with her spoon, grateful that the sweetness obliterated the Life Saver's aftertaste. Frannie watched her eat, but Frannie only dipped the spoon into the bowl and took it out again, never putting it in her mouth. Ella cleaned out her bowl and eyed Frannie's.

Finally the buzzer sounded. Again, Mrs. Gulliver let the person in without asking who it was. The girls followed her, leaving Frannie's pudding and the spoons on the kitchen table. Mrs. Gulliver opened the door as Joe Da Silva lumbered up the hall.

Frannie ran to him and hugged him hard. Her head barely came to his chest. Joe stared at Ella, said nothing.

"Where's my mama?" Ella demanded.

"Hospital," Joe said, coming inside the apartment. His broken English and heavy Portuguese accent made his speech difficult to understand. Ella could decipher maybe half of what he said. Only her mother seemed able to clearly communicate with him.

"I want to see her! Let's go."

"No oose," he said.

Oose? What was "oose"? "What do you mean?" Ella's voice was shrill.

"No oose," he tried again.

This time she understood. "No use? What do you mean there's no use?"

"She's gone, baby," Mrs. Gulliver said. She leaned over as if to embrace her but Ella shook herself free. "Ella, come here, baby."

Ella backed away from them and stood in the middle of the living room as if afraid to be too close. The walls contracted to pinpoints. Outside a siren wailed.

She looked from Mrs. Gulliver to Joe, who people could say was her daddy from now till forever. It would never be true. She just wanted her mother. "Gone?" she said. "What? Gone?"

"Dead," Joe said. His goatee quivered. His cheekbones were high and pale. Tears welled in his eyes.

Her world closed in even further. "What did you do to her?"

"She dead," Joe repeated.

"She's dead?" Ella repeated. "What do you mean?" Some terrible part of Ella had expected this. The secrecy, the policeman, the calling of Joe, not Tempie.

And an even deeper part of her screamed out, remembering her thought the night before. *I wish you were dead.* There it was, manifested, materialized. Tempie was dead. The word was so terrible and so enormous. "She's not dead," she said. "I just saw her. She was washing sheets this morning." Her mother couldn't be gone. How could someone cooking meals, listening to Connee Boswell, fussing at her, scrubbing sheets, be dead? It was impossible. But her mother had winced in pain. *What you gon' do*, her mother had asked her, as if she'd known.

Her mother had told her, "Don't 'spute my word," and Ella had hatefully talked back in her mind. *I wish you were dead.* Ella's thoughts had been unspeakable, blasphemous. Now the realization was ripping into her: as soon as she'd thought those words, she'd cursed her mother, and she'd spited God, who'd commanded, *Honor thy father and thy mother.* She'd cursed herself, too. She deserved every terrible punishment that would come to her.

For years, in quiet moments, Ella would unearth the dark specter that gleamed like obsidian, hard as diamond, immovable as a planet, and she'd hold it out, its mirrored surface reflecting back a sorrow so vast that she could float upon it: *Had she killed her mother?*

"I know, baby," Mrs. Gulliver said. She was twisting her hands in her skirt, looking as if she wanted to stride across the room, but Ella lurched backward, wrapping her arms protectively around her body. She couldn't bear to be touched.

"You never took care of her," she told Joe. She wanted to blame someone—anyone—but herself. "You a white man so you ain't got no excuse for letting my mama down. She worked herself to death taking care of you. I hate you and you ain't my father!"

Her chest felt close to bursting. *It's my fault*, a voice kept repeating. *It's my fault she's dead.*

"Come here," Mrs. Gulliver said, reaching, and Ella took another step away. She was standing far away from them now, near the window. She could go no farther.

Frannie was in Mrs. Gulliver's arms, weeping. Ella stayed where she was, a body's length or more from any of them. Shadows hovered just out of sight.

"Come on now, it'll be alright," Mrs. Gulliver was crooning to Frannie. "Hush there. You need to be strong. Your father needs you now."

"We ain't family," Ella told her, and then to Joe, "I want to see her. I don't believe you. You just don't want us to see her. But nobody's gonna keep me from my mama."

Her stepfather was shaking his head. "She gone," he said. "We go home."

"I'm not going with you," she told him, wrapping her arms more tightly around herself. "Which hospital is she at?"

"We go home," he repeated, and tears brimmed, slid down his cheeks. He wiped them away with the sleeve of his faded gray overcoat. The elbow had worn through and a bit of red wool calico shirt poked out. Ella wanted to rip at the hole, shred the sleeve entirely.

"I'm going to see her," Ella said. She looked around for her own coat. "I'm going to find her."

"Joe, the girls need to see their mother or this is never going to end," Mrs. Gulliver said.

"No, she gone now," Joe said. "You remember her alive," he told Ella. "Come home now." And then, looking at Mrs. Gulliver, he said more gently to Ella: "Please."

Years later, she understood what Joe had wanted for her. He

believed that the living should be with the living. He wanted her last memory of Tempie to be full of color and spirit. Later, Ella understood that he was trying to protect Ella—protect her mother's memory. Later, she'd realize what burdens were on Joe: no steady job, now no reliable income, no close family to help him arrange a decent burial and memorial service. But right then, and for years afterward, she hated him. She needed to see Tempie's body, needed to assure herself that her mother hadn't just left them, hadn't just disappeared.

A commotion started up in the doorway as Charles and Annette burst in. "Mom," Charles said, "You wouldn't believe what—" he stopped, staring at them, and then his eyes caught Ella's. He asked her, "Is everything alright?"

"No," she said. She hugged herself tighter, as if more certain than ever that all the disparate parts of herself—the rage and grief, the sorrow and guilt—would shatter her whole. "Everything's not alright."

Mrs. Gulliver said to Charles, "Mrs. Da Silva passed away." She was still holding Frannie, rocking her back and forth. "Joe, please let the girls stay with us tonight."

Passed away. That phrase, the ring of resignation in it, threatened to undo Ella entirely. *Passed away*: she tried it out in her head, as if it were a foreign language.

"The girls, they come home with me now," Joe said.

Mrs. Gulliver was telling her stepfather that it would be no trouble, that the girls shouldn't be alone, that surely he had much to attend to, that being free of the girls underfoot would only be helpful. Ella couldn't quite hear her, couldn't quite process him standing there, listening to Mrs. Gulliver, considering.

"Okay," he said at last. "The girls, they stay here tonight. Tomorrow morning I come for them." Then to Ella, "No school tomorrow."

Mrs. Gulliver said, "Of course. Let's just give them tonight, okay? And they can come back here anytime. Anytime."

Charles and Annette were still standing by the door. Annette's mouth was open a little. Mrs. Gulliver made plans with Joe, and he went to embrace Frannie. She unglued herself from Mrs. Gulliver and clung to him, weeping. He gestured for Ella, but she stood apart.

After plans were made and set upon, Joe put on his hat and left. Ella leaned over toward the window to watch him, and only then remembered that the window looked out onto a fire escape and the back alley, not their apartment on School Street.

⟶

A few years ago, Tempie had been in a car accident. Some children were playing in the street as a car barreled toward them. She'd leaped into action, pushed the kids to the side, and the car had struck her a glancing blow on her side and back. She'd been black and blue for days, and ever since had winced when she had to carry heavy loads, like the laundry bags. Maybe this accident had somehow killed her. Ella needed to know how she'd died.

She refused to cry. The room now seemed enormous, as if the walls and the plastic-covered white couch were too far away to reach. She wanted to see the body. See for herself that her mother was really "gone." After dinner—food she never remembered eating—she asked Mrs. Gulliver for another helping of pudding, and Mrs. Gulliver filled Ella's bowl. She sat alone in the kitchen, spooning it in mechanically. The sweetness soothed the ache in her, and after some time she started feeling sleepy, still holding the spoon. Mrs. Gulliver guided her to Charles and Annette's room, to a makeshift bed made from folded blankets and extra winter clothes.

Frannie was still sobbing but finally fell asleep. Ella lay next to her, staring up at the ceiling silvered in the reflected glow of the streetlights. Charles had barely spoken to her, as if she were diseased, as if she were a liability (and that voice deep inside her agreed with him: she was a terrible girl, she deserved this). When she was smaller, she'd often stayed over and they'd whispered and laughed until well after midnight, but tonight it was as if she were deaf, or sick. Something to be pitied, but not touched. That, too, was how she felt about herself.

The silence was a weight that pressed her down. If only there were music. She played Louis Armstrong in her head, "Blue Turning Grey Over You," where the singer misses his beloved. For the first time that day, tears warmed the sides of her cheeks. She stared up into nothing. Her mother had loved music. She'd loved how the Boswell Sisters' tight harmonics wrapped around each other. Outside the kitchen, her mother only ever sang in church, loud and unapologetic, raising her voice to the Lord; and Ella next to her would feel her own voice twine with her mother's. She'd been proud of her mother's voice, so rich and assured, so smooth.

Ella thought of the gospel hymn, "Amazing Grace." Quiet, her voice no more than a rumble on her tongue, she whispered the words.

Maybe her mother was happier now. She knew that the church mothers, who always wore white, would tell her, "She's in a better place, child, she's with her Lord." The church ladies were right, no doubt. Any place was better than School Street, with its boiling cauldrons of wash water and the lye burning her hands, and the heavy endless laundry stained with other people's lives. But her mother couldn't have wanted to leave Ella and Frannie.

She didn't even know how her mother had died, except that she'd collapsed at work, at the Silver Lining Laundry. She wondered if her mother had been alone. She hoped someone tried to help her. Did Tempie cry out for Ella?

She imagined her mother's last moments bent over the stewing wash bins of stained sheets, the heat beating against her face. The rolling boil had a rhythm to it, and as Ella lay there in the dark, in this first night of the rest of her life, she pictured her mother, just before she collapsed, mouthing the words to "I Found Million Dollar Baby (In A Five and Ten Cent Store)." She'd heard different versions of the song before, but Miss Fanny Brice's version was all the rage right now. She wasn't sure why she thought of the song, but the melody was in her head and would not leave, a song about unexpected love and spring rain.

She held on to that image of her mother singing, and tried to forget the song that Tempie had been singing when Ella had last seen her, Bessie Smith's "Down Hearted Blues," a song that spoke of weariness and hardship and heartbreak. A life that had never been lived. The price of living had been too high.

Ella squeezed her eyes tight, trying to convince herself that in her last moments, her mother had heard music.

3

Silence, Except for a Sparrow

January 26, 1932

The day after her mother's funeral, Ella woke to silence, except for a sparrow flitting about on the fire escape, chirping earnestly. For an instant she thought she heard the soft brush of her mother's house shoes, but it was only the eerie quiet of total stillness. Her mother should have been mixing pancake batter or cornbread, and preparing Joe's Eight O'Clock coffee if it had been a good week. She would have been humming her spirituals or one of the popular songs she listened to on the phonograph. She should have been calling Ella's name. That was the worst part. No "Ella" from her voice.

It was as if Ella, too, no longer existed.

She lay in bed, waiting for her stepfather to stir, to wake her. The windup alarm clock next to her bed pointed at 6:30, then 6:45. Her mother would have been standing over her by now.

She waited.

Seven o'clock. Joe should have been out of bed. His job unloading shipping containers off a river barge was still new, and she knew that he needed to be at work—he'd gotten two days off to deal with her mother's death, but that was it. Perhaps he'd already left. Perhaps he'd gotten drunk the night before and passed out on the street. He'd torn up the living room a few times over the years, after her mother had lugged his dead weight through the front door. Ella hoped that she wouldn't have to do that. She refused to carry him like her mother had.

Yesterday Ella had stayed away from him, resentment simmering. If he'd only been more help to Tempie—if only they'd all been more help to Tempie—she'd still be alive. Tempie had always been slightly dazzled with him just because he was white. But he'd never pulled his own weight.

Ella had never known her natural father.

Long ago, back in Virginia, William Fitzgerald had left Tempie and Ella when she was three. Soon after, Tempie had taken up with Joe Da Silva, then a gentle Portuguese immigrant who barely spoke English. Tempie never talked about William Fitzgerald's disappearance from their life, and Ella had given up trying to ask questions. Tempie had understood Joe's pidgin English and had given him a home and, eventually, his own daughter, Frannie.

Joe had, over time, become her papa. When she was small, he'd lift her onto his knees, comically try to braid her hair with his thick fingers. He'd take walks with her and sometimes even bought her chocolate ice cream, her favorite. He was a big man and handsome— high cheekbones, glittering smile, broad shoulders. Swarthy, olive-skinned, but white nevertheless. He navigated through the world with white man authority. Their household held more stature be-cause of him. The neighbors deferred to Tempie when they sat out front, and greeted the family with respect on the street and in the neighborhood.

When Ella was a toddler, he'd persuaded Tempie to move from Virginia up to Yonkers, settling them in an Italian neighborhood where he felt at home. Sometimes neighbors would mistake Tempie for Joe's housekeeper; and sometimes, when the family wasn't with Joe, people they didn't know hurled racial slurs at them.

This never happened when Joe was with them.

The breadlines often stretched long down the street, around corners, but their family rarely stood in them. Tempie's regular job at the laundry, supplemented by Joe's more spotty work, paid the bills.

Ella wasn't sure when her relationship with Joe had changed. In the past few years he never braided her hair anymore and only bought her ice cream when he bought it for the rest of the family. She was okay with the changed relationship—she was older now, and had friends—but she missed the loving way he used to grin at her, grab her hand in odd moments, and rub her hair the wrong way. Well, perhaps now that Tempie was gone, in their shared grief Ella and Joe would grow closer again.

At 7:15—now she worried that she and Frannie would be late to school—she tossed back the covers and went in search of him. Joe had told them last night that they'd have to go to school today, and he had to go to work. Life had to go on.

The tiny apartment was dark and cold without Tempie. Even the swish of Tempie's layered skirts as she moved about had created warmth. But no mother had started the stove, no mother made cornbread, no mother boiled hot water for the laundry she'd taken in to earn extra dollars.

Joe was sleeping on one side of her mother's double bed, clutching tightly to her mother's pillow as if trying to hold on to something that wasn't there.

"Hey," Ella said, touching his arm, terrified for a moment that he had died, too. But his arm was warm and he stirred against the sheets. Ella exhaled. "Don't we have to get up?"

He rolled over, opened one eye, mumbled something. She thought he'd said, "Breakfast."

"Aren't you going to make it for us?" she asked. "We've got to get ready for school. We're going to be late."

"You make," he said. "Ten minnit."

"I don't know how to cook," Ella said. "Mama did the cooking."

"You make." He closed his eyes, squeezed the pillow to him.

"I don't know how to make anything," she tried again. "And I have to be in school."

"Do it," he said. He didn't open his eyes, and something about his tone made Ella not want to argue.

He was the adult—he should be the one making breakfast. She only knew how to make simple meals: hominy grits, eggs, toast. Tempie usually prepared the more elaborate breakfasts like cornbread or pancakes, both from scratch. Her mother had always told Ella that she was going to teach her to cook. "Really cook," Tempie would tell her, "the way my mama taught me." But Ella had had no interest in learning. Besides, her mother was usually too exhausted to chase her down and drag her into the kitchen. Still, Ella was willing to try.

With relief she remembered that neighbors had left casseroles and cakes, stews and soups. The tiny icebox was filled, as was the interior of the hulking stove in the corner. More platters glittered on the fire escape, frozen in the January cold. She unwrapped a Depression cake sweetened with raisins and cut out three big chunks. It was dry and crumbly, and they had no butter. No tea, either. Joe liked his Eight O'Clock coffee—they still had a little left—but Ella just stared mistrustfully at the coffee pot. She had no idea how it worked, and wasn't going to try. At twenty-five cents a pound for the coffee beans, she didn't want to mess it up.

Ella grew resentful as she prepared their cold breakfast, banging pots more loudly than necessary on the stove and slamming the cabinets. When Frannie peeped into the kitchen, Ella barked that breakfast wasn't ready yet.

The funeral—closed casket—had been small, as if a shameful secret, and in an unfamiliar storefront church, since Joe didn't have enough money to hold services at the Bethany African Methodist Episcopal Church. The Gulliver family, Tempie's sister Virginia, her daughter Georgie, and a few other friends attended, but many of their neighbors and her mother's acquaintances shied away as if to spare them embarrassment.

Ella, Frannie, and Joe had sat in the front row. The paid minister had droned on about "taken before her time" and "at peace with the Lord." The coffin stretched in front of Ella, but she couldn't fathom her mother lying immobile inside the pine box. She imagined that any minute her mother would yell out that she was trapped, Ella would rush to the coffin and rip off the lid, grab Frannie, and the three of them would tear out of this mistaken world. Her mother could not be dead.

Before she quite realized what she was doing, she was sliding out of the pews and running up to the casket. She was shouting something—"Mama, I'm coming"?—but afterward she couldn't even remember. She was at the casket and trying to pry up the lid before anyone else reacted.

It was nailed shut. Her fingers scrabbled in the seam but couldn't pry it loose.

And then the adults—Joe, the minister, Aunt Virginia—were pulling her away. Aunt Virginia wrapped her arm around Ella and sat with her out in the entryway until she finally grew calm enough to rejoin the service.

At the grave site, as the wind blew stark in her face, a sparrow had hopped about, chirping and looking for seed. It looked so much like the bird that lived on their fire escape, but of course that was impossible. The sparrow had bounced on the frozen grass, glancing one way, tilting its head the other. Ella couldn't stop watching it, how it seemed more alive than she was. The cemetery had smelled of snow, but only a few flakes fell from the dense clouds. The wind buffeted them and Ella dug her fingers deeper into the pockets of her coat. The seams had given way and the inner lining was rough on her fingertips. She huddled close to her sister, bumping shoulders. That was some comfort.

Now, as she banged around in the kitchen, Ella was grateful that Tempie's friends had at least sent condolences in the tangible form of food.

She yelled into the quiet of the apartment, trying to sound like her mother. "Breakfast! Come on, you two! Get up. Time to get going!"

Movement came from the bedrooms, and a toilet flushed. In the meantime, Ella wolfed down her piece of cake, not even tasting it. She put the other two pieces on plates and set them on the kitchen table. Then she cut three wedges from a macaroni, cheese, and hot dog casserole, and wrapped them in scraps of wax paper for their lunches.

Back in her bedroom, Frannie had fallen back to sleep. She'd been sleeping for ten, twelve hours a night in the days since Tempie's passing. "Come on, you gotta get up," Ella told her, pulling out a skirt and blouse for Frannie that her mama had ironed, folded, and left neatly in the bureau. Ella would have to iron now. "I left you a piece of cake. It's on the table."

Frannie sniffed, as if she had a cold. "I want Mama."

"Well you got cake instead." Ella slipped into one of her good skirts, combed her hair with her fingers. It seemed like too much work to brush it. "You'll like it. It has raisins."

Frannie was no longer trying to dress. She was sitting now at the edge of her unmade bed, head down, hands dangling limp between her legs.

"Come on. Get dressed," Ella said.

Frannie didn't move. She was crying, but quietly, and something broke inside Ella. She found herself sitting next to her sister, wrapping her tight, pulling her close. Frannie sobbed into her shoulder. "Why did Mama leave me?" she said, her voice muffled. "What did I do bad?"

"You didn't do anything," Ella said, rocking her now, Ella's own words *I wish you were dead* haunting her even now. "We have to be big girls. We have to get dressed and we have to go to school. You know Mama would want us—" Her voice cracked and she had to take a second to finish. "Want us to go to school."

Although Frannie sometimes left after Ella—Frannie had a friend down the street who she'd meet, and they'd walk together—today Ella waited for her to shrug into her sweater, pull up her socks, and tie her shoes.

"You gotta eat," Ella told her, handing her a piece of the Depression cake, which Frannie held in one hand. "You can eat it on the way."

No way her mama would have let the girls have all that cake, Ella thought, and for a moment the grayness lifted around her.

On their way out, Ella stopped by her mother's bedroom. Joe was where she'd left him, head still under the covers. He'd used the bathroom and returned to bed. "Papa," she said, a name she'd called him until she'd become a teenager and realized he wasn't her real father. Now "Papa" sounded even more distant from her, but she was grasping for someone to hold on to. "I left you a piece of cake on the table. You gonna be late."

He didn't stir, didn't respond.

Frannie slipped past her. "Papa? We're going to school now, okay?"

He rolled over, blinked. "See you," he said. He sounded either asleep or hopeless, or both.

4

You Rascal, You

Late January 1932

The food ran out ten days after the funeral.

Until then, the days unfolded in a grief-addled blur: Ella carving up the neighbors' offerings, then heading to school with Frannie, then heading home in the afternoons. She held herself tightly, avoiding everyone, afraid she'd burst into tears at the first sign of someone's pity.

Joe never mentioned Ella working in the laundry, and Ella didn't remind him. Perhaps he didn't even know. So she'd planned on making additional money by dancing. It was too soon to practice her steps with Charles, too soon to dance at the Yonkers clubs or check out the latest steps in Harlem, but sometime—soon—she'd start up again.

She missed Charles but still wanted to be alone. In the quiet afternoons when she returned from school, she'd sing along to the Victrola, play Louis Armstrong, the Boswell Sisters, trying to escape the gloomy uncertainty of being motherless. In music she recalled Tempie's strong vibrato, her tapping feet, and her world, for a few moments, became solid again.

It wasn't just dancing that Ella loved. It was music. The bebop bounce of jazz, the lushness of the orchestras, the elegance and upbeat charm of ragtime, the broken-hearted despair of the blues: all of it gave her joy. A clarinet playing on a street corner would lift her spirits; the sudden roar of the big bands was guaranteed to send her heart thumping in unison. Although she'd wanted to be a dancer ever since she was small—her mother always encouraged her—singing also came easily. Ella would listen obsessively, over and over, to a single song. The Boswell Sisters became her own favorite, and she practiced all the songs in the hard, swinging Boswell style.

As the days passed, neighbors stopped by, paid their calls, and collected their dishes and trays and platters. One night, when she went to pull out something for supper, the empty icebox terrified her. She didn't understand why Joe hadn't gone shopping, and she worried that he was spending all his wages out drinking. Except for a few bottles of his beer, the shelves yawned vast and desolate. The kitchen cabinets were similar: a half box of oatmeal, a half tin of flour, a few elderly cans of peas. She didn't know what they'd eat. The entire idea of dinner seemed beyond her, impossible as dancing with James Cagney or singing in a movie. She didn't know what she could cook with these ingredients. She had no turnips, cheese, hot dogs, or macaroni, and no money to buy them.

She panicked, wondering about Joe's reaction. He'd always been perfectly civil to her; there was no reason for her to be so worried, but there it was: she was frightened. He hadn't been the same since her mother passed. He seemed frustrated by his inability to communicate, frustrated to be eating leftovers, frustrated that Ella and Frannie weren't Tempie.

She pulled down the cardboard container of Quaker Antique Oats and set them to simmering on the stove, then boiled some potatoes and carrots.

Ella was beginning to have a sense of just how much Tempie had done for them. It should have been obvious but it wasn't, not until suddenly the tasks were undone if Ella didn't do them herself. *I'm so tired,* her mother had said that last night.

Half an hour later, the oatmeal was ready, the potatoes and carrots steaming. It wasn't a great dinner, but Ella was proud of it. She had cooked and set the table like Tempie. She'd decided that she was grown up and could discuss the bills and the rent with Joe that evening.

She'd just finished putting out the food in serving dishes when Joe burst in and shrugged out of his overcoat. He didn't greet her, stomped instead to the icebox and opened one of the last bottles of Columbia Beer. Just a week ago the bottom shelf had been stocked, but now only one bottle remained.

"What this?" he said, looking at the set table.

"It's dinner. I cooked it like Mama. We don't have a lot. I need to go shopping," she explained.

He grabbed a spoon, leaned over the pot of potatoes and carrots, dipped the spoon in, and tasted. He rolled his eyes, spat it out onto a plate, dropped the spoon on the floor.

"I work all day and you feed me this?" He towered over her.

"It's all we have," she said, backing up a step. "We need to go food shopping. Anyway, I don't know what to buy and you didn't give me any money."

"Food taste like—like mud." He gestured but she didn't understand. "You do what Mama do."

"I don't know what she did," Ella said.

That set him back. "You buy," he told her, pulling a handful of coins out of his pocket and slapping them on the table.

"It's too late now," she said. "Stores are closed."

He stared balefully at her oatmeal. "Work hard today. No oatmeal, you hear? Real food."

"Well this is all we have," she said.

He didn't answer, looking instead pointedly at one side of the couch, where a pile of Ella's and Frannie's clothes lay in a heap. "This house a mess. You clean. Like your Mama. It your job now." He kicked their shoes and clothing to the side. "Stinks. This place."

He took one more look at her and at the room, and shambled out of the apartment, slamming the door behind him.

In the sudden emptiness, she glared at the oatmeal, wanting to be mad, but Joe was right. The apartment was a mess. Clothes clumped in the corners, the trash can spilled over, and Tempie's favorite lamp was broken, crouched on the floor in the corner, its shade cracked. She wondered if Joe had broken it.

A year or so ago, her mother had brought the lamp home, so proud of it. "This looks like a Tiffany lamp," her mother had said. "You see the cut of the glass and the different colors?" She trailed her fingers over it, admiring. "It's not a real Tiffany but for me it is. Remember, there's more to life than what you see around here. There are Tiffany lamps."

Until that last night, her mother had always fed Ella's dreams, told her not to give up. There was the "never give up" poem, in red ink, folded next to her bed.

"You're better than me. You gon' be more than a colored laundress," Tempie would tell her, stroking her hair. "You're goin' places 'cause you have talent and I'm telling you so. But talent ain't enough. You have to want it bad. Don't you ever quit trying to make something of yourself."

Ella had grown up hearing this kind of encouragement. Her mother had even ventured out a couple times to local Yonkers clubs to watch Charles and Ella perform. Sometimes she'd even dance with Ella in the living room. Ella remembered one time, several months ago, when Tempie had put Ma Rainey's "Black Cat, Hoot Owl Blues" on the phonograph, raised her skirt, and began swaying back and forth to the blues music. Then, effortless, she swung her hips around and her feet slid into a tap-dance shuffle.

"You think you were the only one who could dance?" Tempie grinned at her. Ella must have looked dumbfounded. "I'll have you know that I was known for my fine legs and my smile." She twitched her skirt. "I had boys and menfolk lined up to dance with me." A shuffle, hop, and ball change. "Bet you had no idea."

"No ma'am," Ella said, and her giggle burst into laughter. Tempie laughed, too, hands on her hips, shaking her head.

The music ended, the needle bumping on the inside track of the record. Her mama lifted the needle off, closed the lid. "Me and your auntie wanted to have what they called a minstrel act. Your grandma would talk on about Scott Joplin and his ragtime piano. We was about your age. We didn't know nothing."

"So you wanted to be a dancer, too?"

"Dance some, sing some," Tempie had said. "I know you want to dance."

Ella nodded, suddenly feeling shy.

"Don't be embarrassed ever about wanting to make something beautiful for the world," her mother had said. "If that's what you want, you got to make it happen. Even if it's hard, and it'll be hard. But if you want it bad, you can do it."

Tempie had promised her the chance to pursue her dreams, and then backed down, gotten Ella a job at the laundry. The feeling of having been betrayed welled up in her all over again.

Still standing in the kitchen, she slid into a time-step-shuffle, just to do it. She would dance—she'd trap her dreams, catch them, and then follow them to the end of her days, just like Mama had promised.

She tried a Lindy Hop shimmy into a grape chain. One of her outstretched hands knocked into a plate that had been left precariously on the edge of the counter. It whizzed back, clanking into other dishes and knocking over a half-filled glass of water.

With new eyes Ella turned to the kitchen, where she'd left the crusted pot of oatmeal. Dishes piled in the sink and on the counter, days-old food scabbing the plates and glassware. The floor was sticky and the air rich with the sweet rot of garbage. There wasn't much soap left to clean with. Without ammonia, vinegar, or lye she couldn't make new soap. She checked in the bathroom and under the kitchen cabinets.

Ella had never envisioned herself sweeping, washing, or ironing, but she realized that was how Joe saw her. She felt unmoored, as if without her mother she'd lost her own identity. She didn't know who she was without Tempie fussing at her, brushing her hair, kissing her, telling her she was pretty.

"You can be whatever you want to be with your dancing self," Tempie would tell her.

Her dancing self would have to clean the kitchen. And Frannie could help.

"Frannie, get out here," she yelled, and when her sister appeared, Ella ordered her to take out the garbage while she tackled the dishes. The next few hours, the girls scrubbed and cleaned. They ate most of the oatmeal, carrots, and potatoes, leaving a serving for Joe, and went to sleep before he came home.

Joe's slam of the door at midnight woke Ella, the thump of his boots on the floor, the rustle of his coat as he flung it somewhere, probably onto the couch. Hopefully he noticed the apartment was now tidy, all the dishes washed and dried and tucked back in their cupboard. Probably he was sorry he yelled at her. Probably he'd come into their room, see if she was awake; or, like he used to do, lay one hand gently on her forehead in apology; or perhaps he'd kiss her forehead, thinking she was asleep.

Instead, he stomped into the kitchen, wheezing and coughing. The floorboards squealed under his weight. He'd gotten heavier lately, and she could often hear him breathing when he performed even simple tasks.

Now in the kitchen, opening the icebox, Ella could hear Joe gurgling down that last beer with the icebox door open. On the stove she'd left him his plate covered with a clean cloth. His belly was probably full of the hot meal he'd have gotten somewhere, a dinner of meat and potatoes, thick bread with butter, and maybe even some chocolate pie for dessert. She wasn't resentful, though. She felt sorry for him. Sorry for herself, too. They both missed her mother.

She knew he wasn't a bad man. Even in her grief she recognized his loneliness, a twin to her own. Her mother had been his lifeline. Tempie had always been the buffer between him and everything else, including her daughters. Despite his hopes that an Italian neighborhood would give him a sense of home and place, it was really

Tempie who gave that to him. She was the connection between him, the bewildering bustle of Yonkers, and the overwhelming customs of America.

In Portugal he'd lived on a farm. His family had two cows, a goat, and dozens of chickens. They made goat's milk cheese. Yonkers was horns blaring and mean brick buildings blotting out the sky.

Joe was at the bedroom door. "Where food?" he said, his voice loud in the dark.

Frannie was asleep, or faking sleep. Joe's voice from earlier in the evening echoed in Ella's ear: *Your job now. Like Mama.*

Ella got up quickly, slid past him, closing the door to the bedroom. In the kitchen she pointed to the plate. "It's right here," she said. "You want me to heat it up for you?"

Now he'd apologize, she thought. He'd say that they would have to forge ahead together. That they were still a family, even without Tempie to nourish and sustain them all.

"It cold," he said and she realized that he was very drunk. "I work hard. Want my hot food."

"I'll heat it up," she said, picking up the food, preparing to put it into pots and warm it on the stove, but whether on purpose or by accident—she never knew—he knocked her hand and sent the plate spinning out of her grasp. The oatmeal made a vicious streak on the linoleum tile. The carrots and potatoes bounced and skittered under the sink.

And the plate shattered, shards everywhere. "You made me drop it!" she yelled at him.

She moved toward the closet to retrieve the broom and he grabbed her arm. "You clean!" He pointed to the floor, as if she didn't see it.

It was the middle of the night. Her mother was dead. Her step-father was drunk. She was fifteen years old. It all seemed too much. The distance between what she'd envisioned for the night—Joe's apology and a moment of bonding—and what had happened felt like two separate realities.

She said instead, "No. I no clean," mocking him, pulling her arm away. His paw clamped onto her arm again, thumb digging hard into her shoulder. His breath was a rasp, hot on her neck.

She yelped and tried to snatch her arm back; he tightened his grip. His fingers pressed against the bone of her arm.

"Let me go," she told him, looking up, staring him down. She could feel him recoil, feel him almost release her. She shook herself free. "Don't you hurt me," she told him, backing up to get the broom. "Mama would never let you hurt me."

He slapped her face—hard. She had turned toward the pantry, so she didn't see the blow coming. She crashed into the stove and the wall. "Your mama not here. This my house," he roared. "You do what I say!"

She held her cheek and glared at him, furious and terrified. Rage and powerlessness brought her to tears even more than the pain radiating in her temple and left ear.

"Too bad," he was saying. "You work. Like Mama. You clean. Still mess." He pointed to the floor, to the pile of dirty laundry that she and Frannie had heaped up in a corner earlier that evening.

Slowly she staggered to the broom closet, extracted the broom, swept up the shattered plate and the carrots and the biggest potato chunks. Slowly she filled a bucket with water and found a rag and sponged up the oatmeal. She thought the rag was dripping water and realized that her tears were spattering on the floor. Joe watched her, saying nothing. She could feel him gloating, sure that he'd bested her.

He had.

She was lost in her own grief, so perhaps that was the reason she didn't realize until long afterward how the death of her mother must have changed Joe so dramatically. While Tempie was alive, he was a decent man. Lazy, maybe, not great at work, but he was reliable. After Tempie had gone, the rage that may have always been there—disappointment over his life, frustrations that Ella would never understand—tore through. When food regularly appeared on your table and you went to sleep every night in a bed, it didn't cost you anything to be civilized. But once the food stopped appearing, the laundry stopped being cleaned, the bed you slept in belonged to a stranger, then the niceties might disappear as well. Life, Ella was slowly learning, had a way of showing up mean and hungry.

The next morning, Joe woke both Ella and Frannie as if nothing had happened. "Get up," he told them from the doorway, and disappeared.

Ella stirred stiffly, face throbbing. She sat up.

Frannie gasped. "Wow, it's really bad."

"What do you mean?" Ella said.

Frannie pointed to her cheek, and Ella delicately touched her face, which pulsed as if it had its own heartbeat. In the mirror she saw that her left cheek was black and blue, and her ear had a ring of dried blood in it. She couldn't imagine how to explain it away. She felt nauseated for a moment.

In the kitchen, Joe sat at the table, waiting to be fed, arms akimbo and legs spread. She didn't speak—just pulled the pot from the dishrack, poured in the oatmeal and water. The silence lay cold between them like rancid milk.

"You stay home. You clean. You buy food," he told her.

She wanted to tell him that she and Frannie had already cleaned last night, but she didn't. She couldn't believe that he didn't notice the garbage was gone, the dishes washed, the tables dusted.

"I don't have any money," she said instead.

He threw two dimes and a nickel on the kitchen table. Enough for a day or two, no more. "This won't buy us much," she said.

"Your mama buy." He pointed at her. "You buy."

She was about to say, "No, I'm going to school," but his face was set. Her cheek prickled with pain. She would stay home, clean. She would go shopping. She'd just miss two days of school: tomorrow was Friday, and she and Charles would be playing hooky to practice their dance steps at his apartment.

She stirred the oatmeal until it was ready, poured it into three bowls, set the bowls on the table. They had no milk or butter, so she laid down a dish of salt the way her mother used to when they had nothing better.

Frannie appeared in the doorway wearing her school clothes. Normally she'd be chattering, complaining about homework, telling them about her friend Maisie and how Maisie wanted to play a trick on Tommy at school. But now Frannie was silent, too.

All three of them ate without speaking.

Joe struggled into his coat and sauntered out. Left his bowl, grimy with a few flattened oatmeal grains, on the table. Next to it, a scum of beige pooled on the table beneath the spoon.

A few minutes later Frannie ran out to meet Maisie and walk with her to middle school.

Ella was alone. She cleaned the breakfast dishes. She mopped the kitchen floor.

Then she went to the living room, pulled out her mother's records: Bing Crosby and Louis Armstrong and, of course, the Boswell Sisters. The record covers were glamorous, suave, elegant—the people on these albums never spilled oatmeal, never wiped clean an ear ringed in dried blood. Some of the covers were dusty, so she pulled out her rag and dusted them front and back. She dropped the first record—"I Found a Million Dollar Baby (in a Five and Ten Cent Store)"—on the phonograph.

Feeling defiant—she wouldn't let Joe boss her around, not her— she played one song after another. When the opening bars of "I'll Be Glad When You're Dead, You Rascal You" floated into the air, she closed her eyes, breathing in the music. When the needle reached the center of the phonograph and buzzed into the hiss of static, she listened to that side of the record again. She played it over and over. After the third or fourth time, she started singing along, focusing on every tone and beat, trying to imitate, impersonate, utterly disappear into each of the singers—each breath and each phrase, each tremolo and vibrato. At first it was difficult to sing; her cheek pained her. But the more she sang, the more it loosened up, and the more the world refilled with possibility and hope.

Her mother was gone and her stepfather was proving to be a brute. All Ella wanted to do was dance. But now, right now, this music made everything, for this moment, seem right.

5

Boiling to Vapor

February 4, 1932

Laundry took most of Ella's day. Although she'd certainly helped Tempie out, this was the first time she'd done it on her own, with the emptiness of the apartment caving in around her. But she supposed that making things clean was in her blood. She hauled out her mother's big cast-iron pots, set the water to boil. Before she added the clothes—there were so many—she watched the bubbles materialize on the bottom of the pot, float as if desperate to reach the surface, lift, and then open, the vapor curling like feathers into the air.

She had learned in chemistry about water molecules: heat them and they turn from liquid to gas. But, she wondered, how did the molecules choose which ones would become gas? She imagined a larger, more important molecule in charge, tapping the little water molecules on the shoulder. *You shall be air, and you, and you.* The molecules in the front row, closest to the heat, were tapped.

Were most deserving.

It's always easier, looking back from the distance of years, staring down from the penthouse of success, to say, "Of course you should pursue your dreams." *It's easy enough to say that of course you should try, of course you shouldn't give up no matter what life throws at you. But when you're a young colored girl living one step away from the street, when your mother has died, when nobody around you is thriving, is successful, is dreaming big dreams, how do you keep your own dream alive?*

When you stare at the other boiling molecules around you, and none of the others is even aware that there is a way out of the steaming pot, how do you keep your eyes fixed upward? All her life she would ponder this. She would do what she could to encourage young voices to reach up, to never yield; but then, right then, with a plantation field of laundry in front of her, her hope of dancing professionally felt doomed.

But she refused to be bedeviled by what appeared impossible. She put Cab Calloway's "Minnie the Moocher" on the phonograph, prancing around the kitchen, pretending she was dancing like Cab and repeating his calls: "*Hi de hi de hi de hi, ho de ho de ho de ho.*"

Into the water went Joe's shirts and underwear, yellowed and stinking, stains rippling out into the water. She added bleach and soap, and the kitchen hummed with the smell of Tempie's work, which sweetened the kitchen air. She imagined herself as one of those slinky, long-legged, yellow-toned Cotton Club dancers, and she imagined that rich white men were after her. She grabbed a hair rag from the laundry, wrapped it around her neck, and high kicked. She rinsed and scrubbed, hung out the clothes on the fire escape to freeze and, hopefully, to dry as she re-swept the apartment, dusted the end table in the living room where the Tiffany lamp no longer sat, and organized the empty pantry with the handful of kitchen staples she'd purchased that morning.

Someday she'd be one of those Harlem Greenwich Village loose and gay women, a real flapper. She knew she was a good dancer, athletic and fearless, able to drop into a split and leap into a flip. She would be the water molecule closest to the heat. Under pressure she would rise. She would evaporate, disappear forever from this place.

She practiced the step that was tripping her up on the Lindy Hop (it *was* toe-ball-heel) and Josephine Baker's banana dance, rolling her hips around and gyrating her torso. Without Charles to counterbalance her, she whirled too quickly, overcompensated, and fell. A splinter of pain stabbed through her jaw but she ignored it, imagining herself dancing with feathers waving in her hair, holding hands with one of those handsome, smooth-faced Nicholas brothers—or both of them. She'd be in the middle, wearing one of those white lace dresses with the deep bodice, ostrich feathers nodding in a tiara above her head, and she would be standing at the top of a staircase. One brother would hand her off to the other as she descended, the audience expectant, hushed, waiting. She'd tap-dance down, imitating the Nicholas brothers' suave slides left to right, and then a shimmy to the front of the stage. Everyone would be watching her.

The music made the chores bearable, and soon it would be tomorrow. Soon enough, she and Charles would be earning money dancing, and she'd be helping to contribute to this new household, and Joe would need her and stop doing things to make her despise him.

Hopefully by tomorrow the swelling in her face would go down and her arm wouldn't hurt. Hopefully by tomorrow the threat of tears behind her eyes would begin to lessen, if only slightly.

By evening, all the piles of laundry were clean and draped around the kitchen and on the lines strung across the fire escape. The

apartment sparkled, and dinner was only slightly overcooked macaroni and a very small piece of ham, which she gave to Joe. He sat
down and ate, never seeming to look around him, no "thank you" or
grunt of acknowledgment. But he didn't hit her again.

On Friday morning she made breakfast for Joe, Frannie, and
herself—scrambled eggs and toast—and left "for school" before Joe
headed out for work. She waved to Mrs. Bascombe and Mrs. Hancock,
nosy neighbors she was sure were spying on the family now that her
mother was gone.

As usual she met Charles on the corner of School Street and Nep-
perhan Avenue, and they followed the road up the hill to Maple
Street and into the warren of side streets. But instead of turning left,
into the gates of the high school, they continued straight up the hill
and trekked over to Cochran Park. They'd hide out until they were
sure that Mrs. Gulliver had left for her hairdressing job, and then
they'd let themselves back into Charles's apartment to practice their
dances and laze around for the day.

As they trudged through the slush, Ella was careful to keep her
wooly hat pulled low over her eyes, hiding the black-and-blue mark
which had brightened into a squeamish yellow. Her left eye was
bloodshot from a broken blood vessel. But before they reached the
school, Charles caught sight of her face and his eyes went wide.
"What happened to you?" he asked, suddenly serious. "Is that why
you stayed home? Because you didn't want anyone to see your face?"

"No," she said, heart sinking. She'd spent a lot of time examining
herself in the mirror, gotten so used to the swelling and bruises that
she thought that perhaps it wasn't as bad as she'd first believed. If on
the off chance someone did comment, she'd been rehearsing poten-
tial stories: should she say she'd run into a door frame, or she'd hit an

open kitchen cabinet, or she'd tripped and banged her head on the coffee table?

Charles's words destroyed those thin hopes. Hearing the awe and sympathy in his voice made tears well up. "I'm okay. Just hit my head." She turned away, staring down the street, where a bus was letting passengers off.

"Let me look," Charles said.

"I'm fine," she repeated.

He held her shoulder, and the momentum of her walk spun her around until she was facing him. "Did Joe do that?"

Tears streaked and burned. She wiped at her good eye but the left one was throbbing. She couldn't help but nod.

"What'd he do?" Charles said.

"He—" she gulped. "He punched me. He said we was lazy and didn't clean up like Mama did. He hates me."

"He never acted like this before, did he?"

She shook him off and started again down the street.

Charles had to jog to keep up. "He can't treat you like that. He can't."

"He can," she said. "He did."

"Well—" he paused and she left him behind, so he had to catch up again. "You can't stay there."

"Where am I goin'? What am I gonna do?"

"You can stay with us."

"There's barely enough for the three of you. Even if I worked it wouldn't be enough. I couldn't do that." She paused, thinking. "Anyway he wouldn't let me."

"What you mean?"

The words slipped out of her. "He wants his food on the table and his laundry clean and me sitting there, looking like my mama. He treats me like I'm not even family, just a washerwoman—a—servant. Doing his bidding."

Charles shook his head. "He hit you real good."

"I gotta do it, too. You think Frannie would if I left? He might do the same to her. Even if she is his own flesh and blood. He might take it out on her. She's just a little kid."

"I dunno," he said. "But you got to stop crying. We gotta figure this thing out."

"You shoulda seen him. He turned into a big old white man." A cold wind tugged at Ella's hat. "My mama died and I have to live with him," she said after a minute. "I feel like I don't know him now."

They turned the corner into the park. A handful of trees spread cold shadows into the morning. The sun was mercilessly bright.

"You can't dance tomorrow," Charles said. On Saturday night they were supposed to perform at the Breakneck Club, about half an hour's walk away.

"What you mean?"

"I mean you can't dance looking like that." He gestured at her face.

"It ain't that bad."

"Yeah it is," he said.

"Well we can practice," she said fiercely. "We can learn the steps. Let's go to Harlem tonight and tomorrow night and every night we can. Learn everything. We'll be boogie-woogie dancing machines."

She could tell he didn't want to argue with her while she was in this state. "Okay," he said. "You can work on your Suzy Q. I told you that was a mess."

"I'll work," she told him. Then she made him promise not to tell anyone what had happened to her. "I tripped," she said. "That's it."

They wandered around the park, staying well within its confines while late stragglers headed to work or to school. They tried to find a solution to living with Joe. The best option seemed to be to move in with Tempie's sister, Virginia, who lived in Harlem with her daughter. Perhaps her aunt could take Ella and Frannie both—but then Charles would be far away. "I'd come visit," he said. "We'd still dance."

She eyed him doubtfully and shrugged.

His breath was two plumes of smoke blowing away in the winter morning. "You ready to head to my house?" he asked. "I think she's gone."

"That's what I'm here for, fool," Ella said, mimicking a Lindy Hop dancer named Diddley, who was always first in line to get into the Savoy. Even if she couldn't dance, the prospect of checking out the latest moves that evening lifted her spirits. "Nothin's gonna stop me." She exhaled and watched her frosty breath vanish into the sunlight.

6

The Savoy, World's Finest Ballroom

February 5, 1932

The brilliance of the marquee seemed to go on forever: infinite, shimmering, exhilarating—burning so brightly that the air tingled. *Savoy, World's Finest Ball Room.* Ella had no doubt it was. Below, in slightly smaller letters, read: *Featuring the Chick Webb Orchestra.* She loved Chick Webb—he was a tiny drummer, and his music was infectiously danceable.

A long line of people waited for entry on the corner of 140th Street and Lenox Avenue. A white police officer rode back and forth on a tall horse, maintaining order. White patrons wearing tuxedos and beautiful gowns arrived in chauffeur-driven limousines, bypassing the line. One woman had on a glittering tiara of diamonds and topaz. She looked right at Ella, who tried to imagine what it would be like to be her—white, rich, and beautiful, with a handsome man holding her arm as she glided up the carpeted walkway.

The night was warm for February. Charles wore a black coat

whose worn hem he'd sewn so it looked almost new. She didn't know how he kept the scarf he'd tossed around his neck so pearly, but he looked as elegant as the men in front of them. Ella glanced down at her own tattered brown coat. She pulled her red cloche hat as low over her eyes as she could. The hat's stiff brim all but concealed one eye, so she felt normal. Hopefully people would just see the red of her dress—Tempie had sewn it for her a few months ago and Ella wore it proudly—and the crimson of her lipstick.

She wished she could perform, but she'd be strictly observing tonight, then she and Charles would commandeer a corner, practice a handful of stagy steps so they could show them off the following week, when her arm was better and her face healed.

As they drew close to the entrance, Charles took Ella's arm. Diddley, one of the better-known Savoy dancers, was already there, first in line. He was a tall man with a large nose and terrific, agile moves that Charles envied. His arms and legs seemed barely attached to his torso, so he could twist with the music's rhythm in a way that, to Ella, seemed magical.

"What dis be all about?" Diddley shouted when he saw them. "Yaw look cold." Without losing his place in line, he shuffled into a restrained kick-and-slide, doing something dramatic and impressive with his left heel. Ella made a note to try it once they were inside, where Diddley could show it to her.

"Dancing! That's what I'm here for, fool!" Charles yelled back, repeating Diddley's pet phrase. The bouncer, who was just getting ready to open the doors, burst out laughing with them. They'd seen him around—people called him "Whitey" because of the thick white streak in his otherwise coal-black hair. He seemed to have a soft spot for Ella and Charles, and let them all in.

Inside, the lobby's enormous crystal chandelier sparkled like a relic from a different world, a place more glamorous, more glorious than Yonkers. A pink marble staircase swept upward, and Ella and Charles, buoyed by the crowd, floated up to the enormous second floor that spanned the length of the entire city block. The walls and ceiling glowed, mirrors reflecting face after face, white and black, so the dancing mob seemed endless.

As they threaded their way through the dancers, she was fascinated not by the back flips and the hip twists but by the *smiles*: everyone seemed celebratory, surprised by joy, as if enchantment had reached out, tapped each person on the shoulder, given him or her the one nugget of news that would most delight them: *that beautiful dress you saw last week in the shop window, the one with the gold and blue spangles, it's hanging in your closet*; or: *here's a box of a million dollars cash*; or: *your mother's made a miraculous recovery and she's home now baking you shoo-fly pie.* Everything—anything—seemed not only possible, but probable. She just had to reach out, grab what she most desired, and pluck it from one of the crystal sconces that almost reached up to heaven.

The dancers' feet thundered rhythmically on the mahogany floor, and the big band sound of "Moonlight and Magnolias" rose above all else, sung by Charles Linton. Ella couldn't wait for the release of the phonograph recording of the song. She wanted to play it over and over. Everyone glittered. In women's hair, ostrich feathers curled, silver and pearl waving through the crowd.

They wove farther into the ballroom, sliding past a white couple doing the windmill with point-and-curls.

"We're way better than them," Ella said.

The man looked vaguely like Clark Gable, and the woman had a hairstyle exactly like Tallulah Bankhead's. The couple's hands snapped in time to the music, but neither, Ella told herself, had the spunk that Ella and Charles possessed.

"Hey," Charles said, "There's Frankie Manning. Let's introduce ourselves."

Frankie, one of the most innovative Harlem dancers, stood beyond a white woman in a short black-and-white beaded dress. He was tall—a head taller than Charles—and slim, sporting high-waisted trousers with a crisp pleat and an old-fashioned button-down shirt. His two-tone, midnight black shoes were the height of Harlem elegance.

"No," Ella told Charles. "Not tonight. Next time." She touched her bruised face to remind him that she was staying out of the limelight.

But Charles either didn't hear or ignored her because he was dragging her forward, saying, "Hi Frankie. I'm Charles Gulliver, and you have the best air step ever."

Frankie was turning, shaking Charles's hand, looking over at Ella. "Nice to meet you, Charles, and who's this beautiful lady?"

She tucked her chin, kept the brim of the hat low across her vision, so all she could see was Frankie's shoes. They were shiny and midnight black.

"I'm Ella," she said, holding out one hand. He took it. "Ella Fitzgerald."

"Haven't I seen you two around?" Frankie asked. "You really cut a rug."

"It's Ella," Charles said. "She's really good."

"Okay, Ella," Frankie said. "Want to strut your stuff? Show me what you can do?" Without waiting, just like Charles a moment ago, Frankie was pulling her toward the dance floor—not to the Corner, where the Savoy Lindy Hoppers flaunted Hollywood moves, but to the main part of the ballroom.

Any other night, Ella would have sold her soul to the devil to dance with Frankie Manning. Tonight, though, she couldn't. She would dance when she didn't have to wear this stupid red hat to hide her disgusting face and bloodshot eye, when she could lift her arm over her head without wincing. Better to take another opportunity than to blow this one forever, even if the opportunity never presented itself again.

She braced her legs, tugged against him. "I would," she said, "but I hurt my arm the other day. When I dance with you, I want to be great." She looked up at him from under the hat, and his eyes widened. She was close enough that she could count the hairs of his sparse mustache.

"Damn, girl, you sure did hurt yourself. What happened?"

"I fell," she said. "Twisted my arm, too. But I'll be back next week. Look for me."

The orchestra was jamming in high gear, the lead trumpet slow-wailing with a New Orleans gutbucket sound. The percussions were tight, Chick Webb's steady foot keeping time as they erupted into the syncopated jam, "Jungle Mama."

"I will," Frankie said.

A moment later he gave them both a jaunty wave and disappeared into the throng, moving toward the Corner.

"Come on," Ella yelled to Charles, grabbing his hand with her good arm and following Frankie. As usual they stood on one side, watching the top dancers perform. Normally, they would then go onto the main dance floor and try to duplicate the steps, but today they were going to use a back hall on the way to the restrooms, since Ella felt self-conscious.

On stage, the musicians' conked hair and sharkskin black suits looked straight out of a Hollywood movie. Behind them a painted golden tower loomed, mythical and fairytale-like. In the foreground, a tiny man both played the drums and conducted the band, his hands and arms blurred with energy. There he was—Chick Webb himself.

The packed room of dancers moved in sync with each downbeat of Chick's foot. Ella needed to shake her shoulders to the rhythm, to the southern blare of the horns. Her feet needed to strike out on their own. If only her arm and shoulder didn't ache so badly.

Halfway to the Corner she caught sight of an older woman in royal blue satin, rocking her head in time to the music. She sat alone at one of the tables clustered on either side of the orchestra. As Chick Webb took a solo on the drums, the woman's eyes locked with Ella's. Goosebumps rose on Ella's neck. As if dragged on a string, she threaded through the dancers toward her.

"Where you going?"

She ignored Charles, heading toward the woman.

Dancers blocked her view, and then the table reappeared but the woman was gone. Ella could have sworn she'd seen her mother sitting there, dressed up in her favorite royal blue, smiling, "Puttin' On the Ritz," as Ella remembered her mother saying whenever she dressed up, as if her mother had finally found a Tiffany life.

"I saw someone . . . ," Ella started, trailing off.

"Who?"

"I'm alright now."

"You sure?"

She'd been imagining things, she told herself. They returned the way they'd come, past a full table of mixed races, white and Black, rich and poor, all clapping hands, stomping feet, and shouting at the dancers. "Do dat thang! Be real cool, daddy!" The enthusiasm had a thick sweetness to it, a warmth unlike anything she'd ever experienced outside the Savoy. She wanted to bob up like a cork on the tide of its contagious bounce. Even if you weren't dancing, you sat at a table on the side of the floor, waiting for your turn and itching for your chance. You tapped your feet, you snapped your fingers to the thump of the bass, breaking into the next dance with the orchestra pulsing alongside you, all of you one body of movement and sound. Whew diddy.

A chorus of saxophones, trumpets, and trombones blasted their electrifying intro to "My Sweet" by Louis Armstrong, the heavy African beat of the drums followed, and the orchestra converged into down-home swing music.

Frankie Manning led a tall, light-skinned woman to the center of the floor. The woman wore a red, square-shouldered, A-line dress and Keds. The music burst forth, and Frankie tossed the woman in a dazzling aerial throw. She landed on her feet, pivoted to a slide through Frankie's open legs, emerging fully on her feet and then shuffling effortlessly into the shimmy.

"You get that?" Ella yelled to Charles, never letting the dancing couple out of her sight. "See?" she said. "That's what we got to do. If we do that, we'll have all the money in the world."

"I wish I could see it again," Charles said.

They kept watching. Late in the song Frankie and the woman performed the air slide—the same aerial throw, pivot, and slide.

"I think I got it," Charles said.

"Good. I'm not sure of the landing but let's try it."

At the end of the song, as Frankie and his partner bowed to the applauding crowd, Ella and Charles slipped back to a niche by the restrooms. The music was fainter here but the bass still thrummed in Ella's throat like a second heartbeat. She tossed her hat in a corner and leaped into Charles's arms as a handful of people watched.

The air slide looked effortless when Frankie did it, but it was much harder than it appeared, especially since Ella's injuries made her clumsy. It took half an hour before they felt like they had it, and twice Charles barely managed to catch Ella before she leaped head-first into a wall.

"Girl, what your boyfriend do to you?" one woman called to them, apparently thinking that Charles had beaten Ella up or had dropped her.

"Wasn't him," Ella said. "He rescued me."

The woman nodded approvingly.

They practiced the throw and dozens of other steps, Ella pushing through the pain, pausing to get water, periodically making their way back to the Corner to watch another virtuoso couple perform. Usually Ella and Charles picked up a routine or two, but this night Ella felt like they had five passable segments. Every time Charles wanted to rest or call it quits, Ella asked him for one more time. The specter of Joe loomed behind her. They both were dripping sweat and exhausted when, at three a.m., Ella relented.

She always left the club by one a.m. at the latest, but tonight was different. Tempie hadn't made her promise to be back by two, and she wouldn't be there waiting up. There'd only be Joe, who'd never given her a curfew, and he was probably drunk and sound asleep anyway.

A little after four-thirty in the morning, Ella snuck into the apartment, slipping her key in slowly, cracking the door so it didn't squeak. She'd assumed that Joe and Frannie would be in bed. Instead Joe was sitting up straight on the couch, fully clothed, still wearing his coat. All the lights were on. He was asleep.

As she stood in the doorway, trying to figure out if she could sneak by him, he opened his eyes, stared at her, at first unseeing, and then recognition washed into his face.

"Where you been?" he said.

"Dancing. The Savoy."

"You didn't ask."

She'd never asked him, only Tempie.

"You're not my father," she told him, and tried to bluster past him, giving the couch a wide berth, but he was shifting his weight, he was standing, he was looming over her, blocking her way to her room.

"Leave me alone," she said, and then louder, "Leave me alone!"

"Who gave you dress?" He caught hold of her arm, the one he'd grabbed the other day, and she mewed as he wrenched her back. "What this?" He wiped the lipstick off her mouth with his palm and fingers.

Ella glared at him, refusing to respond.

"You whoring for money? Give me money," he said.

"I was practicing! I was at the Savoy! Mama let me!"

"Now Mama gone. Stay home. You clean."

"You know I dance!"

"Your mama just bury and you dance? You stay home."

"No," she said. "I dance! Mama let me!"

He raised his fist to punch her and she pulled away, slipped out of his reach. He grabbed again, with the other hand, caught her other arm, twisted her to the floor.

She screamed and scratched at his face.

He dragged her across the room. Vaguely, she caught sight of

Frannie hovering in the doorway, fists to her face. Perhaps she was crying but Ella couldn't hear over her own shrieks.

Joe must have seen Frannie, too. "Go to bed," he shouted, and while he was distracted Ella twisted away from him again. She was close enough to the kitchen to stumble in, Joe at her heels. She flung herself toward the kitchen drawers, fumbling for her mother's butcher knife. Her hand closed around the handle just as Joe came at her. "Come on," she shouted at him. "Come on, you low-down cracker!"

Joe backed through the doorway and Ella followed, the knife thrashing out. "You ugly and mean—come on!" Another stabbing blow back at him. "I got somethin' for your cracker ass. Come get it!"

She jumped back and Joe, face red, hands trembling, came toward her. Weirdly, for a few strides his pace mirrored hers, as if they were sliding into a foxtrot. It disoriented her, and that was enough for him to knock the knife out of her fist. It clattered against the wall.

"Cracker, cracker, cracker!" she screamed, and Joe grabbed her by the throat and smashed her against the kitchen wall. The back of her head hammered against the doorframe, and then he slammed his body against hers. His breath smelled like beer and something dead. He let go of her and she collapsed to the floor. He shivered above her, a seething mass of venom.

Then he grabbed her hair and dragged her to the front closet. He threw her in like garbage down a disposal chute. Her head knocked against the clothes pole.

He locked the door.

7

When You Can't Catch Your Breath

February–April 1932

For hours she sat on the floor, in the dark, breathing in the dusty odors of sweaty shoes and mildew. She had howled, screamed, rammed herself against the closet door; it stood unyielding. She had pleaded—with Joe, and later with Frannie—to let her out. As the closet walls closed in around her, the backs of coats or sleeves brushed the top of her head, and she thought of Tempie, lying in her grave, the coffin walls tight and unforgiving. She felt Joe's presence outside the door and was utterly helpless, totally at someone else's mercy, which made her panic again, but this time, instead of pounding on the door, she took one deep breath, then another.

"Amazing grace," she whispered, and the sound of her voice gave her confidence. "Amazing grace," she started again, louder this time, and then sang the whole verse:

Amazing grace how sweet the sound
That saved a wretch like me
I once was lost, but now I'm found
Was blind but now I see

Eventually the hysteria lessened. It didn't disappear; it sat with her, almost consoling.

Some time later she woke, still in the closet. The night had faded and a cold light slivered below the door. Joe was talking to someone at the front door. She wanted to yell, tell the visitor that she was here, but something made her keep quiet. She was careful not to move her legs or body, which throbbed from where she'd hit herself. Then she heard Joe leave, heard Frannie's voice, and the front door creaking shut. The deadbolt clicked. The apartment was silent. The light beneath the door now revealed enough so that she didn't feel like she was floating, disembodied, half-suffocated. If she squinted long enough, the doorknob glowed in front of her, the tarnished brass rosette held by two screws. She tried unsuccessfully to insert a fingernail into the narrow slot. She searched for any tools Joe might have kept in the closet. It was hard to maneuver, and she groped blindly, eventually fumbling across one of his toolboxes, a handful of screwdrivers inside. One fit the slot. The screws loosened, turned. She wriggled the rosette, then the half-knob, and eventually it fell off. With a tiny pop the latch gave and the door opened. The air was cool and sweet.

Later she wondered if brutalizing her was Joe's way of coping with Tempie's death, but all she knew then was that he would hurt her, and would keep on hurting her, perhaps until she was dead, too.

She realized something that night in the closet: Joe didn't want to kill her for dancing or for coming home late. He wanted to kill her for wanting to be more. To him she was only a poor nigger girl, someone to wait on him.

She would fight back. She would succeed despite him. She would dance, become a famous Lindy Hopper, perform in the Corner at the Savoy, buy a brownstone in Striver's Row, and never, ever come back to Yonkers. Frannie would move in with her, too, and then he would be left with exactly what he deserved: nothing.

Ella had busted that closet door open. One day she would bust open bigger doors.

Joe and Frannie returned after a few hours. Ella had prepared lunch—peanut butter sandwiches—and no one said anything about what had happened.

Later that afternoon she caught him examining the closet door, but she'd replaced the screws and it looked the same as it always did.

Frannie, too, pretended that nothing had changed, but one night as the girls were getting ready for bed, Ella asked her, "When you heard me in that closet, why didn't you let me out?"

Frannie didn't answer, buttoning her nightgown, but then mumbled, "I didn't know what to do. I was scared."

"But you heard me hollerin' for you."

"I don't want to talk about it," Frannie said.

"We're sisters," Ella told her, "and Mama is gone. She'd want us to take care of each other."

Frannie nodded.

"I'll take care of you," Ella said. "But help me next time, would you?"

They both knew that there would be a next time, unless Ella escaped first.

The next few weeks Ella was as humble and fawning as Stepin Fetchit. Joe must have thought she had mended her ways; she was going to cook, clean, and mind what he said. She'd go to school when he said. Stay home when he said. Whatever he said, Ella would do. She would even stop dancing.

For the time being.

Mrs. Gulliver gave her some rudimentary cooking lessons, and after a while the tortured silence between Joe and Ella eased into apathy and disinterest. Ella was a good housekeeper, cleaning the apartment and preparing his food. Finally, almost a month after he'd thrown her in the closet, she asked if she could go dancing on Saturdays and bring the money back to him. He begrudgingly agreed.

"But bring money. All to me," he told her.

That Friday night, she and Charles left School Street to head down to Harlem to check out the dancers. She stopped first at her Aunt Virginia's apartment on 145th Street, a few blocks from the Savoy.

Virginia and her daughter Georgiana lived on the third floor of what once had been a luxurious building on a block of beautifully appointed row houses with elaborate cornices and majestically carved front doors, but the neighborhood had by now fallen on harder times. High ceilings and coffered moldings hung above broken plaster and holes in the stairwell. Ella had once overheard Auntie complaining to Tempie about how difficult it was for her to meet the rent, but when Tempie had told her to move somewhere affordable, Auntie told her that she needed to live in "rooms that breathe."

"I want to be able to entertain in style," Auntie had once said to Tempie when the family came to visit. "You know how I love my tea service."

Virginia worked as a nurse's aide in the emergency unit at Harlem

Hospital, where even white police officers went for medical treatment. Virginia's hours were long and irregular, so Ella never knew if Virginia would be home to hear her knock. That evening, to her relief, she was.

Aunt Virginia opened the door and folded Ella into an embrace. "Honey, it's been too long." She released her, stood back. "You look pretty tonight," she told her. A tall, high-cheekboned, full-figured woman with mahogany skin like Ella's mother's, Auntie rarely smiled and even more rarely laughed. Tonight she seemed tired, the bags under her eyes prominent, but her hair was smooth and sleek, neatly arranged, her faded cotton housedress pressed. "You heading to your dance club?" Auntie didn't hold much with dance clubs: too easy to fritter money away, with a lifestyle of loose women and stolen husbands. Her husband had disappeared years before, so Aunt Virginia alone had to provide for herself and her daughter.

"Yeah," Ella said. "Charles and me is going back to the Savoy to learn some new steps."

"Yes, not 'yeah,'" Aunt Virginia said. "And it's 'Charles and I are.' Not 'Charles and me is.'"

"Yes ma'am," Ella said. "Charles and I are."

Auntie nodded approvingly. "Charles? Where is he?" She peered around Ella, down the hallway.

Unlike everyone else Ella knew, Aunt Virginia spoke hypercorrect English, enunciating each syllable. She didn't hold with slang or poor diction; her daughter Georgie had regular elocution lessons, and Virginia would correct Georgie, and Tempie's daughters, if they didn't speak clearly.

"He's running some errands," Ella lied. Charles was waiting outside. "I'm meeting him later."

Auntie nodded and backed into the apartment.

The front door opened directly onto a sitting room that Aunt Virginia called her "parlor." A French provincial sofa and two matching burgundy velvet armchairs sat primly on a Persian rug. Along one wall, above the unusable fireplace, an ornately carved mantel held up porcelain figurines and, prominently, a photograph of Virginia and Tempie as small dark girls hanging on to their grandmother. Everything except the photograph, Ella knew, had been given to Aunt Virginia by white women who Virginia had taken care of when they were ill. Only guests of a certain level of social significance ever sat in this room. Auntie kept it clean and proper to receive important folk like her church minister, the magnificent Adam Clayton Powell Sr., or the white folks snooping on those rare occasions when Aunt Virginia needed to ask for public assistance.

Auntie led the way through the parlor, back into the real living room—a small space with a kitchen along one side. Here the furniture was more threadbare, but still immaculate. Virginia gestured to Ella to sit down in one of the chairs. She sat across from Ella, folding her hands like she expected to be put upon with bad news.

"I love your French roll," Ella said, trying to start out with a compliment, to ease Aunt Virginia into this conversation. "You keep your hair so nice. You using Madame Walker's hair cream and hot comb?"

Aunt Virginia loved everything French. "That's so sweet you noticed. It's so expensive but it's the one thing I'm going to afford." Aunt Virginia patted her thick roll of hair, so similar to Ella's mother's: probably from the Cherokee blood, Tempie had once told Ella.

Ella hesitated, and then started in. "You know I'm almost sixteen now and I have to start looking for work and times are so hard—there's no work in Yonkers. I'm thinking there might be work in Harlem."

"You're still in school, of course?"

"Yeah," Ella said.

"Please don't say 'yeah'. It's common."

"Yes, ma'am. I'm still in school."

"Where would you stay?"

"Well that's just it," Ella said, clutching her hands in her lap. "I could stay with you and Georgie and even help out with the rent from my dancing on the side and I'd clean your house like nobody's business."

Auntie did not look convinced, but she didn't seem totally opposed either. There was hope. "Who would do the housework and cooking in Yonkers?"

"I don't want to stay there," Ella said, picking at the cuticles of her left hand.

"Oh, honey," Auntie said, "I know it can't be easy. But you can't leave your sister and your father at a time like this. They need you more than ever."

"He's not my father," Ella said.

"He thinks of you as his daughter." Auntie's voice was so gentle.

Tears stung Ella's eyes. "Since Mama died, I can't do nothin' right."

"'Anything,'" Auntie said automatically. "He's just being a man. Look at me."

Ella met her aunt's gaze. She was so desperate—so filled with hope and defiance, so frightened, and so in need of something better in her life.

"That's what men do when life gives them a bad turn." Something about the way that Aunt Virginia delivered the sentence made Ella feel like there was a meaning that Ella wasn't quite understanding.

"They don't know how to do otherwise," her aunt went on. "People are always looking for them to be strong—so men get mean. Don't pay him any mind. He'll get better. You just be a good girl."

"He's gonna try to kill me," Ella said. "He's hit me a bunch of times." She looked down again, trying very hard not to cry. Even if weeping might soften her aunt, Ella didn't want to seem weak in front of her.

Virginia stood up and pulled her up as well, wrapping her in a hug. "I want you to know that you are my beloved sister's firstborn and my niece. We are family. I don't want anything bad to happen to you or Frances."

Ella relaxed into her, breathed in her comforting scent of talcum, sweat, and a mother's embrace. Auntie was the closest person to Ella's mother she'd ever have again. She closed her eyes and didn't speak.

Aunt Virginia's arms were strong around her. "This world is in trouble. Until lately you've been busy dancing and being young, but look around you, honey. People are starving. Colored people are being lynched, right up here in the North, even after we thought we got away from Jim Crow. But it followed us straight to Harlem."

Ella didn't know what this had to do with living with Joe, but she nodded all the same. She hoped her auntie would never let her go.

Aunt Virginia rocked her from side to side. "We thought things would change after the war, with our colored soldiers dying for this country. But I'm afraid, sweetie. I'm afraid it's going to get worse before it gets better. Worse for everyone. Me and Georgie are barely getting by."

"Is it that bad?" Ella said. "Even for you?"

She knew her auntie worked long hours, but she never seemed poor. Ella knew that Auntie invited Mrs. Thomas from the fifth floor and Mr. Angus from down the block for every Christmas and

Thanksgiving dinner, since they had nobody. Plus she made care packages for older folks in the neighborhood.

Auntie was saying, "We sat down to soup bones the other night."

"Soup bones? That's it?" Ella knew that people had to do this, but somehow it didn't seem that Aunt Virginia was one of them.

"That's what we do when times are hard. We do what we have to do." She took a deep breath. "But Joe? He's a good man. He puts food on your table and a roof over your head. Now we need you to keep a roof over your head by taking heed of what he says."

"I could help, Auntie," Ella pleaded. "I could help you. Make extra money so you'd have good things to eat."

"I know. I know. But Joe's a decent man and—"

"He's not, he's not decent at all—"

"Yes he is," her aunt said firmly, and Ella didn't know how to argue. "He's keeping a roof over your head and keeping you fed."

"But he hits me," she said again. "He—"

Aunt Virginia was staring off over Ella's shoulder, face blank, talking over her. "Try to understand what he's going through. He'll come to himself."

No matter what else Ella said, Virginia remained firm: Ella should stick it out. Joe was a decent man. It would get better.

Soon Ella left, went dancing with Charles.

She was home by midnight. Joe was waiting up for her, but when she came through the door he grunted and shambled off to bed without saying a word.

The conversation with Aunt Virginia only made Ella more anxious to get out of Yonkers forever. It was as if seeing a light at the end of the tunnel gave her the courage to keep moving forward, even if it turned out that she had to march through an entirely different tunnel to get there. It was almost enough to know that there was, indeed, light.

Meanwhile, Joe had gotten accustomed to ordering Ella around, and she'd gotten used to biting her tongue and performing whatever menial task he asked of her. If she didn't move quickly enough, he might lash out with a light cuff to the back of the head, a menacing grab to the back of her arm, nothing deeply painful, just enough to let her know that in his house, he was in control.

One evening, he barged into the apartment in an especially foul mood. His feet thundered on the floorboards. Ella didn't ask how his day was—she never did.

Frannie, who was in the kitchen with Ella, tried to slip into their bedroom to escape. Ella was making rice, black-eyed peas, and potatoes for dinner, and couldn't get away. "You wait here," Ella told Frannie, refusing to be alone with him. "Dinner's about on the table."

"I'm not hungry," Frannie said.

"Get the plates out."

Frannie pulled the plates from the cupboard, set them on the table. Neither of them spoke, but both looked at each other out of the corners of their eyes. Ella held her breath.

Joe collapsed into the kitchen chair, waiting to be served. Frannie was by the icebox.

"Get Joe a cold beer," Ella told her. Ella had to lean over toward Joe to spoon the food onto the plates, but kept herself as far away as possible.

Frannie sat down and began to eat.

Joe was examining the black-eyed peas as if Tempie hadn't cooked them several times a week. "Fork," he said to her.

There was a fork next to Ella's plate, and one in Frannie's hand, but Frannie must have forgotten to set one out for Joe. And that was apparently all the justification that Joe needed.

Before Ella had a chance to turn to the cutlery drawer, he grabbed her arm and slung her to the other side of the room. She banged against the counter, caught herself from falling. By the time she'd recovered, he'd taken her fork for himself and was shoveling rice into his mouth.

One Saturday in early April, Ella and Charles went to see a matinee at the Loew's. "You pay attention and don't just sit there," Ella told Charles.

This wasn't just for fun.

They were studying the dance steps.

Anise Boyer prayed for luck by rubbing Harlem's Tree of Hope on Seventh Avenue; and Ella put herself there, with Anise Boyer. Ella and Charles had placed their feet on this same ground, but now, seeing it up there on the screen, it was magical, even sacred. Suddenly the glamor of that world seemed attainable, reachable. She and Charles would make a pilgrimage to the Tree of Hope and rub it for luck, and their dreams would come true. They could design their own world. She felt exhilarated, uplifted, empowered.

She studied Bojangles's tap dancing and the Cotton Club's chorus line, trying to adapt new dance steps.

On this Saturday night they performed at the Troubador, showing off their Lindy Hop, interspersed with the shimmy and the bee's knees. The crowd seemed to love them, applauding with every shake of their hips and flutter of their hands. Ella did a round-the-church to a split, then slid through Charles's bee's knees. That brought down the house. At the end, Ella performed what she referred to as the "Snakehips Fitzgerald," transitioning into her version of Katherine Dunham's Tribal African dance; and Charles, the African Prince, lifted and spun her in the air before she landed and, hand in hand, they bowed to the crowd.

Ella was sweating and still breathing hard when Ernie paid them each their seventy-five cents—a whole week's salary for the working man—and told them how great they were, how much the crowd adored them, how people were asking about when they'd be dancing next. *Could they come back next Friday as well?*

"We're booked Friday," Ella said. She had a calendar of all their engagements in her head, but kept the appointments in a small notebook back in her room. "We could come next Saturday, though."

"Done," Ernie said, and poured them each a bottle of Coke, on the house. Their engagements were coming in now. Ella could do this. She'd be a professional dancer in no time.

8

The Tiffany Lamp

April 1932

Ella's feet didn't quite touch the ground when she let herself into the apartment just before her eleven p.m. curfew. She figured Joe would be asleep, but once again there he was, sitting on the couch waiting for her. A prickle slid along her shoulder blades, and she straightened.

"Hi," she said. "You didn't have to wait up. I made it in time."

"Where money?" he said.

Ella fished in her purse, handed him the three quarters, careful that she didn't touch his bare skin. Soon she'd be gone, she promised herself yet again. His fist closed around the coins, and he grunted, stood up, and shuffled off to his bedroom.

The following week was unremarkable. He slapped her once when she burned the milk and smoked up the kitchen, punched the wall—but didn't break the plaster—when he wasn't happy with her dusting, and screamed at her when she was late getting his supper on the table. All in all, it was a week that she tolerated only by hanging on to what Auntie had said about heeding his word.

Until the next Saturday around five, when his key rattled in the door, his feet thumped on the floorboards, and the couch sighed under his weight.

She'd be leaving within the hour to dance with Charles at the Shim Sham Club, and was in her room working on her dress for that evening. Frannie was down the street at Maisie's. Now Ella would have to walk past him to the kitchen, heat up the beef and potatoes, set the table for him. It wouldn't take more than fifteen minutes. She'd go to Charles's and wait with him before they headed out to dance.

In the meantime, she readied herself by slipping into Tempie's royal blue dress with the sequined hem. Her mother had cobbled the dress together from laundry castoffs. When Tempie had fitted the dress to her, six months ago, Ella's bosom hadn't been quite as full. That afternoon she'd let out the seams as much as she dared, but it was an effort to breathe. Still, the color looked great on her and the beaded sequins sparkled against her skin in a way she thought fetching.

Tonight was the Shim Sham Club's Lindy Hop competition, for a cash prize of five dollars, which would mean money for new clothes, not hand-me-downs, and an entrée into bigger competitions. They'd gotten better at Frankie's air step, working it into their routine, and they hoped that someday soon they'd even outperform Frankie with it.

Now she opened the door to her room and peeked out. Joe was sitting on the sofa as usual, half asleep, feet propped on the coffee table and *Daily News* spread across his chest. She tiptoed past him and he cracked open his eyes, then must have realized it was her. He struggled up. "Where you go?"

"Going to make your dinner," she told him. "It'll be ready in a few minutes. I'll call you as soon as it is."

"You cook like that?" He gestured to her dress. Her breasts felt very exposed and she resisted the urge to cross her arms to cover them.

"I have a competition tonight, remember? First prize is five dollars."

"No dance," he said, crossing his arms over his chest as if he could read her mind.

The door to the hall was behind him, and she imagined racing through it, closing it firmly behind her, marching free out into the world. She wouldn't fight him, not yet.

"Okay," she said. "But let me make you dinner." She'd sneak out, if she had to, while he was eating. And once she came back with five dollars—well, two-fifty, since she'd split it with Charles—perhaps he'd forgive her.

She edged past him toward the kitchen, already choreographing how she'd drape the towel to hide her chest, how she'd stand in the corner where he couldn't see her from the couch.

He reached out, touched her shoulder. She froze, anticipating a blow, braced for it.

"You look like your mama," he said. "Beautiful."

Ella didn't know what to do. She knew how to think about him slamming her in the face or throwing her across the room or locking her overnight in a closet; but a compliment?

She stepped back and he moved in closer, now touching the sleeve of her dress. His thumb seemed huge. Thick, coarse hairs sprouted from the back of his hand.

He didn't seem angry at her. He looked at her the way he used to, when her mother was alive: with kindness, a small smile on his lips. She thought about him trying to braid her hair in the evenings, and how they all would laugh, even when he pulled too hard by accident and it hurt, because she knew he didn't mean to harm her. She thought of the wooly hat he'd bought her and how she said she hated it but she didn't. Not really. While it wasn't the black cloche hat she wanted, it was warm and she needed a hat to wear every day. Her red cloche hat was for dancing. Joe had loved her mother. He was the closest thing she had to a father.

"This color Tempie favorite." He smiled down at her, and for a moment he seemed handsome again, even if his teeth were stained with cigar tobacco. She found herself wondering, not for the first time, if her mother really had loved him. He was a white man, though, after all.

"I need to make your dinner," she said, trying to duck around him.

His eyes were glassy. He was drunk.

Joe the Drunk could go two ways: he could lash out meanly, or he could fall asleep. Once, he'd staggered in from wherever he'd been and grabbed Tempie around the waist and raised her dress in front of the girls. Tempie had gotten angry with him and sent them to their bedroom. They could still hear the slaps and, sometimes, Tempie whimpering; but neither of the girls had seen what was going on.

"You be nice," Joe was saying. "I be nice." He pressed her against the door. His breath smelled like rotting meat, strong and rancid.

Ella slipped underneath his arm into the kitchen, terrified he'd follow her, but he didn't. A moment later the sofa springs sagged again.

Donning the kitchen towel, she heated up his dinner, stirring the potatoes as quickly as possible, as if the motion would heat them faster. She waited for him to lurch in, but when she peeked out, she saw he'd fallen asleep.

In a moment his plate of roast beef and potatoes steamed on the kitchen table, a knife and fork neatly aligned on top of a folded napkin. She shrugged out of the towel and was into her coat and out of the apartment before he opened his eyes again.

The spring air was luscious and warm as she and Charles ran down School Street for the trolley.

Ella and Charles stumbled into the Lindy Hop contest at the Shim Sham Club in Harlem. They applied immediately, paying the ten cents to enter. Usually they started their dance routine with a wide-legged shimmy that slid into their Lindy Hop, but once Ella studied a crowd of young fit men and women all gyrating with style and flair, she convinced Charles to let her start the routine with her snakehips. Then they could segue into the Lindy Hop and their arsenal: air step, shuffle, Blackbottom into cakewalk, shimmy with jazz hands, and back to a wild, spontaneous gallop of the Lindy Hop swinging out into a frenzy.

When at last their turn came and the band burst into "Minnie the Moocher," they busted loose, eager to show what they could do. Perhaps it was the crowd or the lights, perhaps it was her lingering memory of Joe or her desperation to forget him, but something felt different in Ella. Her fingertips flew higher, her joints looser, her timing sharper. The crowd clapped and hooted, and Ella could actually feel their enthusiasm like a string that yanked her taller, pulled her like taffy into the splits and the turns. It was glorious, heady, and she didn't want it to ever end.

But end it did. They won second prize and two dollars.

The high of winning lasted most of the way uptown on the A

train, almost to the Yonkers Trolley stop. As they neared Yonkers, though, Ella remembered Joe's comment from earlier that evening, the way he'd looked at her, and her chest fluttered: *You be nice. I be nice.*

—

"I don't feel so good," she said aloud, only partially aware she was even speaking.

"You pull a muscle?" Charles said, peering over at her. She shook her head, stared out the window at the blackness of the underground speeding past them. She didn't want to tell Charles that she was worried about going home. It was after one in the morning, two hours past her curfew, and Joe had told her not to leave the house. She prayed that the dollar in her pocket would appease him.

She wanted to say all this to Charles, but speaking it would ruin the memory of their triumph at the Shim Sham Club. Like a mantra, she counted the new steps she'd worked on: one, move; two, hold; three, move; four, swing; five, move; six, kick; seven, move; eight, spin. Then shimmy, turn, jazz hands, shuffle, and kick to heaven. Yes ma'am, she was a dancing fool—and soon she'd be a rich dancing fool. She had to be. With Auntie refusing to take her in, being out on her own was her only hope for escape, and she knew if she didn't get out soon, Joe was going to do the worst thing, a thing so terrible she couldn't even think it to herself.

In Yonkers, they got off the otherwise empty trolley car to a night of stars hanging from the sky like lights on the Savoy marquee. Charles walked with her up to the front door of her apartment building. Their footsteps rang out in the silent street, and Ella's feet were like bricks, too heavy to lift, the closer she got to home. She wanted Charles to walk her inside but knew it would do no good. Charles couldn't help her.

Inside, the stairwell echoed with dread. No neighbors peered out, and this one time she wished they would. It was the heart of the night, and she was praying that Joe was snoring in his bedroom and wouldn't be sitting on that couch, his legs spread, owning the room, waiting for her to come in like a supplicant, waiting to pounce on her for money.

The sofa was empty. She breathed out in a rushed gasp, so grateful that she'd be able to make it safe to her bedroom and surprise him in the morning with her windfall. A weight lifted from her back as she closed the front door carefully behind her.

She shrugged out of her coat, hung it in the closet. Two steps into the living room, she realized that his bulk had filled up the doorway to his bedroom.

"Oh," she yelped, and then tried to recover and act normally, speaking fast. "You scared me. Guess what? We got second place! I made a dollar tonight. Here." She fumbled in her purse for the money.

"You make money?" he said, not moving.

"I said I did, didn't I? Second place, and some people came up to us afterward and said we should have gotten first. But here's a dollar. Take it."

"Is this all money?"

"Yes," she said, and this time the coins dropped into his open palm. She closed her purse and edged past him down the hall to her bedroom.

He followed her. He grabbed her arm, her wrist, pulled at her.

She froze. Stopped breathing.

"Come," he said, pulling her—dragging her—by the wrists to the couch. "Sit," he told her.

"Let's talk in the morning," she said, too loudly. "I'm really tired. I gave you the money."

"You think about what I said?" He sat, pulled her down next to him.

"What do you mean, what you said?" She leaned as far away from him as she could. She knew what he meant: *You be nice. I be nice.* But she wouldn't make this easy for him.

"I said I be nice to you."

"Okay," she said, hoping if she agreed he would come to his senses after a good night's sleep. "Great. I'll see you tomorrow. You got your money."

She tried to stand but his hand was around her upper arm, holding her down. "I miss Tempie," he said.

Ella, too, had never missed her mother more in her life.

"I know." She looked toward the hall, toward her bedroom, as if she could go where her eyes went.

"She gone now. You here." He paused, his eyes on her face, then dropping lower. "I need you."

She struggled against his paw on her arm, struggled again to stand. "I gave you the money. You want me to make you something to eat? I can make you something. Cornbread? You want cornbread?"

"You be nice," he said, one hand holding her thigh, keeping her down. "I be nice." He stunk of old cigars and whiskey. "You pretty like your mama." He reached out and cupped one of her breasts. Ella let out a squawk and shoved him hard with strength she didn't know she had. She jumped up from the couch.

Joe grabbed her and pulled her back. "I make you be nice."

She balled up her fists and slammed them into his face like she held a handful of rocks. It didn't seem to hurt him. She thought for an instant that he smiled.

And then he stood, reached out, and wrapped both hands around her neck and squeezed. Hard. Lifting her so her legs swung and she tried to kick him.

Her mouth was open and she was gasping but nothing was happening. The air had vanished from her lungs and she flailed against him.

After a moment that seemed to last forever, he dropped her. She collapsed to the floor, half on her back and half on her side. She would fight him, but first she needed to breathe. Joe was above her now, on top of her, ripping at her dress, the royal blue fabric digging into her neck for an instant before giving way.

"Tempie favorite color," he mumbled, somehow seeming both far away and nauseatingly close, and he plunged his head into her bosom. No one had ever touched her there before. The bristle on his cheeks and jaw scraped her chest as if she were being dragged across gravel.

She was pushing him away, beating at him with her fists, and he was kissing the side of her face. His lips were wet and cold. The mass of his body imprisoned her on the floor, one leg was between hers, forcing her legs apart. She gulped for air, screaming.

He tilted his head up to look at her, examining for a moment as if surprised to see her under him, and slapped her, hard, on the cheek and jaw. Then he slapped the other side. After a few more blows she stopped fighting.

Joe was wrangling up her dress and fighting through her undergarments, pulling off her slip, and groping under her bloomers. He rose off her an instant to shift his angle and she twisted her legs under him, kicked him hard in the stomach. He fell back for a moment but as she crawled away he threw his weight on her, pinning her.

"Why you do this to me?" she tried to say. "Please stop." She pushed against his shoulders on top of her.

"You mine," Joe said.

Her mother's cracked Tiffany lamp curled above them on the side table; it wasn't supposed to be there, but there it was. As Joe struggled to tear off her bloomers, she scooted forward, closer to him, more intimate, but now they were so close that he had trouble forcing her bloomers down, so he moved onto his knees, ripping at them, they were down around her ankles and the wooden floor was cold on her skin. He was fumbling with his pants, shoving them down, using one knee to wedge her legs apart.

She was reaching over and grabbing the lamp—

She smashed it against his head. Once, twice, and a third time, even harder.

A crack as if the world were splitting apart: glass and metal shattered, and Joe's blood spattered against her and he grabbed his head and collapsed, moaning.

Ella pushed him off, slid out from under him. He lay with the remains of the lamp speckling around him, and then she was in her bedroom fumbling through her drawers for her clothes, her red cloche hat, her pair of good shoes. She stuffed them into a canvas bag. Frannie sat up in bed silently as Ella fumbled under her bed for her other pair of good shoes, because she'd need the shoes for dancing, and Ella was shaking and was afraid she'd be sick but there was no time to be sick, no time to pause.

"I'm getting out of here," she told Frannie. She could hear Joe moving and groaning out in the living room, and it would be only moments until he was reeling into the doorway, blocking her. "I'll get you out of here, too. I promise."

She sped down the hall. Joe was climbing to his feet but she was faster, darting around him, grabbing her coat, leaving her wooly hat in the corner like something that had been run over in the street. She was out the door now, down the hall, down the stairs two at a time, and out into the cool spring Yonkers night.

It was late. The trolley had stopped running, so she walked, tears and snot and blood—hers or Joe's, she didn't know—streaking her face, dripping onto her coat and onto the sidewalk. She tried not to think, tried to focus on her breathing. She counted her footsteps, counted each block. She followed the trolley line all night until, near dawn, she reached the final outpost of the New York subway line. The glowing green globes seemed like the most glorious lights she'd ever seen.

Soon she knocked on her Aunt Virginia's door in Harlem, carrying her canvas bag and holding closed her torn coat. Her aunt, thank goodness, was home, and after a moment she opened the door. A look passed between them: an understanding that connected Black women for generations; and her aunt—like the mothers, grand-mothers, sisters, and all the other womenfolk before her—let Ella into her safe harbor.

Part 2

9

The Tree of Hope

April 24, 1932

Ella first saw Zukie Cabell the day after she moved to Harlem.

She'd spent the previous day resting, nursing her bruises. Auntie and Georgie went to church and then visited neighbors, so Ella had the apartment to herself. She bolted the door after they'd left, just in case Joe came after her. Her whole left side ached, and she had scratches at her waist and left shoulder.

Aunt Virginia never asked what had happened between her and Joe. That night she'd added a pillow to Georgie's narrow bed, but Ella slept so wildly, tossing and turning, that she woke her cousin. The next morning Georgie complained that Ella was fighting in her sleep. From then on, Ella slept on a pallet Auntie had fashioned on the floor so they could sleep separately.

Auntie's primary concern was Ella's education. "I'll have to enroll you in the Wadleigh School," Aunt Virginia told her, which was where Georgie attended.

Ella begged to start next week. Give her just a few days first, Auntie? Please?

Auntie relented with a hug and a kiss on her forehead.

The next day, Auntie made her peppermint tea before she left for work. Ella felt like a princess, savoring the tingle of the tea and lounging on the parlor's burgundy sofa. The tick of the antique clock on the mantelpiece was loud, each click a relief, another second farther away from Joe and Yonkers.

She lay on the couch for another hour, each breath a release, and finally decided to stroll down Harlem's Boulevard of Dreams on a weekday, escorted by an April sun and serenaded by all that was Harlem. She stopped first at the Tree of Hope on 131st and Seventh Avenue—the broad-leafed elm with its buds growing green and full, not yet bursting, the exact spot that Anise Boyer had stood in the movie she and Charles had seen and what felt like a lifetime ago. Like Anise, Ella rubbed its smooth bark, and thought of how many other dreamers' palms had caressed it. She closed her eyes tight and wished for luck. Now that she was living in Harlem, it felt like all of her wishes to be a big-time dancer could come true.

As if that weren't enough, just a few minutes later she walked right past Ethel Waters, striding along the sidewalk as if she were everyday Harlem folk—if everyday Harlem folk wore full-length furs. Diamonds fluttered from her ears, sparkling over her shoulders like the beginnings of a halo. Miss Waters had starred in *Rhapsody in Black* on Broadway, and she was the most glamorous Negro woman that Ella had seen in person.

Ella took this sighting as an omen that better times lay ahead for her, too.

Later, Ella would come to understand that there was nothing like seeing someone who looked like you succeeding at what she loved to do; it turned on a light switch in an otherwise forbidden room, broadcasting a message, *Yes, you, too, can shine.* Women, colored women like Ella, were on the stage and in the movies, breathing the same air she breathed, and their feet were touching the very ground she walked on. She, too, would shine, she told herself.

And she was in the one place in the world where it seemed possible for a colored girl to shine: Harlem.

Down bustling streets lined with beautiful brownstone row houses, some as magnificent as castles, colored people lived, people of all hues, from blue-veined to dark, every one of them nurturing grand expectations. No small-town Yonkers nobody, where your biggest hope was to one day clerk for a grocery store or sweep a floor. Here people rubbed the Tree of Hope on their way to big-time possibilities, like auditions that would land them in the spotlight.

And on their way to the jackpot they would saunter down the sidewalk with movie stars. *That's how close your dreams were: they'd brush your elbow as you turned a corner or loitered in front of a shop window.* Of course Ella would be a famous dancer at the Savoy, just like her mother had promised, back before the fight and before Ella's world had disintegrated.

Now she explored the streets, swaying to music that trilled from clarinets playing on street corners. Harlem would offer its treasures to her now that she no longer had to leave it each night. She was home.

Kids her age, clad in glittering imitation ballroom clothes and ragtail top hats, tap-danced for nickels and dimes seemingly on every street corner. She was like them. They, too, wanted more from life. Many lived together in an area they called Black Broadway along

Seventh Avenue, between 130th and 140th Streets. They were art-ists, she'd learn in the weeks and months that followed, determined to make it with their talents.

On one block, she stood to watch a boy about her age tap-dance like a young Bojangles, confident in his bandy twist, back flap, and ball change. Tall and heavyset, he was still quick on his feet, light as a ballet master. *Hot dog,* she thought. He must have started dancing in the cradle. He'd be a perfect partner, if only he weren't so grubby. His clothes were tattered, the armpits black with sweat; spots and food stains splashed his shirt. Ella ached with missing Charles. He had been her steadfast partner and now she had no one. This boy was her first glimmer of hope that she might be able to scrounge up someone else. He would never replace Charles, of course, but maybe he would work for now.

He ended his routine with a barrel roll, twisting his torso and ex-tending his arms like a windmill. He delighted the crowd—the coins rang on the sidewalk and in his hat. A couple of smaller kids went from person to person, hands extended, collecting more. One big, mean-looking girl, hair standing with tufts on her head, was also tak-ing the money. She stared threateningly at Ella.

When he finished his routine and the crowd applauded, the big girl drifted to one side, so Ella eased up to the boy and introduced herself. "Those were some amazing steps," she told him. "What's your name?"

He grinned at her, revealing a missing front tooth. "Hey thanks. I'm Boss Man." He was out of breath, wiping sweat from his forehead and cheeks.

She was suddenly conscious of how close he was standing to her, and could smell the sweat of him—bitter, like old onions, but not unpleasant. "Boss Man? Who you the boss of?" She breathed him in deep.

He waved his hand at the crew of kids, all still rustling the crowd for money. One little boy beat the ground rhythmically with two sticks. "It all me. These is my steps." He tapped the side of his head. "All out of here." Spinning around twice, he broke into a split, and then stood, his legs scissoring together as if he were being pulled up by an invisible rope. "And I makes all da money," he said. Then he started coughing—coughed so loud and so long that people turned to look.

"Are you okay?" Ella asked him.

"Sho is. It was raining hard last night when I fell asleep. Musta got something in my throat."

"Can you show me that move?" Ella said. "How did you get up from the splits like that?"

"My moves is gold. I don't just give 'em away. What you gonna give me?" He looked over at the growing crowd and at the mean girl, probably his girlfriend, eyeing him.

"I can get you into the clubs, and you can make a whole lot more money there than on the street. I need a dance partner. What you say?"

"Can you dance? I don't wanna be dancing with no girl can't dance."

Ella broke out in her Fitzgerald Snakehips for him. She caught sight of the big girl, and put her everything into it. The kids and a few pedestrians watched. A few clapped.

"Okay. I'll think about it," Boss Man told her with a wink. "You ain't half bad."

"Who is you?" The big girl was in her face, a cluster of braids standing up like boulders in an open field. "What you want here?"

"Just looking to dance," Ella said.

"She want a dance partner," Boss Man told the girl. "She say she can get me into the big clubs. Like the Savoy and the Lafayette."

"What you want wit dat?" the girl spat. "Dem folks acting all high and glorified."

"Might be good," Boss Man said. "She dance a whole lot better than you."

"If you want you some lovin' from me you best not tangle wit her," the girl said.

He winked again at Ella. "You come find me and maybe we'll try us a practice. See how you do."

"Okay," she said. The girl gave her the evil eye again but Ella just grinned at her. "See you soon, Boss Man."

He started to dance, and soon the crowd was back, clapping and stamping. Ella slipped off. She could hear the audience's roar halfway down the block. She hugged herself tight, thinking that she'd found her new dance partner.

Oh, she loved this place, where colored folks' industry and talent were welcomed and celebrated. Barbershops, grocery stores, pool halls, and beauty parlors were two to a block, sometimes more. Business owners with no storefronts sold ice, shined shoes, peddled their own food—southern, Caribbean, or Harlem homestyle—right on the street. It was their town, their culture, their Mecca, a medley of lives and lifestyles. Cobblestone streets, tired but steady horses pulling ice, junk wagons, men and women dressed to the nines riding in new Ford cars. Garbage can fires warming the homeless. Black people had found a place to breathe and simply be. Harlem was home.

And then, about an hour or so after she left Boss Man, she caught her first sight of Zukie Cabell hightailing it out of a barbershop. She'd never seen anything like him. For a moment she thought that he was the flamboyant big band leader, Cab Calloway, in the flesh. In the movies, dressed in white, he seemed shining and clean and somehow bigger and more alive than anyone else she'd ever seen before—until she saw the man leaving the barbershop.

He was grinning, white teeth flashing along with his rings, as he tucked something in his jacket, waved nonchalantly to the men inside the barbershop. That first afternoon, she didn't know who he was, what he would mean to her, but she noticed him. Some people turn the air silver around them; a silence, an ache, glow in their vicinity. Sometimes it's enough to be in their presence, and sometimes you want them to notice you; but always you want to be near them, to be acknowledged by them, as if the touch of their eyes will make you brighter, more yourself.

That day he wore his signature cream suit jacket and matching trousers, with cream-colored spats, and cream-colored laces to match. He was too bright for dirt to settle upon, as if he didn't quite inhabit this world.

She would see him again that weekend, at the Lafayette, and that would cement her fascination with him, but that first afternoon he summed up all that Harlem could be: glittering, ripe with opportunity, golden with hope.

But her early optimism in this new Harlem life was tempered almost immediately by reality, which kept looming in front of her, undeniable. The gloss of Harlem was like some of the clothes that Tempie used to take in for laundering: seeming at first tightly woven and strong, but when submerged in soapy water, revealing worn patches, darned, threadbare, torn.

That evening, when she returned to Auntie's from wandering the streets, she found her pulling garbage for the landlord, which she did every Monday and Thursday. On other evenings, Auntie was mopping the hallway, polishing the mailboxes. Weekends she'd take in laundry, hanging other people's sheets and blouses surreptitiously behind interior doors. Her nursing salary didn't cover rent and electricity, so Auntie used a jumper cable to keep the lights on. If the landlord caught her, he would bribe her to pay more rent or might kick her out.

Even more frightening, Auntie often seemed as tired and worn as Ella's mother had been. Harlem wasn't all dreams and possibilities. A few days after her arrival, desperate to keep her Auntie rested, Ella took over as many of Virginia's chores as she could.

Soon it was Ella mopping the floors and pulling the garbage. She'd stay up late to clean the apartment and wake up early to make Georgie's breakfast. Auntie would not only be grateful for Ella's presence, but would need her. She was never, ever, going back to Joe again. She couldn't even think about what might be happening to Frannie up in Yonkers, and she told herself she'd rescue her sister as soon as she was able.

When she first arrived in Harlem, she thought that she could earn money as she'd done in Yonkers, by demonstrating dance steps with Boss Man. But in Harlem everyone already knew the dance steps— they were dancing those steps every night. So that wasn't an option. When she broached the subject of dancing on street corners, Auntie told her that was "common" and not something that Ella would be doing.

But none of that stopped Ella from dancing.

She'd gone looking for Boss Man on his corner, but he hadn't been there. She recognized one of the street kids and asked him where Boss Man was. The kid shrugged, kicked at a broken piece of glass on the sidewalk, didn't answer. She wandered the streets, but never found him.

By now she'd been at Auntie's for a couple of weeks, and her bruises were healing. That evening, when she asked Auntie if she could still go to the local clubs to dance, Auntie gave her a curfew. "I want you home and in bed by nine," she told Ella. "You need a good night's sleep to get a good day's education."

"The bands don't really start playing till after ten," Ella protested, but gently. She was worried that any disrespect would send her back to Yonkers. Auntie never threatened this, but the understanding lay between them. "If I have to be back by nine, I won't get any dancing in."

Auntie considered and relented. "Okay, on weekend nights only, you can be out until ten. But no later. I don't want you breaking my curfew, miss."

That didn't mean that Ella was allowed to go alone to the clubs. If Charles were there, that would be one thing, but Charles was up in Yonkers and "there isn't any way that a fifteen-year-old girl is going by herself into those places," Auntie told her. "With all those grown men? And if you come back home with King Kong on your breath. . ." King Kong was the local hooch, bottled and sold throughout the neighborhoods.

Since she couldn't find Boss Man, Ella asked the only boy she knew in Harlem, a hulking bumpkin from upstairs nicknamed "Woofie," to accompany her. Auntie approved. "He's a good boy," Auntie told her. "Always doing what his mama asked. And a good student to boot. You could do worse than go with him to your club.

Maybe some of his sense will rub off on you." He was tall, and Ella worried he'd be clumsy, but at least he'd be a dance partner.

The real dancing wouldn't begin until much later, but that Friday, just after eight thirty, she and Woofie slipped into the "Rennie"—the Renaissance Ballroom—where several couples were already twirling to "Basin Street Blues." Ella led him to the center of the room as the clarinet serenaded her. She held her arms up in dance position.

He stared at the floor.

"What, you not dancing?" Ella asked him. "Come on."

Half-heartedly he raised his arms, took her left hand in his right. As the crooner on the dais sang, "Won't you come along with me, to the Mississippi? We'll take a trip to the land of dreams," she waited for Woofie to move off into the basic foxtrot, but he'd been planted in that spot and seemed too terrified to move. He rolled his eyes at her, whites showing.

"Come on," she said again, pulling him back into the step, left-right-left-side-together. His feet unstuck and he shambled after her.

Ten seconds in, she realized he actually knew only that very basic step and seemed unable or unwilling to learn more. Every time she tried to pull him into a dip or get him to twirl her, he planted both feet as if bracing for a torrential wind, leaned back, and stared at her blankly. By the end of the song she was dancing around him, swaying to the music, eyes half closed, making up her steps as he stood in the center of her orbit like a rock in the middle of a rushing stream.

And that was when, again, she caught sight of the man in the cream-colored suit.

He was standing near the bar, talking to commanding-looking men who Ella later learned were the club's managers and assistant managers. She noticed that it wasn't just her who was looking at him—it was women, and other men, too.

The man didn't appear to notice. He was smiling at something one of the men said and nodding his head to the beat of the music.

Then, so effortlessly and so smoothly that Ella didn't even notice how it began, like a wave retreating or a bird lifting off in flight, he was holding the hand of a flapper girl and they were drifting into an easy foxtrot, and then into a relaxed grapevine, she bending away and back toward him, feet light and gliding. It seemed as if she, too, were a speck of foam carried along in the tide of his relentless charm, lifting her up and out and onto the dance floor, where they spun and gyrated so fluidly that soon an empty space of onlookers opened up around them.

It wasn't the girl, Ella realized—she could barely keep up. It was all him, his light brown calfskin spats like a sand-colored blur, his shoulders spreading like wings.

"Who is that?" she asked Woofie. He said something that Ella didn't catch. She wasn't really listening. She elbowed her way closer to watch.

People were calling out, "That's it, Zukie! That's how it's done!"

The song ended and applause fluttered around him, and he waved to the crowd, effortless and nonchalant. He put the girl's fingers to his lips in a gesture that was both chivalrous and mocking.

Then he was gone, standing there until suddenly he wasn't, and the room seemed dimmer in his absence. Even his dancing partner looked around for him, confused.

This was Ella's introduction to Zukie Cabell. He would embody everything of those days: beauty, grace, inexorable charm, and uncaring self-regard—like giving a top hat to a man down on his luck, knowing full well he will pawn it for something to eat.

But that would come later. On this night she knew none of this and was glowing and dancing all the way back to Auntie's, Woofie three paces behind.

—

The Wadleigh High School for Girls, down on 114th Street in Central Harlem, was a twenty-minute bus ride away. The enormous brick public school offered an exceptional education for colored girls. Unlike almost all other schools in the city, Wadleigh fully embraced integration, with white girls sitting next to colored girls, using the same water fountains and the same bathrooms.

Auntie was adamant that Ella, like Georgie, attend. They couldn't afford a new plaid skirt for her uniform, but Auntie asked her friends for hand-me-downs; and, with Ella, stitched together three ragged skirts into one that looked almost new. True, the green and navy stripes didn't line up precisely, and if you looked closely you could tell where several tears had been mended, but Ella was proud to smooth it over her legs.

"This is where you'll get yourself a real diploma," Auntie told her. "No telling how far it'll take you. You can be a teacher someday. Or a lady lawyer. You buckle down and pay attention to your education. Reading and math in particular. Who knows how far you'll go."

All of Auntie's education, and all of Tempie's, hadn't gotten them very far, Ella wanted to say but she held her tongue. She liked school, and having an education as a backup was only prudent. The girls were nice enough, although in close quarters, many of the colored girls looked hungry and put-upon. Fewer white girls attended than she'd imagined, and those were mostly from the neighborhood.

She was determined to be the model student and the model niece, so every morning she was up well before sunrise, sweeping the kitchen and tidying the living room; and every afternoon she'd wash and hang out Aunt Virginia's stockings and nursing uniform. She ran a lemon oil cloth over the furniture so often that the carved back of the parlor room couch took on an oily sheen. After a couple of weeks, Aunt Virginia gently suggested that perhaps once a week was enough to dust the furniture. Ella relented, but plumped the cushions extra high and even ironed their undergarments.

The next Saturday night, and the next, she dragged Woofie back to her clubs: Minton's, and then her beloved Savoy. She kept an eye out for the cream-suited man, Zukie, but didn't see him. She knew that Woofie wasn't going to work out as her dance partner, and she had never found Boss Man again. She wrote repeatedly to Charles to ask him when he could get down to Harlem, but only received two regretful postcards in reply: he couldn't come the first weekend because he'd hurt his leg, and the second weekend he wasn't feeling well.

A quiet sense of panic began to percolate in Ella's chest—she didn't know how she could make it as a dancer if she didn't have a partner.

Some of the boys on Black Broadway were talented, but grimy. They seemed to be living on the street. Auntie wouldn't approve of them at all, so she steered clear. Which didn't leave a lot of options, since she now attended an all-girls school. "Just you sit tight," Auntie told her one evening when she was telling her how difficult it was to keep up her dancing. "You'll find someone. Besides, you should just teach Woofie. I think he's sweet on you."

Woofie, with the cow's body and the dopey expression, his mouth half-open. What magical routines could he perform, how could he flash and glitter in the dance hall lights when he could barely follow the simplest steps?

She worried that her dancing would grow rusty, but she was more worried about her survival at Auntie's.

Ella had thought that Auntie lived well, and that Tempie had scraped by. After all, Virginia was a trained nurse with only one child, and Tempie was a laundress with an unreliable husband and two children. Ella soon realized that Auntie's life felt more precarious than she'd realized. A velvet sofa and a nonworking fireplace didn't mean enough cornmeal to make cornbread, or enough money to hire an exterminator. A week after she'd arrived, sleeping with Georgie in the pristine bedroom with clean white linen, Ella woke up to squeaking and black eyes staring at her. Terrified, she nudged Georgie awake, who screamed. Auntie came charging into the bedroom with a broom to chase a large rat that had gnawed through the floorboards. They dragged the bureau over the hole, but that didn't stop the cockroaches: no matter how much boric acid Auntie sprinkled in the corners or in the cabinets, they always reappeared.

Auntie, like Tempie, worked long hours; but unlike Tempie, she didn't have Joe to supplement their income. She had higher rent and food bills, too. Learning about Auntie's finances made Ella begin to question that last night's fight with her mother. Maybe things *had* been bad with her mama and Joe—maybe Tempie hadn't exaggerated that they needed Ella's income. The doubt crept in, and would creep in for years: that Tempie hadn't been trying to sabotage Ella's dreams, but was only trying to keep them alive, so Ella would have the bare necessities of food and shelter.

The world in 1932 could often be terrifying. One day, as Ella headed home, she passed an old man slumped against a brick wall, so skinny his bones pressed through his thin pants. His eyes were wide open, as if he were bewildered, and he didn't appear drunk. He caught Ella's eye and bared a gap-toothed grin at her, then jerked his hand out like the flapping wing of an injured bird. Something about the gesture—the rhythm, the open fingers—reminded her of a dancer's open hand, stretched out under a spotlight, and horror and pity danced around her. Perhaps this would be her in a few years.

She groped in her pocket for a nickel, handed it to him. He nodded, and then his face closed up and went sullen. He hated the handouts, she thought. He hated having to rely on other people. She couldn't blame him. The bread lines in front of the churches or storefronts stretched around the block.

One day in early May, when school let out, she didn't take her usual city bus back to Auntie's. Instead, she wandered over to 116th Street and passed Minton's, which was blowing swing music onto the street. The band practiced during the day; outside, a guitar player strummed an acoustic guitar.

Almost before she was aware of it, Ella began to dance a whole eight-bar dance step, feet breaking time and arms pinwheeling.

"You sure can dance, little thang," the guitar player told her. She grinned and did a soft-shoe tap dance, segueing to a slide.

"You might be able to get work in the club if you can dance to a full band," the guitar player told her. "You might even be able to open our act if you have a dance partner and a routine."

There it was again: *if you have a dance partner.* She did a spin to cartwheel, flashing her arms into jazz hands, and then she bowed, as if on stage. The guitar player gave her a thumbs-up. When he took a break from playing and went inside, she ran to the nearest bus stop so she could get her chores done, wondering how she could get Charles to come to—or move to!—Harlem.

10

Ain't Quittin' on the Ballroom Floor

May 14, 1932

Ella plain missed Charles. Despite their promises to practice, she'd only seen him once, two weeks after she'd left Yonkers. They'd arranged to meet at the Savoy and had performed their favorite Lindy Hop routine. It hadn't gone well. She'd left early because of Auntie's curfew, and Charles had gone home promising to trek down to Harlem more often. But then he'd written letters, begging off. She wasn't sure she believed him.

She kept writing to him, catching him up on her daily life, trying to encourage him to visit. And in the second week in May, she wrote him another note, telling him that she'd try to come to Yonkers the following weekend. She'd take back routes to avoid Joe and wear a hat to hide her face. They could spend the day dancing and perhaps head back to Harlem to the Savoy that evening.

On Saturday, after she'd completed all her chores for Aunt Virginia, she took the subway and trolley back up to Yonkers. It was a gorgeous May morning, the sun radiant, the day warm on her face, thawing her hands and mood. Auntie had hot-combed her hair and twisted it in a French roll just like Georgie's. Ella felt pretty in a clean white dress and hat. Her brown-and-white striped oxfords— regulation footwear at the Wadleigh School—made her feel grown up and glamorous. Auntie had gotten them from a nurse whose daughter had moved away and left them in the closet.

This was the first time she'd been back on School Street, and she was surprised at how little she'd missed it. Her life in Yonkers seemed like it had been so long ago, but she yearned for Tempie. Just to be where her mother had been, to breathe that air and touch the same sidewalks. She felt brave and a little foolhardy to come back. It was late morning, so who knew where Joe was right then. She could run into him on the street. So she tucked her head between her shoulders and kept the brim of her hat low across her eyes, just in case. The low brick apartment buildings, row upon row, seemed to smirk, dream-like, at her. Her heart beat fast.

She wanted to see Frannie but hadn't figured out how to manage it. She was embarrassed by what had happened—Joe forcing himself upon her, Frannie pretending to be asleep. Perhaps Charles could help Ella see her.

When she got off the trolley, she headed directly to Charles's. He opened the door with a dramatic flourish, hugging her tight and slightly longer than was necessary. She hugged him right back.

He hadn't told his mother that Ella was coming—if Mrs. Gulliver had known, she would have been home, and practicing their dance steps would have been impossible. They had the apartment to themselves.

The living room looked exactly the same. She'd only been gone a month. It felt as if time mocked her, as if nothing had changed.

Yet it somehow surprised her that plastic still covered the white couch, that porcelain figurines still stared down from the shelves. She focused on the spot where she'd stood when she'd heard of Tempie's death, and where Joe had stood, how he held his hat and wouldn't look Ella full in the face. Perhaps it had been a mistake to return.

Charles placed Fats Waller's "Ain't Misbehavin'" on the phonograph and took a few forward quicksteps, holding up his arms in dance position. "Come on," he said, but her feet didn't quite manage to move. She wasn't ready to dance just yet. She wanted to talk.

"How's your mom? How's Annette?" They were both out shopping.

"They're fine." He shrugged.

"The street dancers in Harlem do so many things we haven't seen in the clubs. You've got to come down and see them—they're incredible. There's this one girl over on 124th, she does this twist and spin with the Lindy Hop. It's great! If we work the steps into our routine, we're going to be stars. The Savoy is going to be begging us to dance in the Corner. I know it."

"That sounds fun," he said. "It's great that you're finding us new steps."

"Why did it take so long for you to answer my letters?"

He looked away. "I hate writing."

"But we have to stay in touch. We have to practice. We have to be a team."

"Then shouldn't we dance?" he said, grinning. He took another swallow from the glass, went over to the phonograph, and put the needle back to the beginning. He held up his arms again.

Within moments they were anticipating each other's moves, the way they'd used to. They practiced the Charleston for a good half hour, the swivel step, Johnny's Drop, and Savoy kicks. By the end, despite some initial clumsiness, it was all flowing. At last, Ella called a halt and flopped down on the couch, which crinkled uncomfortably beneath her.

Charles got them fresh glasses of water. "You seen your papa lately?"

She shook her head. "He's not my papa. Besides, I didn't come all this way to talk about him. I sure wish we had a telephone. It's so hard to do this."

"My mom wants to get a party line. She said when that happens, we have to be careful because Ma Bell will have our business all over town." Mrs. Gulliver had talked about getting a phone for ages, but had never done so.

"How much does it cost?" Maybe Ella somehow could purchase a telephone for Aunt Virginia. That would be a daily reminder of how important Ella was to the household.

"I dunno," Charles said. "Three dollars a month? Five?"

Three dollars a month might as well have been a million. She wouldn't think about it until they were dancing regularly again.

"Let's go to Minton's," she said, folding herself into his arms and sliding easily backward into the basic quickstep. "I was talking to the assistant manager. We can open up for a band there if we show them our routine."

"I don't know," he said, spinning her. "Our routine is so old. We haven't practiced in how long? And there's so many new dance moves out now. We have to catch up."

"We'll catch up," she told him fiercely, her face inches from his. "We will. You just have to come down to Harlem more."

He looked away, over her shoulder. "Your papa isn't doing well. My mom saw him the other day and she said he looked terrible. Like he wasn't sleeping and lost weight."

"I told you I don't want to talk about him," she said. "I want to dance. Plenty of money there. We can do rent parties. Dance outside the clubs. Entertain people before they go in. Then the managers can see how good we are. And we get to meet all these new people and people who dance like us. You have to come. You have to!"

He spun her around in a fast turn and she landed hard. The phonograph skipped in the middle of the bridge of "Ain't Misbehavin'."

Charles ran over to rescue the record. "I don't know," he said, his back to her. "I just don't know if I can do it."

"What do you mean, you don't know?"

He fumbled with the record.

"Don't you want to dance with me?" she asked.

"I guess I do," he said as if he were trying to convince himself, and her. "I don't know."

Anger simmered in her face, which was suddenly hot. She'd somehow expected this. "What *do* you know?"

"I'm doing my best," he told her.

"That ain't good enough," she said. "Everything's different now. I have to make money. I have to earn my keep. I need to be ready."

"Ready for what?" He stood by the record player, and seemed as if he were trying to retreat behind the Victrola.

"Ready for the big time," she said.

"I don't think you live in the real world," he said. "Every time I spend fifty cents going to Harlem, I take that money out of my mother's pocket."

"What are you saying? Are you telling me you're going to stop dancing?"

He was looking at the floor. "Dancing is for fun. I guess I don't think of it like you do."

"What about competition money?"

"I heard those big competition money contests are going away. Connie's Inn already stopped theirs."

"I don't believe you," she said.

"The country's in a depression. My mom's lucky to still have a job. We have to cut back. I have to look for work, since I'm the man of the house." She stared at how his hair curled around his temples, around the small fold of his earlobes. He suddenly seemed impossibly distant, as if he were standing on the subway platform and she were on the train, disappearing into the night.

She could feel it; she'd moved on, or he had. They were not dancing in lockstep anymore. She was burning to be more, to be better, to live a life beyond Yonkers. She could see him sweeping floors at a hardware store, stocking shelves, becoming a store clerk after high school, finding a nice girl and marrying her, settling down. The man of a house. There was nothing wrong with that, but she knew it wasn't for her.

She tried again, one last time. "You can dance. Dancing is work."

"Steady, real work," he said. "Like a newspaper route, or in a grocery store. Or being a janitor." She hadn't ever told him—told no one—of that last fight with her mother, but here Charles was, parroting Tempie. Settling for a regular paycheck. It was as if all the world were conspiring, forcing her to choose the safe path. The known path.

Ella found her vision blurring. She distracted herself by looking for her hat. She'd dropped it in a corner of the tiny foyer. She pinned it on. Her best friend, her dancing partner, was going to harness his dreams to a broom. Well, she wasn't going to do that. No broom would ever sweep her away.

"Where you going?" Charles had followed her. The music had ended and the relentless hiss of the spinning phonograph spilled out from the living room.

"I'm leaving," she said. "I'm not quitting. I don't care about a Depression. I see people in Harlem who don't care either—like at Minton's. Or at the Savoy. Or on the streets. Everywhere." She opened his front door with fingers weak and a little sweaty. "They make music and they dance to live. And that's where I'm going. I don't need nobody to take care of me. You want to be a janitor? Go 'head. I don't need you."

"Hey, Ella, hold on a minute. You know I don't mean—"

The door slammed loudly behind her in the hallway. She kept hoping he would open it, kept expecting him to call to her, to say that of course he'd be dancing with her, that he wanted more, too.

The elevator arrived. She stepped in and the doors closed. Charles's door never opened.

Okay then, she'd have to dance without Charles, would have to put all the thoughts about having just lost her best and only friend out of her mind. She'd have to find a new dance partner. Boss Man. Zukie Cabell. It felt like another door was permanently closing in her life, but she would force another one to open.

Out on the street, she automatically turned up the sidewalk to 72, her old building. She halted a few feet away. Nothing had changed. The building didn't care that she'd left. Its faded red bulk ate up the sky, vacant-looking and lonely. Frannie might be home. She decided to risk seeing Joe—she was desperate to see her sister again. Besides, Frannie was younger and innocent. The thought of Joe going after her made Ella slide her front door key into the lock and head up to the apartment.

In the hall outside her old apartment, she paused again, couldn't decide if she should just go in or should knock.

She knocked.

A moment later Frannie opened the door. She launched herself into Ella's arms.

"Hey, it's okay," Ella said, and then repeated it over and over. Somehow this was what she'd expected from Charles, and that made her hug her sister even more tightly. "It's okay."

Frannie squeezed back.

"I've missed you so much!"

"Can I come in?"

"Yeah," Frannie said. "He's not here."

Ella slipped inside. The floor could use sweeping and clothes were piled next to the couch, but everything looked like it had when she left. "Are you okay?"

"Yeah," Frannie said, sounding unconvinced. "I'm okay."

"Doesn't sound like it. Is he being mean to you?"

She shook her head. "He's okay. I'm okay. Really. I just miss you, is all."

"I miss you, too. You've got to get down to Auntie's. Come for Sunday dinner."

Frannie beamed at her. "I'd like that a lot. How's Auntie?"

"She's good. Georgie's a pain though."

"Georgie's always a pain." They shared a grin. They both liked Georgie, but she could put on airs.

Ella prowled the apartment. The dishes were washed in the kitchen, and the counter was clean. Frannie was doing a nice job. Ella was relieved. She didn't know why she had found these kinds of chores so difficult to do for Joe, or why he had never been satisfied with what Ella had done—because she'd certainly tried. She'd kept the apartment as tidy, or tidier, than Frannie.

"Are you coming back?" Frannie asked.

"No. I came up to practice with Charles. I couldn't tell you I was coming because I figured he'd read your letters."

"You can write. He never looks at the mail anyway."

"Then I'll write," Ella said. "Every week. Or more."

"That would be great," Frannie said. "You can tell me what crazy things Georgie did."

They both laughed.

"Are you cooking?" Ella asked.

"I'm not here all the time. But I know how to cook eggs and easy stuff. Papa picks up something on his way home. Bread or a meat pie if he has the money."

Frannie answered the unspoken question. "I eat at Maisie's house most nights. He lets me stay over. He never says nothing. It's like he doesn't even care if I come home."

At least there was food—bread, oatmeal, flour—in the pantry. Onions, potatoes, and a few carrots in the icebox. But the apartment felt damp and chilly, despite the warmth of the May day outside.

Ella sat down at the kitchen table. She felt slightly amazed at how she'd ever lived here. Now she saw the appeal of Auntie's burgundy sofa, the high ceilings and fireplace. This apartment was so small. Her bedroom with Frannie was a closet, and the kitchen was half the size of Auntie's. "How are you? Are you going to school?"

"Yeah, I'm going to school. I guess I'm alright. Papa hasn't been good though. He keeps missing work."

"Is he paying the rent?" Ella asked.

Frannie slid into the chair across from her. She shrugged. "I don't know."

"What's wrong with him?"

Another shrug.

—

Frannie looked at the kitchen wall. "I wish you'd taken me with you."

"I wanted to. I will. Aunt Virginia doesn't have much money but I'm trying to get a job. So I can bring you."

"You mean it?" Frannie said. Again their eyes locked.

Ella nodded. "I mean it."

"I hope so."

"You're my sister," Ella told her. "No matter what happens."

"You should go," Frannie said. "I don't know when he'll be back."

Ella stood, relieved. "Come here," she said, and hugged Frannie the way that her mother used to, and the way that Auntie had when Ella appeared on her doorstep: tight, long, and never wanting to let go.

11

Eyes Like Fresh Pennies

May 21, 1932

On Saturday night, Ella dragged Woofie to Connie's Inn on 131st and Seventh Avenue. They went down to the cavernous basement, which had been converted to a dance hall. Usually it was whites-only, but during certain hours, it opened to colored folks.

They'd been dancing for about twenty minutes, Ella hauling Woofie's bulk around the dance floor in a pathetic attempt at a Charleston—he refused to pick up his knees or swing his feet— when she caught sight of Zukie Cabell leaning on the bar, his head tilted back in a laugh, his white teeth flashing as he shook his straight black hair out of his face. Blue light from the dance floor flickered and danced across him, as if he were under water, or part of the sky.

They moved past him once, and then Ella maneuvered Woofie around so she could stare at the café au lait man again. He really did look like Cab Calloway. She studied him, the clean line of his shoulders, how he leaned on the bar, one toe balanced to reveal scuffed leather soles. She realized a second too late that she'd stopped dancing, and Woofie smashed into her, sending her sprawling, knocking into another couple. "Hey," Woofie apologized. "What happened?" He leaned forward to help her.

She barely noticed his outstretched hand, because Zukie Cabell himself was standing over her, right behind Woofie, and then was in front of him, holding out his hand, his sugar-cream face so animated. A large green ring glittered from a forefinger. His eyes, so close, were a tawny shade of rust, like fresh pennies. His hand was smooth when she took it, strong as he pulled her to her feet, deft as he lifted her into dance position.

"May I have this dance?" he said, voice soft but gallant. He acknowledged Woofie with a nod, and then turned his copper-bright eyes back to her.

Mesmerized, she realized she was dancing—that he'd done the same thing with her that he'd done with that other girl a few weeks ago. He was the most compelling man she had ever met, maybe a half-dozen years older than her, but he was a man, not a boy. She had to remember to breathe or she would pass out.

He led her in a foxtrot through the Duke's "It Don't Mean a Thing If It Ain't Got That Swing," and Ella willed her nervous feet to remain untangled; she felt so clumsy. He smelled manly and wild, sea spray from Coney Island mixing with whiskey and tobacco. He held her close, hand warm on the small of her back.

"You're a good dancer," she said. "I'm Ella. I just moved to Harlem and I'm looking for a dance partner."

"You are, are you?" A laugh rumbled in him, and she could feel it thrum through her, too: like an engine purring, or a cat, or a bass-line in a song.

"I want to dance in the Corner. In the Savoy," she said.

"You do, do you?" he said, spinning her out and then pulling her close. His voice was exactly the way she'd imagined it would be: smooth and low, but with a spark of light running through it, like his eyes.

As the last strains of the melody fell around them, he tilted her into an exotic, long dip. She kicked one foot in the air, toe extended, like she saw the best dancers do.

And then the music ended, and he tilted his head slightly, and kissed her fingertips without quite touching his lips to them, and slipped away, leaving her standing in the middle of the dance floor, alone, as Woofie waved at her from the sidelines.

"We have to get home," Woofie said, coming up to her as she tried to follow Zukie. Where had he gone?

"We have a few minutes. Did you see where he went?"

"Who?"

"Who! The boy—the man—I was dancing with. Where did he go so fast?"

"Zukie? He right there." Woofie pointed to a dark corner of the club, and Ella shuffled around to get a better view. There Zukie was, half-blocked by a large woman in a bright red dress. "He's over there. Taking care of his business, I guess."

"Hold on. You know him?" Ella asked.

"Everybody know him." Woofie sucked on his teeth. "Zukie Cabell."

"Zukie Cabell," Ella repeated. He glowed under the blue light as he leaned against a wall and wrote something down for a dapper-looking man. "It's such a lovely name."

"Your auntie won't like it."

"What do you mean?" Zukie would be the perfect dance partner. Auntie would love him—his cleanliness, his beautiful clothes, his polished shoes.

"He's a numbers runner. I coulda been one, too." Woofie said, as if trying to minimize Zukie's value. "Come on, we have to go now. My mama and your auntie gonna be waiting for us. It's almost ten o'clock and I always get you home on time."

"Wait a minute. Give me a nickel."

"For what?"

"Give me a nickel," she repeated, one eye on Zukie. It looked like he was getting ready to leave. She danced impatiently in front of Woofie as he fished in his pocket.

"Oh my God, wait a minute." He finally handed her a nickel.

Zukie had finished talking to the men at the bar and was waving casually at them, sauntering away, around a corner toward the exit. She ducked around dancing couples, dashed in pursuit. She caught sight of him now flirting with the hat-check girl, leaning over the banquette as she giggled stupidly up at him, all lipstick and eyes as she handed over his hat, a cream-colored fedora with a white band and a pale blue feather poking up, as if a bit of sky had landed on his head.

Ella held back, feeling shy. This gorgeous, tall, broad-shouldered man wouldn't want to have anything to do with her.

But he'd danced with her. He must have found something in her that he liked. And he said that she was a good dancer. Well, maybe he hadn't said it in words but he danced with her like he knew she could dance, and that meant something, didn't it?

Her legs were moving across the floor and she was in front of him, holding out her nickel.

He didn't seem at all surprised to see her. "Hi, Sassy Feet," he said.

"Sassy Feet?" Ella asked. "Who's Sassy Feet?"

"You are. Funny girl." He burst out laughing. "What's your name?"

"Ella." She'd told him already.

"Do you know my name?" He stood over her, grinning down. There was that wonderful scent again. Whiskey, tobacco, and man perfume.

"No. Yeah. Zukie Cabell." Ella couldn't help grinning back. She prayed she didn't look silly.

"Then you know what I do." He moved even closer to her, and Ella didn't mind a bit. The orchestra was playing the instrumental version of "Harlem Holiday."

Ella swayed back and forth to it. "Numbers runner," she said, almost giggling. The band and Zukie made her giddy.

"Do you want to place a bet?"

"I want to do everything you do. I want to play numbers."

"You don't look like you play numbers."

"I want to learn. Can you teach me?"

"Come on, kid, keep your nickel." Zukie walked away, a "See you around" floating out behind him as he slipped up the steps and the door closed. Suddenly the vast dance hall, which moments before had seemed mysterious and magical, now felt harsh with smoke, glaring with noise that was no longer music.

Woofie was next to her, holding her coat. "Come on," he said. "Let's go home." She handed him back the nickel. When they reached the street, she looked again for Zukie, but he'd disappeared.

They wandered home, the brownstones of Central Harlem quiet shadows behind the streetlights. Their footsteps rang out on the sidewalk. She asked Woofie, "How you know Zukie Cabell?"

"He wanted me to be a numbers runner. Said I could make a lot of money."

"Why wouldn't you do it then?" She thought about how desperate Auntie was for money.

"That's gangster life," Woofie said automatically, as if he'd heard someone say this many times before. "You don't want nothing to do with them people."

Most people in Harlem played the numbers, from mailmen to teachers to Auntie's church folks. A winning bet could be worth six hundred dollars. She didn't quite understand how it all worked, but knew that you bet your pocket change that a handful of numbers would win. She did understand, though, that almost everyone gambled in Harlem—including Aunt Virginia. But as far as Auntie was concerned, it wasn't dignified and she certainly didn't want it to be common knowledge. Auntie prayed up her numbers right out the Bible, and discreetly gave them to Mr. Herbert, the newspaper man, when she purchased her *Amsterdam News* on Mondays and Thursdays. It was just something she did in passing. She never made a fuss about it. It was like adding milk to her coffee—newspaper and numbers. Ella had thought that Aunt Virginia spent so much time with her Bible for religious reasons only: now she knew better.

"Zukie said I'd be good at numbers because of my size and all." Woofie was big, easily over six feet tall, and filled out, although it was more flab than muscle. "He said I had what it took to be a player."

"You think you're a player?" she asked cautiously.

"Nah," he said. "I don't have the right attitude. Players is mean."

"Zukie Cabell doesn't seem mean," Ella told him.

"He ruthless. That's what my mama says. Ruthless." It didn't seem like a word that Woofie was familiar with, and certainly didn't seem to describe Zukie.

"Could I do it?"

Woofie started laughing, hanging on to a lamppost. "You? You think you're ruthless?"

"I'm serious," Ella told him, frustrated at how difficult this conversation was, but feeling the warmth of hope spread across her shoulders like a cloak. "You have to help me. I need money. Can you talk to him for me? Tell him that I want to be a numbers runner." Maybe this would be her way in: work for him as a numbers runner, and then he could dance with her, too. It would solve all of her problems at once.

"There ain't no girl numbers runners," Woofie said. "They want men. Big men. Girls get hurt or in the way."

"I won't get hurt," she told him, wheedling. "Will you help me? Come on, Woofie."

A long pause. They passed a wrought iron fence, and he trailed his palm along it, the rhythm faint and cool in the darkness. From behind them came the distant sound of sirens, musical and ominous at once. "Okay," he said at last. "I'll help you. But you gotta promise not to tell my mama. I don't want her worrying."

The following Wednesday, Woofie stopped by her apartment after school. It was the last week before summer break. Ella was lying on the burgundy couch, the fan turned up full blast next to her. She was just about to start cleaning. Auntie wouldn't be home till late, so Ella would be making dinner as well.

Woofie stood in the center of the room, grinning his big, toothy grin, and didn't say a word.

"What you all smiling about?" Ella said, turning back to the fan.

"I talked to Zukie. Got a meeting set up."

"You did? Really?" She jumped up and gave him a big hug. She'd almost forgotten that she'd asked Woofie to introduce her—she'd just assumed he'd forget or wouldn't do it.

"You sure you want to go into this racket?" he asked her. "It can be ugly. You ain't seen ugly till you see these folks on full display."

She thought about ugliness, and about the beauty of the cream-colored dancer who'd kissed her fingers. "I do," she told him. "I have to find a way of making some real money. Last night Auntie barely ate so me and Georgie could have dinner. I got to do something."

"Well, just be careful."

"I can work as good as a man." She'd learned that women rarely became numbers runners—most of them were men, imposing, able to slip through the shadows, lethal as butcher knives. But Zukie Cabell didn't look lethal: he looked magical, enticing. If Zukie could do it, so could Ella.

"I don't know if he'll take you," Woofie said. "But you're meeting him at Alfredo's Pool Hall. Saturday, at noon."

"Okay," Ella said. Now she felt intimidated. "Can we go together?"

"Mama don't want me over there in that pool hall," he said. "Don't be late. You never want to be late with those people."

She found out later that her debt to Woofie was greater than she'd imagined. Zukie at first refused to meet her, doubted that a girl could run numbers. Woofie, somehow, talked him into it: bribing him with a half-slab of ribs, corn on the cob, greens, and Mama Tillie's secret-recipe potato salad.

That Saturday, Ella must have changed clothes five times before she felt comfortable in a simple tan skirt and white blouse. Only after she was on the street heading toward the pool hall did she realize that she was wearing Zukie's colors. That was a wonderful sign, she decided.

When she arrived, Zukie was in the middle of a pool game against a husky man in a stunning gray suit. A huge black fedora shaded his face, and he wore shiny patent leather shoes. He was frowning at Zukie, who breezily knocked one ball after another into the pocket. He was, as usual, clad impeccably in cream.

Most of the people in the pool hall were dressed in fedoras, silk suits, and signature gator shoes. A handful of women in glittering skirts perched on stools around different pool tables. The women laughed and waved their hands about, but didn't seem to speak much.

Ella presented herself at Zukie's pool table. He didn't notice her at first, and then that smile, deliberate, barely touched the corners of his lips.

And as if in answer, there was that feeling in Ella again: a tingling sensation in her belly, a rush of happiness, a longing to pull herself up to him and align her body next to his—from the very top of her head to the soles of her feet—and stay there forever.

Zukie hit the eight ball and all eyes were fixed on its roll into the pocket. The onlookers roared. Zukie's opponent hollered, "That ain't right, man, you can't win no three games in a row!"

"Relax," Zukie said, racking his cue. "We don't have no beef. You can pay me when you have it. We sweet." Then he turned to Ella. "Hello there, Sassy Feet."

He remembered her, and she loved it.

She didn't immediately register that the black fedora man now had his hand on Zukie's shoulder and was spinning him around, yelling, "No, nigga, what you know? You using hoodoo or something?"

Zukie didn't waste time. He didn't even talk. He reached for the pool cue he'd just racked, and knocked the fedora off the man's head with one hand as he broke the cue across the man's head with the other. The man stumbled back and grabbed his head. Women screamed. Seconds later spider lines of blood snaked down the man's arm. A big man who looked like a bouncer pulled him away, sat him down in a corner.

Zukie stood there, holding one end of the pool cue, observing. Once the man was seated, Zukie said to Ella, seemingly without any concern, "Come on, let's blow this joint." He strolled out, no blood on him, although now the man in the corner had it dripping onto his collar. Stunned, Ella followed. Perhaps Woofie was right. She had no idea what she was getting herself into. Zukie was more than a suave dancer, a sharp dresser, or a captivating man. He was lethal. He just didn't look it.

The air was sunny, fragrant with oncoming spring. Zukie strolled up Lenox Avenue, took Ella's arm as if they were on a date. "I hear you want to get into the game. Tell me why."

Ella was caught off guard. She'd been thinking about the fight in the pool hall, and then focusing on the feel of her hand tucked against his bicep, his nearness. "I'm hungry," she said. "That's why."

"If you're not hungry, this isn't the racket for you. It's no fool's business. You could get killed. Or worse."

Ella suspected that Zukie wanted her to ask what was worse than being killed, but decided that she probably knew—and if she didn't, she didn't want to. "I learn quick and I listen."

"You have to carry a lot of cash. People will be laying to take that cash from you. And they'll do anything to get it."

"How much cash?"

"A lot," Zukie said. "More than you ever seen in your life."

"How much would be mine?" Excitement jolted Ella's spine.

"A shitload. But people might try killing you for it. Stabbin' you from behind or shootin' you." Zukie pantomimed a knife blade sliding into the back of Ella's skull, then drew his fingers into a gun, fired into Ella's face.

Ella didn't blink.

"You sho look all innocent," Zukie said. "Nobody will suspect you. At least for a while."

"When can I start?" Ella asked.

He laughed out loud, the sound bouncing off the storefronts. Two girls turned to look. A June day had never seemed so bright, so filled with possibility. "You know something, Miss Sassy Feet? I like you," he told her. "And you know something else? Our business needs something different. Lots going on in Harlem, and we need to maneuver. Not attract attention. Having a girl running some of the numbers might help with that."

He studied her. She felt her face flushing. "Maybe you could help us out." She could see him considering, weighing options. Then abruptly he turned, resumed walking, and she had to trot a few steps to keep her hand from slipping away from him. "We're gonna meet my boss. Let's see what he thinks of you."

"Your boss?" Ella hadn't thought that Zukie would have a boss.

"Yeah. He's the one who takes all the money to the banker. But you don't need to concern yourself with any of that right now. All you have to do with your pretty self is stay cool and listen. Answer his questions and don't lie. That's all."

"Now? We going now?" Her voice went up a little, whether from nerves or terror she wasn't sure. But she was sold on Zukie. He had called her pretty. No one, even Charles, ever told her that she was pretty.

"Good," she said, her voice lower, trying for a more casual tone. "I can do that."

She followed Zukie to 135th Street and Lenox Avenue where, on the corner outside the subway entrance, a man wearing a purple suit leaned casually against a mailbox. He had a toothpick in one corner of his mouth. Lazily he eyed Zukie, then Ella.

"That's him," Zukie said, nodding.

Ella realized that she recognized him.

From church.

Zukie's boss, who she later learned was one of the most notorious numbers runners in Harlem, went to the Abyssinian Baptist Church. When Ella had first arrived in Harlem, she'd been intimidated by the block-long line of parishioners. It was a far cry from the small store-front Yonkers church that Tempie attended. The most dignified colored people—doctors, lawyers, politicians—worshipped here. Appearances were part of the worship: well-pressed suits, hand-tailored dresses, women's hair hot-combed and clipped back with jeweled barrettes. No wonder that, every Sunday morning, Auntie agonized over their appearances: dresses were starched crisp, and Ella's and Georgie's legs were oiled, not ashy. They had a special pair of white socks with lace at the hem that they folded down in a perfect ring above their ankles.

Reverend Adam Clayton Powell Sr., the pastor, was revered not only in Harlem, but throughout the country. People said that in his church, one not only heard the voice of God, you also heard what foolishness man was getting himself into.

The first time that Ella accompanied her aunt and cousin, one man stood out: tall, with conked hair. Something about the way he swaggered down the aisle in his purple suit and huge lavender fedora made him seem wickedly alive. One of the ushers followed him, asked him to take off the hat, and Ella glimpsed gold cuff links.

She couldn't resist asking her auntie about him as he settled onto a bench four rows in front of them. "Who's that man in purple?"

"Don't pay him any mind," Aunt Virginia told her. "He doesn't belong here."

Just before the sermon began, Aunt Virginia went over to speak with some friends, and Ella repeated the question to Georgie. "Who's that man? He look like the devil."

"Well, maybe he is the devil."

"Is he rich?"

"You bet he is," Georgie said. "He probably is the devil for sure."

Now on 135th Street, the devil himself was standing in front of her, again wearing that purple suit, leaning back against the brick wall. His arms were crossed and he had a toothpick in his mouth. Toothpicks, Ella had learned, could tell you a lot about a person. The more skilled they were at twirling that toothpick, the slicker they were. This man was a master, flicking it from side to side like an antenna.

"Hey, boss," Zukie said to him. "This spry filly thinks she can run numbers. She wants to work."

The man's eyes traveled her body, down to her school shoes. It suddenly felt as if the world had sped up: people hurried by more quickly, spoke and snickered more loudly. Down the block a woman in a beaded yellow evening dress screamed at a scrawny man cowering in a doorway before she stormed away. Her dress glittered like a walking jewel, out of place and surreal in the daylight.

And then the man in the suit was speaking, voice higher than she'd expected. "You know anything about numbers, sweetheart?"

No grown man had ever called her "sweetheart." She was pretty and now a sweetheart. She felt grown. Standing next to him, with Zukie, she sensed that great things were about to happen—and happen to her.

"I know that everybody does it," she said, "and that it's dangerous. And that I can make a lot of money."

"You good at math?"

"Real good. That's my favorite subject," she lied.

"You good at counting?"

"Anything with numbers I'm good at."

"This is a position of trust. Of honor. You know why, sweetheart?"

That word again. She could listen to him say it all day long. She shook her head.

"Because people are entrusting us with a lot of their money. Money they can't afford to lose. They rely on us to take their numbers and their money and to pay them when they win. They trust me. Trust Zukie. They have to learn to trust you." He looked her up and down again. "Hmph," he muttered, considering.

"They will," Ella said confidently. "Give me a shot."

"Half the people around here don't have jobs. For some people, this is how they stay alive."

Down the street the yellow dress had disappeared, but three girls walked hand in hand behind their mama. Ella felt newly important, tied to the lifeblood of the city. She would keep people eating, keep roofs over their heads.

"Your job, sweetheart, would be to collect these Negroes' numbers and their money, and you bring them to me. You place their bets with me, got it? I'll pay the winner myself. Understand?"

The word "Negro" sounded odd in his mouth. Ella didn't hear the word much outside of school, and it made her uncomfortable—too close to "nigger." She preferred "colored."

"Where do I find these people?"

"That's my business." Smoothly, elegantly, he twirled his toothpick from one side of his grin to the other, and then back. "I'll tell you where to go. You work for me and the less questions you ask the better off you be, got that? But you gotta be straight bout what you do—and what you damn well cain't do."

Ella didn't understand, but didn't want to appear slow to catch on. The man's eyes darted from side to side, bouncing off her and on down the street. Zukie was the same way, but he was more elegant about it. It seemed to Ella that even when they were talking, their minds were way ahead of hers, and thinking thoughts she couldn't begin to follow.

"Be sure you understand who you're working for. Me. You got that?" He stepped back from her and assumed his Big Nigger street pose.

"Got it," Ella said.

"Nobody get in trouble if they know what they're doing, okay?"

"Okay," she said.

"And this is the big one: Don't lose the goddam money, or the numbers."

"Okay."

"You don't ever lose them," he repeated, shifting the toothpick again from one side of his mouth to the other. "You write everything down in your book. Show her your book," he told Zukie.

Zukie slipped a hand into his jacket pocket, extracted a small beat-up notebook, its cover faded and creased. Inside were rows of names and dollar amounts. Between sheets, a few pieces of carbon paper would keep duplicate records for accuracy.

"You don't let nobody touch that book," he told Ella, pointing. "You don't let nobody even know you got it. The cops will use it as evidence if they catch you. People will kill you if you lose it." He stared at her, and his gaze was intense.

"Okay," she said, nodding this time, hoping to please. "Can I ask one question, though?"

He looked at her hard. "Didn't I tell you not to ask questions?"

"Yes," she said. "But can I know what I'm supposed to call you?"

He hollered with laughter. "Yeah, you can ask me that, sweetheart. That is something you need to know. You call me T-Bone. T-Bone Fletcher."

She figured she could ask another question. "How much money can I make?"

"If you got a tight game, you can whiplash twenty to thirty dollars. A day."

This was the first time either T-Bone or Zukie had given her a hard number. Ella had to lean against the brick building wall, scrabbling with her fingertips in the mortar joint to keep upright. Aunt Virginia could retire from the hospital, could stop mopping floors; she could buy that telephone. Ella could call Charles if his mother ever got that party line. Maybe he'd want to dance again.

"You still interested?" T-Bone was asking. He'd turned his shoulder to the street, surreptitiously flipping through his own battered book, making marks on some pages.

For a moment she couldn't even breathe, held tight on to the building. On thirty dollars a day, there would be no Depression for her or for Aunt Virginia. And she could dance. She'd be working with Zukie, dancing with him at clubs. She'd be a regular at the Savoy, dancing in the Corner in no time.

Zukie rubbed her shoulder. "Get outta yo head. You game? This is work, Miss Sassy Feet."

"Sassy Feet?" T-Bone echoed.

"That's what we gonna call her. Miss Sassy Feet. She love to dance."

"You do, do you?" The toothpick flicked to the other corner of his mouth, and then back. He peered down at her and smoothed his lapels. There was something sly and a little terrifying in the glitter of his pupils, in the way he blinked at her, so slowly, like a wink with both eyes. It made her uncomfortable, but she ignored it. This was how city people were. Thirty dollars a day!

"I do," she said. And then daringly, "Maybe Zukie can dance with me sometimes. At the clubs."

T-Bone and Zukie both laughed. "You think so, do you?" said Zukie. "You won't be goin' to the clubs. You going to be working the day shift. The clubs is way too dangerous for a girl."

That set her back, but only for a moment. "I'll be working with both of you though, right?" she said, but what she meant was, *I'll be working with Zukie.*

"Yep," T-Bone said. "Zukie'll be your boss, just like I'm his. Like I'm both of yours. You'll report to him. Give your money and numbers to him. Or to me."

"I want it," Ella said, and then repeated, "I want to do it."

"Good. We gotta see how you built," T-Bone Fletcher told her. "You goin' on a run with Zukie. You watch what he do. Then we know what you made of. Cuz Kool-Aid don't pump in either one of our hearts." He pointed his long finger to himself and then at Zukie, and then, continuing the gesture, extracted a silver flask from inside his suit jacket pocket, offered it to Ella. "You ever had King Kong?"

Ella looked at Zukie, who shrugged. "Take a swig."

Hesitantly Ella tilted back her head, let a few drops of the bitter liquid hit her tongue, then gulped down a mouthful. It tasted like motor oil and burned wood, but then the flavor lessened, became almost lemony, almost like molasses. A moment later her head felt lighter. The worry and self-doubt rolled away. She beamed at them both, did a couple steps of an Irish jig.

"There she go, Sassy Feet!" Zukie said, grinning back at her. Now they were both smiling at her. Their approval was a rowboat she could clamber into, like the rich people did in Central Park. They would protect her. She would be a different person. Fearless. She wasn't going it alone anymore; she was willing to do whatever they wanted.

12

Harlem Streets

Late May–July 1932

The King Kong had long stopped burning Ella's lips and tongue by the time she got home, but a sweet aftertaste still lingered. She savored it as she waited for Auntie to return from the hospital. Only this morning, Ella had been a child, but now she'd tasted the dark promise of numbers running, now she'd strolled the streets on the arm of a handsome and respected and—yes—feared man. She trembled on the cusp of learning the secrets of adulthood. The way Zukie looked at her made her believe that she was not the only one thinking it.

The mantelpiece clock had already chimed nine o'clock before Auntie's key rattled the front door. She was thin-faced and out of breath from climbing to the third floor. Ella met her on the threshold, hung her purse in the closet as Auntie sat on the sofa and slid out of her nurse's shoes with a sigh.

"Good day, Auntie?" Ella asked her, shutting the closet door.

"Same as usual," Auntie said. But her face was gaunt, a muscle twitched under her left eye, and her veined skin seemed thin and fragile.

"What would it cost to bring Frannie here?" Ella said, unable to contain herself a moment more.

"Frannie?" Auntie repeated, as if she didn't know who Frannie was. "What do you mean?"

"Could Frannie come and live with us?" Ella tried again.

"She needs to stay with her father," Auntie said. "You know that."

"Well, what if Joe said it was okay? What if she wanted to come and he was okay with it?"

"There isn't room for her," Auntie said. She pulled off the other shoe.

"We could both sleep in Georgie's room," Ella collected the shoes and set them neatly by the door. "On the floor. It's cozy there."

Auntie laughed, squeezed Ella's upper shoulders in a hug. "It's not a long-term solution, is it?"

"We could make it work," Ella said, leaning into her. Auntie smelled of sweat and antiseptic, and Ella imagined miles of hospital corridors, Auntie wrapping a blanket around an elderly woman. Soon, perhaps, Auntie wouldn't have to do this. "Frannie and Georgie could share the bed and I could keep sleeping on the floor."

"We could if we had to," Auntie said. "But Frannie's okay where she is. With her father."

"What would it cost to have a new apartment?" Ella tried. "One with enough room for all of us."

Auntie thought a moment, looking at her and looking past her, at the wall. "That'd be probably thirty, forty dollars a month more. Then there's her food and clothing, unless Joe paid for that."

"Would fifty dollars a month do it?" That was two days' worth of her salary. Only two days!

A smile softened Auntie's lips. "Is there something you're not telling me?"

"No," Ella said, not meeting her eyes. Those dreams were beyond her reach—she knew this—but she couldn't stop reaching. Above all else, she had to strive. To try. To rise. "I just wondered."

"Don't you be getting any ideas," Auntie said. "Might as well be a million right now. Unless you rob Hamilton Bank."

"Of course not," Ella said. She didn't want Auntie imagining, even for a moment, that she was doing something illegal: it was too close to the truth. How would she keep it secret, when everyone would soon know she was running numbers? She couldn't worry about that right now. "I was just thinking."

"Well, if you're just thinking, think about another two hundred and fifty dollars a month. And then we can have a bigger apartment and food on the table. Buttermilk biscuits and fried chicken every night. Even some August ham."

"What's August ham?"

"Watermelon, honey."

"Okay," Ella said. "I love your fried chicken. I still don't know how you do it with just salt and pepper."

"It's the lard," she said, hands on her thighs, leveraging herself into standing. "It's the lard."

Ella led the way to the kitchen, where she'd left the baked potato for Auntie's dinner covered with a cloth.

Two days later she met up with Zukie and started following him on his runs.

From the outside, Zukie's work might have seemed effortless, but Ella soon realized how much was involved, and why they'd hired her. Zukie, leisurely sauntering down the street, was performing the work of two, maybe three men: handling numbers for the stores and beauty parlors by day, and the nightclubs and bars by night. If Ella worked out, she'd take over some of the day rotation—a teenage girl would be less conspicuous in beauty parlors and grocery stores.

As they went from one place to the next, Ella calculated. Fifty dollars a month would work out to about thirteen dollars a week. If she worked twice a week, she had to make six or seven dollars a day. That felt like Auntie's million: impossibly out of reach. And hadn't T-Bone said she could make up to thirty dollars a day?

Zukie's day run began at Sybil's Beauty Salon on 131st Street, a honeycomb of Black women immersed in gossip, husband and men trouble, and laughter good for the soul. The bell chimed over the door when they entered, and all the women turned toward them. Several called out, "Hey, Zukie. Who's your girlfriend?" Ella liked the attention. Zukie just grinned. Like dirt or trouble, the idea of her being his "girlfriend" seemed to just roll off him.

As soon as Zukie appeared, the bustle ceased, and only partly because of his intense maleness. Everyone knew him as the man who could make them rich. A woman might be in the middle of a hot-comb, shampoo, or styling, but the sight of Zukie sent her hand into her brassiere or her pocketbook, telling Zukie to give Lady Luck a kiss for her. Often as not, the woman would angle a way to try giving Zukie a kiss as well.

But despite how relaxed he seemed, Zukie never stayed at one place long: he zoomed in and zipped out, bestowing grins and waves, but all business, collecting the money, tallying everything in the small book he tucked away in his jacket pocket, a thick leather wallet in another pocket.

Then they went to Harry's Barber Shop a few doors down, and got a similar welcome. After that, the Ambrozine Palace of Beauty. By the end of the run, Zukie had accumulated two fat wallets: one filled with coins and bills, and another with slips of paper scrawled with numbers and names. He wrote everything down carefully in his notebook. The more full each wallet became, the more Zukie watched where he went, checking behind himself constantly. But he did it all so casually that Ella honestly didn't realize that he was so vigilant.

They turned from 135th to Lenox, Ella chattering about the Savoy and wanting to dance in the Corner, when she suddenly looked over and Zukie had disappeared. No—he was behind her, slipping back the way they'd come. She spun around to catch up. "Hey, where you going?"

"Hush," he said, and he was behind a lamppost, and quicker than she could grasp it, he was pulling up a pant leg and slipping the wallet into an elastic band just below his knee, and tucking the book under his coat, in the small of his back.

"What you doing that—"

"Hush," he said again, more firmly, not quite admonishing, but enough to make her flush with embarrassment. A second later he was ambling back down Lenox, passing two white policemen. He touched the brim of his cream-colored fedora to them, his eyes never meeting theirs, and in a moment he and Ella were past them and moving on. "That's what you do," he said. "You don't get caught."

"That was smart," she said, admiring.

"Everyone's against you and you can't ever forget that. The police will haul you in and you'll get robbed if you walkin' blind," he told Ella, showing her how to watch her back, to peer around corners before heading down the street. "You have to scope out everything and everybody. And change your run. Because they'll learn it and lay in wait for you. And if they catch you, Sassy Feet, it won't be the story you want. You see that dude?" Zukie nodded at a man across the street, talking to Melvin from Melvin's Hardware. He wore a white, wide-brimmed hat and plaid pants. His gator shoes gleamed. Ella suspected they were real crocodile and must have cost a few hundred dollars.

Loud as hell, Ella thought. "Yeah, I see him."

"That's Country."

"Country?"

"That's his name and that's what I said. He look all friendly, right?"

"Yeah, in a funny way."

"He ain't funny. He got more bodies than Obee's Funeral Home."

"What does that mean?"

"Murderer. That's what it means."

She started to speak, and he laid one finger, so gentle, against her lips. She could feel the touch of his finger everywhere on her. He seemed unaware of his power. "Listen," he told her. "Don't speak. It's all about developing your street senses. What you feel in your gut. Don't just walk down the street, even if that's what people think you're doing."

He reached around and pulled her close. Her breasts touched his chest. "Make sure nothing happens to you," he said, and his eyes were bright sparks, warming something up in her.

And then he let her go, took a step back, sauntered off as if nothing had happened between them. She had to quicken her walk to catch up, tried to see behind herself with the back of her head.

Along their rounds, she shared her dreams of dancing with him— finally asked him, abruptly, as they left Gladys's Hair Boutique, if he'd dance with her some night.

He opened the door to the street, stashing away the numbers and money, and seemed to only be half-listening. "Dancing don't pay the landlady or support my lifestyle," he said, turning left and up the street again. "At night I'm working. The clubs are my bread and butter. My personal time is something else. Sometimes, when I feel the music, that's when I hit the dance floor. But T-Bone and I have an understanding. Spending all my time all night at one club, dancing with one girl—well, that ain't the business we in. I'm there to make money."

"Do you work every night?" she asked. Her voice shook a little with disappointment. All her plans were now threatened.

He straightened his lapel, stared at her expressionless. "Maybe some nights I don't."

"Maybe then you can dance with me."

"Maybe," he said, opening the next door, this to Miss Bettie's Spoonbread, and Ella relaxed slightly. That "maybe" would have to be enough.

Late that afternoon they hunted T-Bone down on Seventh Avenue, where he was watching a few girls dance a ragged version of the Lindy Hop. Ella thought privately that she was far superior, but T-Bone seemed taken with them. Zukie passed along the money and numbers.

T-Bone slid a handful of bills into Ella's hand. "Put this away," he said.

She squeezed the bills, warm and sweaty and infinitely comforting, tightly in her palm, before tucking them under her blouse. "When can I do this again?" she asked him.

"Mondays and Thursdays," Zukie said.

"Okay," she said, breathless.

"Be ready Thursday," T-Bone said.

"I will," she promised them. Out of sight, she ducked into the doorway of Thomford's Soda Fountain. She wished she could go in, but it was whites-only. She pulled out the wad of cash. Eight dollars!

She was well on her way to earning that fifty dollars a month for Frannie. For all of them. It was more money than she'd ever had in her life. She wished she could get some ice cream to celebrate, but she was taking this all to Auntie. She tap-danced a sequence onto the sidewalk, then slipped into an Irish jig. This was the life!

She returned to Aunt Virginia's feeling powerful and blessed. Walking around for a couple of hours had made her almost as much money as Aunt Virginia made in a week. Sure, she was scared, and she suspected that there was far more involved than T-Bone or Zukie let on. But she'd earned that money. This was a new beginning—for her and for Auntie. She just had to learn the streets, the seen and unseen, and soon it wouldn't feel odd or dangerous or difficult.

She pulled out two dollars to buy groceries, stuffed the rest in an empty glass jar she'd found in Auntie's cupboard. They landed with a tiny rustling thud that made her feel powerful and sneaky. She was embracing a secret life. Auntie wouldn't approve, even though Ella didn't understand why Auntie was against making money any way you could.

Plus she'd get Zukie to dance with her—and if he wouldn't, she'd find someone who would. If only she didn't feel so guilty for doing all of this behind Auntie's back.

By the end of June, Ella had her own run: from 116th to 118th Street and Seventh Avenue, up to 131st Street to 134th Street and Lenox Avenue.

That first week on her own, despite Zukie's warnings, she was cocky, giddy with her new fortune, thinking of that glass jar she'd hidden under Georgie's bureau, the dollar bills and coins slowly filling it. It was only later that she'd realize how obviously inexperienced she was. She was a perfect mark.

So she was strolling down Lenox Avenue just before noon, crowds around her. She wasn't in a back alleyway, in the shadows, behind a waste bin or half-hidden by an awning. A group of men were on the sidewalk playing three-card molly, and she stopped for a moment—*just a moment!*—to watch, and when she reached for her purse, it was gone.

She screamed, grabbing at her clothes, her voice echoing down the sidewalk. Horror blasted her in waves, first hot and then cold. *The money was gone.* She panicked, racing back down the street, asking the street people and passersby, "Have you seen my purse? It's green and small with a rope handle." Heads shook. She flew back to the men, hollering, asking again if they'd seen it. They shook their heads, grinning monstrously, and one stomped his foot and shouted, "You got took!"

What would she do? How would she replace it? Now it seemed impossible that Frannie could come to live with her. But that might be the least of her worries: what would Zukie do, what would T-Bone do, when they found out that she'd lost the numbers and the money?

She weaved around the men, dashed over to the next street corner, peered down it. No signs of a purse, and no one was running away or even acting suspicious.

Sweat dribbled down her neck. Her armpits were sticky and wet. The men stared at her, knowingly. Harlem stood still, mocking her, while she panicked.

She had to get control of herself. She couldn't be seen losing her cool, couldn't give up her street savvy—even if she didn't have any. She took a breath, and then another. She thought the situation through: she'd already delivered her morning take to T-Bone, so the thief had stolen less than ten dollars. And she realized she had all of the clients' numbers in her notebook.

Relief surged through her. Only the money had been lost. She ran home, pulled a handful of bills out of her glass jar, and went out and bought a new purse and a belt to wrap around her.

That day she learned how to front: when trouble hit, act like nothing was going on. Then no one would know she'd been robbed.

Harlem streets bragged about takedowns, she knew, so it was only a matter of time until Zukie and T-Bone learned what had happened—but by then she'd have made more money for them. She still had twelve dollars left.

Soon she settled into a routine, and the running got easier. Saturday mornings were her busiest time; she needed to start by eight o'clock, well before the gangsters and thugs woke up and started prowling. Bernice's Hair Salon and Natalie's Beauty Parlor were packed with women reveling in their only day of freedom, their hair being marcelled and waved, their nails trimmed and polished, their laughter gusting up from one chair and catching on to the next until the narrow rooms boomed with hilarity. Slim Goody was often there, too. He sold stolen clothes for affordable prices door to door in the beauty salons; the freshly coiffed women would wear his dresses at night at the Lenox Lounge or Leroy's Cabaret.

Ella's biggest client was Sister Bernice, who placed numbers twice a day as well as at night, winning so much money over the years that her clients came to her salon not only to get their hair done but to get a variation of her number.

"What your number today? So I can put a dime note on it and get rich too," a woman demanded as she bent over the sink. The other women around her clamored, "Yeah, tell us the truth, Sister Bernice!"

Bernice had sidled up to Ella, handed her a slip of paper with "8—4—3" on it. Ella tucked it in her wallet.

"None of your business," Sister Bernice told the crowd good-naturedly.

"You gonna tell us?" one woman asked Ella.

"Miss Bernice's numbers are between her and me and God," Ella said.

The laughter bloomed around her.

In mid-June, Miss Bernice had bet four dollars and won $2,400: enough money to pay her rent for a year, feed her family of five, and maybe even consider renting the storefront next door, expanding Bernice's with a dozen more chairs.

A week after Sister Bernice's big win, Ella met Miss Adeline. Chain-smoking and heavily perfumed, Miss Adeline bedecked herself in the filmiest of chiffons, like something out of a movie picture, and her fingernails were always perfectly lacquered. She should have been dainty, fragile, a gossamer feather easily tossed in a passing breeze, but her pancake makeup and marcelled hair covered a scar running from her right ear down her jaw. The way that she stubbed out her cigarette, firmly and with no extra motion, made Ella believe that Miss Adeline was not one to cross lightly.

By morning, as she sat in the chair at Natalie's Beauty Parlor, Miss

Adeline reached into her black lace brassiere and handed Ella a bet for twenty bucks. No one had ever placed that much money on one bet with her. Adeline's twenty-dollar bill smelled of perfume: thick and exotic and adult. A single bet of twenty dollars was a huge step up—this could be the beginning of bigger bets for Ella, more lucrative payouts.

"Play it straight on 646 tonight," Miss Adeline told her, lighting a cigarette and squinting slightly at Ella. "You know the kind of work you do is dangerous for a young girl." She paused a moment, considering. "You're not so bad looking."

"I make good money," Ella said, looking down, flattered.

"I bet you do." Miss Adeline said. "Why don't you come by my place on Thursdays? Maybe you'll be good luck for me."

Ella's head swam slightly: not only a twenty-dollar bill, but a new regular customer, all her own. Wait till Zukie and T-Bone learned she was bringing in new clients!

On Thursday, Ella knocked on the door of the address Miss Adeline had given her. She was confused—the place seemed to be a grocery store. During the day, she learned, Miss Adeline tended a storefront grocery, selling canned goods, cigarettes, and newspapers; at night, the brownstone's second and third floors transformed into a brothel she called the Parisian House, and the basement became the Chateau, a speakeasy hawking jazz, gambling, and of course prohibited alcohol.

Most colored brothels in Harlem were between 127th and 135th Streets, with red Christmas lights dangling off their fire escapes all year long, and Ella crossed paths often with the working girls. Some would bet their numbers with her as they strolled down Lenox Avenue, telling her that there was good money in their profession, and it

wasn't as dangerous as numbers running. This might be true, Ella
thought, but this wasn't a profession she was heading toward. Prosti-
tution inside houses didn't seem so bad, but many women, especially
colored women, weren't so lucky. They peddled their wares in cars,
alleyways, and public restrooms.

But Miss Adeline fascinated her: she stood on her own, not
propped up by a man. When Ella could, she studied Miss Adeline,
tried to imitate the way she turned her head, unfaltering and no nonsense; how she'd stub out her cigarette, or pull herself out of her chair
with a firm grip, instantly rising onto her feet. Ella suspected that no
man could just walk into the Parisian House and do whatever he
pleased. Miss Adeline had rules, and suffered no fools breaking them.
Ella also supposed that Miss Adeline was packing heat in the purse
she carried tight under her arm. Probably something small and dainty
looking that could blow a hole three feet wide in a man.

The Parisian House became part of Ella's regular run. She'd show
up in midafternoons, when most of the girls were awake and home,
and while most of the men were at work. A dark-skinned man with a
black suit and white carnation in his lapel usually opened the interior
door to the brothel. His name was Monty, and he regularly bet a
deuce whenever he saw her.

Ella slowly grew more comfortable with the clients, learned to
love their banter. Their good humor buoyed her and made her grin
as she hustled from beauty shop to brothel to soda shop.

"You tell Mr. Henry to come around here with some more King
Kong," Natalie of Natalie's Beauty Parlor told her. "We dying of thirst
in here." Ella would sometimes bring Mr. Henry's illegal, home-
brewed liquor to some of her better customers.

"I'll tell him," Ella said, trying not to laugh, and already heading to her next customer. By one o'clock in the afternoon, no matter what, the money and bets had to be in T-Bone's pocket, so he could take it to the policy banker and the winning number could be announced no later than three o'clock. Ella was never late.

One evening in late July, Ella returned home and found a group of school-aged kids hanging out on the front stoop. She knew a couple of them from the neighborhood, and recognized the rest, but had never said more than a handful of words to any of them. Tonight, though, the air was misty with twilight; sounds came soft, the air was sweet. She leaned against the balustrade, smiling a little, listening to them talk. It was a group of six, five boys and one girl.

The girl, Gardenia, was about Ella's age, although she appeared much older. She wore pancake makeup a few shades lighter than her skin tone, so her face seemed brighter, shining behind her full red painted lips. She was shapely, thick and tall, with a big behind that jiggled when she walked. Ella wished she had a jiggling behind, too. Virginia had warned Ella several times to steer clear of her: she had no supervision from her father—whom Ella had never seen—and she dressed in clothes more suited to an older woman—beautiful, store-bought clothes. And Gardenia was always smoking and drinking and hanging out with boys. Tonight, for instance, she wore a red A-line dress with a wide flair skirt and deep bodice that pushed up her breasts. A red belt cinched her waist.

"Nothing good is going to come to that poor child. Don't think she's having fun because it's not fun to be thought of as the loose girl of the neighborhood," Auntie had warned. But Ella was fascinated. The boys seemed to love her, and brought her presents—candy and flowers, mostly. Auntie saw that as suspect as well.

Now Gardenia was in the middle of the boys, which included

Chester and Devon from downstairs. She had a red thick-petaled rose in her hair, and was laughing.

"Hey, Ella," she said when Ella made no move to slip past her and go inside. "Come sit by me. You want some candy? Leroy just gave me this." Gardenia showed her a small bag packed with penny candies, and patted the cement stair. The boys made room. "Did you boys know that Ella here is a great dancer?"

"Oh, I'm not that good," Ella said modestly.

"That's not what I saw the other day. You was dancin' good as that kid Norma Miller who's always sneaking into the Savoy."

Norma Miller was a few years younger than Ella, but already a dancing prodigy. Ella wanted to meet her, but their paths hadn't crossed yet. The boys started talking about different dance steps, and Ella joined in, laughing with them for half an hour before Auntie came home and dragged her inside.

"I don't want you sitting with that girl," Auntie told her again. "She's common. She's not a good influence on you."

Ella wanted to say that she was working for mobsters, feeding the gambling frenzy of everyone in Harlem, Auntie included. But she didn't.

July's sweltering heat flattened the city, and Ella stayed out of the spotlight, speeding from one venue to the next, collecting her bets and cash. She was making as much as eighteen dollars a day, giving ten dollars of it, or more, to Aunt Virginia. The rest she tucked in a waxed paper bag inside the glass jar she'd wedged under a loose floorboard beneath the bureau. She had $61.48.

Numbers running took up most of her day, but many evenings she'd drag Woofie or one of a few other neighborhood boys she'd met—she'd never found Boss Man again—to the clubs: Connie's Inn, the Shim Sham Club, Basement Brownies, and of course, the Savoy. She sometimes would cross paths with Zukie, and he'd whirl her around the floor and then, as usual, disappear.

In this summer of her life, though, everything—numbers running, dancing, even her growing attraction to Zukie—had a soft unreality to it. Every night she'd hit up against the brutal hardness of this new life she was living, a life without her mother, without her sister, without a home. Above all else, she wanted somewhere to belong, to fit in without question. And that summer she sought it. In beauty parlors, or soda shops, or sidewalks, or in the clubs at night.

No place felt right. Not even the Savoy felt like hers anymore. Tempie's death had unmoored her, as if the soles of her shoes didn't quite connect to the pavement, as if the blanket she pulled over her shoulders at night hovered a hair's breadth above her skin and did not keep her warm.

She yearned for something but didn't know how to describe it or search for it or make this ache fade away.

So, every night, she'd unroll the pallet on the floor; every morning she'd roll it up and tuck it against the wall, next to the bureau: it was as if she were camping out, lodging there temporarily, until God got wind of where she was and decided to come for her. Only if she kept shopping and hanging out the laundry and ironing and folding, as if in penance, did the apartment feel, briefly, as if she might one day be allowed to live there and feel like she was part of a family, loved and cherished. By running numbers and doing Aunt Virginia's chores, she would earn her way into a home.

She was desperate for Auntie's love, but she always felt like an outsider and by that summer was beginning to feel it was a lost cause. Georgie's plate always had the larger portion of mashed potatoes, the nicer piece of chicken. Auntie's hands went out automatically to smooth Georgie's hair and wrapped around her when Auntie got home while Ella looked on. If both Ella and Georgie talked at once, Aunt Virginia would tilt her face toward Georgie.

Georgie didn't need to work like Ella did. Instead, she went to summer school. "Education is the ticket," Auntie would tell both of them, but Georgie was the one who got to learn while Ella hustled in the streets, mopped the floors, prepared the meals. Georgie would always be Auntie's daughter, and Ella couldn't let her guard down and get comfortable as long as her cousin watched her every move, judging her.

Ella had never been close to Georgie. She acted so proper. Ella rolled her eyes at Georgie's ballet and piano lessons even as she envied her. Ella didn't know how Aunt Virginia afforded it, but Georgie was taught skills that Ella thought of as "white people things." Who even knew what "elocution" was, let alone have to take "elocution lessons" twice a week? Some part of Ella knew Auntie would go without electricity before she'd allow Georgie to go without ballet and piano lessons. Auntie didn't want anyone to think of her as common.

As the summer went on, Georgie treated her more and more like a maid. One day she stood in the kitchen, examining the dress that Ella had washed, acting more like a middle-aged white lady than a thirteen-year-old girl in a much-darned school uniform. "You need to smooth them while you're folding them," she told Ella, about her dresses. "That way it's easier to get the wrinkles out when you iron them. Just don't burn them, okay? I found a burn but didn't tell Mama."

Ella wanted to throw the plate she was washing, but just scrubbed harder at the sink.

Georgie, behind her, pirouetted, pretending to practice her ballet lessons.

Ella let the plate fall into the sudsy water. "You call that dancing? I'll show you what real dancing is." She started off with a shuffle tap, segueing into the shimmy and then the Charleston, gyrating her hips and thrusting her fingertips to the ceiling.

"That's gut bucket dancing," Georgie said, pressing her lips together like a rich white girl from high society. "I'm going to be a debutante. They're announced in the *Amsterdam News*. You have to look a certain way and Mama tells me I do and you don't."

"What kind of certain way?" All Ella's anger and outrage collapsed like the plate, drowned in dirty water.

"I look like Katherine Dunham," Georgie was saying, looking past Ella, out the little kitchen window as if she were gazing out at her public. "I look like Anise Boyer. My skin tone, my hair, and my figure." She patted her hot-combed hair. Aunt Virginia had not hot-combed Ella's hair, and it was short and unruly.

"Oh, that don't mean nothing," Ella said, louder than necessary, as if trying to convince both of them. She envied Georgie's petite figure and grace, the queenly way that Georgie bestowed smiles on people when she walked into a room. Georgie knew how to manipulate people, charming them with a hand on their arm, with a lilting laugh or a giggle. People did what Georgie asked. Ella turned back to the dishes, scrubbed them harder, and ignored Georgie's pirouettes and pliés.

She brooded, waiting for Auntie to get home. Georgie ate and went into her room to do her homework. Ella had made dinner, of course, and took extra care that the roast beef was slightly tender, the collard greens lightly salted, and the baby carrots had a dab of butter melting on them. They were all eating better now that Ella was contributing. They had meat—neckbones or hog maws—on Sundays now, with their collard greens and black-eyed peas. Sometimes Mrs. White from down the block would give Ella a homemade sweet potato pie when Ella collected her numbers. Ella savored the thick crust and the sweetness she knew she'd earned and which was meant just for her.

She waited until Auntie cut her roast beef into neat slices, folded a couple into her mouth. Then she said, "Georgie's always trying to show me up."

Auntie finished chewing before she spoke. "You're older than she is. What did you expect? You're here now and she has to share everything she once had to herself. You're almost grown, honey. Act like it."

"I'm only fifteen. I'm still a girl."

"That's grown. Georgie is the little girl in this house."

That hurt. What was she doing, if not acting like she was grown? She was working with gamblers and hoodlums, weaving her way through criminals. All so Auntie could eat roast beef.

She pulled the chair closer to the table, laid her elbows on it, propped her chin on her fist. The tabletop, freshly scrubbed, gleamed before her. "When can Frannie come?"

"Aw, honey—"

She'd told Auntie that the money came from dancing on the sidewalks.

"My dancing's been making good money," Ella said.

She didn't know if Auntie believed her or not, but that was the thing about Auntie, Ella had learned: she was all about appearances. It was enough for her if something seemed to be what it was. She either didn't want to know, or actively avoided burrowing into the dark secrets, uncovering the messy twisting reality beneath the whitewash.

"Frannie's place is with her father," Auntie said. "I told you that."

"She's miserable there." Ella didn't know if this was true or not. Ella wrote her every few days, but Frannie never wrote how she felt. Her letters were more *I am fine, how are you?* Ella read between the lines and decided that Frannie couldn't tell the truth, couldn't say what Joe was doing, or doing to her. "Please let her come. You said if I made fifty dollars a month—"

"Yes, but it's summer," Auntie said. "Soon you'll be going back to school, and that's what you're going to focus on. Your education."

"But I'm making all this money dancing—"

"Music won't get you far," Auntie told her, finishing the roast beef. "Your mother and I learned that lesson. Music is a dead end. You slip up, you break your leg, and then what do you have? Nothing, is what. But do you know what will see you through? Education, Ella. Do you know who W. E. B. Du Bois is?"

"No," Ella said. What had education ever gotten her aunt? A

nurse's aide degree, terrible work hours, and rats gnawing holes in the floorboards.

"Well, you need to know. If you stay in school, you might become one of the 'Talented Tenth.'" Auntie was always talking about the Talented Tenth—how one out of every ten Black men or women could have leadership qualities and lead their people into a better life.

"I'm not a man," Ella said. "I can't be one of your Tenth."

"It means colored women, too."

"I'll never be one of them," Ella said.

"You're already talented. Look at how you dance. And you're just as pretty as you want to be."

"Really?" She looked up from the tabletop, where she'd been idly drawing patterns with her finger on the linoleum. "You think I'm pretty?"

Auntie had finished eating and was sitting back in the chair, watching her. "Of course. We don't have unattractive people in our family." She dabbed her lips with the napkin, the napkin that Ella had washed and ironed.

"How is education going to help me dance?"

"I know you didn't just say that. Nobody wants a dancer who can't read or who doesn't know what the artists are doing in France or Italy or even right here in Harlem. Dancing is more than just dancing. And besides, you need something to fall back on. What if you get hurt?"

"I'm young," Ella said. "I won't get hurt."

"Getting hurt is the least of your worries. Education is your way out. I needed that diploma to go into nursing—white people tried to keep me out but I had that piece of paper. One day I want to be a licensed nurse and do more for my patients than change bedpans. I might even become a doctor."

Auntie must be living in a fantasy world. Ella had no chance of ever becoming a doctor, and didn't want to be one. She could barely find the time to sleep. How would she be able to study, and how would she pay for it? Plus she felt the call of the streets, the action in the city. All of this Ella wanted to say, but fear locked her tongue. She never risked a fight with Auntie. She'd fought with Tempie, and look what had happened.

Auntie was talking. She leaned over the table, cupped Ella's chin, forced Ella's gaze up to meet her own. "Do you understand, Miss Ella? Education means a better life. Take your intelligent self to school every day and open those books."

"But what about money?"

"Education," Aunt Virginia repeated. "That's what white people have that we don't, and we have to fight to get it. When you can read and write and decipher numbers like they do, you can create your own opportunity and earn your own respect."

Ella had heard this speech before, and let it roll over her. In her eyes, white people wouldn't respect her no matter how many books she read, no matter how clear her diction or whether she could quote from Paul Laurence Dunbar or not.

"People respect me because I'm in medicine," Auntie said. "Although I mop floors and pull garbage, I'm not known as a cleaning woman. I'm known as a nurse. White men can't pull the wool over your eyes because you're so ignorant you can't read, and they can't underpay you, because you can count your money. Every day those white doctors and nurses have to respect me because I don't use gutter language and I carry myself like a lady. I don't use slang or chew gum in public spaces. I use the King James's English and enunciate my words. You want to sound well read, educated, and refined."

"Yes ma'am, Auntie," Ella said dutifully, more convinced than ever that education would never be the answer for her: dancing was her escape out of poverty.

13

Stoopin'

July–September 1932

All through the summer, Ella heard that her stepfather Joe had been unwell—he'd stay in his bed all day, several days in a row, before stumbling off to whatever job he'd managed to scrounge up. Later, Frannie told her that he often couldn't make rent after Ella left. Ella had sent Frannie money from her numbers running, proud that she was contributing to both Joe's and Virginia's households. But Ella hadn't known the extent of Joe's debts and illness.

He was too proud to go to a doctor, and kept insisting that his bad health stemmed from something he ate, or a pulled muscle in his back. Frannie said that he tried odd homemade remedies from Portugal: stews involving eggshells and raw meat, or chicken feet and soup bones. Frannie had to prepare it all, the reek pervading the apartment even if she left open the back door to the fire escape. The whole situation sounded terrible and repulsive, and Ella was more anxious than ever to get Frannie out of his house. If only Auntie would agree.

On July 26, Joe climbed out of bed and tottered to work. He had no appetite that morning. The chicken feet that Frannie gingerly boiled for him still lay curled and clutching air on the plate. He staggered through the door of the metal shop where he'd found work for the past few weeks, waved to the foreman, and made his way to the back.

He collapsed halfway across the room, and was probably dead before he hit the floor.

When Child Protective Services came to Auntie's apartment, Ella wasn't home—she was out running numbers. She learned of Joe's death from Georgie that afternoon when she returned.

"Your daddy died," Georgie said bluntly the moment Ella had gotten inside.

"What?" she said. Perhaps she'd misheard. The heat was sweltering and all she'd been thinking about was a tall glass of water.

"Uncle Joe." Georgie repeated. "He died this morning. Mama's up in Yonkers getting Frannie."

"Joe's not my daddy," Ella said.

"I don't know where she's gonna sleep," Georgie said, looking back into the apartment as if another bedroom would suddenly manifest itself.

"What happened?" Ella asked.

None of this made sense, and she had to lean against the wall. A mush of emotion poured through her: sorrow tempered almost by a vicious glee. *Served him right.* But sorrow won out. Joe's death somehow cemented the loss of Tempie even more deeply. Now she had only Aunt Virginia. There would be no going back to that life in Yonkers, even if she wanted to. She could take all those horrible memories and stuff them in the closet that he had put her in.

"I bet Frannie's gonna sleep in bed with me," Georgie said. She and Frannie were less than a year apart, and had always gotten along—often rivals, and often bickering, but still close. "Sure hope she doesn't roll around and try punching me the way you did."

"What happened to him?"

"Don't know. The lady that came for Mama just said he died and can Mama come get Frannie," Georgie said.

Ella got her glass of water, went back to the couch, and sat. On the mantelpiece the family photographs—her mother, Auntie, her grandmother—peered down from the frames. All women, all with dark, haunted eyes; but they were all together, a family. With Tempie gone, and her grandmother, too, this now seemed over. But they could make a new family. After all, Frannie was finally coming to live with her. Ella couldn't decide if she should cook a celebratory supper or if that wouldn't be fitting. Well, they'd both be hungry, and this way Auntie could see what a help Ella was, how having Ella and Frannie wouldn't be a burden.

"Let's make a nice dinner for them. What do you say?" Ella asked Georgie. "I'll even make fried chicken."

"You don't make it as good as Mama," Georgie said skeptically.

"I'm gonna try with just salt and pepper, the way she do." Ella rummaged in her purse, pulled out a few dollars. "Go down to the store and get some chicken thighs and some potatoes. We got greens. Maybe we can even have a pie." Ella loved sweets.

"What kind?"

"What kind you want?"

"Sweet potato."

They trooped to the kitchen and Ella rummaged through cupboards. There was a little molasses—it might be enough for a pie, especially if she filled it out with some breadcrumbs. "Sweet potato it is," she said. "I'm gonna start cooking so it'll be ready before they get here. I'll give you a list for what to buy. You hurry straight back so it'll all be ready by the time they get here."

And that was how, early that evening, Auntie and Frannie returned to Harlem and found the apartment redolent with fried chicken and freshly baked pie.

Ella was in the kitchen. Before she had a chance to set down her platter of greens, Frannie was in her arms, hugging her and weeping. Her face was puffy and her nose kept running.

When, half an hour later, they sat down to eat, Frannie only picked at her chicken, but both Auntie and Georgie complimented Ella on it.

It was surreal, having Frannie there. She'd come once for dinner, back in May, but this felt very different. Harlem was now her home, too. Ella had part of her family back.

"Frannie is going to sleep in the room with both of you," Auntie said to Ella and Georgie, and then to Georgie, "She'll share the bed with you."

Georgie rolled her eyes, and Frannie elbowed her. "No snoring," she told Georgie.

"Your cousin doesn't snore," Auntie said. "And that's not ladylike."

"Bet *she* will," Georgie said.

"Girls, no fighting," Auntie said. "I'm not sure how we're going to make it, but we're going to. No question about it."

Ella wanted to say something—how she would contribute—but she felt like they already knew.

The next weekend the four of them went back to Yonkers. Auntie made arrangements to sell what little furniture there was.

Ella folded up the three handmade patch quilts that Tempie had sewn, and a coin purse made out of beige and white tapestry fabric. She also pulled out the lined sheet of paper that Tempie had given her a few years before, with the "never give up" poem in red ink. She'd have that framed one day, she decided: once she was a famous dancer.

—

With Frannie living in the apartment, the pressure on Ella to earn income—both to support Frannie and to move into her own place—was more intense. More often than not, Auntie Virginia would sleep on the sofa in the parlor. Georgie gave up her bedroom to Frannie and Ella, and Auntie and Georgie would share a bed; but because of Aunt Virginia's late nights and irregular hours, Auntie didn't want to awaken Georgie. Four people in the apartment was too many people. The bathroom was always in use and food disappeared at an alarming rate.

And the August heat was unrelenting. Like a constant slap in the face, a fist thrust down their throats and lungs. Harlem folks cooled themselves by opening up fire hydrants, bathing in the makeshift waterfalls; children danced in and out of the flowing water. Stray dogs and cats shook their coats onto the pavement. When the police roared by, people just stood in the streets observing as the sirens shrieked past. People wondered idly who had been stabbed, or shot, or arrested in the latest mob wars.

Finally, August faded into a slightly cooler September and school started back up. Ella usually missed a couple of days every week to make her rounds, but did go to school most of the time. The girls her age now appeared silly and empty-headed—like she used to be. They were worried about dresses and boys. Ella worried about how to not get evicted, and whether Hector the Mooch would get paid on his betting numbers on time. Now Ella felt more at home with the matrons and the shop girls who always called her by name and waved paper and cash her way. Her purpose had legs, and school was only getting in her way.

—

In mid-September, Ella returned from her numbers run and found Aunt Virginia sitting on the stoop. She never thought that she would see her auntie sitting outside on a step, common-like, with her legs slightly open, and Ella thought she smelled a slight hint of alcohol on her. Ella was carrying a bag of groceries—a small pork roast, some greens, and yams—and she set the bag next to her on the step.

Aunt Virginia smiled blearily up at her.

"Help Auntie up," she said. Ella noticed her aunt had put on weight. It looked good on her.

Ella picked up the groceries, and together they climbed the steps to the third floor. Auntie paused on each landing as if the climb exhausted her. Inside, the apartment's air felt still and sullen, stale.

"Come have a cup of tea with me," Auntie told her. "We need to talk."

Ella put the food away as Auntie prepared the tea, moving slowly as if carrying bricks on her back. She placed the teacups down on the table, adding two teaspoons of sugar. She'd never been able to afford sugar until Ella had come, Ella knew, and it made her feel good.

Auntie took a sip and sighed. "There's nothing like a cup of black tea to soothe bad nerves," she said.

"What's wrong?" Ella asked. She was nervous, always slightly anxious that Auntie would take offense over something that Ella did or said, and throw her out. Ella would work harder. She'd bring in more income. Ella was worth keeping.

"I had some bad news at work today." Auntie took another sip. "I'm so tired. I've worked my whole life and I don't deserve this."

"What happened?" A new tension sprung up in Ella: how could she help?

"They cut my shift in half," Auntie said. "They said the hospital is near bankruptcy."

"You don't have to worry about money," Ella said, relieved and proud. "I can pay the rent until you get back on your feet. And maybe even after. It's okay."

"It's not okay," Aunt Virginia said. "What little dignity I had, being a nurse's aide, is being taken from me. They say I can make some extra money cleaning the hospital. A cleaning woman. Something I've worked my whole life to stay away from." She looked so deeply sad. "You be more than that."

So this was what all of Auntie's talk of education was getting her. Ella couldn't help feeling the tiniest bit gleeful. She knew that education wasn't the path for her. But she said only, "Cleaning is okay, isn't it?"

"In a hospital full of sickness, being a cleaning woman is one of the most perilous jobs out there." Auntie laughed, but there was no joy. "I can die from cleaning the hospital. All those operating rooms. And they don't give us no gloves."

Any gloves, Ella thought. Auntie always drilled correct English into her. *You show the world that you're educated*, she'd say. It was disorienting, hearing Auntie speak so colloquially.

"I can support you," Ella repeated. "I'm making good money."

Auntie nodded. "Yes, but there's this, too."

Aunt Virginia pulled an envelope out of her pocket, laid it on the table. Ella recognized the Wadleigh insignia.

"This is from Wadleigh," her aunt said unnecessarily. "You know what's in it?"

"No." All of Ella's enthusiasm and goodwill seeped out of her.

"According to this letter, you're not in class a majority of the time."

Ella stared at the tabletop. She'd polished it that morning, and it gleamed.

"The school wrote me a letter." Her aunt sounded more exhausted than angry. "You've only been back in school for three weeks, and they've already sent a letter to me about you."

Ella took a gulp of tea.

"Just tell me the truth," Auntie Virginia said. She moved her own teacup out of the way, leaned on her elbows on the table. "Don't lie to me."

"Please don't be mad at me," Ella said. "I been bringing you money home and food home, haven't I? We can't eat on what Wadleigh teaches."

"You know that education is the way to a better future," Aunt Virginia said.

Ella looked at the kitchen table and said nothing.

"What troubles me more, or as much, is that you've been deceitful," Auntie went on after a moment. "First, it's lies, then what's next?"

Ella stood up, wanting to run, move, escape. This was how she, as a numbers runner, handled trouble: she disappeared before it could catch up with her.

"Don't you dare dismiss yourself in my presence," Aunt Virginia said. "Sit your Black ass down." Suddenly Aunt Virginia wasn't tired.

Ella had never heard her this angry or improper. Ella sat down.

"We are not an ignorant family," Aunt Virginia told her. "We get as much education as we can, regardless of what is happening around us. Do you hear me?"

"Yes, ma'am."

"I must admit, we need the money you bring in here with God-knows-what-you're-doing-besides-dancing, and I don't want to know. But I do insist that you go to school. You can't miss out on this opportunity to raise yourself up and it will only happen if you get your education."

"Yes, ma'am."

"Don't 'yes-ma'am' me. You better do it. I don't want another letter from Wadleigh telling me you're not in school. The next warning, they'll call the authorities and it will be out of my hands. They'll take you from me."

Ella stared at the teacup. It seemed impossible to provide for Aunt Virginia, provide for the household, and stay in school. But if she didn't stay in school, the authorities would pick her up. She didn't know where they'd take her—she'd heard rumors of reform schools in the Bronx or upstate where they treated the girls—especially colored girls—like animals. Less than animals. Beat them and starved them.

She needed to work weekends and evenings, then. Less work during the schooldays. That was the only solution, she decided. Would T-Bone let her change her schedule? She needed the money from him. "Okay," she said, her voice barely audible even to herself. "I'm sorry, Auntie."

"I know you are," Virginia said, and the anger had gone, and her aunt laid one hand softly on Ella's. "You're a good girl. I know you're trying as hard as you can."

Ella wiped her eyes and her nose with the back of her hand.

"But you have to stay in school," Auntie said.

14

A Man Should Dance

October 1932

Ella reduced her numbers running to Tuesdays and Thursdays, and a longer run on Saturdays. It meant she had little time to study, but that didn't bother her. In the meantime she was feeding the whole family, and Frannie was going to school and giggling at night with Georgie. Life didn't seem that bad.

But she was dancing less and less, and that made her anxious. She wouldn't become a famous dancer if she didn't dance; and she still hadn't found a partner. She tried a handful of boys she'd met, but none of them were serious like Charles.

And then there was Zukie.

"Sometimes." That's what Ella remembered Zukie telling her when she asked him if he went dancing. She remembered, too, him saying that dancing would distract from the real business of collecting his clients' numbers. When she'd see him at the clubs, she'd catch his eye and she'd push her dance partner into a few barrel turns, or she'd surge into a tap routine, arms flailing, loose-limbed, grinning at him from across the dance floor. He'd look her up and down, smile that laid-back smile, twirl his toothpick in time with the music. Once, when she broke out in the Fitzgerald Snakehips, he'd put his hand up. "Stop now, Miss Fitzgerald, before you cause a traffic jam."

In mid-October, late one Saturday afternoon when she was handing over her bets, she said to him, "You working tonight? Because a man shouldn't work all the time. It ain't good for you."

"True gospel," he said, pulling at the lapels of his cream-colored overcoat. He'd told her it was cashmere, and it was the softest fabric she'd ever touched. She wanted to touch it again, wanted him to wrap it around her and pull her close. "It's unbalanced," he agreed. "But what's a man to do?" Something about the way he was looking at her, with his copper-bright eyes, made her think he was flirting. He did flirt with her sometimes, and she tried to brush it off, tried to be adult about it—she knew he flirted with all the girls—but she always felt he looked at her in a different way. As if she were more special than the others.

"A man should dance," Ella said. They were heading up Seventh Avenue, and she was about to turn west to head across town, when all of a sudden he wrapped his hand around her waist, pulled her into him. The cashmere bumped against her cheek, warm and comforting as a bath. She wanted to submerge herself in it.

"Well, guess what," he said, his voice a rumble she could feel in her breastbone. "I agree. A man can't live by bread alone. So you and I, Miss Sassy Feet, are going out on the town tonight. We doin' the jitterbug until the midnight hour."

"We will? For real?" She was so thrilled that she hugged him back. She didn't want to mention her ten o'clock curfew.

"Yeah, for real."

She broke out in a shuffle-shimmy, her feet a blur, swiveling her hips, and hugged him again. "What time?"

"Daddy-O," he said, one arm casually slung around her, "what have I just done? What did I let loose?" He burst out laughing and shrugged free of her. She ached to press her cheek against that cashmere again. "OK, Sassy Feet. Calm down. Meet me at the Rennie at eight. And dress up." He continued down Seventh Avenue and waved at her without turning around—he definitely had eyes on the back of his head.

Ella caught his hand wave as if she were grabbing a star, clutched it tight against her chest the whole way home. Finally, everything was coming together. Frannie was living with her, she was making decent money, and now she'd have a boyfriend. She wasn't quite sure what love felt like, but if it was what she felt like being with Zukie, she wanted as much of it as she could get.

Now she needed to figure out what to wear tonight.

No one was home. Who knew where the girls were, and Auntie was at work. She flung open her closet, shuffled through the hangers. Her three dancing dresses seemed suddenly too threadbare. Her other two dresses were too schoolgirlish. She pulled out one, then another. Maybe the maroon with the white collar? The collar had sweat stains and wasn't classy enough. The light blue one had that tear—mended, true—on the side. She could wear a belt to cover most of it, but didn't she have anything better? Nothing would suit. Panic rumbled in her.

Auntie's closet smelled faintly of mothballs and church ladies' perfume. She scanned the handful of dresses, clicked one hanger after another, pulled out a few and held them up. They all seemed too old for her, but seemed better suited to an adult than Ella's own schoolgirl clothes. Besides, she'd filled out a little more lately, and Auntie's clothes would fit better.

And then she saw it: a bright green teal, chiffon and heavy silk, with a deep bodice and flared skirt. A pattern of rhinestones sparkled on the sleeve. Ella couldn't imagine Auntie—sensible Auntie in her sensible white nurse's shoes—wearing such a dress, and knew that she'd never let Ella wear it either. But she had to impress Zukie tonight. She had to convince him to be her dance partner.

——

Well, maybe it wouldn't fit. She pulled off her everyday numbers runner skirt and blouse, stepped into the sea-green lake of fabric at her feet. It felt exotic and lavish against her skin. Although the hem hung low and the bodice was still a little loose, having the extra room to stretch out her arms when she was dancing would be for the best.

Since she didn't want to run into Auntie or the girls, wearing Auntie's dress, she packed the dress in a shopping bag along with a hairbrush, Madame Walker's Pomade, and a tube of Auntie's purple-red lipstick. She left a note for Auntie and the girls that she'd be back before curfew, and that there were enough leftovers in the refrigerator for dinner. In the meantime she'd hide out at Miss Bernice's until it was time to go. Maybe Miss Bernice would give her a discount on a styling.

By seven forty-five she was heading over to the Rennie—the Renaissance Ballroom—dreaming of all she wanted to be: a dancer, famous, rich, independent, free.

He was there when she arrived—more beautiful than ever, holding court in a cluster of women. Of course he wore his signature cream colors. Her own teal dress would contrast perfectly against him on the dance floor. She elbowed her way through the other women—Gladys Jones, Becky Oliver, and Tabitha Banks among them—and planted herself in front of him, breathless. "You ready?" she said.

When he looked at her, she could see admiration in his eyes, and then he did a double-take. "Lovely, Sassy Feet," he told her. "You sure look divine. Gorgeous."

"You like it?" she said. Miss Bernice had straightened her hair and pulled it up in a high bun, and loaned her a pair of dangling rhinestone earrings, like Ethel Waters's. The silk chiffon dress still loose, and she spun around, the rhinestones glittering and the skirt flaring out and pushing up against the other girls. Auntie's kitten heels were tight but didn't hurt—not yet, at any rate.

"Yeah, I love it," he said. "Love it." He offered her his arm. "Sorry, ladies, I'm taken tonight. Miss Ella Fitzgerald and I are gonna show all the dancers how it's done."

"You save me a dance," said Tabitha Banks, batting her eyelashes at him.

He shook his head. "Miss Fitzgerald gets to decide. I'm all hers."

Ella could barely swallow around the pounding in her throat. She held up her head as tall as she could—she'd never felt so proud, and didn't think she'd ever been so terrified, either.

The enormous open-air dance hall, covered by a tent, was a Harlem landmark: from the outside it glowed like a gigantic lampshade. Inside, a casino was on the left, and a dance hall on the right. Tonight he escorted her under the tent, to the dance hall, where the Fletcher Henderson Orchestra's "Sugar Foot Stomp" vibrated in the night.

She wasn't walking, she decided. She was actually floating. Zukie's hand tethered her to the world she knew—without it, she was ready to float away in the slightest breeze, a teal bubble lifting toward the ceiling. Only his hand, holding hers, and the familiar cream-colored shoulder an arm's length away, kept her in check.

The bass came in hard and thrumming, with a beat so undeniable that she couldn't help but rock her head in time with it, and then Zukie spun her around and they were dancing—he was guiding her, swinging out, the Charleston's steps and lifts, the breakaways and barrel turns effortless and so familiar. The bass, drums, and horns blared out like a magic carpet that was lifting her toward the pink canvas, a luminous, immense pink sky above her.

"Let me show you something," Zukie said as he swung around from her and did a few barrel turns and then began tap dancing to the swing beat of the orchestra, his feet moving faster than she had ever seen anyone perform. He was a prodigy and didn't care. "How about that, Sassy Feet?"

Not to be outdone, Ella polished off her Snakehips Fitzgerald, gyrating her hips, tap dancing, and then shimmy sliding right up to Zukie. A space began to clear around her as other dancers gave them room, and then formed a circle.

Never had Ella been the center of this kind of attention, the focus of cheering, the applause like something that she could bite into, like bread. The orchestra surged into Louis Armstrong's "All of Me" and she and Zukie were cartwheeling arms and grins, hands reaching as she swung out, spun back in, dipped in close and then out again. People were cheering them on, applauding, hands beating out a rhythm.

"New Orleans," and then "I Don't Stand a Ghost of a Chance with You," and then "How Deep Is the Ocean," each melody a new burst of energy for her. Sometimes there was an admiring crowd around them, and sometimes it was just her and Zukie and the music, and all she could see was his face, those lips. How handsome he was. *Never forget this*, she told herself, trying to hold this moment, this music, this man, tight against all that had come before.

At the final strains of "Night and Day," he lifted her into the deepest dip she'd ever done, the back of her hair touched the floor and one leg stretched out into the air. He easily raised her back to her feet, and the crowd cheered again. She joined in. He shook his head, grinning at her. "Sassy Feet, you're wearing me out."

"You want to take a break?" she said. Auntie's shoes were stabbing her insoles. She suspected her feet were bleeding. But she wouldn't let on, and wouldn't stop for anything.

"Can we?" he fake pleaded. "You're killing me here. I'm not as young as I used to be."

"You see how special we are as a team?" she asked.

"You think so?"

She couldn't see his face, but her arm was securely under his. She had to almost jog to keep up. Dimly she felt the pain in her heel, ignored it. "That was some kind of applause," she told the side of his jaw as he led her through the crowd. Was it her imagination or did it part for them, like royalty? "We got more attention than the orchestra," Ella said.

"Just for a moment, maybe."

"We can make more money dancing together than running numbers," Ella said. "Those dancers at the Savoy? They're making a lot. And it's a lot safer, too."

He turned briefly, his eyes gleaming at her. "You're something special, that's for sure."

In all the darkness that would come after, for all the years that would follow, his words that night rang in her ears: *You're something special, that's for sure.* If only she could have held on to it, captured his voice in a recording, folded it into a blanket that she could unfurl and wrap around herself again, forever: if only. But time raced on, and she in all her innocence went right on, rather than holding tight, but she remembered this moment always.

She said, answering him, "We're special together."

By now they were at the edge of the crowd, near the bar, which served Prohibition liquors if you knew who to ask. But he'd only ordered water, and the orchestra's drums beat around her, and the wind of the horns drew her close to him. Her body tingled and she swam in Zukie's scent.

She tilted her face up to his, and he leaned down, his eyes so bright—never had she seen eyes so bright—locked onto hers, as if searching for a place to land. She could see tenderness there, and kindness; and if this was love, she yearned for it. He was so close to her, leaning closer, their lips only a hair's breath apart—

And then the orchestra's drums blasted in the air and he stopped, eyes on hers.

He was going to kiss her. She knew he was.

A trombone lifted into a melody—"Willow Weep for Me"—and a moment later a saxophone joined in, and then the clarinets, and then the rest of the band. He looked away.

The nearness of him lingered, unrequited, unanswered, impossible, between them.

She couldn't leave it alone. "Will you be my dance partner?" she repeated. "We can do it. We really can."

He glanced over her shoulder, then glanced again. She turned to look, but the couples were curling around him and she couldn't follow his gaze.

"What is it?" she said. "Come on. Let's dance."

"No." He seemed distracted now, looking out at the crowd. "This is just fun. Nothing serious. I don't want to be a dancer. I told you that." He looked at his watch. "It's getting late. Come on. Let's blow this joint."

"Can't we stay a little bit longer?" she asked.

"I don't have time for this. I gotta get back to business."

"I thought you were going to take tonight off? You said we were going to jitterbug all night."

"My jitterbugging is done," he said. "And I never said that I was going to take the night off." There was a hardness now to his face, a dismissiveness. "We're done here. Can't you see that?"

"What just happened between us? We were amazing. Don't you feel that?"

"Nothing happened between us," he told her. "And nothing ever will."

And he left her there, slithering out and away from her, into the night.

She'd been in another world, a world of music and romance, and he'd thrown her out. He'd slammed the door and stood before it, immovable as a boulder, blocking her from possibility and hope. He wasn't Prince Charming anymore.

She ran after him.

But he didn't wait for her. By the time she'd reached the Rennie's front door, he was halfway down the block, his cashmere coat open to the darkness, the coat tails rippling behind him.

The heels of her shoes felt like shards of glass in the soles of her feet. She didn't know why she'd bothered trying to wear these shoes for him, why she had ever thought that she meant something special to him.

She watched him go, watched him disappear around the corner, not even looking back although she knew that he knew she was looking at him.

The next time he saw her, and the day after, he treated her exactly the same as he had—mildly flirting sometimes, and other times like his sister. She didn't trust either way he acted. So he just wanted to be friends—fine. She'd just be friends with him. She didn't need him anyhow. She'd try to move on.

But for the rest of her life, Ella hated "Willow Weep for Me."

15

The Scent of Lavender and No Good

October 11, 1932

The next Tuesday, Ella slipped into Miss Adeline's after school.
The scent of lavender buffeted against her. Miss Adeline loved po-
mades and potpourris—"Life can look good *and* smell good," she'd
tell her girls. Ella took a deep breath: this was her last run of the afternoon, and although she had to get her numbers back to T-Bone, Miss
Adeline's felt more like a respite than work. On the gramophone,
Bessie Smith was growling "I need a little sugar in my bowl." Ella
could feel her voice, and the bass, strum deep in her chest.

Of course, all the shades were drawn. The shades were always
pulled down. Heavily shaded lamps—they reminded Ella of her
mother's Tiffany lamp—glowed from tiny tables. Gilded mirrors
twinkled from the walls—supposedly to better display the girls'
charms, but Ella suspected it was more so Miss Adeline could moni-
tor even the most secret corners of the rooms: although the men
were allowed to drink, the women were not. Miss Adeline's house

was known for cleanliness and class. Most of her customers were white, including the police—although the police didn't have to pay much to Miss Adeline, Ella had heard.

Ella was taking Agatha's and Missy's bets when another girl, tall and buxom, descended the carved wooden staircase, wearing a ruby red, low-cut evening gown trimmed in white feathers and gold sequins. The rest of the girls were lounging on couches. Ella didn't recognize this new one, but the girl seemed to recognize her. The girl's lips tipped in a full-on grin when Ella's eyes met hers.

And then she recognized Gardenia, gussied up like a runway model out of a foreign fashion magazine. Ella realized only then that she hadn't seen her sitting on the stoop for a while now. "Well, hello, stranger," Gardenia said.

"Gardenia," Ella said. "Where you been?"

Gardenia sat down on the sofa, patted for Ella to join her. Ella glanced at the door. She couldn't stay long; she had to be two blocks over very soon. But she could stay for a minute.

The sofa was made of soft, silky material. Ella could have easily gone to sleep on it. "Where you been?" she repeated. "I was going to ask Auntie if she saw you."

"Silly," Gardenia said. "I's sitting right next to you, ain't I?"

Ella wasn't sure what to say. "Are—um—are you—are you working here now?" The other girls were looking at them both. Ella never sat down on sofas with the working girls. She started feeling anxious. Where was Miss Adeline?

"Started last week. Miss Adeline takes very good care of me."

"Why?" Ella's voice was louder than she'd intended, and she softened it. "You don't have to do this, do you?"

"My papa never came home," Gardenia said. "He been gone

over a month." She stared at a painting on the other wall, as if somehow bypassing Ella's judgment, as if not wanting Ella to ask further
questions.

"Are you—" Ella hesitated—"Are you a sporting girl now?" The
answer seemed obvious, but Ella had never known a girl who had
gone to work for a place like Miss Adeline's.

One of the few men—they were all white, since white people
could pay more than coloreds—was eyeing Gardenia and Ella. He
started to approach. Ella stood up, and so did Gardenia, but Ella
backed toward the door, and Gardenia swayed to Bessie Smith's
voice, clearly watching the man. He was perhaps fifty, gaunt, with a
few gray hairs sprouting from his chin and thick gray hair in his ears.

"I be with you in a minute, Mr. Bernard," Gardenia told him, and
the man stopped halfway across the room, eyes going back and forth
between them. Ella was taken aback. It was as if Gardenia had learned
some special charm to make men do what she wanted.

"Come on," she told Gardenia. "You don't have to do this."

She tried to grab her hand, but Gardenia snatched it away.

Gardenia rolled her eyes and scoffed. "I know what I'm doin.'"

"Do you?" Ella said. "Because from what I hear the girls that live
in the brothels end up out on the street, sooner or later."

"Well, for me it'll be never," Gardenia said. "And what you doin'
here anyway?"

"I'm just here for Miss Adeline's numbers," Ella said. She'd had
another thought she'd been mulling over as well, and this conversation with Gardenia was clarifying it in her head.

"Well you can make a lot more here than you can tryin' to be a
man in the street. You'll end up with a bullet in you, that's for sho."

Better a bullet in me than what's going in you, Ella thought of saying, but didn't want the conversation to get ugly. She didn't want to fight. So she said, "I know what I'm doing. Besides, my sister's come to live with us. I want to be there for her."

"Well, there's a lotta work around here." Gardenia moved close to Ella.

Miss Adeline's voice broke over them. "Posey, honey, why don't you offer Bernard a drink," she said, staring at both of them.

"Posey's my working name," Gardenia muttered to Ella. "See you around." She sashayed toward the white man, hips swaying exaggeratedly, and slipped her hand under his arm like she knew what she was doing. She led him over to the bar. Ella tried to watch—Gardenia seemed so sophisticated, so unlike the carefree girl who laughed and teased on the front stoop—but Miss Adeline was in front of her, handing her money and numbers.

"Miss Adeline," Ella said, "could I talk to you?"

Miss Adeline paused, holding out her bills. "Everything alright?"

"Yes ma'am. Just had a question to ask you in private."

Miss Adeline was wearing some kind of vanilla perfume, and as she turned and led Ella into the back of the townhouse, Ella breathed her in. She wished that Miss Adeline had been her mother—strong and decisive, pursuing her own goals, never doing someone else's laundry—and then came to her senses: she didn't want to know what compromises and sacrifices Miss Adeline had made to run her own brothel.

The kitchen opened up to the rear courtyard, with a narrow back porch. Half-rotted floorboards gave alarmingly under their weight. Below, in the small rear garden, two Doberman pinschers prowled on chains. They didn't bark.

"You ready for a job, sugar?" Miss Adeline said when she closed the door behind them. The dogs trotted back and forth, staring.

"Maybe," Ella said.

Miss Adeline watched the dogs. "Everything's okay, boys," she told them as they looked up at her. Then she said to Ella, "You're going to have to change the way you dress. You can't dress like a schoolgirl. And your manner is too rough and unpolished. That won't work here. I can train you, though. And I can help you pick out some new clothes."

"I was wondering if there's anything else I could do to help," Ella said.

"What you mean?"

"I was thinking that you could use some more eyes out on the street. I know the area. Know the neighborhood. Know people who don't belong," Ella said.

For many weeks she'd been mulling over her situation, trying to figure out where to pick up more work. The conversation with Aunt Virginia about missing school terrified her—she had to keep showing up, even though her grades were in the toilet and she couldn't care less about any of the classes. But she didn't want to intercept any more notes from Wadleigh threatening expulsion because of her absences. Didn't want to disappoint Auntie.

Numbers running felt more and more dangerous. A few weeks before, another big-time runner took a bullet to the back of the head. Ella was constantly scuttling from one venue to another, heart in her throat, terrified she'd be next.

But it was last weekend, that glorious and awful evening with Zukie, that fully cemented her resolve to ask Miss Adeline for a job. She knew, without question, that Zukie would never be her dance partner. He was beautiful and extraordinary, and he would never be hers. There was no use trying to pretend otherwise. Ella was many things—a dreamer, a romantic, an innocent—but she was also practical, and it was time to look elsewhere.

She'd find another dance partner. She needed to find another way to make money. Brothels and speakeasies needed people to keep watch.

"I could be a lookout. Watch the street in case the police come. I know your people already, or most of them."

"A lookout?" Miss Adeline barked a laugh, and both dogs looked up at her. "I wasn't expecting you to say that."

"I can work nights and weekends," Ella said. "I know a lot of your regulars already. And I know the cops. I can stand outside and dance and we can figure out a signal I can give to Monty." Miss Adeline did have both a brothel and a speakeasy, so she was doubly exposed, as Ella knew.

Miss Adeline shifted her attention from the dogs to Ella. "How soon can you start?"

"How much can you pay me?" Ella asked.

16

Bitter Street, Harlem

Fall 1932

Autumn descended. October and then November were cold and dark. Only a year ago, Ella had been a schoolgirl in Yonkers, her biggest concern being what dance she should practice at night. Now in Harlem she spent a few afternoons running numbers for the mob, her evenings and weekends keeping watch for a brothel, her mornings and afternoons cleaning and doing chores at home, and her nights terrified that Aunt Virginia couldn't afford to keep her apartment, even though Ella's income supplemented Auntie's nicely. Georgie and Frannie tried to get jobs, but neither had any luck. Finally, Frannie made some money delivering the *Amsterdam News* on Saturday mornings, but the route was short and the income was paltry. Ella suspected that Georgie didn't try very hard.

As the nights came earlier, the Harlem streets grew bloodier for the gangsters who controlled the avenues. Ella was only a small-time numbers runner who never needed to do more than hand her numbers to Zukie or T-Bone, or sometimes to a couple of other men who worked with them—JJ Jones, Preacherman, or Big Caesar—so she hadn't paid a lot of attention to what was going on in the street. But in early October, the same night she was out dancing with Zukie, Big Caesar got gunned down; and a few weeks later it was Preacherman.

These were people she knew, and this terrified her. She wanted to float above the violence erupting through the gambling halls at night. So she asked questions of Miss Adeline, of Miss Bernice, of many others, until she pieced together what was going on around her.

From conversations with the women on her route, and chats with Zukie and T-Bone, she learned that a battle actually was being fought in the bars, bordellos, and back rooms of Harlem, a war between the Negroes and the whites.

Years ago, colored folks had been in charge of the numbers racket. The Italian and Jewish mobs thought Negroes were poor and disorganized, and ignored Harlem until they found out how much money the Negro mob was making. They allowed "Madame Queen"—her real name was Stephanie St. Clair—to run the numbers game. Ella had only seen her from afar, sitting with her entourage on Sunday at the Abyssinian Baptist Church. She was taller than most men. She dressed like a white woman, with long pearl necklaces and rhinestone earrings; her flapper dresses sparkled like a living stained glass window. The Queen put advertisements in the *Amsterdam News*, demanding voting rights and ending police violence. She was as good as a Baptist minister, visiting the sick and shut-ins, eating pigs' feet with the community in juke joints, hiring folks desperate for work. No one in their right mind would talk bad about a colored woman who gave food to the starving, or paid electric bills to turn people's lights back on.

About a year ago, a Jewish mobster named Dutch Schultz, backed by the Italian mob, demanded control of the racket money in Harlem. He sent out an ultimatum: Madame Queen, and all the other colored policy bankers, must work for him. There was no other option.

But everybody with any Harlem street sense knew that Madame Queen would never back down.

So now Dutch Schultz was systematically making good on his threat. If you were a Queen's man, you were a dead man, people said.

—

T-Bone, and Zukie, and therefore Ella, were Queen's men. Ella had known this from her first weeks running numbers, but it had never seemed that critical to her—until now.

A few days after Preacherman died, Billy Herk—a legendary gangster, numbers runner, and vicious enforcer—was strangled in broad daylight, in front of dozens of people, including several police officers. Herk's murder was casual, blatant, and utterly cold-blooded. Afterward, Dutch Schultz's henchmen didn't hide, didn't run. Herk's killing was meant to send a message, and it worked. Madame Queen's street runners were horrified, defecting immediately to the Dutchman. Harlem residents questioned in hushed whispers what kind of people had the balls to squeeze the life out of the Herk for everyone to see. And, almost worse was knowing the police would do nothing except turn their backs, walk away, and collect their bribes from the Dutchman.

Now Ella and Zukie were the only young runners left in this

part of Harlem. And the school authorities were cracking down on truancy. Aunt Virginia's threat always felt close. Outside school, matrons in official uniforms patrolled the playground, with police officers and a paddy wagon parked nearby.

In the second week of November, soon after Herk's killing, Ella met Zukie outside the subway at 125th and Seventh Avenue. School had let out for the day, and Zukie now often accompanied Ella in the gloom of the late autumn afternoon. After the dance at the Rennie, Ella had been awkward around him, uncomfortable, but Zukie was always the same, breezy and casual and as easygoing as ever.

Zukie had taken a bus and as he descended the steps, Ella was struck by how fragile he seemed. Beneath his cream-colored suit, beneath the cashmere overcoat, his shoulders looked hunched and thin, no longer the wings she'd once admired. But his smile was as free and full as ever. "Hey, Sassy Feet," he said.

"You're late," Ella told him.

"Yeah, well." He strolled down 116th Street toward Minton's, and she followed. Trash and scraps of paper blew against their legs. The buildings leaned over them. Many of the top windows had been broken.

"We owe Mrs. Jackson fourteen dollars," Zukie told her.

"You got it?"

"Of course. Right here." Zukie nodded at his clothes, where the money was hidden somewhere.

116th was broad and empty. They liked it because they could see in all directions, just in case. They turned up Lenox for a block, to hit 119th, toward Mrs. Jackson's. She had a babysitting business in her living room.

The brownstones closed in around them. It was just a block up. Soon, Ella told herself, they'd return to the light and bustle of 116th.

Just then, from the direction they'd come, a black sedan screeched up, the rear passenger window lowered.

"Look out!" somebody screamed.

A white hand came out the window, and it held a long barreled pistol.

The car was moving quickly. Ella didn't have time to even think. She leaped behind a pile of broken furniture that clumped on the curb. Zukie was right behind her.

But as Ella dived for cover, two shots rang out. Instinctively she covered her head, curled up in a ball.

The car squealed off, and for an instant the world—the air, the street, Harlem—went silent.

Then, Ella uncurled, opened her eyes. She hung onto a splintered chair leg for balance. Nearby, a crumpled heap of cream fabric lay shattered on the cement. For an instant Ella couldn't quite figure out what it was, but then saw the arm, the fingers curved, the twisting angle of a hip, a knee.

The cream color bloomed: bright, impossible, scarlet; the fabric soaked up the vibrant red and let it go, a pool trickling onto the sidewalk.

Ella staggered over.

Zukie lay there, face up, one arm outstretched, one leg bent impossibly behind him.

The top of his head was gone.

Blood and bone spattered beneath him. His eyes were open but his mouth said nothing, and his eyes were seeing nothing.

Ella stood there, trying to breathe, staring down at him, at this man who she loved and wanted to dance with and wanted to hold forever, trying to decipher some last message on Zukie's handsome, vulnerable face.

She was half a block from Minton's, and tottered over there for help, everything a cream-colored, blood-spattered blur. Vaguely afterward she remembered the people from Minton's making her leave Zukie in the street. They warned her the police would want her as a witness and she could end up in jail, or the murderers could circle around and come for her. Someone hailed a cab, and she jumped inside, too terrified and nauseated and heartsick to do more than hang on to the car door as it sped north back to Auntie's.

This was what her life had become. Earning twenty dollars a day didn't seem worth having her head blown off. Didn't seem worth it, at all.

And Zukie. Handsome, dazzling, beautiful Zukie.

HER NEXT STEPS WERE MECHANICAL. SHE GOT OUT OF THE CAB. She looked up at Auntie's building. She couldn't go through the front door. She was too afraid to go home. But she didn't know where else she could go. Rain was coming. A silky blast of wind brushed her face. Somehow it was night: hours had passed and Ella didn't know how, or where she'd gone. The sky was full of stars. She wondered if all of those tiny pinpricks were souls, how those souls—even if murdered—rose to heaven, was one of them Zukie now?

Later that evening, when she finally opened the door to Auntie's apartment, no police waited for her. Georgie and Frannie were playing jacks in the parlor. Georgie at least had made dinner, but Ella didn't eat. Auntie wasn't home.

The next weeks passed in a blur, and now it was December. No one sought out Ella to take her witness statement for Zukie's death. T-Bone just shook his head, lips tight, face grim, and gave Ella some of Zukie's route. "We don't talk about street matters," he told her. "Talk walks."

The entire situation—the war for Harlem, her numbers running, school, Miss Adeline's, Aunt Virginia—seemed impossible for a fifteen-year-old girl to navigate, but Ella didn't know how to free herself. This, she thought, was the real meaning of depression.

She didn't tell Auntie about Zukie—they still didn't speak of Ella's numbers running. But Auntie's job was paying less than ever, and more pressure than ever was on Ella to earn money just so they could eat. Ella had started skipping school again to take bets in the morning, when the gangsters were still in bed; and the afternoons and evenings she hung out on 134th Street, watching for raids on Miss Adeline's.

She intercepted another note to Auntie from the Wadleigh School: *We would like to set up a meeting at your earliest convenience to discuss Ella Fitzgerald's continued truancy. As you know, we believe strongly that a young girl's health and well-being depend on her being . . .*

She threw it away without reading the rest.

Soon Ella was missing at least one day a week at school, sometimes more. She wasn't able to focus when she was there, and she'd given up entirely on homework. She intercepted yet another letter from the school to Aunt Virginia, tore it up without reading it.

Still reeling from Zukie's death, she knew that she had to figure out another source of income. She looked more and more at Miss Adeline's sporting girls, but couldn't bear the thought of what they did with those men.

Even dancing had lost its charm. She tried to imagine making real money at the Savoy, tried to imagine loving what she was doing every day, but it was too disheartening. The world felt gray and distant. When she closed her eyes at night she often saw that cream-colored jacket: blooming, blooming, blooming.

17

Something Wasn't Right

November 17, 1932

A week before Thanksgiving, Ella skipped school again to gather the numbers from the beauty parlor route. T-Bone hadn't been in his usual spot so she'd had to track him down to one of his favorite bars over on 133rd. He'd been ugly drunk and had barely paid attention when she'd handed off the numbers and money. He didn't double-check the tally, either.

A wind was blowing cold and damp in her face: it smelled of winter and garbage as she let herself into the apartment building, made her way up the three flights of stairs. Her face was chapped from the cold. She was exhausted—she'd been up late the night before. Miss Adeline had asked her to watch the corner because a group of VIPs were in the speakeasy. The ragtime piano tinkled faintly from the basement, but she didn't even try to dance. She hadn't danced in a few weeks. The money Miss Adeline offered was an extra ten dollars, but Ella had stayed out until almost three a.m. Now weariness bit at her bones. In the stairwell another chunk of plaster had broken off. Crumbling white powder trailed down several steps.

Later, she'd wonder if she should have realized something wasn't right, even then. Would she have noticed, had she studied the street more carefully? *Eyes in the back of your head*, Zukie had told her: maybe she needed eyes at the top of her head, too. Perhaps she could have deciphered the hieroglyphics in the plaster dust, like tea-leaves foretelling the future. As it was, there was nothing: no different smell, no warning bell, no shadows in the corridor as she trudged to the apartment door. She let herself in.

The living room parlor was full: Aunt Virginia, Georgie, Frannie, a tall white stern-faced woman, and a white policeman she didn't recognize from Miss Adeline's. She tried to back up, close the door, disappear, but in the hallway another white policeman appeared, blocking her escape. She looked from them to Auntie. Auntie's eyes were stern and sad, and Ella couldn't read her expression.

"Ella, come in here, please," Auntie said. She seemed smaller. Defeated.

Down the hall the policeman approached, his footsteps loud and heavy on the ancient tile.

Ella went in, closed the door in his face. She tried to figure out if she could get past the crowd, get to the fire escape. But so many people blocked her way.

The stern-faced woman was from Child Protective Services.

She was here because of Ella's truancy.

The two policemen had arrived to question Ella about Zukie's murder.

Ella never learned if it was pure coincidence that Child Services and the police had arrived together, or if it had been orchestrated ahead of time, in some moldy bureaucratic office somewhere. Later, she would imagine the conversation:

The Fitzgerald girl? We have a report that she's running numbers and may have been involved in the death of Alonzo "Zukie" Cabell.

You talking about Ella Fitzgerald, the ward of Virginia Fitzgerald? That's the same girl that Wadleigh School reported with chronic truancy and behavior issues.

"Oh, Ella," Auntie said now. She started to say something else but one of the police officers was talking over her.

"Miss Fitzgerald," he said to Ella, "you need to come down to the station with us. We have some questions for you."

"Auntie—" Ella began, and the room erupted in shouts and wails: Georgie and Frannie. The two police officers were coming toward her, one had grabbed her right shoulder and the other was holding her left arm.

"Don't give us any trouble, girl," the tall woman from Child Protective Services said.

She had $295.86 in that glass jar. If only she could get to it. "Can I get something from my room?"

"Your aunt will pack some personal items for you," the woman said. She was brusque and burly.

"But —"

"Come along now," the woman told her. The policemen loomed behind her.

"Can I say goodbye to my sister and my cousin?"

The woman considered this. Ella couldn't believe that even this simple request was so unreasonable. Eventually the woman nodded, and the policemen let go of her, and Ella took two strides to Frannie. She hugged Frannie tight.

"What did you do?" Frannie whispered.

"I'm gonna come back for you," Ella whispered in her ear. "Promise."

"How could you do this?" Frannie said.

How. How else could she have tried to help, to keep them together, to keep them safe? Ella didn't know how to say any of this, so she closed her eyes and breathed Frannie in.

Everything was happening so quickly. She wouldn't, for hours, have time to understand what she was feeling—the utter loss that was engulfing her, the grief and regret and desperate hysteria—all she could do was repeat to the top of Frannie's head, "I'll come back for you."

Eventually she had to let go. She hugged Georgie too, and Auntie. Neither said anything to her, and she squeezed her eyes tight. When she let go, Georgie grabbed Frannie. They hugged each other. Tears were rolling down Frannie's cheeks but she didn't wipe them away, and somehow the sight of them, gleaming on her skin, made Ella feel even more desolate and alone.

Then the officers were manhandling her down the stairwell, over the plaster dust, and out into the street.

"I want my Auntie," Ella said, but hopelessness clamped over her lips, making it difficult to even speak. "I want my mama," she said, but wasn't sure if she said it out loud. "You can't do this to me."

But they could, and they did.

They shoved her into the back of a police car that was now idling on the corner. Neighbors peered out the window.

They drove her to the 28th Police Precinct in Central Harlem and locked her up in a cell in the back of the station. All the other cells around her were empty. Ella lay awake on the thin cot, too broken and too frightened and too hopeless to sleep, trying to figure out how to escape. If only she could get to that glass jar, to those three hundred dollars, no one would ever see her again.

The next morning, the sun streamed through the small window in her cell. She was given oatmeal and bread. A tall white policeman escorted her down the hall to a small office full of steel file cabinets. A white female truancy officer—not the same woman from last night, this woman had mousy brown hair and a haggard expression—didn't give Ella her name. On her desk was a file, and Ella guessed the file was hers.

"Miss Fitzgerald, you've been quite a busy young lady," the woman said. "You miss more school than you attend. And the police want to question you about the death of Alonzo Cabell, too." She shuffled pages. "You've missed school for a total of twenty-four days in the last two months. Our records show that the school sent half a dozen letters to your home, but apparently it hasn't made a difference."

"What you gonna do?" Ella asked. She tried to channel Zukie: casual, hardheaded, giving away nothing.

"We're going to help you lose that attitude, for starters," the woman said, not bothering to look up from her paperwork. "You'll have plenty of time. You're going away for a while. The court order's already signed."

She gestured to an official-looking piece of paper, with a seal on it. Ella couldn't read it upside down, and didn't want to.

"Where's my Auntie? You can't send me away."

"I'm afraid we can," the woman said. She didn't sound regretful. "Missing school, no living parents, and consorting with known criminals and prostitutes? You're headed upstate. To the Training School for Girls."

Ella had heard of this place: the girls had talked about it, jokingly, at Wadleigh. A reform school. *You better not get sent to the Training School,* the girls had said. *They lock you in the basement, and that's if you're good.*

She jumped up from the desk, backed away toward the door. "No I'm not! I'm getting out of here!"

But when she opened the door, two more white police officers were waiting.

Part 3

THE NEW YORK TRAINING SCHOOL FOR GIRLS

Wet Dogs and Old Milk

Perhaps if Ella had known that famous people would be among her best friends, that she'd one day go out to lunch with Marilyn Monroe and sing with Duke Ellington—whose records she listened to all the time—maybe then she would have had more strength that morning when she had to mount the bus to the reform school.

Had she only been more sure of her life, had she only envisioned what lay in store, perhaps then she would have felt less ill, less certain she was some kind of walking curse.

But now she was blind to her destiny, and she knew nothing but cold, and a hurting belly, and a sick, nauseating dread.

Ella was on the bus, and the bus stunk of white people: of wet dog and old milk just before it turned sour. She usually only noticed their odor when it was raining; but on this cold, miserable November day, the curdled aroma of the four white girls hit her like a bottle in the face the moment she climbed onto the school bus. The white girls were all wedged into their seats, two and two, like Noah's animals, their pale faces congealing, blue eyes drifting over her, thin pink lips set in smirks.

Row by row she slouched her way toward the rear, where a boyish looking girl, mocha tan, with straight black hair, glared at her. "You know how to use a brush and comb?" She turned to her seatmate, a dark-skinned girl with thick braids down her back. They ignored Ella.

She sat down across from them and stared hard out the window, hoping that if she didn't notice anybody else, they wouldn't notice her.

Yes, Ella felt like saying, *I know how to use a brush and comb.* But she hadn't touched them since she'd left Auntie's three days ago. Her hair stood up in coiled knots, uncombed, and her skirt and blouse were badly in need of laundering. She felt like she'd staggered up from a filthy street corner—which wasn't that far from the truth. And now that she was seated, she could smell her own stench. She'd spent the last two days in a foster home where a woman had locked her in a bedroom only slightly bigger than a closet, with no window, and had thrown in a plate of tasteless mush three times a day. She was allowed out four times a day to use the bathroom, but never had a chance to bathe or comb her hair.

Outside the bus's window, endless rows of squat, red buildings folded into themselves, brick facades flashing into wood siding, and then into open fields. Ella had been to the country several times: Yonkers was close to the suburbs where her mother and Joe had taken the girls for outings. She'd paddled her bare feet in creeks and they'd picnicked beneath tall trees in the summer.

Out the steamy bus windows, the fields and woods of this country glowered back at her, ominous and unwelcoming. The trees, barely budding, bent beneath the wind and rain as if they were already broken.

She tried to imagine how Zukie would conquer this, all casual brash and dare, but thinking about Zukie, like thinking about her mother, started an ache deep inside her; so she turned her face away from remembering how he was so alive one moment and then snuffed out the next. She'd hoped for a romance with him, and that hadn't occurred; but now, with a little bit of distance, she sometimes wondered what would have happened had he lived—maybe they would have gone dancing another time. Maybe *then* he'd have kissed her. Maybe, maybe, maybe . . . all meaningless now. He was gone. All his beauty and bravado did not keep him alive.

Death had stalked Ella so much she was sure it was waiting for her around every corner. First she'd lost Tempie, then Zukie, and she wondered if she'd be next, since it was breathing all over her. Grief was cold and metallic tasting on the roof of her mouth. It wouldn't disappear no matter how many times she swallowed.

The world rattled past, bleak and distant. She tried not to look at any of the girls on the bus. Tried to tell herself that it would be okay, that she'd get through this, that it would be an adventure. *Adventure*: the word didn't seem to reflect anything about where she was heading. Her stomach cramped, and she felt sluggish and achy. She was lightheaded from fear, or perhaps she was getting sick. That was all she needed, on top of everything else.

If the place was as awful as she'd heard, she told herself, she'd escape. She'd live on the streets. She wouldn't be able to go back to Aunt Virginia's, since the authorities would look for her there, but she was crafty. She'd figure it out.

The fields stretched out endless and gray. The road bumped

along next to the vast expanse of the Hudson River, the water drifting sluggish as oil, and then the bus turned back through the broken fields again. Mist and rain obscured most of the view.

They'd been traveling for well over an hour when she noticed a stain on her dress. In the middle of her lap, a pinprick of dark red bloomed on the light blue fabric. It must be a food stain from the past couple of days. But ten minutes later, the red stain had flowered, doubled in size.

She looked over to see if either of the girls on the other side of the aisle had noticed. They hadn't, not yet. Horror amplified terror and embarrassment. As surreptitiously as possible, Ella pulled up her skirt. Her bloomers were red with blood. The back of her skirt was soaked. She knew what was happening. This had never happened to her before, but Aunt Virginia and the working girls and the girls in school had their "periods." They said it was horrible and now if she let a boy do it to her, she could get pregnant. She would bleed every month from now on until eternity. Ella knew all this. Still, she somehow never expected it to actually happen to her.

A low voice said, "Pull your dress down." The mocha-tan girl had noticed. Ella glanced past her—the girl's seatmate's eyes were closed; she seemed to be sleeping.

Ella instantly pulled down her skirt, gathered her torn coat around her, leaned back as if unconcerned. "Don't mess with me," she said.

"If I was you, I wouldn't put my business in the streets," the girl said. Her lips were swollen and shiny, and she kept licking them. Ella wondered if someone had punched her in the face.

It didn't matter. Ella knew that she couldn't let herself get walked all over, especially not in the beginning. She'd learned that much from Zukie. "Mind yo own business," she told her.

The girl slid over, tall and gangly, halving the distance between them. "If you want a rumble, you met the right one." Her voice was loud, shocking in the bus's silence. In one motion the white girls in front all turned to look. The girl's seatmate opened her eyes. They were bloodshot.

"Sit down and shut up," Ella hissed. "See what you done, girl?"

"Don't call me 'girl.' Name's Sweetbread."

"Don't nobody wanna know your stupid name," Ella told her.

The bus hit a bump and sent Sweetbread sprawling back into her corner. The white girls tittered and turned back to the front.

"Let's see how you do when you get up out of that seat," Sweetbread said.

Ella was thinking the same thing. She had to figure out how to get off that bus without everyone else seeing her bloodied clothes. She imagined everyone snickering, and her stomach dropped again. She tucked her coat around herself as tightly as she could.

The ride was endless. The white girls, who for a moment had been laughing at something, talking in extra loud voices, as if they owned the bus and were riding along for amusement, had fallen silent again.

Finally the bus turned through a heavy pair of gates and climbed a steep hill. They'd left the city in early morning and it probably wasn't even lunchtime, but Ella felt like they'd been traveling for days. Several ornate-looking brick buildings leered down at them. An old Black man was sweeping the front steps of the biggest one across the lawn. He looked over when the bus drew up, but then kept sweeping, ignoring them.

The bus driver turned off the ignition but didn't open the door. A few of the girls in front stood up as if expecting to be let off, but when the doors remained resolutely shut, they sat back down. Ten minutes passed.

Finally, the door sighed open and a rail-thin white woman stepped inside, introduced herself as Ma Ramsey. She wore a nurse-like gray uniform. "I'm the one person here that you don't want to meet again." She paused as if waiting for someone to speak, someone to ask why they didn't want to meet her again, and then she answered her own unspoken question. "I'm in charge of discipline," she said, and then repeated herself: "Discipline."

The "s" was sibilant and drawn-out, the "n" hummed through the bus like a wasp.

No one spoke.

After a pause, Ma Ramsey read out the girls' names—Sweetbread's real name was Marion Wilson—and assigned them to "cottages." Ella wasn't sure what a cottage was, but imagined something rustic, with a thatched roof, tried to remember which fairytales had cottages in them. But that couldn't be right. More likely, "cottage" was a euphemism for something terrible, like "jail cell."

Ella was in number seventeen.

The girls were to grab their belongings from under the bus—they'd each been allowed to bring a small suitcase, which would first be searched for contraband—and they'd begin orientation at the administration building, where they'd receive their uniforms.

Whites first, of course.

"Well, just don't sit there, girls," Ma Ramsey said. "Get off the bus."

The white girls were all climbing to their feet, shuffling down the aisle.

Ella let Sweetbread and her seatmate get off. She was last. She flicked open her coat to find the blood had stained the entire back, all over her skirt. She could feel herself panicking, gasping for air. Would her blood leave a trail from her seat? Could she stay in the back of the bus forever? Maybe they wouldn't notice her.

Ma Ramsey shouldered her way back onto the bus, her face drawn, her eyes gray and blank.

"Didn't you hear me? I told you to get off the bus."

The bus rocked as she approached, as if she were much larger than she appeared. A long keychain hanging from her waist banged rhythmically against the bus seats. The light seemed to contract around her, and now she was standing over Ella. "I said get up and off this bus."

Ella felt dizzy, lonely, and cold. She couldn't stand up. It was as if the blood had glued her to the seat.

"Don't you speak English?"

She looked at her lap, where her tweed coat hid her shame. "I have my period," she muttered.

"Get up. I won't ask you again. The next time we'll be dragging you off."

"I have my period," she said more loudly.

"You have—oh," the woman said, and paused. "Let me see."

She pulled back Ella's coat before Ella had a chance to grab onto the hem.

"Oh," the woman said again. "Don't you know how to keep yourself clean?" The loathing in the woman's voice added to Ella's humiliation. "You people are no better than animals. Follow me."

Ella didn't look up as she trailed Ma Ramsey down the aisle. Perhaps she was right. Perhaps Ella was no better than an animal.

"Girls, go inside, up that way." Ma Ramsey pointed to the door in front of them. "I'll be just a minute." And then to Ella, "Grab your suitcase."

She led Ella across an open grassy area to another "cottage," which turned out to be another heavily carved brick building that seemed too solid and not at all fairytale-like. Ma Ramsey didn't speak, and the walk across the lawn felt like it would never end. The handles of Ella's small suitcase dug into her palm, and she kept switching it back and forth between her hands. She welcomed the pain—she deserved this, too.

Ma Ramsey bustled Ella into the infirmary, told another white woman—this one white-haired, introduced to Ella as "Ma O'Brien"— that Ella needed to be cleaned up. She pointed to Ella's coat and skirt.

"Another one in heat. Filthy creatures," the woman observed casually to Ma Ramsey. She handed Ella a sanitary pad without looking at her. "Go wash yourself. I'll get you a uniform. Here's a bag for your dirty clothes. We'll need to wash that coat, too."

The uniform was dark blue and faded, with a thick collar and a row of buttons down the front, and a skirt that fell below her knees. She could wear her own shoes, at least. She loved her oxfords. It seemed like they'd been purchased in another life, by another girl.

An hour later Ma O'Brien led Ella over to Cottage Seventeen, angled slightly away from the other buildings but still encircling a central empty space where much of the grass had been beaten into dirt. Number Seventeen was smaller than its neighbors, set slightly lower on the hillside. All of the buildings were grimy red brick, with heavy gingerbreaded trim under the roofs. The trim had once been painted white, but now the paint was peeling, pieces of it dripping down like icicles. It all seemed forlorn, somehow abandoned. Even when the girls were thundering through the rooms, calling to each other on the grass, the buildings still seemed uninhabited, or inhabited by ghosts who had lost their way.

Ma O'Brien knocked on the door of Number Seventeen and stood in the vestibule as if it were too distasteful to enter.

"Go on now," she told Ella, and shouted into the depths of the house, "Rose? The new girl's here. What's your name again?" she asked Ella for the third or fourth time.

Ella told her.

"Ella," Ma O'Brien called out. "Ella Fitzgerald. Rose? You there?"

Inside, the cottage smelled of wet wool and unwashed feet. Ella waited in the foyer, front door open, with Ma O'Brien outside on the landing. The murmur of girls' voices buzzed from somewhere within. After a few moments, a beleaguered-looking white woman, overweight and bulging through her dress, hair pulled back tight off her face, emerged from the central corridor. She wiped her hands on a stained apron. Her face was lined, with dark shadows under her eyes, as if she'd been punched.

"What are you doing there with the door open?" she said to Ella. "Get in here and close that door."

"This is the new girl," Ma O'Brien told the woman, and then asked Ella, "What's your name again?"

"Ella Fitzgerald."

"Ella Fitzgerald," Ma O'Brien repeated. "This is Ma Murphy."

"Well, don't linger in the hall," Ma Murphy scolded Ella. "Get inside. Never leave the door open, the drafts will kill you, you understand? And the heat gets out."

She reached past Ella and slammed the door in Ma O'Brien's face. Ma Murphy wore filthy nursing shoes, something that Auntie would never do. Auntie polished her shoes white every night.

The long hallway smelled of mildew and cleaning solvent. Ma Murphy made her way heavily upstairs, using the banister to haul herself up each step, leading Ella to a room at the end of the hallway. As soon as Ma Murphy opened the door, a blast of freezing air hit them, but she made no mention of drafts.

"This is your room and you keep it clean," she said, edging to one side to allow Ella to go in ahead of her.

The room was so narrow that Ella could almost touch the side walls. A rusty iron bed crouched on one side; on the other was a small wardrobe missing several knobs on the drawers. Against the back wall, the one window was cracked and had been taped. The wind whistled in harshly.

"Every girl gets her own room." She said it with pride, as if maid service was next.

Ella backed up, bumping into Ma Murphy and grabbing the doorknob. The woman pushed her back in.

"Where you going? I don't want any trouble with you."

"I have to go to the bathroom." She took a step into the room, so as not to touch the woman.

"There's a bedpan over there in the corner."

She pointed to a pan.

"I have my period."

"This is your room and if you know what's good for you, you'll make the best of it. There are sanitary napkins in the dresser drawer." The woman surveyed Ella. "You're one of the Ungovernables. All of you always are."

Ella didn't know what she was talking about, so she said nothing. Flakes of rust from the bedframe sprinkled the mattress. She wondered if she'd have rust in her hair when she awoke in the morning.

"Truancy, right?" Ma Murphy was saying. "You're all always truant. Always skipping school. Never wanting to better yourselves."

All? What did she mean by *"all"*?

"I was trying to earn money for my family," Ella explained.

"Oh sure." Ma Murphy didn't seem to believe her. "Hustling, more like it."

Ella thought about mentioning the dollar-fifty-a-night she'd earned as a lookout for Miss Adeline's brothel, but decided she'd better not.

"Your file says that your family gave you up," Ma Murphy said. "Your family didn't want you."

"That's not true," Ella said hotly. "That's not true at all."

Ma Murphy shrugged. "That's what your admission papers said. Parents are dead, right? Aunt couldn't control you?"

"She wouldn't give me up." But doubt slithered in. Perhaps Aunt Virginia had reported her. Perhaps Aunt Virginia was the reason Ella was here in the first place. Auntie hadn't wanted her, after all. Desolation unfurled through her. Had Aunt Virginia betrayed her? After all the money Ella had given her, all the cleaning and minding of Georgie, after all of Aunt Virginia's talk of always looking out for Tempie's daughters?

Ma Murphy was pointing to the bed, where sheets and a gray blanket, all neatly folded, had been stacked. "Make that up. Jessie will show you how to do it properly tomorrow. It's one of your duties and it will serve you in good stead. Supper's at five thirty sharp, I'll get you for supper when the girls finish their chores."

The door pulled shut and the key turned. Ma Murphy was gone. Ella twisted the doorknob several times, willing it to open, but she was locked in. She took three strides to the window. The room was high off the ground, the window sash nailed to the frame. She could pull out the glass, but the mullions were too narrow to fit through. No one was on the lawn below.

Years later, in the three-in-the-morning insomniac moments when she'd brood over her time at the New York State Training School for Girls, she wondered if it could have been different if she hadn't begun in isolation. If she'd been welcomed, if only in name; if the administrator had lined her up with the other girls and explained the layout of the buildings, the mission of the school; if in those first moments she'd bonded with another newcomer, like Sweetbread. Perhaps the school, as somber and miserable as it was, could have been a place where she belonged. But she never quite shook off the sense that she was an outsider, locked in or locked out, viewing the school and its inhabitants as if through a warped glass windowpane that reflected a disfigured, discarded self. No one—not even her family—wanted her.

Instead of making the bed, Ella perched on the raw, stained mattress, the coils sagging uneasily under her weight. Her misery was bone-deep and too intense for tears. So she clutched the alien fabric of the uniform, stared at the cracked wall a few feet opposite, and realized that their intent was to remake who she was. The cold plaster had been permeated with loss, grief, absence. Everything Ella knew, everything she cared about, had been snatched away: Auntie, and Harlem, and dancing, and Zukie, and Miss Adeline. Only she was left. Weary, she pushed the stack of sheets to one side, shook out the blanket, and wrapped herself in it. She curled into a fetal position, tightening into herself so she would be small, colorless, invisible to everyone's hate. She wanted to disappear behind her tightly squeezed eyelids and never return, to disappear into a world of her own making, Duke Ellington playing endlessly, marquee lights shining, a thousand stomping feet hitting the floor in spins, splits, and shivers.

She conjured the Savoy, dancing with Zukie at the Rennie, the circle of faces, admiring, applauding, as they spun and curled in on each other.

Now, unmoving, lying beneath the rough-spun wool coverlet that reeked of sweat and misery, she spun and dipped and aerial flipped, she slid and trotted and tangoed and tapped, all in her head.

Slowly, the darkness surrounding her eased, and she breathed deeper.

Ma Murphy Blues

November 20, 1932

Hours passed. Thick gray light cut through the windows before the door finally rattled, then opened. Ma Murphy leaned in. "Didn't you hear me? Didn't I tell you to make that bed?"

Ella found herself on her feet. She wanted to explain that being forced into the school, having her first period, all of it had overwhelmed her. She needed a quiet space to retreat, to shake herself loose from despair; but she didn't have the words to soften this woman. Zukie, she knew, wouldn't have stood for someone screaming at him the way this woman was screaming at her now. But Zukie was a man, so it didn't do any good to think of him. And Zukie was no more. Still she clenched her fists, took a stance. Hateful old woman.

Ella would show her.

"Don't you make a fist at me, missy. That kind of behavior is not tolerated here," Ma Murphy told her, taking two steps closer. Then she repeated, as if for good measure, each syllable distinct, "Not. Tolerated."

Ella opened her fist. "I—"

Ma Murphy didn't let her speak. "Let me be very, very clear with you, Ella Fitzgerald. If you ever raise your hand to me again, I'll see that you have no hand." Ma Murphy looked her up and down. "Ungovernable, indeed. Filthy, lazy brawler is more like it. Like all your kind. Well, just know right now: it won't be tolerated."

"I didn't—"

"But," Ma Murphy said, talking over her, "because you're new here, because this is your first day, I'm going to be Christian and charitable. I'm going to give you one warning. One." She held up a chubby index finger, its nails and cuticles gnawed and bloodied. "If you act up again, the next time I won't be so nice. I'll send you to Ma Ramsey." Another frown, as Ma Murphy looked her over. "And one thing you don't want, my girl, is for me to send you to her." Again the threat about Ma Ramsey. Ella didn't know what was so terrible about her, but remembered that thin frame, the keys swaying ominously from her waist. She didn't want to find out.

Ella just kept staring at her shoes. Ma Murphy took another step toward her, pushed up on her so close that Ella could smell her sour body odor, and the aroma of an oily-smelling liquor. Ella wanted to lean back, but didn't dare move.

Ma Murphy was saying, "I don't tolerate laziness and back talk. You thought you was too good to come to orientation, or you would have heard that. This is a place of discipline. Now come with me."

—

The dining room took up the entire back length of the building. Colored girls, all shades, from very light to very dark, all wearing the navy blue uniform with the heavy collar, crowded tight around five round tables. Other girls stood behind a buffet line, serving. When Ma Murphy appeared, everyone fell silent.

"You can sit here." She tapped the back of an empty chair.

Ella looked around the room, caught sight of Sweetbread pointing to a chair at her table. All the girls were watching.

"You really are a troublemaker, aren't you?" Ma Murphy said, following Ella's gaze. "I said sit here. This will be your seat from now on, so make sure you stay put."

No food was on the tables. Apparently, the girls were waiting for Ma Murphy. There was clearly an order to things. Ella took her seat and watched as, first, the table nearest the buffet line stood up, filed neatly in a queue, grabbed their plates and made their way down the line. Here, the girls behind the buffet tables dumped small scoops of baked beans, boiled potatoes, and boiled cauliflower on their plates. Dessert was a thin slice of bread, no butter. Then, the second table went; then the third. Ella was at the fourth. She stared disbelievingly at the tiny dollops of vegetables dumped on her plate.

They returned to their seats and waited, silent, heads bowed, silverware shining, until all the tables had been served.

"Anna Mae, would you like to say grace?" Ma Murphy said.

A girl at the first table bobbed her head and mumbled something. After a few minutes, she said "Amen," which the room repeated, and then they attacked their plates.

Under the clatter of cutlery, the girl next to Ella—round-faced with pigtails—introduced herself as Faye.

"Don't you be talking loud, Murphy can hear what you're thinking," she told Ella, and continued cheerfully. "What you here for? I'm Ungovernable. They caught me selling liquor and bones."

"They say I'm Ungovernable, too, but they never caught me breakin' no law."

Ella thought briefly of Aunt Virginia, wondering again if she'd turned her in. "Truancy." She paused, then confessed, "But I was also a numbers runner."

"Like in gambling?" Faye seemed impressed.

"I had a German Luger," Ella lied. It had been Zukie's gun, but that was almost the same as Ella having one.

"Most of us are here for truancy," Faye said. "But Lizzie there—" Faye nodded at a heavyset girl whispering on the other side of the table—"she came here pregnant and had the baby. They took it away and she never saw it. She don't even know if it was a girl or a boy."

"Pregnant?"

"You bet. Lotta girls knocked up. Not in this cottage but you see them outside."

"How old are they?"

"Our age. And Mary Agnes—" Faye nodded toward another table, Ella couldn't tell at which girl—"she's Destitute. A bunch of girls here is orphans, too. What room they put you in?"

"Silence!" Ma Murphy bellowed from the front of the room. All chatter stopped. Ella hadn't been aware of the rising buzz of conversation amid the chink of forks against plates, and chewing.

But after a few moments the whispering began again.

Some of the girls lined up for seconds. Okay then, Ella thought, she could at least get more. She started to stand, pushed back her chair.

"Where you goin'?" Faye asked.

"For seconds," Ella said.

"You don't get seconds," said a skinny young girl on the other side of Faye. "That only for the ones in good with Ma."

"You gon' starve in here if Ma don't like you," said another girl from across the table.

"She right," Faye said. "You betta listen if you want to know what's going on."

Ma Murphy left the room. After a minute the whispering grew louder.

Sweetbread slipped over to Ella, squatted next to her while keeping watch for Ma Murphy's return. "What happened to you?"

Ella shrugged. Now, apparently, Sweetbread wanted to be friends. Well, Ella would take all the allies she could muster.

"You didn't miss much. Just a boring-ass lecture about how this was going to be just like home and how they expected the best from us. The white woman in charge, Mrs. Morse, she one of those do-gooders with a guilty conscience. All talk. Where you sleepin'?"

"I'm up on the third floor."

"I made me two friends. That's them over there." She nodded toward the table she'd left, but Ella didn't know which were the new friends. "Beulah and Gloria. They said that we should try stealing as much food as we can cuz they never serve enough. You get enough?"

Ella shook her head.

"Here." Sweetbread fumbled beneath her skirt, pulled out a thick crust of white bread. Ella bit off a chunk. A girl laughed at them on the other side of the table.

Sweetbread glared at her. "If you keep playin', we'll give you somethin' to laugh about." She went back to her seat.

Ella followed her, still chewing. She figured that Sweetbread could introduce her to these new friends of hers. The more friends Ella could make, perhaps the more insulated she could be—the more the group would help her blend in, adjust. It was like numbers running: she could lose herself in a crowd. The ones who stood out got picked off. She vowed to not stand out.

She'd just gotten to Sweetbread's table when the room fell silent again.

Ma Murphy had reappeared.

She was staring at Ella. Ella swallowed around the lump of bread she'd just bitten into. It seemed impossible to get down.

Then came a smacking sound, wood hitting flesh: Ma Murphy held a paddle, and the sound thundered on her open palm. She hadn't looked away from Ella. "Get over here."

The room had gone utterly still. Ella had the sense that no one could even blink: that they weren't girls anymore; they'd all frozen into stone. Ma Murphy's voice was sickeningly loud, as if coming from several directions all at once. "I warned you, Ella Fitzgerald. You've been here a couple of hours and you're already making a name for yourself. You don't want to make a name for yourself. Insolence, niggardly back talk, and table hopping will not be tolerated. Not tolerated! Didn't I tell you? Didn't I?"

"I didn't do nothin'," Ella said.

"Stepping out of your place is nothing? Sneaking food is nothing? You didn't get more to eat because you didn't deserve to eat any more." Ma Murphy was sweating and her lips twitched spasmodically. "So you have to learn the hard way. Used to be, we would've used a bullwhip on you people. So consider yourself lucky."

She paused, the paddle smacking the fat meat of one hand. Somehow, although Ella hadn't been aware of her moving, Ma Murphy was standing right in front of her now. "Hold out your hands."

Ella's arms seemed both lighter and heavier. Her biceps ached and her fingers tingled.

"Hold them out," Ma Murphy said. "Palms up. And keep them still."

Ella raised her hands, palms up, fingers extended, and before she was ready the paddle was whistling through the air and descending, the sting bringing her to tears. She closed her fingers, the heat in her palms sharp and throbbing.

"Because it's your first day, I'll let you off easy," Ma Murphy said. "You're going to start by cleaning up every single plate and utensil off all these tables, and you're going to wash and dry them. And you," she looked at Sweetbread, "are going to do the same thing tomorrow morning. But you two don't get to do it together. You understand me?"

Ella nodded. Her fingertips returned again and again to the pad below her thumb, where the stinging was worst.

"Dinner is over," Ma Murphy said. "The rest of you have three hours to get your homework and chores done before bed. The girls on dinner rotation will thank Ella and can have the night off." The girls got up and started filing out, murmuring.

"Quiet!"

When they'd gone, it was just Ella and Ma Murphy again. The pain in her palms was lessening.

"Ma Murphy led Ella into the kitchen, a humid, hot room that stunk of cabbage, although they hadn't had cabbage for dinner. Ma Murphy pointed out where the soap and drying towels were, where Ella was to stack the cleaned plates and cutlery. "Get to work," Ma Murphy said. "And you better do a sparkling job. This is the first lesson you'll learn. Be clean. No more sloth or filth."

I'm clean, Ella wanted to say. *I'm a girl.* But the sound of the paddle still rang in her ears and the welts still burned. So she stood, gaze unfocused, silent.

And there, in the middle of the kitchen, Ma Murphy looked back at her with what seemed like pity.

"You're not going to survive this world," she told her. "I can tell right away. You people need to know your place. I'm trying to give you the skills to survive. That means no uppity attitudes, no laziness, and no dirtiness. You'd better clean up this place like you never cleaned before." She sighed, rubbed one hand on her thigh. The other still held the paddle. "I'll be back in an hour. I better see some real progress by then."

Back in the dining room, Ella stacked plates. She wanted to throw them to the floor, yearned to hear the splintering crash.

As Ella cleared the plates, she thought about the days after Tempie's death, when Joe'd made her clean the apartment—how lonely she'd felt. How desolate. She'd survived that time by playing the phonograph. Music had transported her out of despair. But here there were no phonographs, no radios. Music did not live in the grimy linoleum, or the walls with their spiderweb cracks radiating out at irregular intervals.

The dishes were endless, the night stretched out before her. She could feel herself sliding further into hopelessness. Her dreams of dancing, getting out of Yonkers, making something of herself, felt very far away. She had been fooling herself, there was no way of escaping who she was: poor, colored, alone, unloved. And all of it was surely, surely, her own fault.

She carried a stack of plates to the sink, and then another. If only she hadn't wished her mother dead that night. *If only.*

On her fourth trip to the sink, she began hearing Mamie Smith in her head: *There's a change in the ocean, Change in the deep blue sea, my baby.*

Ella didn't have a phonograph here, but she realized that she could always remember the music. She could always remember the feeling of dancing. She shifted her weight in the beginnings of a dance—just a small step here or there—and sang under her breath as she worked through those dishes.

Ma Murphy returned sometime later, when she was most of the way through.

"You're doing an adequate job," she sniffed, examining the plates. "Maybe there's hope for you yet." She disappeared again.

Ella had finished the dishes and was sitting on the floor, eyes closed, hearing "Heebie Jeebie Blues" in her head, when Ma Murphy returned again.

"Finished?" she asked. "Good." She stared at Ella a moment, considering, as if she wanted to say more. Then: "Get to your room."

Upstairs, Ella slid beneath the thin blanket on the unmade bed. The wind battered the cracked window. The rain had stopped, but now the cold of the room stood up and surrounded her. A room of her own should have been a privilege, but she understood that here, at the Training School, it was anything but. This was isolation. She was used to sleeping with the warmth and sounds and smells of others around her—Georgie, Frannie, even Aunt Virginia. Thinking of Aunt Virginia sent another wave of loss through her.

They won't break me, she kept repeating, as if trying to convince herself. *I'm getting out of here as soon as I can.* If she could only figure out where to go. Not back to Auntie's. Almost as if in response, the key turned in the door. The white woman had locked her in again.

No matter. Ella would find her way out. She had to. She could only be herself, and being herself wouldn't work in this place. Staying here would destroy her.

Through the Wetland of Sheets

November 22, 1932

The next day—and all the days that followed—began before dawn. Ella would later learn that the alarm went off at five, but that first morning she only knew that a horn blared out so loudly that she bolted up, blanket to her chin, wondering if this was a police raid. Voices and footsteps resounded in the hall. Moments later the lock clicked and Ma Murphy ushered in a tall, frowning colored girl with unkempt braids. Ella had noticed her last night, sitting at the first table.

"This is Jessie. She'll show you how to make the bed and do your chores," Ma Murphy said. "Now, get up and get dressed." Ma Murphy didn't wait for a response.

Ella was out of bed now, the thin nightgown she'd been issued feeling even thinner than it did before. Without Ma Murphy here, Jessie got up in Ella's face.

"Why you here?" Jessie's voice was heavy, low for a girl. It reverberated in the tiny room.

Ella would soon learn that Jessie was one of the Training School's "enforcers." She had a reputation for fighting and beating up girls, and Ma Murphy used this reputation for her own benefit, siccing the girl on the most difficult wards. When the girls were hard to govern, Jessie did what the school could never get away with.

"What's it to you?" Ella stood her ground, pushed her head back on her neck to give herself more personal space. She could tell that this girl was itching to brawl. Ella wondered what Ma Murphy had told Jessie about her.

Jessie shifted an inch closer. "You knocked up? You a thief? You a ho?"

"Numbers runner," she spat back, standing her ground. "You gonna show me how to make this bed or what?" Ella sized her up. "You gonna get out of my face, I know that."

"Numbers running?" Jessie didn't seem impressed.

"I had a Luger. Had a run in Harlem, with the Queen. You know who the Queen is?"

Jessie shook her head.

"She rules Harlem. Madame Queen. And I was her right-hand man."

"You just an itty-bitty thing," Jessie said doubtfully, looking down at her.

"You want to find out?" Ella got right in her face and didn't blink.

Jesse stared back, lips wet and raw-looking. She was taller than Ella, broad, built more like a man than a woman. After a moment's consideration, Jessie turned, yanked the sheets and blankets off the bed.

"This is how you fold the corner," she said. "You tuck it in here, see? And fold down here. You make sure it's straight and it's smooth.

No wrinkles. And make sure that the corners go in just like this. You do the other one and I ain't showing you twice."

Ella had braced herself, fists balled against her hips. She'd been ready to fight but now followed Jessie's instructions, keeping a wary eye on the big girl.

"If you follow the rules," Jessie said, "we won't have no beef. Don't give Murphy no mess and won't be no mess between you and me. Understand?"

She towered over Ella, leaned in as if whooping her ass would be no problem. "We eat at six so you get yourself cleaned up and be down in the dining room ready to work." Jesse slammed the door behind her.

Now that Ella was alone, she practiced folding the sheets into perfect military corners several times. No way that Murphy woman was going to say she was lazy or dirty. Ella was neither. When she was finally satisfied with the bed, she made her way to the bathroom and then downstairs to the dining room.

That first morning she started talking to some of the other girls. Cicely, a skinny twelve-year-old, had been picked up for vagrancy. "My mama and daddy both leff," she told Ella. "Dunno where they is. Those police picked me up and brung me here."

She seemed soft and untouched, always on the verge of tears. Ella immediately wanted to hug her, but knew better. She had to be cold-hearted and unyielding in this place.

Breakfast, Cicely told her—she'd been there for almost a year now—was prepared and served by a rotating group of girls, who also washed up while the others swept and dusted the cottage.

Lessons began at nine a.m. Ella made Cicely repeat herself, since she didn't believe it the first time. Aunt Virginia, who believed in the power of education to uplift the Negro race, would be outraged. On Mondays, Wednesdays, and Fridays, the colored girls "learned" domestic cleaning. Tuesdays and Thursdays were laundry.

The white girls, in their larger, cleaner cottages, were taught English, math, and home economics. The Training School saw no point in teaching Negroes those kinds of skills. They were only fit to be domestics, after all.

This institution, Ella realized immediately, claimed to be a training school but was really a holding pen to keep colored children in their place until they were old enough to be set loose on the world. There was no pretense of education. She wondered how Aunt Virginia, of all people, could have allowed her to be sent here. Perhaps Auntie hadn't turned her in after all? Or perhaps Auntie didn't know how terrible it was.

On Tuesday, Ella found herself in a cavernous basement, scrubbing sheets with her bare hands on steel-plated washing boards. In a different room, sheets and clothes dripped onto the cement from clotheslines strung like spiderwebs across the ceiling and bolted to the walls. "They call this the hangin' room," Bertha told her. "For hangin' they clothes. But I heard tell that a girl hanged her own self here, too, not long back."

Ella stared respectfully at the strands above them, the clothespins like crooked teeth, jutting out into the air.

"I'll never do this for a living," she told Sweetbread, who was next to her. "Never. My mama died doing laundry and I damn well won't."

"You know it and I know it but they don't know it," Sweetbread said, teasing.

Ella didn't think it was funny.

They trooped back to the main laundry area, where piles of

to-be-washed sheets and uniforms and underthings took up an entire wall. Here she was, doing laundry, just like her mother. Ella felt the urge to grab an armload of dirty towels in the laundry bin and throw them on the floor. For a moment she froze, paralyzed, not knowing how to express her revulsion. She was not going to be a shame-ridden, poverty-driven washerwoman like her mother— and then again, didn't she deserve exactly that? She'd thought, *I wish you were dead*, and hours later her wish had come true. The Bible said, "The punishment should fit the crime." This was exactly what she deserved.

Still, she stood there, unable to move. Frustration, loathing, misery, and an almost-eagerness to get started warred within her.

The other girls eyed her but didn't stop scrubbing.

Cicely, who was behind her, reached around her, pulled out a handful of towels, dropped them in the vat of water.

"Lemme do it for you, Miss Ella," she said.

Near the door, where the remnants of a breeze could brush in, two of the older girls—Jessie and Sadie—were supervising the rest. Bertha whispered to her that Sadie, a pole-thin girl with an enormous head wobbling on top of a pencil-thin neck and narrow shoulders, sometimes shared Ma Murphy's bed, but Ella never knew if that was true or not. Luckily neither girl had caught sight of Ella yet.

"Just wash them sheets," said Thelma, a belligerent, streetwise girl with a forward way about her. "More foul things be happening here than you know. There is two white men that come sniffin' around, and you gonna meet both of them, Carter and Lewis. You want to suck their dicks? Cuz if you don't mind Ma Murphy, that the first thing you be doin'."

Ella stared blankly at her, shook her head. She edged toward the sink, where Cicely was scrubbing towels that seemed to weigh more than she did.

"We call them Carter Lewis—just one name. You know why?" Thelma went on. "Cuz they do dirt together. If you get done by one, you get done by the other. So you git got twice." Thelma's face was fixed and scowling. The water was too hot against the back of Ella's hands. She leaned into Cicely, took back the towels from her, and started scrubbing.

"You don't want them to take you behind the cottage neither, in them bushes," Thelma was saying. She'd turned back to her own sink, and Ella had to strain to hear her over the sloshing and the other girls' chatter. "And you don't want Carter Lewis to get the other old white boys to join them, that's for damn sure. That Duncan?" Thelma shook her head, didn't finish the sentence.

"What about him?" Ella asked. "Who is he?"

Thelma pulled in her lips, let them out as if she were going to say something, but didn't. After a pause she told Ella, "I'm planning to run away." It was like you flipped a switch and Thelma would just keep talking, whether you wanted her to or not. "Colored girls go missing from this place. Since I been here, three gone."

"They escape?" Ella asked. Thelma shook her head.

"They was 'discipline problems.'" She said the words like she was quoting. "Ma Murphy don't have no patience with uppity girls, so she send 'em to Ma Ramsey. That's when they be gone. I'm not gonna risk it. You shouldn't either."

Scrubbing the slippery wet fabric had made Ella's stomach queasy. Images, unbidden and unwelcome, reflected in the water: the bushes behind the cottage, Ma Murphy telling her she wouldn't make it here, and then her mother, scrubbing laundry in the kitchen, choking on the bleach fumes, collapsing in the laundry room that final day.

It was all too much.

Her legs grew unsteady. She sat down on the wet floor, leaning her head against the front of the sink, legs tucked under her, and wondered how she would survive this place. Ma Murphy was right. She wasn't going to survive in this world, let alone this place.

"Miss Ella, please get up," Cicely said. "Jessie ain't seen you yet but when she do, she gonna report you. You don't wanna report on yo first week."

"You sure don't," Thelma said. "Maybe they put you right in the Dungeon. They do that sometimes."

"What's the Dungeon?" Sweetbread asked. Her arms were deep in the sink and she was leaning in to the washing as if wanting everyone to know that she was working hard.

"That where you don't never ever want to go," Thelma said. "That where Duncan like to visit. Some girls never come out."

Ella didn't want to think about what happened behind the cottage, or in the Dungeon, and she didn't want to think about this Duncan. Instead, she took a deep breath full of bleach fumes and humidity, clambered to her feet, immersed her arms in the scalding water, and began to scrub. She saw herself momentarily from above, one of a long line of colored girls, all side by side, bent over stained sheets and scorching, soapy water. An image of the glittering Savoy popped into her head. Life had to be more than this. But the pink glow of the Savoy had never seemed farther away.

Music, Sweeter than Roses

December 1932–July 1933

During Ella's brief hour of schooling, Ma O'Rourke covered ma-terials that Ella had learned years ago. Still, she practiced her penmanship and delighted when Ma O'Rourke complimented her writing.

The only bright spots in her life were the infrequent letters from Frannie. Sometimes Georgie and Aunt Virginia wrote, too, but Ella lived for Frannie's letters.

Dear Ella,

I am fine. Monday we had a English test and I passed with a B. Auntie said I could have a malted milk this weekend. Auntie is fine and Georgie dont like to share. Did you know Mr. Ackers from Yonkers moved two blocks away, I saw him and he knew who I was but I didn't remember him. He is fine, too, and he says hello. Georgie and me play with the Michaels sisters, Missy is a year

older than me and much bigger and she is my new best friend. She
smiles and laughs just like you. And guess what Tammy and Geor-
gie have the same birthday!! Next year we going to have a big
birthday cake for both of them and Missy says that we can have a
party at their house it is bigger than Auntie's. I had french fries
two days ago but don't tell Auntie, Mr. Jones gave me a cup of
them when I brung his paper. I still have my paper route and I
have saved 46 cents in a secret place.

> *I love you and miss you Ella!!!*
> *Frannie*

Ella saved all of her sister's letters, folded them tight, and hid
them in a back corner of her top bureau. In the early morning she'd
pull them out if she awoke before the horn, reread them, and smell
the paper and ink as if she could inhale Frannie and Harlem in a
breath. But then the horn would sound and the day would open into
its routine and drudgery.

Physical education rounded out a few afternoons: volleyball,
swimming, and bicycling from three to five twice a week. Dinner was
from six to seven-thirty, followed by solitary study in her room from
seven-thirty to eight-thirty. The last thirty minutes were for "personal use." Lights went out at nine.

A few times a day, Ella and the other girls would troop from one
cottage to another—for a special announcement, or to pick up laundry,
or to run an errand. She never forgot the first time she saw the pan-
orama that a social worker had told her about after the police had
picked her up from Auntie's. "It's real beautiful," the woman had said, as
if bestowing a prize to Ella, as if this were a place Ella would love to go.

At least in this, the woman hadn't lied.

The first time Ella rounded the corner of the cottage and the Hudson vista appeared, she stopped and gasped aloud. Below her shimmered the Hudson River, its ripples pouring endlessly forward, with the greening hillsides of farms and fields glowing behind. The afternoon sun slanted in distant treetops. Far below, birds winged across the rippling surface of the river, and fish leaped in the late afternoon sunshine. Ella had never seen a view so enchanting.

But mostly the white girls, and the administrators, got to enjoy it. Cottage Seventeen didn't have a view. Still, always there was a sense of space, of vastness, nearby. The light and the air seemed charged with a luminous weightlessness, as if time moved differently up here, as if this place were separate from the world. Sometimes she wondered if perhaps her first idea of fairytale cottages hadn't been that wrong, after all—even though apart from the view there was nothing at all magical about the Training School.

As the weather grew warmer, on some Wednesdays the girls got a break from laundry and were awarded a field trip: traveling to a farm in the Hudson Valley and weeding the fields. They dug into the ground with hoes and shovels, scraping dandelions and weeds away from the rows and rows of vegetables—beans, tomatoes, peas, peppers that were bound for other households, probably in the city. The girls would never eat these. Ella's hands blistered and grew tough.

The white girls, meanwhile, trooped into the farmhouse overlooking the fields. "Where they going?" Ella asked Thelma the first day she saw them.

"They don't have to do field work like us. They white."

"I'm no field hand." She sunk the shovel blade deep and released the handle, which vibrated in the warm June air. "I'm no washerwoman."

Thelma poked her arm. "Pick it up or you gonna be sorry."

Lewis and Carter strolled their way. Both men had brown hair and very pale blue eyes, but that's where the resemblance ended. Lewis was enormous, well over three hundred pounds, and his shirts always had dark sweat stains around the neck and under the arms. Ella didn't know how he could stay so big, given how much physical labor he did every day—he was one of the groundskeepers—but he never lost weight. Carter was much more slender, with rough, pock-marked cheeks that looked painful, as if blistered.

Neither man had noticed Ella yet. She begrudgingly yanked the shovel out of the earth again.

But her resentment simmered. From her perspective, it seemed that the white girls sauntered into a beautiful farmhouse and were taught sewing, knitting, and other ladylike arts. She imagined tea and scones, their pale faces staring from the windows at the Negroes sweating in the sunshine without hats or gloves. The white girls used the indoor bathroom. The colored girls used the outhouse in the back, or squatted in the fields if the men were far away.

On the bus ride home, and all that night, Ella fumed. The sight of those privileged white girls made her want to be feminine, delicate. Wear gloves and carry a parasol. This was well beyond her reach, beyond the reach of any of the colored girls who were preassigned their roles for life. The white girls were learning to be ladies, were learning to be creative and have skills. She was working like a farm animal.

Stop trying to be what you aren't was a phrase that Ma Murphy liked to repeat. Along with *Stay in your place.* But Ella wasn't sure what exactly that meant. How could she know what she could be if she didn't try? Auntie had told her that her people could be more

than shuffling maids, nannies, and shoe-shiners. Ella wanted to believe this.

Weeks passed, and Ella grew more confident. She learned the
routine, knew the women who ran the colored cottages, recognized
the guards and groundskeepers, and kept her distance.

Mrs. Morse, the superintendent who ran the Training School,
stayed near the administration building, or in the white girl cottages. Every so often she came by to give speeches about the power
of education, or the possibility of redemption through learning,
but she made no effort to introduce herself to the girls in Cottage
Seventeen, and never inspected the rooms, or common areas, or
laundry rooms. Perhaps, Ella thought, she actually cared about
the plight of Negroes and just didn't realize how bad those girls
had it?

Ella wondered if she should say something to her, since there was
no point in trying to talk to Ma Murphy. Once Mrs. Morse knew
what the girls were living with, maybe then things could change. All
the girls would have new opportunities. Perhaps Ella could dance as
part of physical education; perhaps she could teach the other girls.
That might help the morale. If nothing else, most of the girls were
sad and homesick: the Lindy Hop and the Charleston would liven
them up, give them something to look forward to.

One early June day she decided to sneak over to the backdoor
kitchen entrance of the main building and introduce herself to Uncle
Clyde during her thirty minutes of personal time, instead of staying
in her room. Ella had seen him sweeping the steps when she'd first
arrived at the school, and saw him periodically since then, but they
hadn't ever spoken. As Thelma put it, "He the old man butler who
waits hand and foot on Mrs. Morse. He has a radio. Sometimes he

lets us into that kitchen of his and plays the music, and boy can he dance. He has tapping shoes and a top hat."

Ella had wanted to meet him, but their paths had only briefly crossed, and she didn't have any opportunity to talk to him.

Uncle Clyde, she reasoned, would have a wider perspective than the wards. He'd worked at the facility for years and had seen girls come and go. He'd know how to get Mrs. Morse's ear. Plus, if he was a dancer, like everyone said, Ella wanted to see his steps.

That evening, before her cottage's back door was locked for the night, she snuck out. She wouldn't have much time, but if she found Uncle Clyde quickly, she'd have enough. She closed the door behind her, slipped around the cottage to the administration building.

The seventeen cottage buildings were arranged in several loose circles around a central green space. The Negro cottages, far to one side, didn't have the magnificent views of the Hudson River or of the village of Hudson nestled on the hillside to the north, but since these cottages were set slightly lower than the others, it was also slightly easier to move undetected around the other cottages until she reached the back door of the main building.

Music, faint but clear, thrummed in the summer air, and Ella hesitated on the back porch, listening. Bing Crosby was crooning from a radio, and she recognized the melody. She'd danced to "Sweet and Lovely" several times, an uncomplicated foxtrot with a simple beat that her feet ached to dance to now. Her heart yearned, too. How long had it been since she'd heard music outside her head—and how desperately she missed it!

How Uncle Clyde knew she was there, she never learned. But inches from her, a man's voice, deep and gentle, said, "Come on in, child."

A moment later Uncle Clyde opened the door. "You don't have to

hide none on the porch. You hungry? I was just about to have a biscuit and some tea."

"Oh, I'm fine. Thank you." Ella was on her best behavior. The
music washed over her with a comforting warmth that she could feel
on the back of her knees and against her eyelashes. The kitchen was
enormous: on one wall, rows of cast-iron pots and pans gleamed
from racks. The largest stove she'd ever seen hulked nearby. The
kitchen cabinets ran clear up to the high ceiling, which had a tin
pattern stamped upon it. The room was cozy and nurturing, smelling of bacon and cinnamon, and had a homeyness about it that she
hadn't felt anywhere else at the school. For a moment, Ella allowed
herself to believe that Tempie and her grandmother and Frannie
might march through one of the swinging doors as if they owned the
place.

"I'm Clyde. They call me Uncle Clyde."

He was sixty or seventy—Ella didn't have a sense of his age—
with thin gray curls around a shiny bald pate. He moved smooth and
sure, with broad shoulders and an athletic frame that made Ella wonder if he were actually much younger than she'd first thought. He
poured himself some tea from a kettle on the stove, then sat at one
end of the large kitchen table, placing his biscuit and cup firmly in
front of him. She continued to stand.

"Can I help you with something?"

"I'm Ella. Fitzgerald. I was hoping to talk to you for a minute."

"Oh, sit down, honey, and rest yourself."

She sat down at the table, let out a breath she hadn't realized she'd
been holding.

"Do you like music?"

"I sure do." Ella stood again and performed the Maxi Ford: jump, shuffle, jump, toe, tapping a few steps to the music, keeping her el-bows tight and her hands on her hips.

"Oh, my, who taught you that?" Uncle Clyde stood and did a dou-ble Maxi Ford, the tap sequence effortless and unexpected. "Bet you can't top that," he chuckled, then settled himself at the table, took a sip of his tea.

Bing Crosby ended, and Ethel Waters came on with "I Got Rhythm," a classic Lindy Hop. She launched into the combo that she'd done with Charles. Her muscles remembered the steps as if they'd been just waiting for the opportunity.

Uncle Clyde laughed out loud. "You sho can dance but I don't want you gettin' into no trouble. You need to be gettin' back."

"Can you teach me some of what you can do?"

"That why you come here tonight?"

She nodded. "Partly. I want to get your advice on some things."

"What kind of things?"

"It's—well—how we colored girls are treated. Laundry and field work. I heard that Mrs. Morse—"

He shook his head, interrupting her. "Ah, honey, this is a longer conversation than you gots time for. You need to get back before lights-out. But you come and see me real soon. I want to see those steps you just did. I just might learn somethin'."

Ella was grinning and giddy. The gloom lifted, if only for a moment.

"Thank you, Uncle Clyde. See you soon." She flitted out the door, and made it back minutes before the lights were turned out and the doors were locked.

Three nights later she returned to the back porch, and again he opened the door to his kitchen's warmth and comfort. He demonstrated the Buffalo: brush left forward to the left side, eight leaps forward to left foot, a shuffle right forward, and a leap back to the right foot. She'd seen this routine in the past but had never attempted it. Now, she tried it a couple of times.

"I do want to talk to you about Mrs. Morse," she said when they took a break. She had perhaps five minutes before she had to hurry back to her cottage.

"She a fine lady," Uncle Clyde said. "A fine lady."

"That's what I hear," Ella said. She'd only seen Mrs. Morse from a distance. "That's why I wanted to figure out the best way to talk to her about what's going on with the colored girls. How most of the day is laundry and being a maid. How we go to that farm and—"

"Child, what make you think Mrs. Morse don't know about that?" Uncle Clyde said. He leaned back in his chair at the kitchen table, looking up at her. She couldn't read his expression.

"Well, I know Mrs. Morse believes in education. I read—"

"Mrs. Morse know what's what," he said.

"But she wants us girls to get educated. Not just doing laundry—"

"Mrs. Morse do what she do," he said.

"So you mean she's okay with it? She *don't* want colored girls to get an education?"

"We out of time for this tonight," he said, pointing her to the door.

So the next time she could sneak out, four nights later, she tried again. Again, he deflected her.

"You just take care of your chores and finish your time here," he said, which was no answer at all. Finally, she realized that this *was* his answer. That he knew, that Mrs. Morse knew. That they all agreed that this was a colored girl's lot at the Training School. Perhaps the colored girls' treatment was even Mrs. Morse's idea. Defeat and despair battered her.

There was nothing to be done except make the best she could of the situation. She'd dance with Uncle Clyde whenever she could, and that would have to do.

They both knew how to make music with their feet, and his love of dancing was akin to her own. Between the stove and the back pantry, as the radio burbled low, he would show her his vaudeville buck-and-wing steps—explaining that these steps were danced to the banjo; and older steps, like the African worship dance and the Juba, a plantation dance, which were danced to hand-clapping and rattling bones from years and years ago, from before she'd been born. And Ella would demonstrate the modern blues and jazz steps, the Charleston and the shag, and of course her favorite Lindy. Together they danced a simple Maxie Ford combination, his palm warm in hers.

There in the kitchen, he'd often sing or whistle. His joy in his daily life hit her as unexpected and as unfamiliar as being rich enough to shop on Manhattan's Fifth Avenue. Ella couldn't fathom how he could find happiness in such a terrible place.

"How come you so happy?" Ella asked him a week later. "These people don't treat us right."

"I know how they treat you and how they treat me."

They were taking a break from trying the Irish jig, which wasn't that far removed from the syncopation of the buck-and-wing. Now Uncle Clyde let go of her hand, looked at her and away. He seemed to force a smile, which wasn't usual for him. His grins were effortless and beaming. He went over to the radio, fiddled with the dial. "I lost my family when I was sent up North to live with my grandmother," he said, not looking at her. "Never saw my family again so who's so ever I come upon and we set horses, we's family."

"Who taught you to dance?" She gulped a glass of water.

"They tell me I had music in my bones. I wasn't but a peanut when I started dancing in a minstrel show. Everybody around me could dance and entertain white folks. White folks couldn't get enough of us. When we came to town, there was so much laughing, there was no heart for lynching."

"How could you be happy when there's lynching?"

"Let me tell you a secret." He'd been staring down at the radio, but now looked up at her. She moved closer. "Those people doin' that, they don't know what they doin'. Some is crazy and others is lookin' for somethin' that can't be found. I am one colored man, livin' in lynchin' country. But I always finds a way to get along."

She stared at him, disbelieving, not quite sure she was following what he was saying.

"I sets my eyes above," Uncle Clyde told her. "He know and see everythin'. I don't want for nothin'. I gets plenty to eat and these people love me. You know why?"

"Why?" She, too, wanted to be loved, but it seemed so impossible.

"Cuz they can see themselves in me."

Ella thought about this for a moment.

"I want people to love me, too. But I don't think they do here."

Uncle Clyde shook his head. "This ain't a place where there a lot of love."

"Especially for colored people," Ella said.

He didn't answer. This was an answer in itself, she realized. "I'll be here for another year at least," she said.

"You make the best of it. I heard you singin', too. You gots a powerful voice. Your place is there, not here. People will see the good in you when you sing and dance, and they love you for it. You mark my words, they will. You a fine young lady, Miss Ella. A fine young lady."

She wished she could believe him. Sometimes she could really see it. She could feel some magic in her, in the way she was moved to dance, the way she dreamed in music. Anywhere there was music Ella glistened. And every now and then she thought she could see a version of herself sipping champagne, reaching beyond the streets and this raggedy place. Most times, the weary grayness of the days stretched out before her, unbelievably bleak, and the Dungeon's darkness waited at the end. She didn't know how she'd survive another year here.

By then, the routine had taken on a nightmarish familiarity. It was as if she were bolted to a theater seat, her eyes pried open, forced to watch the same grainy film over and over. Except she wasn't sitting in a red velvet seat with a luxurious, special-occasion, five-cent bag of popcorn: she was scrubbing and sweeping and picking up and dusting, and the work was endless and sweaty and backbreaking and—above all else—demeaning.

She wanted to escape but was too exhausted to even try to plot how she would get away, where she would go, with no money, her heavy navy blue Training School uniform making her stand out from the crowd.

But every week or so, no matter how bone-weary and miserable, she managed to sneak over to Uncle Clyde's kitchen to dance for twenty minutes before lights-out. That kept her sane. The old man nurtured a kind of freedom through dancing and music, and she found joy in the radio tuned to WFEA, the big band sounds of Duke Ellington, Benny Goodman, and Glenn Miller. Their music washed over her and Uncle Clyde like a benediction. The trumpet and trombones would slide up the scale, and Ella would imitate the sounds of the horns with her voice, surprising herself by how much she sounded like a horn; and then in syncopation she would tap-dance the notes, singing along.

Dancing, Ella became more and more convinced, was indeed her way out, just as she'd thought a year ago, before her mother died: brush-step, shuffle, tap, pencil spin, shimmy-sham on down the road. Dance away from despair and desperation. Yes, sir—this was the way.

Visiting Uncle Clyde one evening in July, she managed to hear one of the new president's Fireside Chats. It was about something called the National Recovery Administration and went over Ella's head.

"That man just makes me feel real good. Trust you me, he's good for this country and he gon' get us out of this Great Depression. And Eleanor Roosevelt—what a lady," said Uncle Clyde.

She shrugged. She'd seen a blurry photograph of the new president and his wife, but they had nothing to do with her. They wouldn't whiten dingy sheets or remove collar stains and didn't know any dance steps she could imitate.

She wanted only to feel Uncle Clyde's hand over hers as he spun her on one leg, arms and legs catapulting in all directions. Then, for those brief instances, a light glowed within her, a hope that fed her for days afterward. But the time with Uncle Clyde flew by too quickly, especially in these summer months when the daylight's intrusiveness made it much harder for her to creep over to his kitchen.

In odd moments of the day, or when she didn't head over to Clyde's, a few girls—Thelma, Faye, and Cicely were the most usual—would sneak over to gather in Ella's room, or in the back stairwell, and Ella would demonstrate a few dance steps while one of the girls kept watch. There was no music, of course, so Ella would impro-vise, humming or even singing one of the many songs she knew by heart, the words and melodies like a yearning, so familiar and so unexpected. But the dancing never lasted long, and often the girls— Ella included—were too spent to do more than lie on their beds, bones throbbing.

One July morning she was pouring extra bleach on Mrs. Morse's sheets in the basement to make sure they came out pure white. The sheets had to be rinsed over and over because they couldn't have any lingering bleach smell. Mrs. Morse had a special lavender rinse, just for her linen. She was so busy she barely realized that Carter had come in, was talking to Jessie and Sadie, and a moment later they followed him out of the laundry room. For a few minutes, work continued, but without the weight of the older girls' ever-present watchfulness, the others started slacking. Ella stirred the lavender water idly with a finger, watching the ripples spread.

After five minutes, when the older girls still hadn't returned, Ella decided she'd had enough.

"We shouldn't be doing laundry day after day, and for what?" she asked Faye, who was at the adjoining sink. "We ain't twenty-one. We ain't white. But we sho can dance. Let's have some fun."

Thelma, who kept threatening to escape but still hadn't attempted it, overheard. "Yeah," she said. "I want to dance. What steps you teaching today?"

"Listen up," Ella said to the room. "When we dance, we also tell a story. You have to start somewhere. I like to start with rhythm."

She pivoted into a shuffle-step and raised her arms elegantly.

"And then we end somewhere. Today we gonna learn the Black-bottom. It's a variation of the shimmy and Lindy Hop."

Louder she said, "Come on, pick yourself a partner. You be mine," she told Cicely, and grabbed her hand. "You step side by side, and right to left, and then you wiggle your bottom like this. And then jump."

And then she moved.

"You gotta do it with heart!" She spun Cicely right, caught her, and spun her back. "There you go! You're going places! We're all at the Savoy Ballroom, in a sea of Lindy Hoppers!" She threw her hands up.

She basked in the movement and the joy from the other girls; vitality rippled through her. Next to them, Faye and Thelma were trying to follow Ella's movements, and beyond them Martha and Bertha and Frannie were picking up the steps, too. Ella had to sing slightly louder so the other girls could hear over the sound of the boiling water. Soon the laundry room was ablaze with partnered dancers giggling as they tripped over their feet, kicked in the wrong directions, pausing to watch Ella and Cicely.

Now, you heard the rest
Ah boys I'm gonna show you the best
Ma Rainey's gonna show you her black bottom

Ella knew she had to stop before they got caught. But one step led to another and the movements felt glorious, and her singing came from deep in her chest, and she sang with relief and joy and, for a moment, hope. After the next phrase she'd stop, she told herself; but then she'd sing another line.

And then, as if she'd always been there, Ma Murphy loomed like a truck in the doorway, Carter behind her, along with Sadie and Jessie, mouths open.

Ella froze, Cicely still clinging to her hand.

"Just what do you think you're doing?" Ma Murphy bellowed.

The girls stopped dancing, dropped hands, heads down.

"You." Ma Murphy pointed at Mary Agnes, a tall thin girl. "Who started this?"

Mary Agnes didn't answer. It was worse to be a snitch.

"Gloria?" Ma Murphy said, taking a step even closer to the girl, towering over her. "Did you start this?"

Gloria, a girl with bad skin and thin hair she kept pulled tight into pigtails, glanced sullenly over at Ella, then stared again at the floor.

Ma Murphy followed Gloria's gaze. "Ella? Did you start this?"

Ella kept her eyes fixed on her shoes. They were the ones she'd come with, black-and-white oxfords that Auntie had given her for the Wadleigh School uniform. "You think you can do whatever you want? You're no better than savages. You're supposed to be working. Doing laundry." Her spit twinkled in Gloria's hair. "Aren't you? Answer me."

"Yes, ma'am," Gloria said.

"Yes ma'am," Ma Murphy echoed in a mocking singsong. "Yes ma'am is right." She pointed at several of the girls, including Ella. "Finish your laundry. Now."

The room was silent.

"You and you," she said, pointing at Sweetbread and Thelma. "You two wenches get no dinner. And you, and you." She pointed to more as she prowled closer to Ella. "And as for you," she said to Ella, and then didn't finish the sentence: she slapped Ella hard in the face. Ella staggered back, grabbed her cheek. "The next time you take it upon yourself to take time away from your rightful work to do that kind of distasteful jungle dancing, I'll show you what it's like to disobey me."

"But that's not fair!" Ella said without thinking, rubbing her cheek, rage blooming in her chest.

"Not fair?" Ma Murphy repeated. "Whatever I say is fair. Whatever I say is right and proper. In Africa you people lived in dirt huts. That's why you don't know how to live a civilized life. And that," she pointed her finger at Ella. The forefinger loomed large, the cracked nail inches from her face. "That's why you're in the Training School."

Ella couldn't articulate her anger and frustration, but she knew what this woman was saying simply wasn't true. Uncle Clyde was loved, and he told Ella that she could be loved, too. These house mothers were trying to rob her of the self-esteem she'd hidden away. Ella knew that colored people had a worthy culture, a rich past, far more than just being slaves. Ethel Waters on Broadway for instance. Or Louis Armstrong. Or Jesse Owens, the young Negro track star, who was winning competitions against whites: he wasn't so much an animal, wasn't so inferior, because he was beating the "superior" white men. Ma Murphy was plain wrong. Ella was worthy of a culture that sang and danced, that competed and won, that was human and not animal.

But Ella could not begin to voice any of this. She could only bury her frustration and fury and say, as quietly as possible, "Yes, ma'am," until the day she would escape.

"Yes ma'am?" Ma Murphy echoed her. "That's it, is it?"

Ella hung her head.

The silence stretched.

Finally, Ma Murphy said, almost reluctantly, "You can wash the clothes until Ma Ramsey gets here." She watched as Ella moved slowly back to her sink, submerged her hands and lower arms in the sudsy foam. The water had grown cold.

22

The Dark

July 14, 1933

Her fingers found no purchase on the fabric—her hands had lost their strength. It was as if all inside of her was trembling, shaking with something more bone-shattering than fear. She stood over a sink of sopping sheets and pretended to scrub.

She was four rows away from the door where Jessie and Sadie would sneak out for smokes. No way could she get through in time. Could she crawl under the sink, fold herself inside herself until she just disappeared?

And then they were there, Ma Ramsey and the two thugs lurking behind her. She knew Duncan on sight: dark-haired, mustached, with a sharp jaw and gray-blue eyes, and a way of moving that seemed almost too lithe, too slippery. At first she was so scared she couldn't remember the other one's name—he had close-cropped dark curly hair and a thin beard that had only patchily grown in. But then it came to her. Eric.

Duncan smiled at her. Out of pure reflex, the rabbit bolting before the fox, she fled: heading toward Jessie's smoking door, and out, toward freedom.

"Hey," one of the men called, "stop her!"

But none of the other girls' hands grasped at her, none of the other girls tried tripping her up.

Jessie and Sadie blocked the door, Jessie's hands in front of her chest, palms out, as if to catch a football, and Ella was on them now, her shoulder barreling into Sadie. She was stumbling onto her knees, and then she was on the stairwell, taking the stairs up two at a time, three at a time, she was on the first landing. One more flight up to go and—

—and a hand was on her calf. She cried out, tried to shake free, but they dragged her down. She flung herself forward, arms outstretched on the steps, reaching for the iron banister, as they pulled her back.

"No!" she screamed, flailing, and unbelievably one of them laughed. Duncan. She was close enough to see that one of his front teeth was gray with rot.

"I love it when they fight," he whispered. She wasn't sure if he was talking to her or to himself. She could taste his rot on her breath. "I hope you fight like that tonight."

Eric was behind him, along with Ma Ramsey. "Bring her up," she said, "Faster to take her out this way anyway. Thank you, Ella, for saving us the trouble."

One man on either side of her, they hoisted her by her armpits so that her feet swung, kicking. She squirmed, tried to aim for their legs, and got a few good blows in.

"God damn she's fierce," Eric said, grunting as her shoe caught his leg.

"Better fight now," Duncan said conversationally. "I like 'em feisty. Plus it'll wear her out."

She was so alarmed that she thought she'd be sick, wished she could be sick so they'd back away from her. Her stomach tightened and churned, but no bile came up.

They were outside, in the bright July day, Ma Ramsey behind them. "I have to admit that I'm disappointed in you, Ella Fitzgerald," she said. "I'd heard reports that you were one of the smarter ones. I had my hopes that I wouldn't be seeing you here."

They were partly across the open space now, the grass already dead and brown. Beyond them, hazy in the summer humidity, the Hudson poured down endlessly through the valley. Close to her, three sparrows pecked the dirt, flew away. A breeze lifted off the river, reeking of fish and mud. "But I guess I was mistaken."

They turned away from the light, following a path toward another building, smaller than the others and slightly set apart from the rest.

"Here we are," Ma Ramsey said, and she unlocked the door.

This cottage seemed empty. Its narrow hall was similar to that of her own, but damper smelling. Ma Ramsey, Duncan, and Eric led her to a door that opened down to a steep, narrow stairway. A moldy smell rushed out, and then a wave of colder stale air.

"Now this is no place to fight," Eric said from behind her, as if anticipating Ella's reaction. "Steep stairs like these? You can break your neck."

One of the men pushed her ahead and she stumbled onto the first riser, then took a step downward. The stairs creaked loudly with every step.

"These things is gettin' weaker by the day. They better replace 'em or somebody is going to fall right through," Duncan said. His voice was high, almost like a woman's.

At the bottom of the staircase, the basement opened out into a roughly oval-shaped room. A single light bulb hanging off-center didn't quite illuminate the closed doors set deeply into the wall, which seemed more shadows than doors. The floor was hard-packed dirt.

"Is this the Dungeon?" Ella asked. She shifted back on her heels and could feel Duncan and Eric on the stairs above her.

"This is a place," Ma Ramsey said, "for you to reflect on your lot. It's the place that will give you the opportunity to do better."

The two men carried her toward one of the farther doors.

"No, not there," Ma Ramsey said, and the men stopped.

"What?" Duncan said.

"We'll put her in Five."

"Five? Are you sure?"

"Yes, Duncan, I'm sure," Ma Ramsey said crisply.

"Damn," Duncan muttered under his breath. And then louder, to Ma Ramsey, "I think she'd be more comfortable in Three."

"We're not paying you to think," Ma Ramsey said.

They changed directions, opened another door. Duncan said something else, and Ma Ramsey replied, but Ella didn't hear what it was. What was in Three? And what, dear God, was in Five?

"What are you going to do to me?"

"We're not going to hurt you," Ma Ramsey said. "We're just going to give you some alone time. Allow you to get your priorities straight."

Ma Ramsey's thin hand was on Ella's shoulder, shoving her inside. Ella tried to resist but she was already off-balance and tumbling into the room. As she fell, the four walls leaped around her, and a pail glimmered in one corner. Then the door closed and the weak light disappeared completely. She was left in the dark.

Silence.

"Let me out," she screamed. "Let me out!"

She clawed at the door, scraping at something that crumbled between her fingers. The hard-packed dirt floor was somehow sticky and damp, uneven with bumps and rivulets where who-knew-what had channeled a course.

When they'd taken her down here, she'd heard a voice calling out, but now, no matter how loud she yelled, she could hear nothing in return. Perhaps she'd imagined the voice, or, maybe they had freed that other girl when Ella arrived.

Her back to the wall, knees to her chest, she grew quiet and listened to the darkness for footsteps, for voices. She opened her eyes, closed them. It didn't matter. The darkness seemed less of a color than a texture. It vibrated. She wanted to bite at it.

After some time—she had no way of judging how long—she groped around the tiny room, knocked over the pail, set it back up. Hesitantly she sniffed. Old urine and feces.

The room's walls were smooth concrete. A few spots seemed rougher, as if the cement were crumbling, but she couldn't dig any additional chunks out with her fingers. No light, no air, no bed—just a dirt floor. She felt like she had walked into a place of nowhere. Nothing existed except her breathing.

She crawled back to the door, leaned against it. For a moment she allowed herself to wonder when they would come for her. How long would they leave her here? A melody, formless and rough, less a tune and more of a cry, curled in the back of her throat.

Amazing grace, how sweet the sound
That saved a wretch like me

Her phrasing, clear and pure, reverberated in this terrible place. She let herself wonder: had God truly forgotten her?

I once was lost but now am found
Was blind but now I see.

Time did not pass.

The blackness stayed still and silent. If she did not sometimes listen for her pulse and feel the breath in her nostrils, she would not have known she was alive.

She wept and sang, and she used the pail. Its smell made her retch but she forced herself to sit next to it, to breathe in the redolence of her own excrement.

When Duncan came for her, she would be ready. She would coat him with her filth before he coated her with his.

Hours passed, or days. The bolt finally thudded back and someone set down a cup and three small pieces of bread. She braced for Duncan to follow but the door slammed shut again and she was alone. She took five small sips of the water, chewed only a bit of the bread. She didn't know if or when she'd be fed again.

She drifted in and out of sleeping, waking, singing. More bread appeared, and then more. She must have been there for two days at least now, or perhaps three. She could smell herself, but welcomed the aroma as further proof that she was still alive.

She became so sensitized to sound that she immediately could tell when people were moving outside, when the person was coming in to bring her bread and water, remove the empty cup and the pail when it grew full.

So when she heard a girl's voice, and Ma Ramsey's, and the

rumble of men, she crept to the door, listening. She wanted to call out but was panicked by the possibility that the men—Duncan— would be coming for her, too.

She couldn't make out the girl's words, but the pleading tone was unmistakable. After a while, silence loomed again. The men had gone.

"Hello?" Ella yelled. Faintly she thought she heard a response but couldn't understand what the other girl said. "I'm Ella."

She couldn't hear the girl's reply.

Ella tried repeatedly to call but could never quite understand what the girl was saying, so eventually she gave up.

More bread and water came. Then, sometime later, voices roused her from sleep. Their words were comprehensible now—perhaps the other girl's door wasn't closed? Ella didn't know.

"Leave me alone," she heard the girl shriek, and the desperation sent Ella's pulse racing. "Please!"

A rumble of male voices, and then, very clearly, Duncan's. "Shut up, nigger."

Ella scooted back from the door, fingers digging into the wall. Fear broke over her, cold and hot. She didn't want to be next. She hated Duncan with his rotten teeth and groping fingers. She imagined sneaking up behind them, hitting them over the head with a shovel that magically manifested in her grip. She clenched her hands, which were slippery with perspiration.

More voices, the girl pleading. Ella was bathed in sweat now, her fingers slipping on the concrete. She pressed herself against the door, once more, to hear.

And then came a scream, louder now, hopeless and ragged, sobbing.

"Leave her alone," Ella yelled, unthinking, punching at the door, and then jumped back, afraid that the door would open and that Duncan would be silhouetted there, his rotten teeth catching the light.

Silence. Then a man's voice, chuckling. Then silence again.

Ella squeezed her eyes closed, opened them. It didn't matter.

Time passed, but she knew a hellish presence lingered on the other side of the door. She prayed it would not open.

"Ella." Duncan's voice, a singsong, caressed the darkness. "Oh, Ella. You in there, sweetheart?"

She backed up as far as she could, fingers scrabbling for the pail. She hoisted it, half-full, to her chest.

"You're next," Duncan whispered. "You ready for me, sweetheart? Ella?"

She waited, but he didn't say anything more. After a long time she realized that he had gone.

She never heard the other girl again.

23

Sparks in the Black

July 1933

Between her eighth and ninth servings of bread, her first bubbles appeared. They started out as tiny silver things, sparks in the black, that would disappear when she looked directly at them; but soon they did not vanish, and grew fuller, rounder, glistening with rainbows. Bubbles boiled around her, bouncing off her hair and cheeks.

She laughed out loud, reached out for them. But like kittens or butterflies they scattered before her outstretched finger—wary, or with their own agendas.

Most of them tumbled down, vanishing near the floor, but a few others, impossibly, floated upward, pink and mauve sheens reflecting nonexistent light. They disappeared but did not pop. She was certain of this. They glowed, and splashed, and vanished, but she could never quite figure out where they'd gone, and meanwhile others took their places, tumbling through the emptiness of the night.

They made her feel light, free. She wondered if the girl who'd cried out could see them, too. She wondered if she could float away with them. *Amazing grace, how sweet the sound.*

She started the second verse, not even realizing she knew the words, but one line followed the other as if she'd known them all her life. Perhaps she had. Singing unfettered her. Opening her lips to the night, pouring out the words in the melody, connected something deep within her to the universe; and at the same time, it made her feel impossibly free.

> *'Twas grace that taught my heart to fear*
> *And grace my fears relieved*
> *How precious did that grace appear*
> *The hour I first believed*

This time, when she sang, she lost herself entirely in her voice. She could levitate on top of a note, sustain it, and ride away on it. She was one of the bubbles floating in the updraft of her own breath. She had no body; she had no mouth or tongue; she was, purely, her own voice. She was centered, sure, and the melody echoed around her and became her.

There was golden blue sky on her closed eyelids and the shimmer of the moon on her upturned cheeks. She opened her mouth wide, taking a deep breath, and effortlessly some deep part of her assailed the world with the might of her voice.

> *My chains are gone*
> *I've been set free*
> *My God, my Savior has ransomed me*
> *And like a flood, His mercy rains*
> *Unending love, amazing grace*

Her voice sustained the scale, from high to low, notes lifting up in that dark and terrible place; and her loneliness and terror vanished. Usually, when Ella would sing a song, she'd mimic the voices of the other singers Ethel Waters, Connee Boswell, and even her idol, Louis Armstrong—but in this dark moment, she heard a voice she had never heard before: clear, soft, hugging her with feeling. It was as if her emotions—terror and loneliness and grief and despair—were doing the singing, not her; and, yet, it *was* her. It was her own voice, straight from some central space inside her that she hadn't even realized existed. It was some place bigger than her heart, but centered in her chest. She listened to it, felt herself adrift within it.

Love is all I am, she found herself thinking, not sure what she even meant. *I listen to my heart.*

There in the total blackness, she'd never felt so assured of her voice before. It *was* hers. Not Ethel's, not Connee's, not Louis's.

Her very own voice.

Her own way of singing.

She was a singer, too, she told herself.

She sang other songs—"He Is King of Kings" and "I'm a 'Troubled in the Mind"—and invented songs of her own. One she became fond of:

Someday I'll look into my eyes
and I'll find myself
in the perfect place

Six days after they locked her in, Duncan, Ma Ramsey, and Eric returned.

She was sitting, legs outstretched, against the back wall, singing the song she had composed, "One Million Miles High," and blinking in the light. This week had utterly transformed her. She was a singer now, as well as a dancer, singing into a future she had to believe in if she was to survive this place. More important, she knew now that she could endure the worst and still she would not be beaten.

24

A Special Dance

July 1933–September 1933

Back at Uncle Clyde's the following week, she tried to tell him about the Dungeon, and about the girl whom she'd heard in the darkness.

Instead of the sympathy and outrage she'd expected, he shook his head at her. "You gots to keep yo mind on yo chores. You gots to mind these people."

"But—"

"You show me that step you tole me bout—what you call it? The Cincinatus?"

"The Cincinnati."

"Why don't you show me yo Cincinnati?"

She never tried bringing the Dungeon up with him again.

But he loved her dancing, and started asking if she could come on Tuesday night, or Thursday.

In mid-September, just as the leaves began to flame crimson and gold, he asked her to come for a "dancin' visit"—as he called them—on Saturday night, which was unusual. She usually saw him on weekdays, when everyone had a normal routine, so she'd done her best and had made it early, soon after supper.

The Jack Benny radio show was playing Ted Lewis and His Orchestra's "We're in the Money" as she peered in through the screen door. The kitchen seemed unaccountably crowded. Uncle Clyde, wearing a top hat and white gloves, was tap dancing, keeping time with the bass and snapping out his hands with each trombone or trumpet blast. Four white girls were trying to keep up, two pairs swing-dancing clumsily in the space in front of the stove.

Uncle Clyde must have been watching for Ella. As soon as she saw them, he was saying, "Come on in," and waving her close. Then he presented her to the others, proudly: "This is my Ella."

These were all white students—Ella had seen them, probably ridden the bus with a couple of them, but she didn't know their names and hadn't ever really spoken with them before. The white girls kept to their cottages, and to the nicer areas of the Training School. "Hi," she said to them now, embarrassed but basking in Uncle Clyde's warmth.

A tiny blond girl with enormous blue eyes dashed over, and then back to Uncle Clyde. "Is this really her?" she asked him. She was a year or so younger than Ella. Her grin was infectious. She bounced back to Ella. "Hi, Ella," she said. "I'm Renata."

Ella nodded warily.

"Girls, make yourselves comfortable," Uncle Clyde told them. "Let me introduce you to Ella Fitzgerald. She's going to be a famous dancer someday. Just you wait."

They were all watching her, but it didn't seem to be with the same kind of frowning intensity that most of the white girls looked at the Black girls. This room seemed welcoming, friendly even.

"Ella comes to us by way of Yonkers and Harlem," Uncle Clyde was saying. "You ever hear of the Sekundi dancers from Yonkers?"

They shook their heads.

"Well, have ya heard of Harlem?"

"Harlem!" the girls squealed, nodding. The Savoy Ballroom, the Apollo Theater, the Lafayette, the Cotton Club: the dance halls' names were so familiar that Ella's knees almost buckled.

Duke Ellington's "It Don't Mean a Thing (If It Ain't Got That Swing)" blasted from the radio, and Ella broke out into the Charleston.

An athletic red-headed girl named Courtney jumped in with her, and soon they were all dancing.

Uncle Clyde had Ella show them her Lindy Hop, shimmy, and snake dance. The white girls tried to imitate. Ella broke down the steps, her movements fluid and effortless.

"That's how ya do it," Uncle Clyde kept repeating. "See that, girls? That's how ya do it."

The half hour flew by, but soon Ella knew she would have to go. The other girls had to get back to their cottages as well.

As they were filing out, Renata hugged her. "You're a star," she said loudly, and all the other girls nodded, enthusiastic. For a moment she felt welcomed, felt like she could have a place where she had never thought she could fit or belong.

On the porch, a sparrow perched on the railing, bobbing up and down as if it had been listening to the music. It was dusk—the bird must be disoriented with the lights from the buildings. Ella took three steps toward it, almost touched it before it flew away into the night.

Unbidden, she heard her mother's voice, and remembered that old lamp in her apartment in Yonkers: *It's not a real Tiffany lamp, but for me it is. Maybe you can have a Tiffany life. Remember, there's more to life than what you see around here. There are Tiffany lamps.*

25

The Charleston Sizzling in Her Veins

October 12, 1933

Ella was still humming "Minnie the Moocher" as she snuck back across the lawns in the October dark. She crept in through the back, up the stairs to her room, and opened the door.

Ma Murphy waited on the bed. She looked up companionably, as if she were a friend or a confidante, about to whisper secrets and plans.

Ella froze.

"I told you not to sneak out, didn't I?" Ma Murphy said, genial, friendly, warm, which was how she talked whenever she disciplined the girls.

Ella had learned by now to look down at her feet rather than answer or betray any emotion.

"But you didn't think our rules applied to you, did you, Miss Fitzgerald?"

Miss Fitzgerald. The words of her name, terrifying in their mildness, in their familiarity, now smacked against her face. Her oxford shoes were badly scuffed, the formerly white leather now a gray brown. She'd never again be able to get the shoes clean enough. Why hadn't she tried to escape before now? What had she been waiting for?

"You did this to yourself," Ma Murphy said, slightly sad. "Breaking the rules will not be tolerated. I told you that." She paused. Ella didn't move, didn't breathe.

Ma Murphy continued, "Perhaps after tonight you'll be more open to obeying the rules. In listening to what I say. Well," she sighed, standing, brushing her hands against her thighs as if to wipe them clean, "I warned you. You can't say I didn't." She swept past Ella. Up and down the hall, the other girls' doors were sealed like tombs. "Wait in here," she told her, pointing to the bed. Ella tensed her muscles as if to flee but the bolt slid home, locking her in.

She waited. The room was too small to pace. She stared out the window, where a light burned in one of the far cottages. From down by the river, on the other side of the building, out of sight, came the ghostly wail of the evening train, heading somewhere, anywhere, but here.

She could imagine what was coming: the Dungeon's oblivion, the silence. She told herself that she could get through it. A few times the past few weeks she'd almost longed to see those pink iridescent bubbles, to tap into that part of herself that she could only reach in darkness and isolation, so although it would be bad, she would face it head on.

But what if this time Ma Ramsey let Duncan into the room? What if all the men—Eric, Carter, Lewis, the others—all stormed down to the basement, unbolted her door, unbuckled their pants? What then?

At last the door unlocked and Ma Ramsey's dark-rimmed steel eyes glared at her. "I thought once would enlighten you. I was wrong. Girls like you would rather die than change. That's sad. Really sad. I'd like to say that 'two time's the charm,' but quite honestly, Miss Fitzgerald, I don't see any hope for you."

She took a step into the room. Behind her, shadows flashed: Duncan and Eric, no doubt.

"You are a recalcitrant negress." Ma Ramsey studied everything in the room except Ella: the faded and stained walls, the cracked window, the bureau with Ella's other uniform folded neatly in a drawer. "Perhaps beyond rehabilitation. Since you refuse to adhere to a work schedule or clean up after yourself. Since you sneak around, refuse to follow orders. Your attitude is wrong. You think you're better than the others, don't you? Because you can dance, 'cut a rug,' as your people call it."

Ma Ramsey was rail thin, with a head like a crow's: her nose a huge beak, hair pulled tight over her skull, white skin stretched over her bony face. Her words chopped at something at Ella's core, but Ella had learned to keep her face impassive.

"Who do you think you are?" Ma Ramsey asked. Then she slapped her, hard, across her upper cheek and temple.

Ella stood up from the bed and swung back, smacking the older woman's nose and chin, and then Ma Ramsey was raining blows on her, and Ella was hitting back, trying to grab her arms to make her stop.

"What have I done to you?" Ella screamed. "Why are you doing this to me!" She broke free, backing toward the window. The room was suddenly filled with people: Lewis and Carter behind Ma Ramsey, and all of them staring at her, mouths agape, panting.

No one spoke, Ella's breath—and Ma Ramsey's breath—loud in the narrow room. She imagined that none of this was happening. She'd slipped into her nightgown, washed her face and hands, and slid into bed. Ma Ramsey and these men would leave. She tried to hang on to the feeling of Renata calling her a star, of Uncle Clyde's admiration, of the Charleston sizzling in her veins, but it had taken flight beyond her reach, like that bird that had disappeared into the night.

"Now, my girl, you're going to learn how to behave," Ma Ramsey said.

"Come on," Carter said. "Let's go."

"I'm not going," Ella said, backing up even more toward her cracked window. The wind whistled through it almost companionably. She looked around for a weapon.

"Wanna bet?" Lewis asked her.

Both men lunged at her, although there wasn't enough room for the three of them against the back wall. Carter had his forearm around her throat, bending her over. She couldn't breathe. "Get your stinking hands off me," she whimpered.

"Let's get on with this." Ma Ramsey had regained her breath. "Don't put up with her nonsense. I don't have all night."

Somehow Ella was in front of Lewis, her arms pinned behind her back, and then she was in the hall—all the other doors resolutely shut fast—and then down the stairs and outside. The night was everywhere, the barest light glimmering in from a few cottage windows. It was as if they were the only people alive in the world.

"Come on, missy," Lewis's breath was hot in her ear. She wanted to scream, claw at them, but Lewis's hands were tight on her upper arms, her wrists turned up behind her back. At each step, pain skewered her shoulders.

"I hate you," she whispered. "I hate all of you."

"Oh, she speaks," Carter said, leading the way. They were near the cottage now.

"You heading to Miss Opportunity," Lewis said. "Mrs. Morse says you coloreds living in 'Opportunity Cottages,' haha. You gonna see your opportunity. You goin' to where girls like you disappear. Or die if youse lucky." Then he started laughing, and the laughing turned into coughing.

Carter turned back to him, fumbled in a pocket, pulled out a small brown bottle. "Here," he said, offering it to Lewis. "I'll hold her."

"Naw," Lewis said. "I want my head clear." He cleared his throat, hitched his hands higher and more brutally on Ella's upper arms, pushed her in front of him.

Ma Ramsey had gone on ahead and waited for them on the narrow front porch. "Take her downstairs and put her in Eight." Then to Ella, "You, miss, are going to wish you never put your hands on me. You will curse the day you met me." Her eyes were wide, an endless black tunnel, and her hair had come undone. She looked unhinged.

Ella was so frightened now that she couldn't have stood on her own, even if she wanted to; her legs had turned boneless, her muscles no longer would do what she asked. How had she ever managed to dance, with legs as rebellious and useless as hers?

Lewis and Carter dragged her inside.

"You think she'll make it?" Lewis had a southern drawl that she always had trouble understanding. Some of the other girls whispered that he was in the Ku Klux Klan, had donned white sheets and burned crosses in colored people's yards, had even lynched a man. Now those whispers circled back around her.

"Please let me go. I can't go back in there. Please!"

"It's too late for that, honey chil'. " Lewis's breath tickled her ear, his hands firm on her arms.

They reached the cellar. There was the oval space, the off-center light bulb, the ring of closed doors.

This time they dragged her to the other side, to a door that seemed wider than the others.

This cell was lit, and a wire and a light bulb snaked in, a switch by the door. Somehow the light made the room even more terrifying than the others. There was also no pail.

There was, however, a hole about the length and width of a human body. Just a rough outline, the clods of earth loosely ringing an indentation. A shovel leaned against one damp-streaked wall.

"It's time to dig your own grave," Ma Ramsey said. "That's what we do with girls who really are Ungovernable. You have proved yourself beyond redemption."

"You're evil and crazy," Ella said. "I'm not—"

"You see over there?" Ma Ramsey nodded to a corner of the room. "That's where a couple of other girls like you are buried. Just like you. They wouldn't listen and they had to pay the consequences. Just like you're going to do."

There did seem to be two or three higher, body-length humps on the ground. Ella's breath came fast and she swung around to fight, to flee, and then a high shivering zipped through the air—

—and a strike against her back, sharp like nothing she'd ever felt before. And then another.

It was an electric extension cord, and it was hitting her over and over again, and Lewis was in front of her gripping her hands, pinning her. She fell to her knees. Four or five blows, and then six, and she hung from his grasp on her wrists, the pain like nothing she'd ever felt, like another person was burning flesh from her back, like it couldn't possibly be a part of her.

She was shrieking, sobbing, trying to twist away—

—and then the lashing ceased.

"Dig," Ma Ramsey said. "Or next time I won't stop."

Ella picked up the shovel, sank the blade into the earth.

The soil was loose, clumped, and came out easier than she'd expected. She was used to shoveling and hoeing at the farm, and she wondered if the reason that the colored girls had been sent to the fields to begin with was so that they'd develop the strength and prowess to dig their own graves.

Ma Ramsey and the men stood over her. Ma Ramsey kept folding and refolding the extension cord.

Beneath the loose soil, about three feet down, the dirt was harder packed. The shovel rang against the crust. "That's deep enough," Ma Ramsey said. "Now clean it out. You should know how to make something clean by now."

Ella circled around and shoveled out the dirt. Lewis stood close behind. She kept eyeing the door, trying to figure out how to make a break for it, but Carter was standing in the doorway, smoking, and grinned when he caught her eye.

After she'd cleared most of it off, she started slowing down, looking for a way out. She might as well go down fighting: she'd slide to the left, duck under Carter's arm, and—

Lewis pinned her arms at her side, and quick as a striking rattlesnake, Ma Ramsey was wrapping the extension cord around her wrists, pinning them behind her back. She screamed, fighting. They wrapped the cord around her body, over and over—how long was the cord?—and tied it off around her ankles.

"There we are," Ma Ramsey said. "Hush your squalling. It won't help."

Carter and Lewis were on each side of her, lifting her up and lowering her into the grave. She twisted, struggling, trying to get out, but the walls of the grave were too high. Her back burned and flamed. She must be bleeding into the dirt. She howled again.

Someone stuffed a rag, tasting of oil and copper—blood?—into her mouth. Twine wrapped around her face, holding the fabric in place. She shook her head to dislodge it, shoved her tongue against it, but it would not come out.

They started filling in at her feet, working their way up. Chunks of dirt fell around her legs, against her stomach. Carter was kicking the clods, and Lewis was using the shovel to pack the dirt around her.

She was twisting, struggling, hitting her head against the ground to try to lift it higher.

"Stop banging your head, idiot," Carter said. "Won't do you no good."

She could barely breathe. She tried to inhale through her nose. The dirt rained down, her legs and feet had disappeared. Her chest and head were still uncovered.

Then they paused.

"You come from dirt," Ma Ramsey said. "You should be able to survive. If you listen. For a change."

Lewis and Carter were on each side of her, pulling Ella up by her shoulders, so in a moment her head was above ground level. Then they started packing in the rest of the loose dirt around her chest and shoulders, burying her to her chin.

But not burying her face.

"You are uncivilized and filthy at your core," Ma Ramsey said.

"You live a beastly life. You are disobedient and lazy and expect to have something for nothing. No matter how many times we try to lift you people up, you revert to your godless ways. You've got to find your place in God's country, and your place is in humility and service. Do you understand, Ella Fitzgerald? Humility and service."

By now the shovelfuls were packed tight around her chest. Only her head was above the ground.

"I'm going to give you some time to think about what you've learned here today," Ma Ramsey said. She and the men were moving toward the door, abandoning her. Carter propped the shovel back against the wall.

Ma Ramsey flicked the light switch off and closed the door of the cell behind them.

26

White Girls Only

December 9, 1933

The town of Hudson was like something out of a fairytale: little shops lining the main street, cafés with colorful pastries in the windows, snowflaked doors opening into restaurants where picture-perfect fires burned in diminutive fireplaces. The townsfolk strolled easily as if they owned the world, stopping to chat, holding mittened children by the hand. There was even a Santa Claus, tall and full of cheer, shouting "Ho, Ho, Ho," waving, waving, waving.

It felt utterly surreal to Ella, as if she'd landed in a different universe, in a different dimension where people walked on their hands and removed their mouths to speak.

Ella couldn't believe that they'd let her go Christmas caroling in Hudson, but Ma Murphy had said that as a treat for her excellent behavior, she'd be allowed.

"Besides," Ma Murphy said, sniffing, "Ma Jacobs asked especially for you. She says she could use your voice. We want to put on a good showing."

The Training School went caroling annually—it was usually the choir run by Ma Jacobs, but they let a few other girls come along. The choir was for white girls only, of course, so "other girls" meant the colored ones with decent voices.

So Ella had nodded, said, "Thank you, ma'am," and had trudged behind the others in line for the bus. The Training School was a short walk from the town, but they took the bus anyway—it was probably too far for some of the house mothers to walk. Now Ma Jacobs checked her roster as each girl boarded. The white girls sat up front and the three colored girls—Faye, Anna Mae, and Ella— headed to the back. Ella folded her hands neatly on her lap, looked out the window.

Two other house mothers got on, as well as Carter, Duncan, and Eric. The adults all sat in the front: women on the left, guards on the right.

"We will arrive in ten minutes. I expect everyone to be on their best behavior. Remember you represent the Training School."

Then Mrs. Morse stepped in, wearing a bright red-and-green Christmas sweater, with green mittens. Cheerily she announced, "Thank you so much for caroling today. It's going to be a fine day. When you arrive, the Hudson Café will give you hot chocolate and a holiday sweet. Have a good time! Remember you represent the Training School for Girls! I expect all of you to be on your best behavior!"

Seven adults, Ella noted. Including Mrs. Morse.

Have a good time! Ella replayed Mrs. Morse's words as the bus rumbled down the drive and onto the main road.

She'd wondered again if Mrs. Morse knew about what went on in the Training School. She'd wondered if the other house mothers knew. She'd wondered if the world knew.

She'd figured that they all knew. That this *was* the world, a place of sadistic neglect, abuse, and torture. A place that bred isolation and despair. None of these girls on this bus would raise their hand to help the girl sitting next to them.

As the brown and gray fields flashed past the bus windows, she had envisioned Ma Ramsey rising up from the Dungeon's graves, her face twisted in a malicious grin, to tower over the treetops, over the school and village of Hudson. She could reach down and pluck off one girl at a time, do whatever she wanted with them. Bury them or rape them or lock them away and starve them. How many girls were buried, for real, in that cellar?

The memory of that night in the Dungeon grave seemed like a leering man who never left, who tucked himself into bed with her at night and who held her toothbrush with her in the morning. He whispered in her ear as she lay sleepless and he blew through the crack in the window as she stared out into the night. He whistled with the train's breath as it passed. When she'd fall into a brief fitful sleep, he'd twist up behind her eyelids and sprinkle dirt on her legs so she'd launch herself, breathless, out of bed, a scream sawing at her lips.

She did her best to be in open space as much as possible. In rooms without a clear exit—like the pantries or bathrooms, or the laundry room with the door closed—she grew twitchy and nervous, felt the weight of the earth on her chest, constricting her breathing.

Now, slowly, surreptitiously, making absolutely certain that the other girls didn't notice—Anna Mae and Faye were sitting together and were talking about marshmallows; Anna Mae had never had one and Faye was telling her that last year they'd had a marshmallow in their hot chocolate—Ella slid her hand into her pocket, palmed the handful of coins, a cylinder tied tight in a rag to keep them from jingling. She'd squirreled together $1.63, which was impressive in a place that didn't use money for transactions, a place that had no use for coins.

Girls were supposed to turn in all money they found while doing laundry. It was an automatic paddling if Ma Murphy caught you. Ever since she'd arrived at the Training School back in November and found herself in the laundry room, Ella had stuffed each penny or nickel—once, incredibly, she'd found two dimes—into her shoe. Then, each night, she'd wedge the coin into a gap in the back of her bureau, where the molding had warped. Had Ma Murphy or Ma Ramsey—or any of the girls, for that matter—pulled the bureau away from the wall, they would have seen coins studding the entire rear, from crown to foot. Over time the molding had loosened; now the brad nails barely held. She lived in fear that the nails would pull free entirely, that the coins would rain from the cabinet in a recriminating jingle. Then Ma Ramsey really *would* bury her alive.

But Ma Ramsey would never, ever, get the chance, because there was no way that Ella would ever go back to that place again. She didn't know how, but today, as they sang their Christmas carols and "Yes ma'am'ed" and sipped their hot chocolate in dainty ladylike sips, "because that, girls, is how white people drink their chocolate," Ella was going to escape.

The bus lumbered down Main Street, stopped on a corner, and one by one they descended. Ella had been to Hudson twice before with her cottage, so it wasn't utterly unfamiliar, although it had never seemed so disorienting as it did that day. The cool air seemed warm with the smoke of fireplaces, but wind blew through her thin coat. The girls had been given scarves and mittens at the last minute, just for appearances at the square, and Ella was grateful for them. Snow—ice pellets, really—began to fall, rattling on the sides of the bus and sparkling on the sidewalk.

"Here you go, girls," Ma Jacobs said as a scrawny woman in a lambskin coat and an apron doled out small steaming cups.

"Thank you, ma'am," Ella said, bobbing slightly into a curtsy when the woman gave her one. The woman looked over her head and didn't say "you're welcome," the way she had to the white girls.

There were no marshmallows, either.

The girls milled about and Ella stood near the bus, scouting for her opportunity. The adults were in a loose circle around them, obviously watching for anyone to escape, but everyone was smiling and sipping. Duncan looked friendly, benign, like any white man—not like someone who would sneak into a locked dungeon and pin a girl down and have his way with her, the way he'd done with that other girl when Ella was in solitary. Carter didn't look like someone who would try to bury you alive; he was grinning at something one of the white girls had said, and his hands were holding a harmless steaming cup, not the handle of a shovel.

Church bells rang out, and Ella counted the chimes: it was noon.

The girls left the cups with the woman—Ella placed the cup on the tray so the woman wouldn't have to touch Ella's skin and bobbed another thank-you-ma'am curtsy—and followed Ma Jacobs into the middle of the Hudson square.

They huddled together in the center of the open space, with the fairytale buildings around them and the snow dusting their hats and shoulders, and Ma Jacobs led them into "Hark! The Herald Angels Sing," "Silent Night," and "O Come, All Ye Faithful." The townsfolk stood before them, applauding, joining in, the breaths of the girls and the crowd spiraling up together into the air like feathers, like laundry fumes.

Apart from the three colored girls, everyone else in Hudson was white. How could Ella blend in with the crowd, sneak away, unnoticed?

O come, all ye faithful, joyful and triumphant!
O come ye, O come ye to Bethlehem

Pain lanced her stomach, anxiety and fear churning. Beyond the singing, beyond the man at the edge of the crowd who'd hoisted his toddler on his shoulders for a better look at the carolers, the monstrous figure of Ma Ramsey loomed like a giant helium balloon—like Felix the Cat or Santa—from Macy's Thanksgiving Day Parade.

Dashing through the snow
In a one-horse open sleigh

The words boiled up, round and clear, from her throat as she edged to the side, away from Mrs. Morse and the housemothers. But escape was impossible. Carter and Duncan were smiling and nodding along with the music, but watchful behind the girls, and space separated the singers from the crowd. Ella and the other two were the only colored people in sight, and she felt as visible as a giraffe, and as ungainly.

The sleet had stopped, and a weak sun briefly appeared, but vanished again in the clouds. They sang another song, and then another. The words were automatic, rote, as panic ballooned in her chest, threatening to strangle her. She couldn't go back but she couldn't get caught while she was escaping, either.

Eventually they caroled their last song. Then came the obligatory applause, with murmurings of "The girls sound like angels" and "Wasn't that the sweetest?," and she was shaking now from the panic that she couldn't get away, and desperation that she absolutely had to. She thought her knees might buckle if she tried to take a step.

Mrs. Morse was leading them back toward the bus. Ella looked everywhere for some way out—surely there was some way out—and Eric was chatting with Anna Mae, and Carter, casually intimidating, brought up the rear, herding the stragglers.

"Time for lunch, girls," Mrs. Morse said brightly, turning away from the bus in the other direction, toward the restaurant.

They weren't going back. Not yet.

They were led through the doors, into the warmth, single file, to a private room that smelled of nutmeg and beef and pastry crust.

In honor of Christmas, they all sat together at one big table, whites and Blacks, the colored girls clustered in the corner but still sitting with the others. Grilled cheese sandwiches congealed on plates, next to cups of tomato soup. Ella tried to remember how long it had been since she'd bitten into a grilled cheese sandwich. It was so delicious that the salt and savoriness exploded in her mouth with actual physical pain. The soup had grown cold, and she gulped it down in three swallows. She pocketed the small sugar cookie.

The adults sat by the door, guards at one table and the house mothers at another. Fat wedges of chocolate cake with thick icing glistened in front of each, and they were sipping coffee, and they were all merry and laughing with each other.

Ella stood up, so abruptly that she almost knocked over the chair, slid past the white girls, and threaded her way toward the door. She stopped in front of Ma Jacobs. "Please, ma'am, may I use the bathroom?" Her hands were clasped, her eyes fixed on her brownish-gray oxfords.

"The bathroom, Ella?" Ma Jacobs repeated.

"So this is Ella." Mrs. Morse, who was sitting next to Ma Jacobs, eyed Ella with benign interest. A chunk of chocolate frosting smeared a corner of her lip. "Congratulations, you sounded beautiful today. I hear you're quite the performer."

"Not anymore, ma'am," Ella said. She didn't look up from her shoes. Negro girls knew their place.

"Oh?" Mrs. Morse said.

"No, ma'am," Ella said, and then, daringly, "my place is doing the laundry. I'm good at it and I love to do it."

"You do, do you?" Mrs. Morse said. "Seems a pity."

"No, ma'am," Ella said. "I'm the one who does the lavender rinse on your sheets."

"Oh, that's you? You do a wonderful job, Ella. I can't deny it."

"Thank you, ma'am." A quick glance, with lowered eyelids, at Ma Jacobs. "May I use the bathroom, please, ma'am?"

"Go ahead," Ma Jacobs said. "Thank you for that beautiful singing today."

"Thank you for inviting me, ma'am."

"I'll come with you." Ma Jacobs slid back her chair.

Ella almost screamed with frustration. "Of course, ma'am," she said, never looking up, "but it's right down the hall. I'll be right back."

"Let her go," Mrs. Morse said. "She'll be fine."

Ma Jacobs leaned over toward Mrs. Morse and whispered, but loud enough for Ella to hear, "You know she's been a discipline problem? She's one of the Ungovernables."

Mrs. Morse nodded and smiled at Ella. "You go and hurry right back." And then to Ma Jacobs: "We have to trust them sometimes, don't we? Otherwise all this teaching means nothing and they really are no better than animals."

Before either woman could say something further, Ella was saying, "Thank you, ma'am," and curtseying, and keeping her head down, and she was out the door, turning right toward the bathroom.

Beyond the doorway she paused, waiting for Ma Jacobs to follow her, but no one did. There was only a burst of laughter. Mrs. Morse said something that Ella couldn't hear.

The back hallway continued to the kitchen, which surely had its own service door, but Ella didn't want to risk it. She'd have to go out the front.

A few feet ahead, busing trays had been stacked neatly on the floor, their pile of dirty dishes and cutlery awaiting cleaning in the kitchen. Efficiently Ella hefted one to her left shoulder, shielding her face; and holding her breath, in one fluid move—one step, two steps—she was beyond the doorway of the private room, and now the main restaurant was looming up around her. Purposeful, she moved toward an empty table littered with three people's leftovers: bowls, water glasses, and one sad sandwich crust alone on a plate. She set the tray on the table as if to bus it, and then smoothly, so smoothly, kept right on walking, head down, waiting for a shout, waiting for running footsteps, waiting for anything. But nothing came.

And she was past the patrons now, level with the hostess stand, and her hand was on the cool metal of the front door latch.

The scrawny woman who'd given them the hot chocolate when they'd gotten off the bus said loudly, "Can I help you?"

"Thank you, ma'am, it was wonderful," Ella told her, not looking at her directly, always knowing her place, always looking down. "They asked me to pick up something on the bus." And she was out the door before the woman answered.

The bus was to the right, but she went left, fifteen steps, down an alleyway along the side of the restaurant, and then to the right, down another street, and down another alley. By now the school would have missed her. Her brown skin marked her in this sea of white people. She needed to find a place to hide.

Down another street, this one more residential, the houses gingerbreaded with big verandas, all open and beckoning in the December afternoon, she grew more and more certain that she would hear a hunting cry at any moment. She tensed for it, ready to sprint away.

But there was no time for further fear. There was no time for anything except to dash up a walkway, wriggle into a gap behind the steps, duck beneath a porch, crawl on her hands and knees in the low space over to the house, curl up tight in a ball, and wait. The warmth of the house glowed at her back.

—

She waited the rest of the day, until night had fallen. She saw and heard no one from the school, although they must have been looking for her. The safest thing would be to get out of town as quickly as possible, but she wasn't sure how best to do that.

For the past year, several times a day, she'd heard trains chugging along in the distance. She'd heard their cries, like dying birds in the night. Now she wandered down Hudson's darkened streets, cowering out of sight before she encountered any passersby. At last there was no one on the road, and she stumbled onto the train tracks, followed them to the train station.

A ticket to New York City couldn't cost that much, and she had the money—but she didn't want to waste it and didn't want the school to be able to track her on a passenger car. She could hop a train. She knew that people did but didn't know how. She'd never done anything like this. She knew that some bore graffiti on their sides—a means for one hobo to communicate with the others. But she didn't know how to read that language, interpret those signs.

She got her bearings and headed north until she found the rail-yard, train cars parked seemingly at random in the wide expanse. She wondered when the next train would come, and how she'd know where to get on it, how to stay out of sight. A train crew patrolled, their flashlights streaking the darkness, but they seemed to spend most of their time sitting in a small building near a gate.

Slipping to the side, where brown weeds between the tracks clawed the air, she followed rails around the side of the yard.

A voice spoke out of nowhere: "What you doin'?"

It was a woman. No, two of them, both white, scarves over their hair, huddling in the shadows, sitting on worn suitcases. They were hobos, like her.

"Trying to get south," she said. "To New York City."

"That's where we're heading, too," the other woman said. "Came down from Syracuse." The one introduced herself as Sue, the other was Jennifer. They were in their late twenties or thirties and asked no questions of Ella. She asked no questions either. She sat down near them, leaned against a barrel.

"When do you think a train will come?" Ella asked after some time.

"We're hoping soon," Sue said. "Should be soon." Below the scarf, her straight black hair fell halfway down her back. She looked exhausted and grimy.

"Don't you worry, hon," Jennifer said. "I've done this loads of times. It's easy. You'll see. As soon as the train comes in, we'll scout for a place. Don't you worry about the guards, they ain't bad. Everybody does it."

They didn't speak much after that. Ella had the impression that neither Sue nor Jennifer knew each other well, but were traveling together for protection. They didn't seem to mind that she was colored, but just to be safe Ella kept her eyes down, said "Yes, ma'am" a lot, and they seemed easy with her.

In the smallest hours of the night, when the moon had disappeared, a train hurtled into the train yard, headlight glaring.

They ducked into the weeds. "Keep your face down," Jennifer said. "That way they don't see the light reflecting in your eyes."

With a roar and a hiss the train slowed, stopped.

"Here we go," Jennifer said.

Ella followed them both, circling the train, hunting for an open car.

And there it was: a boxcar about halfway down, its door partly open, a scattering of straw on the floor. Jennifer went first, giving Sue and Ella a hand.

Five other people were already there. Most were sleeping, but one of the men nodded at them. No one spoke.

The three women crept to the far side of the car. Ella sat, pressing her back against the wall, knees bent, close enough to the other women so that it seemed she was with them.

She took a breath, and then another.

A few moments later the train eased into motion, and Ella was on her way back to New York City.

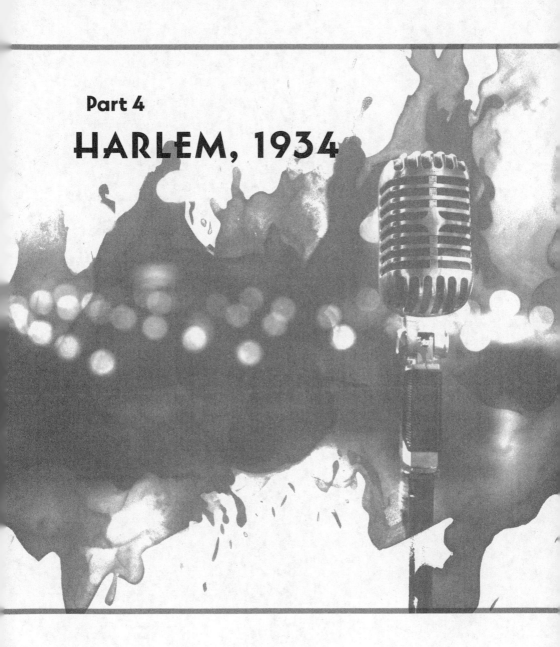

Part 4

HARLEM, 1934

27

The Boulevard of Dreams

December 10, 1933

Early Sunday morning, the train lurched to a stop. One older man yanked open the sliding door. Cold air rushed in, along with the stench of coal and sewage. New York City. The smell was unmistakable. Several people jumped out. Jennifer and Sue nodded to her but didn't seem to expect anything further, and she followed them.

At the edge of the boxcar Ella hesitated, looking up and out above Hudson Yards. Squirrels chased each other between idling train cars, and far away a man shouted. She'd seen this space from above, during a few outings from Yonkers and, later, running errands for Zukie or T-Bone; but she'd never seen it from below, the way the buildings towered over them, the vast snaking rail lines running in patterns that seemed like a road map she could almost follow, a language she could almost understand, and she vowed that she would.

She gripped her roll of coins and leaped to the ground, trailing the others around the side of the yard, through tunnels and passageways, until they emerged from an unmarked door set in a building several blocks away. The others scattered in all directions—she never had the chance to say goodbye to Jennifer and Sue—and she took a moment, getting her bearings, before heading north toward Harlem.

Last night she'd ripped a hole in the pocket of her coat, and now she stuffed the coin-roll through, so it fell down to the coat's hem. If someone tried to rob her, at least they wouldn't find her stash. She wanted to save money at least until she could get that almost-three hundred dollars, trapped beneath the bureau in Georgie's room.

In the meantime, she wanted to savor New York City, rising around her on this cold December morning. She relished the five-mile walk, hungry as she was, exhausted from little sleep and from the terror of yesterday.

Throughout those last terrible months, especially those times in the Dungeon, she'd often imagined returning to New York. She breathed it in now, exulting in the big city smell and excitement of chaos. For months she'd imagined the route she'd take when she returned, and now she enacted it: skirting the far edge of Central Park, where the wealthy white people's apartment buildings towered over the street. White-gloved doormen in broad-billed hats, gold braid glittering on their jackets, glared suspiciously at her as she strutted past.

Up Seventh Avenue, the Boulevard of Dreams. Just after eight a.m., she reached Harlem. Vibrant colored nightclubs, restaurants, and theaters lined thirty blocks, shoulder to shoulder with beauty parlors and barber shops, grocery stores and shoeshine stands.

So early on a Sunday, the stores were closed, the performers not yet awake. From far down the road a horse-drawn buggy crossed, the horse's hooves ringing in the quiet. A car roared past, and a horn beeped. A few boys on bicycles tossed newspapers at front doors.

Despite the serenity, she could feel the energy, the welcome of this place. She was back in a world where it was acceptable—even celebrated—to be colored.

She was home. This was her best chance to succeed. She'd find a way to keep from going back to the Training School if they came looking for her, would lay low until they forgot all about her. Despite the nearness of Aunt Virginia, despite people potentially recognizing her and turning her in, she knew that this was the one place in the world that promised more than a life of laundry detergent and lye, or a broom and dustpan. If she was going to make a living as a dancer, she'd have to do it here. Besides, she had Frannie to take care of.

Harlem bloomed around her as she made her way to pay her respects to the Tree of Hope. People rubbed its bark for prosperity and good luck. So she would, too. To start out her new life.

She reached the elm tree just after nine. It stood tall and leafless in the middle of the street. Lights from a nearby drugstore just opening for the day cast a glow that looked like sunshine upon it, but no one was near. She'd rubbed it for luck in the past, but now went up to it, laid her hand upon it, then the other, and stood there, palms against its trunk, eyes squeezed tight. The depth of her desire, of her desperation, was more than words would allow. She thought about Uncle Clyde, and the girls dancing with her at the Training School.

"Please," she said, and then again, "please," and the wanting overpowered her. She leaned her forehead against the cool smooth gray of the trunk. *Please help. Please don't let them catch me. Please let me find a home. Please.*

She turned up 140th, continued a block on until she finally reached the place that beat like another heart within her. Ella knew that people called it the Heart of Harlem, and it was hers, certainly.

Its marquee was unlit. But it was here, the Savoy Ballroom. She had reached it at last.

At dusk the majestic, block-long building, the engraved windows on the second floor, would awaken. The lights would flash on, and she would come forth in an elegant rose satin dress, ostrich feathers bobbing at the collar, silver dancing shoes sparkling on her feet. Almost as a reflex she swiveled her hips, jumped back, clapped her hands, then slid into a shimmy side to side.

From down the block a man hollered, "That's a great step, kid! Keep it up!"

She beamed at him, then did another shuffle-step. Eventually she realized that she'd have to devise more of a plan: she needed to find a place to sleep, a way of earning money out of sight of Aunt Virginia, the police, and her schoolmates. She was grateful that she didn't look much like the girl they'd known—her hair was much shorter, and she'd lost a lot of weight at the school. Once she had her money in hand, she'd figure out the rest.

She'd thought about running numbers again, but Zukie's death and the ever-present danger—plus the possibility that the police would collar her again—made her decide to steer clear of T-Bone and the gamblers. She'd thought of reaching out to Miss Adeline, but too many of the girls at the Training School had been paid for men to use their bodies. Ella didn't want Miss Adeline to try tempting her into that life. She thought of reaching out to some of the women from her numbers running route, but she was too skittish. They'd seemed like her friends, but she worried that they'd turn her in. And she was never going back to the Training School again.

There was only one option in front of her: she would dance.

On her own.

Back in Yonkers, dancing had been a dream, a goal. It was something she could lean on, until her mother told her that she'd have to do laundry instead. When she lived with Auntie, dancing had been a diversion, a hope, but she was so busy trying to earn money and help out that she couldn't focus on it, even though she tried. At the Training School it had been her only escape from the drudgery and misery.

Now she felt the resolution settling itself around her like falling soot from the chimneys. All she had left was herself. She would dance because she wanted to, and because now she had no other choice.

Uncle Clyde had said that she had talent, and she would prove him right. People could make a living by dancing on street corners or in clubs. Ethel Waters, the most glamorous woman that Ella had ever seen, was brown and tall like her, and not particularly pretty in that white Hollywood woman kind of way—and look what she was doing. Her hit record "Stormy Weather" played all the time on the radio.

The greasy spoon on the corner, below the Savoy Ballroom, opened and Ella went in and bought a hot dog. It seemed fitting that her first meal back in New York would be eaten under the Savoy. It was hot, delicious, and greasy, and hit her stomach right where it needed to. She devoured it in three bites, wishing she could order another. But once she had that glass jar, she'd treat herself to two or three, and a hot doughnut for dessert.

She wandered back to Seventh Avenue. It was now early afternoon, and the crowd swelled around her: bowler hats and canes and beautiful dresses, long mink coats. Whites shared the sidewalks with Blacks. Shoe-shiners offered to polish her shoes, and boys with newspapers cried out the news: "President's latest plan, five cents!"

She found a man selling second-hand clothing in a beauty shop—not one of her former numbers running clients. She traded her uniform, now filthy, for a modest green polka-dotted house-dress. The dress had a little flare to it, so it would spin out when she danced. Once she'd left the uniform behind, she breathed out, hugely relieved. At least she'd blend in better.

On 133rd, three colored boys were tap-dancing, Lindy Hopping, and Suzie Q-ing. They were impressive—one swung himself around a lamppost, kicking up his heels. People—several white people among them—clapped and cheered and tossed coins in the hat. It was magnificent. Money to be made right there in Harlem on the corner. Ella stood and took it all in, then shuffled down to 131st, where a girl in a long blue coat was juggling silver batons and golden balls, the spheres dancing in the air, their light reflecting against the buildings and in the eyes of the crowd.

Ella examined one act, and then another, planning her own debut. She cased her old numbers route and her lookout terrain around Miss Adeline's. New numbers runners—dapper, well-groomed, menacing—lurked in front of the barber shops and pool halls. She steered clear of them, and didn't search out any of her old connections for fear they'd turn her in. She didn't know where things stood with Madame Queen and Dutch Schultz and didn't want to get embroiled in that again. As if to underscore her resolve, she veered over to 116th, passed the spot where Zukie had been killed. The cement was pristine, unstained. Nothing marked where he'd died. Ella looked resolutely forward, toward the end of the block, turned the corner. She would not go that way again.

Her competition had gotten so well-rehearsed, so polished. She didn't recognize their intricate, exquisite steps; they seemed to have graduated from the Frankie Manning School. Perhaps she could join a group, find a partner, then maybe become a solo act. She would steal their routines. It was a dancer's rite of passage to imitate the best and then practice enough to top them.

Time whirled by and, almost before she realized, dusk was beginning to settle over the city. She didn't possess the flashy clothes—yet—to go to a nightclub and didn't want to use any of her precious money for entry fees. Just being near the Savoy, tonight, would be enough.

She wandered the streets, paying close attention to the homeless people, to their carts, their cardboard box homes, their dirty blankets. Just for tonight, just until she got the glass jar, she would construct something for herself. She had to go to the apartment when Auntie wouldn't be there. She had to get Frannie alone. If nothing else, the Training School had taught her to take nothing for granted, to economize and plan. Down the Boulevard of Dreams she drifted, over a few blocks, to a vacant area outside Mount Morris Park. A cardboard tent leaned against a building; one side had collapsed. No one was inside. She circled around it, considering. There were even a few blankets.

It was growing dark. The area was deserted. She decided to chance it, reassured herself that her money stash was buried deep at the bottom of her coat, and slid inside. The blankets smelled of wet wool and body odor; one side was smeared with something foul, and she tucked that at her feet. No one came near. Despite the blankets and the shelter of the cardboard box, she was soon chattering with cold, but it was still far better than the iron bed and the drafty window of the Training School. She didn't think she'd be able to, but almost immediately she fell asleep.

Just before dawn, she woke to darkness and a red-bearded white man standing over her, screaming. The cardboard had been torn back, and he was wrestling the blankets away from her, shouting, "Nigger, what you doing in my house?"

She scrambled up, trying to apologize, but he kept cursing her. When he lunged toward her, hand upraised, she took off running.

He yelled after her, "You niggers stay out of Mount Morris Park! It belongs to the Irish!"

Later that morning, after spending another dime on two rolls with no butter—that cost extra—she elbowed her way into one of the four corners of 125th and Seventh Avenue. White spectators were always passing through, pockets jingling with coins, and the best dancers were always there performing.

She began with a routine that Uncle Clyde always applauded: her signature move, her variation of the snakehips.

"What you doin' on our corner?" Shaggy curls flopped in a kid's eyes, a hulking tomboy part of a brother-sister team. They both looked hungry.

"Nothin'," Ella said. "I just love to watch you dance. That's all. I want to be a dancer."

"You got any jive or hooch?" the tomboy's brother asked, sizing her up while also making sure no one was stealing from their cans on the street.

"I don't touch it," Ella said and didn't back up.

"Yeah, well, get off our corner," the boy said. "There ain't no room for you here. Go past 135th. We don't want to see your face, and don't dance on these corners. They ours."

Several other dancers across the street paused their routines, staring at her, a ragged army preparing to battle. Ella nodded and headed a safe distance away, but she didn't leave. She needed allies. The pair definitely collected money: a crowd gathered around them.

In the afternoon, she situated herself on 114th Street, across from the Wadleigh High School for Girls, lurking behind a metal fence in front of one of the townhouses. She pulled the scarf they'd given her before caroling low over her forehead. Finally the school bell rang and moments later the girls streamed out, all in that well-remembered uniform: white collared shirt, black dress, black stockings. She waited. Finally, ten minutes later—by then Ella had thought she'd missed her—Frannie sauntered out with three other girls. They laughed at something one of them said.

Ella, who'd been poised to leap forward to get Frannie's attention, drew back.

They looked so—she hunted for the word, found it—*innocent*. Carefree. Untouched. These weren't girls who spent their days scrubbing laundry or trying to find a safe place to sleep. These girls had a future. These girls had hope. Ella felt tainted and weary and old. She scuttled back into the shadows.

The trick to getting into the apartment, Ella knew, would lie with her sister. Georgie would turn her in to Auntie, and Auntie would turn her in to the authorities. She could only trust Frannie. And by now the police would probably have come hunting Ella, so she would have to be even more careful.

Frannie headed uptown with the girls. Ella followed, wondering where Georgie was. She stayed on the other side of the street, watching behind her, in case Georgie caught up. But there was no sign.

Her sister looked taller; her hair neatly braided into twin plaits that hung to her shoulders. Of the three girls, she was closest to the street; Ella tried to figure out if she could hide between parked cars and whisper to her. But her friends would notice, of course, and they might turn Ella in.

The girls laughed at something, the short, rounder one in the middle throwing back her head in an open-mouthed guffaw, and their happiness stopped her. She felt so out of place, so alien, like a criminal about to pounce on her victim.

They turned another corner and went down the block, Ella continuing to shadow them. They went into a soda shop on 124th. Ella had been in there several times—it was one of Frannie's favorites, with a chocolate malted she always loved. Her mouth filled with saliva at the thought of a chocolate malted. Once she was dancing, she'd treat herself three times a day, or more.

She hung around a few doors down, on the other side of the street, shadowed behind parked cars and a pile of trash. How long would Frannie stay? Was she working? Her letters hadn't mentioned any work, but her letters were so short that Ella couldn't be sure.

Then she caught sight of Georgie—shining, blouse pressed, very white, elegantly loping down the block in a group of more girls. She looked well-fed and pleased with herself. A moment later they turned into the soda shop.

Ella had lost her chance for the day. Surely Frannie and Georgie would go home together.

Well, she'd try another time. Maybe on the weekend. She'd be sleeping on the street again tonight, and until she got that bottle.

Ella wandered.

First, up to Washington Heights before heading south toward Central Harlem again. She stumbled upon a queue of people in a breadline. She waited her turn for a small cup of soup and a piece of bread, wolfed it down steps away.

By now it was a bit early to sleep, but she didn't want to roam the streets all night. She thought of heading over to St. Nicholas Park, or over to the Harlem River, but remembered from her days at Auntie's that both areas were dangerous, especially for girls. She spotted an empty doorway in front of a closed garment store, stood in the alcove, claiming the space from other homeless people, and finally squatted down, huddling deep in her coat. She dozed off, slumped over.

Before dawn, a white-collared, clean-shaven man in a tweed suit kicked her legs. "Hey. You."

She stirred, rubbing at her eyes. Sleep had been fitful and elusive. Once she'd woken to find someone groping in her pocket, and she'd screamed and kicked out. The person had fled, but it had taken Ella's heart quite a while to stop pounding, and even longer for her to fall back into a light doze.

"Get out of here," the man was saying. "Next time I call the cops. You can get a good night's sleep in jail. How about that?"

28

Lonesome Way Back

December 13, 1933

The sight of Frannie awoke something embryonic and desperate in Ella, a growing reckoning that kept her awake long into the night, huddled under a pine tree in St. Nicholas Park. Two other kids were sleeping there—two girls about her age. One turned her back, cocooned in a blanket; but the other, Dorrie, had a wide, open face, and seemed friendly enough. She'd run away from home in Pennsylvania, and thought she'd find work in New York, but hadn't found anything yet. Thinking of Frannie had opened up an emptiness that made it difficult to pay attention. It was hours before she could fall asleep.

Ma Ramsey's words haunted her, those taunts that Ella was no better than an animal. If Ma Ramsey could see her now. *No better than an animal*: Ella could almost hear her voice, feel her nodding, satisfied. Now Ella truly was no better than an animal, dirty and homeless and worthless.

But with every step she took, every breath she breathed, she refused—*she absolutely refused*—to prove Ma Ramsey right. She was not an animal. She *knew* she could do more. She *knew* she was more. She would never, ever, submit to the world of the Training School.

So the next day she was again lurking in the Wadleigh School's shadow. She'd found a hat and had stolen a tweed overcoat, way too big for her, that hung to her shoes. It stunk of sweat, urine, and wet wool, but blocked out the wind. She kept her head down, like a good little colored girl should, doing her best to call no attention to herself as the school bell rang and the students streamed out into the December sunshine.

Today, though, Frannie waved goodbye to her friends and waited at the bus stop. Ella lurked in a doorway behind her, searching for Georgie or anyone else who would recognize her. The bus came, Frannie boarded, and since Ella didn't see anyone she knew, she paid five cents and followed. Frannie found an empty seat halfway down. In three steps Ella was sitting beside her. Frannie glanced up briefly from the window, turned back to stare out at the pedestrians and traffic.

"Hey," Ella said softly.

Frannie jumped, turned, and a smile split her face as she lunged in for a bear hug. "What—how did you—"

"Quiet," Ella hissed.

Frannie was wrapping herself around her, hugging her tightly, crying. "What are you doing here?"

"I escaped."

"I know. Policemen came looking for you. Auntie said she didn't know where you were."

"What did you tell them?"

"The truth," Frannie said. "Same as Auntie."

"What do they think?"

"I don't know," Frannie said. She leaned back a little to look at Ella. "They didn't tell us. They just said you'd escaped and we should tell them if we saw you. I don't know if I would have even recognized you, though."

"Why not? I'd recognize you anywhere."

"You look different."

"Skinnier," Ella said.

"Yeah," Frannie said with a laugh. "Skinnier, too." The bus roared up the hill. More passengers got on and off. "Where are you staying? What you gonna do?"

"Better if I don't tell you. That way you don't have to lie to them."

"Did you come back for me?" Frannie's voice was very small, and Ella's heart cracked even further.

"As soon as I can, I will." It seemed she was always telling Frannie she would come back for her after disappearing.

"What are you going to do?" Frannie asked again, pleading.

"I'm going away," Ella said. "California." She had no idea where the words came from, but once she said them she almost believed them herself. Maybe she would go to California. One day. Just not yet. "The thing is, I need money. For the bus. To get there."

"Auntie's super worried about money. Ever since you left she's been pulling as many shifts as she can. I'm on garbage duty and Georgie's dusting and keeping the halls clean. And I've got a job after school a couple days a week. I help out Miss Mattie twice a week." She was very proud of it.

"That's great," Ella said. "Is Georgie working?"

Frannie shrugged.

"I need to get into Auntie's," Ella said. "I saved up a little and I left it in my room." After she said it, Ella realized that she no longer had a room. She'd never had a room of her own at Virginia's. Just a place to sleep on the floor.

"I'm not going home," Frannie told her. "I just told you that. I'm going to Miss Mattie's."

"You can give me your key. I'll leave it for you by the front door."

"How will I get in?" Frannie seemed worried, and Ella realized with a pang how young she was. Frannie was thirteen, but seemed much younger.

"Can't Georgie let you in? Just say you forgot it. Will Auntie be there?"

"No, she never gets home before nine now. Sometimes a lot later."

"Give me your key," Ella said, holding out her hand.

Frannie fumbled in her pockets, handed it to her. Ella closed her fingers around Frannie's hand, held her fingers tight.

"Will you write to me from California?" Frannie asked.

"Of course, as soon as I get there," Ella lied.

"I hear there's work there. And it's sunny all the time. There's a girl in my class who moved from San Diego. She says it's really pretty."

"As soon as I get settled I'll send for you," Ella said. "Or maybe I'll come for you myself."

"Don't come back," Frannie said. "If you come back, they'll find you."

"Well, in two years I'll be legal, and then nobody can stop me." She was only sixteen, and two years felt impossibly far away. Two years ago, her mother was still alive, and Ella was dancing with Charles up in Yonkers. It seemed like two million years ago. But in two years, she'd no longer be a minor, and the New York School for Girls would no longer be an option.

"This is my stop," Frannie said. "I need to go."

"Just get off at the next one. Stay one more minute."

So Frannie did, tucking her hand in Ella's and pressing her shoulder into Ella's. "You smell," Frannie told her.

"Yeah, well," Ella said.

"How'd you escape?"

"I snuck away when we went to town one day. Caught the train back. Just like a hobo."

"Wow," Frannie said, leaning harder into her. "Where you staying?"

"Better not to tell you. That way you won't get in any trouble and I won't get caught."

"How will I write you?"

"I'll figure something out." The bus lurched to its next stop.

"I really need to go," Frannie said. "I'm going to be late for work."

"Okay," Ella said, standing as the bus slowed. "I love you."

Frannie hugged her hard. "I love you, too." They held each other tight, and despite herself Ella was crying; they were both crying. Ella wanted desperately to follow Frannie off the bus, to follow her to Auntie's that night, not to steal illegal money, but to sleep in a bed and a place she belonged.

It felt like all of her life was a series of endings, of disappearances— of tiny deaths and enormous deaths—leaving her with nothing but grief and longing, a yearning to spin back the clock, if only by ten minutes. But the clock spun forward, and the bus doors sighed open, and Frannie was gone.

Ella huddled on the bus until the stop on 145th Street. It was a relief to sit there, in the warm space. She thought of staying on to the end of the line and getting off on the way back, but by then Georgie would be back and her chance would be lost. So at 145th she descended, made her way west across the avenues to Auntie's.

She lurked outside for a few moments, searching for police cars, for anyone suspicious on the lookout for her, but saw no one. She let herself in the front door, up the steps. The linoleum had peeled up even more; on a few stair treads, it had ripped off entirely and the metal undergirders glared out like bones, or teeth. The stairwell stunk of urine and mice, and she thought she could hear squeaking, as if a vast hoard of rats nested deep in the walls.

She opened the apartment door as quietly as she dared, but sensed instantly that the rooms were empty. She dashed to Georgie's room, not sparing a glance for anything else—the familiar sofa, the china ornaments, the fake fireplace, all artificial, all making promises and keeping none.

The bureau was still in its spot. In a moment she slid it over. It seemed to move more easily than she remembered, but that must have been her nerves and desperation giving her strength. She lifted the floorboards, scrabbled in the gap.

The jar was gone.

She pulled the bureau further from the wall, and with sweaty hands patted every inch in the space. It had to be there. Had to be. Where else could it be?

The wood was cool and smooth, the space empty. Someone—Auntie, no doubt—had found it.

All of Ella's money, all of Ella's hope, had vanished.

29

Go for What You Want

Winter and Spring 1934

An hour later Ella presented herself at Miss Adeline's Parisian House. She stunk like Auntie's stairwell. She could still feel the sting of Frannie's obvious disgust, trying hard not to cover her nose. The townhouse towered over her, welcoming in its familiarity. She'd hoped she wouldn't have to choose this option, but this was the best possibility for a reliable, safe shelter so she didn't end up in jail, or back up at the Training School.

A few customers were inside, so Ella waited until they left and the store was, for the moment, empty. Inside, Miss Adeline was busying herself behind the counter, dressed in an unassuming day dress with no makeup or jewelry. No one would ever suspect that she dressed nightly in lace, chiffon, and feathers. She looked up when the bell rang. No one else was in the store. "Can I help you?" and then, looking Ella over: "I ain't handing out nothin', so you can take yourself on down the street."

"Miss Adeline, it's me."

Miss Adeline stared at her blankly. "How you know my name?"

"It's Ella. Ella Fitzgerald."

"Ella?" Miss Adeline blinked, shook her head, lips pursed. "Lord have mercy. You don't look so good." She came around the counter as if to hug her, then backed up. "Lord, child, you need a bath."

"I'm sure I do," Ella said. "I don't have anywhere to go."

"I heard they caught you, took you upstate," Miss Adeline said, lips thin.

"They did," Ella said. "I escaped. I can't go back. I can't. You don't know what they do . . ."

"You living on the street?" She didn't wait for Ella to answer. "Come with me."

She circled past Ella, locking the front door and flipping the sign to "closed." Then Ella followed her to the back of the store and up the back stairs to the second level's bordello. Ella had never ventured up this staircase—narrow and steep, the former servants' stairs. "Let's get you cleaned up," Miss Adeline said as they ascended. "You put on clean clothes. I'll leave some out for you. Then we'll get you a good meal and you can tell me all about it."

Ella quickly shucked off the dress she'd bought several days ago, jumped into the tub, scrubbed. Miss Adeline left a pile of clothing just inside the door. It was heavenly to be in a clean, warm room again, to soak in a tub. She wanted to cry, it all felt so good. To be cared for again. She clenched her jaw, scrubbed her face roughly with the towel.

When she was dressed, she went out into the main area of the brothel. A few girls were lolling on couches, but Ella turned her face away so they didn't recognize her—she didn't want to explain herself, didn't want the burden of introductions—and hunted down Miss Adeline back in the miniscule room she called her office. "I need a job," she told her.

"I bet you do," Miss Adeline said. "Come on downstairs. Let's get some food in you. Don't worry. We'll work this out. Tessie will fix you something."

Miss Adeline's part-time cook, Tessie, was also a working girl. She made the most delicious chocolate chess pie Ella had ever tasted. Saliva filled her mouth. Tessie cut her a wedge of roast chicken and some fresh bread. Then Miss Adeline led her to the back porch off the kitchen, where they could have some privacy.

The chicken was so savory she almost wept again: just holding it in her mouth, the warmth of the meat against her palate. And the pie—oh, the pie!—how long it had been since she'd had pie!

As she ate, she looked out at the yard, filled with castoffs and trash, where the Dobermans still prowled, silent and friendly. She wondered if they remembered her—she'd given them a few pieces of chicken sometimes, when she would act as a lookout for the brothel.

"You want to work for me?" Miss Adeline asked her as she ate. "Veronique left and you can have her room. And her clients."

"How's Gardenia doing? I want to say hi to her."

"Gardenia isn't with us anymore." Miss Adeline's lips pulled taut and down.

"Where is she? Did her daddy come back?"

Miss Adeline shook her head. "She's moved on and I hope she's happy. That's all I know."

Ella could tell that she wasn't going to learn any more. "Do you still need a lookout?"

"Where you going to sleep? You can't make enough money acting as my lookout. Wouldn't you rather have Veronique's room? It's at the top of the stairs. Let me show it to you."

"No, ma'am. Thank you. I just want to be a lookout right now," she said. They spoke longer, Ella telling her briefly about the Training School, but not about the Dungeon. She wasn't ready for that yet.

Finally, Miss Adeline agreed to Ella just running lookout again, and fixed up a cot for her in the small pantry off the kitchen. "Beds and bedrooms are for paying girls who earn a living," Miss Adeline said. "If you want to earn money, get you a future, I can get you a nice bed and a nice room. You can even have one right next to the bathtub."

But Ella knew that if she slept in a bed, she'd be required to use it for more than sleeping, and that was not something she was willing to do. The small pantry suited her just fine.

Throughout the winter and spring, her new life rounded out into a rhythm that, slowly, began to heal some of the Training School's wounds—although many would never completely heal.

Many mornings the dogs woke her before dawn, when the milkman left the bottles on the back porch. The dogs were named Mr. Tibbs and Mr. Slaughter, and on the rare occasions she had meat, she'd save them a few pieces. It got so they wagged their stumpy tails and licked their gums every time they saw her.

Then she'd feast on a breakfast of yesterday's crusty bread and tea that she'd warm on Miss Adeline's stove. Sometimes Miss Adeline would offer her a boiled egg, which she never refused. Other times—rarely, to be sure—if the dance money was particularly good, she'd treat herself to a pastry—six cents, oozing with butter—and the memory of flaky crust and the scrim of sugared icing would delight her much of the day.

Some mornings, after breakfast, she would help Miss Adeline on the main-floor grocery store or go upstairs and offer to do chores for the working girls—girls who were her age, some younger—who lay in bed, luxuriating in the damp warmth of their sheets. They would tell her how good they had it, how Ella should try it, and she would smile and shake her head, clear off the bottles from the bureaus or sweep out the fireplaces.

By noon she'd be dancing. Within a week of her arrival she'd struck up a conversation with several girls who danced and sang on the corner of Eighth Avenue and 127th Street. Although the number of dancing girls varied between three and as many as ten, a core group of four or five spent much of the day executing steps to whatever music they could invent: a wax-paper-wrapped comb to make a kazoo; a series of lids for percussion; a couple of the girls humming or singing. Worn hats were set strategically in corners of the sidewalk, opening like flowers to the day and to the passersby's coins. At the end of the afternoon, they'd divide the take. Girls came and went, and felt entitled to different amounts, and that often caused cat fights.

But fighting and bickering were typical of life on the street. Ella learned to accept it. She learned to accept that the girl who pulled her hair today and called her a "a nasty Black ho" would tomorrow hug her and offer her a sip of her ginger beer.

Above all else, though, Miss Adeline herself became a refuge and a mentor to her. She was always impressively dressed, her hair pomaded, her face tactfully made up—dark red lipstick, no rouge or eyeshadow, just a touch of eyeliner—and her nails always polished and elegant. But she was no delicate lily, limpid and easily pushed around—from her Ella learned what toughness really meant: how a woman could be beautiful, gentle, and ruthless.

One Saturday evening just before sunset, as Ella was about to head out to keep watch, she ran into Miss Adeline in the parlor, peering out from behind the lace curtains. Behind them, one of the girls was playing the piano—badly—and singing, also badly, "Ragtime Romeo." Several white men splayed on the sofas were laughing their loud, room-owning laughs, with girls in their laps.

Miss Adeline cast a glance at the room, and then back out the window. Ella tried to peer around her but could see nothing. "Is everything alright?" Ella asked her. Miss Adeline didn't usually stand at the window like that, squinting into the darkness.

Another burst of male laughter from the room. "These are the gentlemen from Paris," Miss Adeline said, tipping her head slightly to indicate the white men with the girls. The Frenchmen had arrived in America a few days before, eager to enjoy Harlem jazz and female company. Ella thought them very glamorous, even if she couldn't understand what they said.

"But there's a rookie cop outside," Miss Adeline went on. "He's getting in the way of my business."

She twitched the curtain slightly.

The Frenchmen needed their privacy: this kind of discretion was something that Miss Adeline guaranteed. The white cop slouching on the stoop of the brownstone across the street, smoking a cigarette, would intimidate her customers—keep new ones from entering, and might frighten away the Frenchmen if they caught sight of him.

"What's he doing on Mr. Henry's stoop?" Ella said.

"It gutter-low-class of him and disrespectful to colored folk," Miss Adeline muttered, glowering at him. "We take pride in where we living." She tightened her lips. "That's a colored man's property and he crushing the geraniums that Mr. Henry worked so hard to grow."

Ella didn't understand what the cop was doing. Most of the cops were already paid off, and the ones who weren't—who'd raid the brothel—were the ones that Ella would keep watch for.

"Cuz he jealous white trash, that's why, and he needs to be told. And I'm gon' do the telling." It was as if speaking aloud to Ella gave Miss Adeline the impetus she needed, because she straightened her shoulders and smoothed her long black velvet jacket over her gray dress as if readying herself. "You're walking over there with me and you keep your mouth shut. Let's hope Mr. Henry don't come outside."

She marched to the door, reached for her feather hat and pocketbook, then smoothed her jacket again and tightened the belt around her dress. She pulled up her garter and stockings, too. Ella half expected her to put Vaseline on her face.

"You ready?" Miss Adeline said, and then she lit a Marlboro, blew the smoke out her nose, and stormed across the street.

The cop, who'd been slumped on one side, leaning against the flowers, straightened up as he saw her. He knew her name, too. "Good evening, Miss Adeline."

Ella almost wanted to laugh, because suddenly he looked scared.

"Don't 'Miss Adeline' me, cracker."

Ella had never heard Miss Adeline speak like this—and certainly not to a white man. All her worries about being so close to a policeman now vanished. Miss Adeline would protect her.

Apparently the cop hadn't either. "What? What'd ya say?"

"Hear me once and forever more," Miss Adeline said, standing very close. She was shorter than he was, but his shoulders were pulled back as if he were anxious to step away. "You betta get your marching orders straight from your boss if you don't know this street and what goes on. Don't play stupid with me even if you are stupid."

His face was flushed. "I don't know what—"

"I'll tell you what. You already gettin' paid and you ain't gettin' a penny more." Miss Adeline suddenly turned to Ella, who wanted to jump back herself. "Do that shimmy," Miss Adeline told her.

Ella broke into the shimmy.

"You see that?" Miss Adeline said to the policeman. "You know what that means?"

He nodded, but Miss Adeline continued anyway. "That means we have a full house and any cop you don't know, you steer them clear from us. If they comin' you let Ella know and she'll let us know. That's your job and you make good money at it."

He stared down at his feet. "Yeah, but what about—"

"What about nothin'," Miss Adeline said. "If you can't do that straight I have no need of you."

"What about more?" the kid managed to say. Ella finally realized that under his uniform he couldn't be more than twenty-two, twenty-three.

"More nothing. You get away from here and stop lookin' at my guests," Miss Adeline said. "Ella, come on." She grabbed Ella's arm and sashayed back across the street.

The evening air was cool, with a pleasant breeze coming off from somewhere, blowing paper and trash down the street. For a moment Miss Adeline watched the wind blow, and then said, "Keep something in mind, sweetheart. Anything you put your mind to, you can do. No matter what everyone else thinks, you gotta just know what you want and go for it. When I was your age, my mama had died and my father was gone, and it was just me and Leroy, my brother, who took sick a lot. I had nobody to help me. Nobody. I was a burden. But I was determined to make my way. I did some things I ain't proud of, and Leroy passed no matter how I tried to keep him—oh, he had the most beautiful big brown eyes and curly hair—but I learned to keep my mind fixed on a task. You do that, too, with your dancing. Don't ever let *never* keep you from doing what your heart wants to do."

This was a small incident, but it resonated with Ella: to believe you're right, to move forward with your convictions, to not let anyone take advantage of you because of a uniform or what might seem like a better social position. Much of life, she learned, was just having the attitude and the confidence to grab onto it.

———

She'd run numbers in these streets; she'd gone to school with the kids and the teachers. Although she recognized people, they didn't seem to recognize her; or if they seemed to, she'd skulk out of sight.

Still, with each passing day, her fear of discovery diminished. She couldn't wait to talk to Frannie again and share with her this new life, but Ella couldn't risk it. If Aunt Virginia had turned her in to begin with, perhaps she'd do so again. If Frannie knew where Ella was, would that mean that Child Protective Services would appear one day at Miss Adeline's, too? Ella wouldn't take the chance.

In late July, her breath flipped and her heart leaped: Aunt Virginia, with Georgie and Frannie in tow, was strolling toward her. They carried colorful bags. She cowered behind the other girls, ducked around a shoeshine stand. Despite the girls around her she suddenly felt starkly alone, as if shoved into a dank cellar with no windows, missing all air and light. Then her family turned the corner, heading uptown, and disappeared behind the buildings.

She wanted to follow them, return home with them, reforge the connection, what she thought of as love. But the specter of Ma Ramsey still lurked around the fringes of her sacred Harlem, and Ella's fear of the Training School overshadowed her need for Frannie.

A few days later, as if Harlem was shining a bright police light on her, three of her former school classmates from Wadleigh approached, walking so confidently that she was sure they were coming to say hello and ask her all kinds of questions about where she had been and if it was true that she'd been arrested and put in jail.

She kept dancing, doing a shuffle-step-jump-shimmy with Frances and Dorrie.

The girls passed her, never even glancing at her.

They didn't recognize her.

Had her appearance changed so much in a year? Her hair was uncombed. She must really look like a bum, wearing tattered castoffs from Miss Adeline's girls. She wouldn't think about it. She would dance and she would find a way to the Savoy Ballroom. Marcus Garvey had once said, "Take the kinks out of your mind instead of out of your hair." Aunt Virginia had loved that expression.

The kinks were her circumstances, which, despite appearances, were vastly better and safer than the Training School for Girls. Self-reliant was what she needed to be, and she would figure out how to thrive. Without Aunt Virginia. Without Tempie. Without anyone.

She'd crawled out of a grave, she'd returned to the living. Being disheveled was the least of her challenges.

30

All Night to Dance

May–October 1934

Of all the girls Ella danced with, her two closest friends became Frances and Dorrie. Frances, a year older than Ella, had been on the streets since her father had diddled her when she was ten. When Frances was fourteen, she'd spent two months at the Training School, but dug under a gap in the fence and hitchhiked her way back to the city. Ella knew exactly where she'd snuck out—a low place in the fence that in her day had been filled in with boulders and rubble. Ella had scaled the pile several times, noted the remains of a faint path winding down the cliffside.

Frances had lived in the other colored cottage, under the more gentle tutelage of Ma Belle, the only colored housemother; and as time passed Ella was able to laugh more freely about Ma Ramsey's gargoyle claws, and the paddling, and the endless laundry suds. But, no matter how close she and Frances became, there were places where they never ventured. Ella didn't know, and never knew, if Frances had had similar experiences in the Dungeon. She thought of the hot meat of Duncan's palm, and how Lewis looked at the girls, and the despairing screams she'd heard that night from the Dungeon's other cell. She didn't ask further, and Frances didn't offer.

Of all the girls on the corner, Frances was the most proficient dancer, muscular and sure, able to cartwheel and backflip, land lightly and kick high, like a Rockette. She was more of a performer than an artist, with a star quality that had people stop their cars on the street to watch her.

Ella's other closest friend was the stocky, heart-faced Doris Combs, whom Ella had met on her first night back in Harlem, before she'd gone to stay at Miss Adeline's. Dorrie wasn't as athletic as Ella or as exuberant as Frances, but she had a slow, lazy, boneless soft-shoe that could go on indefinitely, her fingertips turned up like doves' wings, and when she would dance, her cheeks would lift and her eyes sparkle. She was mesmerizing.

The girls could have gotten more tips if they'd paired up with the groups of boys, strapping and muscled, who performed extraordinary acrobatics on neighboring street corners: twisting up and around lampposts and street poles, cartwheeling and backflipping between parked cars. But although the girls joked about it, they never pursued it; and when the boys would come and proposition them, they would find excuses, put them off. All the girls in her group, Ella realized much later, were damaged; they'd all been injured so deeply that trusting anyone—let alone anyone male—was as alien as imagining themselves blue-eyed and Caucasian, clothed in sequins, or dancing in the front line of the Cotton Club, where only fair-skinned, near-white girls performed.

Except Ella, all the girls slept on the street, tucked in alcoves. Some came from the Hooverville on the Harlem River, and one girl—who came less frequently and one day disappeared altogether—was way up in Washington Heights. She'd carved out a cocoon under the George Washington Bridge and would climb up into the brace work to sleep, dangling like a butterfly's pupa fifty feet in the air. Ella sometimes imagined, with a shudder, hot-breathed men creeping up the bridge's struts, stalking the girl; and none of the others were surprised when they realized that they hadn't seen her for several weeks.

Ella wanted to invite her friends back to the safety of Miss Adeline's to sleep, and once broached the subject. "If those girls stay with you and warm your bed," Miss Adeline told her, "they going to have to pay, same as you. I don't hold nothing wrong with it, but this is a working house."

Ella tried to explain that it wasn't like that and that they were just friends, and Miss Adeline nodded, but was resolute.

Most evenings, on weekends and weekdays, Ella worked her main job: watching for the police for Miss Adeline. She'd perch a few doors down, dance with a hat in front of her; and sometimes one of her friends would accompany her. As soon as she caught sight of a tell-tale police uniform, she'd whistle, bang a trash can lid against the nearby wrought iron fence; and the working girls would bolt their doors, and the johns would slip out through the back alley.

Those first few months, after her escape from the Training School, she had no clear end goal in mind. She wanted to dance at the Savoy, show her steps in the Corner, but that seemed as unlikely as Tempie returning to life and cooking her breakfast. Ella didn't have the clothes to get in the door, and the Savoy bouncer would have turned her away, so she didn't even try. Its nearness was, for the moment, enough.

But as the summer wore on, she began to chafe at Miss Adeline's schedule. It was impossible to dance at the Savoy in the evenings since she had to keep lookout. Sometimes men bumbled into her room off the kitchen, scaring her awake. "There's a perfectly good bed upstairs," Miss Adeline would say, but Ella shook her head or pretended not to hear.

As the late September wind blew down Seventh Avenue, the days grew shorter and the johns were coming earlier and earlier. Ella resented having to stand outside in the dusk and full dark, dancing for herself, or just standing on the sidewalk looking out at the night. She had the talent. She was sure of that. But to perform at the Corner she needed everything.

It all came to a head the first week in October. She'd bundled herself into her pantry as usual, had just fallen off to sleep when she felt a hand on her leg. She awoke with a scream, pulling her knees close, pushing herself against the back wall, but the hand became an arm and a body, falling across her, groping her breast and pawing at the blankets.

"Get off me," she said, pushing him away. "I ain't one of the girls."

Usually that was enough. The john would stop, back up, apologize. But this one was either too drunk or too desperate to care, and he came at her, his weight full across her, lunging through her coverlet, nuzzling at her neck. His breath was like Joe's: stinking, something rotten in it.

"Hey," she said again, pushing at him harder, "get off me." Miss Adeline's bouncer, Monty, took care of the problem johns. But Monty was all the way at the other side of the house, and no one could hear her from the kitchen.

"Please," she begged him, twisting around, squeezing over to one side.

The trick slurred something she couldn't understand, and her blanket was wadded away somewhere. It was just him and her. She wore what she usually wore to bed: a heavy nightgown and too-big bloomers that Miss Adeline had given her.

The nightgown was around her waist, and he was pulling at her bloomers, forcing them down. She wriggled away, trying to put a leg between his, but his full weight was on her, the roughness of his beard scratched at her ear.

"Stop it," she yelled. "Get off me!"

With a snap the waistband of her bloomers disintegrated, and now his hand was between her legs, his knee forcing her knees apart. Again he said something—"Please" and "Be a nice girl"—Ella was too panicked now to hear. She worked an arm free and she was smashing at his face, imagining Duncan's rotten tooth and Carter's lazy smile, hearing Joe's *I be nice, you be nice.* She was fighting them all now, twisting, her knee working free and coming up to hit him hard between the legs.

His breath came out of him in a rush and he folded over.

Before he could swing for her, she clawed away toward the door. "Get back here, you bitch!" he bellowed, grabbing at her foot, but she squirmed free, and in a moment was standing in the kitchen, panting, next to the stove.

She put on Tessie's apron, made her way to the front door, to Monty. He followed her back to the kitchen, but by the time they arrived, the trick was gone.

Next time she might not be so lucky. Just like Joe's house, just like Aunt Virginia's, just like the Training School: she was not safe.

Later that morning, after thanking Miss Adeline, she packed up the small roll of her belongings, closed the pantry door for the last time.

That night, she followed Dorrie back to her wedge of ground in the Hooverville near the Harlem River. She would wash her clothes in the river; bathe there, sometimes, if it were private enough—and if not, there were fountains up on 155th. The water would be cold, but she'd dealt with worse.

But she would have all night to dance, and none of the johns would have an opportunity to mistake her for a prostitute.

When Talent Is Not Enough

Autumn 1934

She might have the time to dance, but the Savoy Ballroom would not have her. She practiced endlessly on the street, perfecting her Shim-Sham shimmy, Charleston Side-to-Side, and Sailor Step until they were as elegant and assured as she could possibly make them; when she would dance on the street corner, people invariably tossed her their change, so she knew she was good.

She was living with Dorrie in the Shantytown by the Harlem River, which some of the residents called the Forgotten Gulch. Dorrie had inserted a tiny wedge of plywood against an overhang, wrapped with a plastic sheet that flapped mercilessly in the slightest breeze.

Those first few nights were fun and welcoming: wedging herself into that tiny space, back-to-back against Dorrie, sleeping on a pile of cast-off clothing. She'd missed the sisterly company, the warmth of another body near her. She also welcomed the protection—two girls could fight a man off far easier than one. Although the Gulch was never silent—a woman's shriek, a man's laugh, a baby's cry, and the incessant coughing—having Dorrie at her back was great comfort.

But soon, more often than not, she slept alone. Dorrie took up with a young man who'd fashioned a lean-to on the other side of the Hooverville, a butcher's son who scrounged and begged and undertook whatever work he could get to make a few coins. He wasn't a performer, although he was attractive, with extraordinarily long eyelashes that curled back almost to his eyebrows, and a slow smile that was hypnotic and impossible to ignore when he turned it on you.

Dorrie was besotted, and after a few days of his turning his smile on her, she began to spend the nights with him.

Ella missed her. She'd been alone in Miss Adeline's pantry, and had been alone at the Training School, and now she felt abandoned.

Because of the river's proximity, there were fearless rats, and lice, and despair. Her clothes grew even more tattered. No matter how she scrubbed, trying out all the skills she'd mastered with the Training School's endless laundry, all of her clothes grew grimy, the colors fading. Ella couldn't stand to look at herself in storefront windows.

She sometimes knocked on doors of her former numbers running clients—Miss Bernice, Miss Nadine, and others—and they would often slip her a nickel or half a sandwich. A few times she washed her hair in the beauty parlor sink. But generally she steered clear of these places. She was ashamed at what she'd become, and hated seeing the pity in the women's eyes.

Worst was the cold. As October folded into November, and the wind blew harder and the temperatures fell, she wondered what she'd do next. Maybe she'd have to knock on Miss Adeline's door again. She'd tried some of the other people that she'd known on her run—

Miss Bernice, and Miss Sylvia—and none of them wanted anything to do with her.

One Sunday evening, her belly full of potato salad she'd gotten at a soup kitchen, she'd combed her hair as best she could, donned her least-patched skirt, shrugged into the men's overcoat she wore now, and made her way to the Savoy. She'd thought of asking some of the girls, but by now she was used to doing things alone; and none of the other girls had been inside the nightclub before. She didn't want them over dazzled, gawking up at the lights like tourists. Sunday nights were usually slower at the Savoy, so she thought she'd have a better shot.

As she'd done years ago, she stood in line. Whitey was still on duty, still checking in the crowd. "Hi, Whitey, remember me?" she said when she reached the front. From inside wafted the melody of a tune that was popular right then—Mr. Hoagy Carmichael's "Judy." A song about spring and new beginnings. Ella had danced to it on the street a few times.

He looked her up and down, no recognition in his face.

"It's Ella," she said. "I used to come here with Charlie. Charlie Gulliver. From Yonkers. Remember?"

He focused on her. She tried smoothing her hair away from her face. She'd often worn it with barrettes. Perhaps that would trigger his memory?

He looked her over, but didn't seem to recognize her.

His eyes were hard and he was already looking past her, at the couple behind her. "The ballroom's full. You gots to go someplace else."

"What do you mean? I'm—"

"I said you gots to go someplace else."

The white couple behind her were a few years older than Ella, the man in a tuxedo and tails and the woman in a white sequined sheath and stilettos. "Next," he said to them, with a big fake smile plastered all over his face, somehow putting his shoulder toward Ella, blocking her entrance.

"But—"

The white couple sailed past. The woman wore an ostrich feather that bobbed and curled above the crowd.

As the music to "Judy" ended, to be replaced by something else, she stood outside the line, unsure where to go. Whitey let others in to rub elbows with Joan Crawford and Clark Gable and Duke Ellington. What was so wrong with her? Her clothes weren't top-notch, true, but they were fairly clean. And she'd washed her hands and face especially.

Perhaps she'd have better luck if she brought a partner. She turned away into the night, away from the Savoy's marquee. Maybe if she was on the arm of Frances's young man then she could get in.

By now Frances, too, had a beau. It wasn't as serious as Dorrie's, but George was a boy who danced over on 126th, in a troop of acrobatic dancers. George liked the girls, and would flirt mercilessly with all of them, but he liked Frances best. She was the tallest and had a great figure. Ella was mousy, with a plain, naked face and scrawny legs, so George didn't pay her a great deal of attention.

Ella first ran her plan past Frances, who had no objection, and then approached George.

"We'll have to practice," she told him. "We can do it with Frances. She can give us pointers."

And so, for a week or more, George would saunter over to their street corner, and Ella would show him Zukie's old moves—which, by now, were dated—and sprinkle in the steps that Uncle Clyde had taught her as well.

They danced to many songs, but one of them was "Judy," the song she'd heard at the Savoy. It became something of an obsession for her, like a Tiffany lamp, something that seemed out of her reach. But if she had ears she could listen; if she had a body she could dance; and now, with or without the Savoy, she would do both.

George and Ella became a team, spinning and gyrating, his fingers tight against hers, his arms strong as he lifted her to the sky.

"You after him?" Frances asked, teasing.

Ella shook her head with a shudder. "The last thing I want is a boy pawing over me," she told her. "You ain't got nothing to worry about."

The next Saturday night, she and George presented themselves in the Savoy's line, Ella in her best skirt, neatly darned—she'd learned needlecraft in the Training School—and although the enormous overcoat was a man's and hung well past her knees, she thought it was presentable enough. George wore dark trousers and a shirt that seemed white until he stood under the Savoy's marquee lights and it yellowed into a grimier, vague color.

But again, as before, Whitey looked her up and down when she reached the front of the line, told her that there was no place in the Savoy for her.

"Come on, Whitey," she begged. "You remember me. Please? Just this once?"

But he shook his head. "Sorry, it's crowded tonight. You'd be more comfortable somewhere else."

Ella could have wept with rage and despair. She was so close that she could taste the vibrant buzz of the electric lights. The bass drummed in her pulse with a heartbeat bigger and stronger than her own.

"Come on," George said, putting one arm around her, pulling her out of line. "We don't need this ol' place anyways. Come on down to the river and let's get us comfortable." He was always practicing, trying to get with the girls, and she usually shrugged him off, but this time his nonchalance, combined with the Savoy's rejection, made her mad enough to shove him back into the maroon velvet ropes. "Jeez, Ella, calm down, wouldya? It ain't that big a deal."

But to her it was. To her, it was everything. She would not give up. The fire for a better life burned in her, keeping her warm in the solitary place by the river; it lit up her dreams.

She kept thinking that the nightclubs would be her way in. Many of the local clubs offered talent shows: you paid an entry fee and performed for a live audience. The winner won a cash prize. The Lafayette and the Regent both offered this.

In September Ella had saved up and applied with Dorrie and another girl, Kimmy Coles, to dance on Connie's stage. But the audience had not chosen them, and all of their money had been wasted.

In November she heard about a talent contest at the Apollo, the new colored theater off 125th. The contest was just starting up, so many people didn't know about it yet. It offered not only a ten-dollar prize, but the winner would perform for a week in front of the audience. The entry fee was steep—two dollars—but since this was the first one, their odds were better. Ella convinced Frances and Dorrie to try out. But rather than each of them wasting all that money on the entry fee, Ella suggested that they each chip in sixty-seven cents and draw straws to see who performed.

"Girl, you ain't got no chance," Dorrie told her.

Ella shrugged. Dorrie had no ambition anymore. She just wanted to lie in her butcher boy's arms, have him repeat over and over to her how much he loved her.

He loved her well enough, that was for sure: she was a couple months pregnant now, and talked about moving in with him, building some kind of home with him in the Gulch.

But eventually Dorrie agreed to try out. The ten-dollar prize would come in handy for the baby, and everyone told her that she soft-shoed and could do the Suzie Q like nobody's business.

The Apollo's audition was on Monday night, but Ella wanted time to prepare. So the preceding Saturday, the three girls—Ella, Frances, and Dorrie—headed over to the new theater to scout it out. Posters four feet high announced the upcoming amateur competition.

They loitered across the street from the marquee, watching the well-dressed crowd coming and going, the women glittering and beautiful on the men's arms. The five-and-dime next to them was open late. Even though it was November, a nativity scene jutted onto the sidewalk. Stuck on a straw bale, a rickety handful of sticks stood in for the manger; beneath, a white-faced baby in a cradle; and Mary in a blue cloak, staring out at the Apollo as if she wanted to dance, too. Joseph stood at her elbow. Nobody seemed to pay attention to the baby—which Ella supposed was alright, since God could look after himself.

"Here," she said, stooping and yanking a handful of blades from the bale of straw. She discarded all but three, kept two the same size and made one slightly shorter. "Shortest straw wins." She led them down an alleyway next to the store, where the marquee's glow did not reach.

"If I win, you just look out," Frances said. Her breath steamed. For an instant the darkness turned white. "Big time here I come."

Ella handed the straws to Dorrie, who arranged them carefully so all ends poked out the same distance. Dorrie wasn't sure she even wanted to win. The winner would have to perform. And if there was one thing Dorrie didn't want, it was to make a fool of herself. She kept repeating the story about another talent show at another club, how the audience had screamed at one girl to get her "fat ass out of here," cursing at her until the girl stumbled away, sobbing so hard she couldn't catch her breath. Dorrie, barely starting to show, was enormously conscious of her growing belly.

"Them peoples sure can be mean," Frances agreed. Not that she was worried: she was the most acrobatic dancer among them, and probably wouldn't be booed off.

Ella tried to figure out which straw to choose. The first straw had a one-third shot at winning. If she went second, the odds went up to 50/50.

Maybe Doris was right. Maybe this was a huge mistake. If you didn't leave the stage fast enough, when the booing rattled the chandeliers, then the Executioner would swoop out, all elbows and soft-shoe and grins, clutching his oversized broom. His feet a blur, he'd tap-dance and sweep you off the stage. He aimed for your ankles. If you fell, the audience would stand up, cheering and stomping and laughing at you. Who would want that?

Ella would.

Desperately.

If she won Amateur Night, she'd have a ten-dollar prize, and the chance to dance for an entire week with professionals on the Apollo's stage. Her life would change. She could wash with real store-bought Ivory soap again.

"Let's do it," Frances said. "I'm gonna be a star. Get outta my way."

Doris pulled her arm out of Frances's reach. "You wait. It was Ella's idea. She go first."

In her pocket Ella fumbled for that last precious Life Saver, still wrapped in its scrap of tin foil. She'd stolen a roll last week. If there was ever a time she needed luck, it was now. Breathing shallowly, praying with each exhale, she popped the Pep-O-Mint into her mouth, sucked in a minty breath.

They wore men's overcoats and castoffs: Frances in men's trousers cinched tight around the waist; Doris in a plaid shirt that hung almost to her knees and a scarf she'd filched from a display rack at Altman's; and Ella in men's boots that rattled and squeaked with each step.

"You ready?" Doris waved the three straws at them.

Ella waited a tiny breath of a second, and—as she'd planned—Frances took her chance, elbowing her to snatch at the far left straw.

Frances swore. Her straw was long and unbroken. She dropped it.

"You out," Doris told her, clutching the last two.

The odds were even.

Doris and Ella exchanged glances.

No matter where she went later in life, no matter the furs and the jewels and the smoothness of the silk gowns, no matter the big band blare of orchestras or the adulation or the cameras, everything always boiled down to here, to this instant that would transform the trajectory of everything that came before and everything that would come after.

Ella would think of this later, sitting in Ed Sullivan's greenroom. That it all boiled down to this: *a willingness to reach out and grab the future, no matter how dark that future might be.* Because there was always that possibility that the future would be lit brighter than she could ever have imagined it.

She reached her hand out through the November air and softly laid a fingertip on the right straw.

A tug, and Ella raised the straw to the light.

32

Take the A Train

November 19, 1934

The line slithered down the block and around the corner to Seventh Avenue. Loud dancers in outrageous outfits practiced complicated routines; singers did vocal warm-ups and belted out entire songs a cappella; acrobats did flips—all the while standing in line on the sidewalk.

Directly in front of Ella, Dorrie, and Frances, a young man in a plaid Zoot suit—gold chain dangling from his waistcoat—did a hard bop, spinning in a tight circle. Several people applauded.

"He thinks he's Cab Calloway," Frances said.

"There's no use staying," Dorrie said, sucking on her teeth. "There's no way you'll make the cut. You should've come earlier."

"We can stay for a while," Ella said. "Maybe they won't pick everyone." She peered at a woman beyond the Zoot suit—an acrobat with ostrich feathers in her hair, her arms and legs bare, despite the chilly November night.

An official-looking woman with a clipboard was working her way down the line. "Your name and what you do," she said over and over, writing down the contestant's responses, collecting their two-dollar entry fee even though it wasn't clear that the contestant would make the cut. The woman behind them said that the Apollo would be choosing fifty amateurs to audition for seventeen slots.

"How many people are here?" Ella asked, sliding into the street for a better look.

"Gotta be two hundred or more," Dorrie said. "Maybe three hundred."

"Not all of them are performers." Ella hoped she was right. "Probably just forty or fifty of them. Most are probably just their friends or relatives."

In a few minutes the organizer reached them. "Name and what you do," she said, not looking up. She was tall and beautiful, with a long black coat that swept the sidewalk.

She gave the woman her name. "I'm a dancer."

The woman looked hard at her. Ella felt suddenly conscious of her men's boots, the raggedness of her overcoat. "What kind?" the woman said.

"Tap, Lindy Hop, Suzie Q, Black Bottom."

"Variety dancer," the woman nodded, as if pleased about something. "You have a partner?"

"No." Ella's mouth was dry.

"Soloist?"

"Yes."

"What song?"

"'Take the A Train,'" Ella said.

"Pick another song," the woman told her. "Everyone's doing that one. A different song would give you a better chance."

It felt as if Ella's luck was finally turning. This woman was helping her—giving her advice, insider information. "Okay," Ella said. "Can you come back to me? And please, miss, may I use the bathroom?"

"No. They're not available for public use. You got your entry fee?"

Ella handed her the two dollars. "How many people are they choosing?"

"Fifty."

"There's more than fifty people here."

"Yeah," the woman said, consulting her clipboard. "Ninety-six competitors. So far. With you it's ninety-seven."

"Oh," Ella said.

She must have sounded as forlorn as she felt, because the woman tilted her head up from her clipboard, really seemed to look at her for a moment. "But we need more dancers," she said. "I'll come back to you. Go choose your song quick." She asked Frances and then Dorrie what they'd be performing, and they explained that they were just there to keep Ella company.

Ella brushed uselessly at her skirt, compared her hand-me-downs with the competitors' costumes. She wasn't even wearing make-up— her face was dry and ashy. Both Frances and Dorrie wore lipstick, but neither had offered to share it.

"You decide on a song?" The organizer was back.

Ella jumped. "How about 'Diddie Wah Diddie'?" she said. She'd just heard some boys playing it that afternoon, and she liked the rhythm.

"You sure?" the woman said, peering closely at Ella again. She was elegant, with clear almond-colored skin and wide-set eyes. Small gold studs glittered in her ears. "That one's not easy to dance to. Why don't you do a crowd pleaser? Like 'It Don't Mean a Thing If It Ain't Got That Swing.' Nobody picked that yet."

"Okay," Ella said immediately. She'd danced to that song many times. "Let's do it."

"Good." The woman nodded, jotted something on her clipboard. "You're forty-eight. You can go in." She gestured up the street toward the Apollo's stage door.

Ella, Frances, and Dorrie skirted the line. Behind her she heard the woman yell, "Okay, people, that's it. The rest of you can come back next week."

Frances and Dorrie weren't allowed inside. They hugged Ella tight, wished her luck. "You come find me after, you hear?" Dorrie told her. Ella said that she would.

Inside, the smell of the theater—a mix of fresh and stale air, of perfume and old sweat, of new carpet and smoke, of anticipation and fear—made Ella's pulse race. This was it. She followed everyone backstage to the audition room, sneaking first into the women's restroom. It had been days since she'd used a proper toilet, and she took a moment to wipe the grime off her face. She combed her hair with her fingers and decided she looked fine, that nobody would know she lived on the street.

The audition room seemed packed, but Ella realized that this was partly an illusion. The back wall was lined with mirrors. An old upright piano leaned against another wall.

Ella watched herself walk through the door. She didn't look as good as some of the other competitors. She pulled her coat around her as if that would help.

"Performers take a seat! Singers here, dancers here, acrobats and jugglers here, variety acts here!" The woman with the clipboard was back, organizing the crowd. Ella slid into the dancers' section, against the far left wall, and stared again at her reflection, at her tattered dress and men's boots and hair that didn't look smooth, shiny, and straight.

The woman explained that the contestants would go up, one by one, and perform for the man sitting behind the folding table to one side. The man, dark-skinned, with thick gray eyebrows and a permanent frown creased into his forehead, nodded once.

"And I'm Maple Brown," she went on. "I'm the talent coordinator. I'll tell you when it's your turn. Jim there—" she pointed to the producer, the thick-eyebrowed man at the table—"will tell you when to stop. Number one, you're up." Ella, at forty-eight, would be near the end. She decided she'd try not to watch the others: it would just make her more nervous.

For a while she shifted uncomfortably on the folding metal chair. She tried not to watch, but didn't have anything else to do, so despite herself she examined the acrobats as they flipped and cartwheeled. She couldn't believe how nervous she was, even if she performed to a crowd every day. Soon, nerves and a full bladder had her in search of the restroom again.

After she used it, she ventured farther down the hall. She had an hour or more, easy, before she would be called to perform; and how exotic and splendid it was, to wander around backstage! The corridor walls, painted black, wound past a few doorways and a stairwell, and then opened to the back of the Apollo's main stage where a band played.

Monday nights, the Apollo—like other theaters in the city—went dark, meaning that there were no audiences. But several professional acts were waiting for a chance to practice. Ella hugged a wall, listened as a singer warbled a Hoagy Carmichael tune, and then watched as a vaudeville performer spun plates and balls on sticks, and balanced them on his shoulders and head.

She was just thinking that she'd have to get back when two impeccably dressed girls in matching yellow sequined dresses took center stage. They looked like twins. One nodded to the band and took off tap dancing and spinning with real professionalism. The other followed an instant later.

"Who are they?" she asked a tall man leaning on the wall next to her. Their shoes were beautiful: the same bright, sequined yellow. Proper dancing pumps.

He couldn't keep his eyes off them, either.

"The Edwards Sisters out of Chicago," he said. They looked like mirror images of each other, and they were fast and polished. It was as if each sister were somehow inhabiting the body of the other, so that when one put up her arm, the other finished the movement in her fingertips. Their feet blurred in complex rhythms and patterns.

"That's their daddy." The man next to her gestured with his chin toward an athletic man standing on one side. "He trains them. He's a dancer, too."

Just then the athletic man called a halt, went over to the two girls, said something, demonstrated a quick step himself, and asked the band to restart four bars back. The girls picked up immediately. Ella couldn't tell the difference: they'd been dazzling the first time.

"They're good," she said cautiously.

"Honey, they're gonna be superstars," the man said.

"And they're going to perform on Wednesday?"

"They're going to close down the show," he said. "They're the finale. You can see why."

She nodded. She could indeed see why, and she felt utterly defeated: at midnight, after the main professional show, directly after the Edwards Sisters, the Amateur Hour began. So Ella would be dancing right after the greatest dancers she'd ever seen. Ella curled her toes in her shoes: no proper dancing pumps for her.

The girls finished their routine, outstretched hands in their brilliant white gloves perfectly aligned, as if tied together. As they struck a pose, the watching performers and handful of spectators burst into spontaneous applause.

By the time Ella returned to the audition room, it had emptied out; and from the doorway she again caught sight of herself in the mirrors: tattered dress, men's boots. She stared at the back of her hands as if expecting them to grow white kid gloves. Maple Brown was leaning against the wall with her clipboard, barking orders to the next performer. There were maybe a dozen people left. The place seemed sadly exhausted.

Ella slipped over to Miss Brown. "Excuse me, ma'am. I'd like to change my act to singer." She started to keep her head down, eyes fixed on her shoes, and then flicked up and met Miss Brown's gaze.

"You can't do that." Miss Brown remembered her. "'It Don't Mean a Thing If It Ain't Got That Swing,' right? You auditioned as a dancer."

"Please?" she said. "I know I can—"

"You signed up to dance. You'll dance."

"I can sing a lot better than I—"

"Well, you'll have to come back to another audition then," Miss Brown said. "I need dancers, not singers." She turned away, called the next act as the soloist finished: number forty-four was a trio of Black boys carrying juggling rings that they spun as they leaped through them.

So Ella would dance. She returned to the metal chair and waited for her number to be called. The other dancers she'd seen were no great shakes, she thought, trying to comfort herself. Hope wilted. She tried to make it bloom: Ella was better than the other amateurs. Everyone said so.

After forty-seven—a singer who lasted twenty seconds before the judge cut him—Miss Brown huddled a few minutes with the judge. Ella saw them looking over at her. The judge nodded. Ella could feel the tingle of nervousness bloom into terror as the man's eyes moved impassively over her.

"Forty-eight," Miss Brown said.

The pianist launched into Duke Ellington's "It Don't Mean a Thing If It Ain't Got That Swing"—a very lively, upbeat tune that usually sent spectators' toes tapping.

She gave it everything she had: sliding forcefully into her jig circle, swingout, and under-the-arch with the ball change. The song wasn't long—maybe three minutes, tops—but the scrawny man at the table called a halt after probably no more than a minute. Ella, caught up in the momentum, continued dancing after the piano had stopped, and then froze, hands in the air.

"You'll do," he said, staring blandly at her. "You're in. See you Wednesday."

Ella was still unable to move.

"Thank you," Miss Brown said. "You can go now. See you back here Wednesday night. Be here by nine at the latest."

Then to the handful of people who remained in the room, "Forty-nine, you're up."

33

Every Hope of Spring

November 21, 1934

It was Wednesday night.

In the Apollo's greenroom directly below the main stage, the syncopated tap-tap of the dancers rattled the ceiling. Singers' voices floated through dimly, and the audience roared—but whether it was applause or catcalls, Ella couldn't always be sure. The greenroom was fetid with fear and anxiety, with a rawness that set her heart pounding. A woman in a red headdress—an acrobat, Ella thought, but perhaps she was a dancer—stood in a corner pressing her face to the wall, talking to herself. A trio doing vocal warm-ups kept repeating the same notes over and over. A contortionist draped his legs over his own shoulders, twisted his feet back onto the floor, and stood up. The movement, vaguely slithering, made Ella queasy.

When she'd arrived at the Apollo five hours ago—they'd told her to be there by nine and she'd arrived at seven—they'd given her the performance lineup: she was first.

"First?" she said, shaking her head.

Maple Brown nodded. "We like starting off with a dancer."

"The first to be booed off the stage," one of the other dancers told her with a smirk.

Ella would be dancing directly after the Edwards Sisters, who would close the "professional" show. Amateur Hour came next.

Of course she'd be dancing directly after them. Because if the universe could throw something in front of a colored woman to stop her in her tracks, the universe would surely try.

Now it was almost midnight, when Amateur Hour would begin.

All yesterday and most of today—ever since the Monday evening audition—she'd become newly sensitized to the Apollo's playbills plastered around Harlem. She hadn't noticed them before, although she had no idea how she'd missed them. The oversized sheets, stuck on every corner, reminded her that the show would be broadcast live over Radio WMCA. That the theater used "High Fidelity RCA sound equipment," whatever that was. That the winner would return for an entire week of performing with the professionals.

She kept telling herself that if she could win—in the ridiculously unlikely event that she won—she'd be a shoo-in for the Corner at the Savoy. No way Whitey would bar the winner of the Apollo's Amateur Night. People would probably pay to see her perform. Plus, with the ten-dollar prize money, she could buy new clothes. Maybe even second-hand dance pumps. She sucked in a breath. She'd made it this far, hadn't she?

Besides, what was the worst thing that would happen if she lost? The audience would boo at her. Maybe even throw something. So what? She'd gone through worse and was stronger because of it. She'd been beaten and starved and groped and buried alive, hadn't she?

And now she was afraid of some man with a broom? She'd leave the stage before the Executioner shuffled on. She didn't need him and she didn't need that audience. She'd march right off the stage and out the Apollo's rear door. She'd head back to the shantytown on the Harlem River and let it swallow her whole. This late at night it would be quiet, a few fires crackling in trash barrels, the river pouring endlessly past, the moon glittering on the ice and the current. By tomorrow everyone—even Ella, especially Ella—will have forgotten this entire mess.

Faintly came the melody from the Benny Carter Orchestra: her mother had purchased his phonographs back in Yonkers. Then the music crescendoed, the brass section holding a last final note; and applause, thunderous and vast, shook the walls. No mistaking that for anything but pure delight.

The Edwards Sisters had just finished their performance.

"Okay, we're up," Maple Brown told the room. "Follow me, please."

Ella at her heels, she led them up a narrow staircase as a single trumpet lifted into "I May Be Wrong" and the orchestra joined in.

I may be wrong, but I think you're wonderful
I may be wrong, but I think you're swell
I like your style; say, I think it's marvelous

This was really happening. Shut down the fear, she told herself. Move your feet.

Soon she was standing in an open space at the very edge of the stage. Miss Brown blocked the way, so all she could see was a sliver of spotlight against the black stage curtain.

Then Ralph Cooper's voice, velvet-smooth and booming, drilled into the farthest corners of the theater, easily silencing the crowd's rumble. "And now it's time for the new program that we're bringing to you tonight. It's Amateur Night at the Apollo, where you, the audience, are the judge and jury!" Ralph Cooper, one of the handsomest men Ella had ever seen photos of, was onstage somewhere, just beyond the curtains. She was about to meet him for real.

The audience howled, heaved in their seats like an ocean of sharks, surging just beyond Ella's sight. They had been waiting.

The voice went on, "But before we get to this evening's victims—I mean contestants—" another roar of laughter from the crowd—"let's give another round of applause to the world-famous Edwards Sisters. Weren't they marvelous?"

The horde thundered.

Yes, Ella thought, agreeing. *They were marvelous.* She thought about the glitter of the Edwards Sisters' yellow sequined dance pumps, how they must have sparkled on the floor. In the spotlights, it would have seemed as if the girls had been dancing on stars.

But Ella would show them a thing or two. Because it wasn't just her, Ella, here: it was all those kids dancing on the street, Lindy Hopping and swinging and Charlestoning for pennies and quarters, for their lives. She was here for them, too.

Earlier that evening she'd spent twenty minutes in the theater bathroom, rubbing at her galoshes with a paper towel, the water darkening the scuffs so the boots had—she'd thought—looked almost polished. Now, under the stage lights, they'd obstinately reverted back, the scrapes and scratches blooming even more obviously without the dirt to obscure them. They were a size too big, and the leather had come loose from her left toe. She'd been thrilled a month ago to find them behind a dumpster. Now she glared at them as if this were all their fault.

"So, folks, here's the rules," Ralph Cooper was saying. "If you like a contestant, you're going to applaud, okay? You're going to applaud loud and long."

The theater echoed with bellows and clapping.

"But if you don't like someone?" the voice went on. "You're going to make that clear, too. Aren't you? How you gonna do that?"

Screams, catcalls, boos, pounding feet.

Maybe, Ella thought for an instant, these colored people, thrilled now to attend this previously whites-only theater, would be kinder to her since she was one of their own.

No, this audience didn't sound kind. This audience sounded mocking and cruel. Eager to have a good time, even at someone else's expense.

Especially at someone else's expense.

"You've got it," Ralph Cooper's voice said. "That's all you got to do. Now let me introduce you to the Apollo's ever-fanatic and fabulative defender of talent and feared enemy of all who left their talent at home. Please say hello to our infamous—" Ralph paused—"Executioner. He'll make sure the contestant doesn't stay on stage a minute longer than they need to."

A blaring siren, the "Bad Talent Alarm," wailed, and even more laughter ballooned up from the audience. From the other side of the stage, in the opposite wings, a tuxedo-clad man who'd been leaning against the back wall suddenly came to life, tap-dancing across the stage as he clutched an oversized broom. He time-stepped into a full-pull-shuffle, each tap of his silver shoes as precise as a heartbeat, as ominous as a snake's rattle, as he danced toward the audience and out of Ella's view.

In a few moments, Ella knew, he'd be tap-dancing and sweeping her off the stage, too.

"Our first contestant hails from right here in Harlem," Ralph

Cooper said. "She's just seventeen years old, and she's here to give those Edwards Sisters a run for their money. Here to dance her heart out for you, please welcome Miss Ella Fitzgerald!"

Her name rang out, echoed in the vast space. She would dance so beautifully, so elegantly, so extraordinarily, that the audience would fall silent in awe. Surely then someone would remember her name. Surely then she would never have to repeat it the way she'd done so many times in the past.

She was marching out into the lights, into the vastness. All those faces, upturned to her. She focused on the standing microphone set up center stage—a black oval shimmering in front of the spotlights' glare. This was what she'd wanted. This was it.

And then, between one step and the next, in a single instant, the entire audition—her entire experience at the Apollo—fell into place. She heard, playing in her head, Ralph Cooper's voice crash around her:

Here to give those Edwards Sisters a run for their money.

Why—why?—*why* had Ella been chosen, out of all the contestants—all better dressed, all better groomed—to perform *first*? Ella with her men's galoshes and tattered dress and the nappy hair that she'd tried, so hard, to brush smooth in the restroom. Why Ella, of all people?

Why had Miss Maple Brown been looking specifically for dancers? Why had she suggested that Ella dance this particular song? Why had that judge said, "You'll do" to her? Why would she "do"?

Of course: so they could laugh at her. She was the first performer, the first dancer, slated to go right after the Edwards Sisters; the comparison between their glittering golden costumes and Ella's threadbare dress no comparison at all. She would wind up the crowd. She would be the first sacrifice to the Executioner. The crowd would cheer with glee as he swept her away, howl with delight as she disappeared forever.

It had all been a lie: all of the Apollo's promise, all of her practicing, all of her desperate desire to succeed in a world where everyone told her that she couldn't. She was just the punch line of a joke.

She couldn't take in the enormity of it. She couldn't catch her breath.

The stage felt like a greedy vortex that would suck her in and under. Beyond it loomed the auditorium, vaster than the Hudson River. Faces bobbed in the reflected light, eyes glittering, mouths agape.

Somehow her legs were moving, the spotlights were in her eyes, and a man was approaching, coming closer. She took another few steps and all the faces were in front of her, smooth ovals like soap bubbles. Three tiers of faces, balcony rising upon balcony, sumptuous with gold plasterwork, and crystal chandeliers, half-lit, glittering over everyone.

She was to dance a few feet behind the microphone, standing stark and lonely in the middle of everything.

And there was Ralph Cooper, even more handsome than his photographs: large dark eyes, a fine nose, square jaw. He was so much taller than she, and he laid his arm across her shoulders, led her to the middle of the stage. She resisted the urge to shake his arm loose.

"Okay, Miss Ella," he said into the standing microphone, "welcome to Amateur Night. You got your dancing shoes ready?"

She wanted to duck out from under him, scuttle over, so she could stride onstage by herself, but she knew better. She would *yes-ma'am*, even now.

Instead, she shook her head.

"I don't want to dance," she mumbled to him, to the half-lit theater, to all the faces turned toward at her.

"What?" Ralph Cooper asked into the microphone. "What did you say?" He was squinting at her, confused, then looking across to where Miss Maple Brown was gesturing and mouthing something that Ella couldn't make out.

A row of light bulbs lit up the edge of the stage, glowing at her feet like a string of electric pearls. She leaned over and spoke into the standing microphone. "I don't want to dance."

Now, finally, she was done yes-ma'aming. She was done with the Training School and keeping her head down and doing what she was told. She wasn't a *filthy creature*, as Ma Ramsey had called her. She wasn't *uppity*. She was a human being, just like they were. Better than most of them, because she'd fought harder, cared more deeply, tried again and again to shake the world into letting her succeed.

She would reach out now and she would make this night her own.

"I don't want to dance," she said to Ralph Cooper, to the audience, to Harlem vast and pulsating beyond these walls.

The crowd roared with laughter. "Get her off the stage!" someone shouted. A few boos bounced like balloons off the ceiling.

"You don't want to dance?" Ralph Cooper repeated, chuckling a little, but sympathetically, so when he asked her, "Well, what do you want to do, then?" she was able to say:

"I want to sing."

Once the words were out she realized she meant them. She'd stood there with emptiness holding her up; the only thing she was sure of was that she didn't want to set herself up for failure by dancing after the Edwards Sisters.

"Singing" felt almost random until she said it, and then it felt impossibly right.

Of course she wanted to sing. Whenever things got really bad—

when Joe had locked her in that closet, when Ma Ramsey had locked her in the cell—she sang. Singing was the key. It had always been the key. She just hadn't realized it until right now.

"You want to sing?" Ralph Cooper repeated.

She nodded, surer of herself. Again the crowd laughed, gleeful and mean.

"Well, Ella, what do you want to sing?"

She hadn't thought about that. What a disaster this was turning out to be.

But she'd been in worse situations. She'd worked with criminals who shot each other in broad daylight. She'd spent days sweating over grimy underpants, scrubbing them against a steel washboard in an airless basement. She'd been beaten and locked away in the dark. She'd been buried alive, and risen from the dead.

Now she was just going to sing a song, and that she'd been doing her whole life. No matter if they wanted her to or not. She didn't need a special ticket or glittering shoes or a handsome dance partner. She needed only herself.

"'Judy,'" she said. "Does the orchestra know 'Judy'?"

Of course Benny Carter's Orchestra knew Mr. Hoagy Carmichael's "Judy."

Ralph Cooper laughed. "I think they can probably do that," he said to her. "Hey, band," he called, "Do you know the song 'Judy'?"

In answer, the piano lilted into the song's opening bars.

"Well," Ralph Cooper said, and now he was smiling at her, for real, this time, "this is Amateur Night, isn't it?"

The crowd laughed, but not so vindictively. It was as if these people understood her in a way beyond words.

She was frantically trying to remember the lyrics to the song, but of course she knew them. She had danced to them on the street for days. She had hummed them after the Savoy had turned her away. Of course she knew them. They boiled in her blood.

"And now, to *sing* her little heart out for you," Ralph Cooper was saying, "Miss Ella Fitzgerald, singing 'Judy.'"

The crowd applauded politely.

Ella opened her mouth and the words were there, and she was singing them.

But her voice was hoarse. Terror and nerves tightened around her throat, turned the notes flat, scratchy, and low. She didn't sound at all like herself.

A boo flew out from the crowd, and an instant later, "Get off the stage!"

Someone barked, and then more joined the first, like the baying of starving dogs. Others hissed.

She stared out into the darkness, wild-eyed. They were against her now. She'd had them for an instant, but then she'd lost them.

"Get off the stage!"

She froze, rolled her eyes at Ralph Cooper, who'd retreated to one side of the stage and now was half-hidden by the curtains.

As if in answer he ambled out, debonair and confident. His tuxedo twinkled in the light like something magical. "Hold on, hold on," he called to the crowd. "Let's give this little girl a chance. She's got something in her." He held out his hands, fingers extended, to quell the audience churning like a vast, terrible monster, and in a moment it quieted.

"You wanna take it from the top?" he asked her, his eyes meeting hers. He was so very kind. She took a breath. She nodded, unable to speak.

This was it. With a certainty that was beyond anything she'd felt before, she knew that this was her last shot. She'd rolled the dice, thrown down what she'd hoped were winning numbers, stacked the decks in her favor. She'd done everything she could think of to even the formidable odds against her when she had, really, no chance of ever winning.

A lost colored girl, an orphan, living on the streets, clad in hand-me-downs, with nothing but hope and a fierce will not to give up, not to give in. How could she fight against a world that forced her mother to die in a laundry room; where gangsters roamed the streets, leaving bullet-ridden corpses in their wake; where hot-handed men would take you into the shadows and grew only more aroused when you screamed; where the school that should educate you believed that because of your skin color you were only fit for laundry; where cold-eyed white women would bury you alive and leave you forever in the dark?

Her mother was wrong. There were no Tiffany lives, not for girls like her.

She took another breath. No. Her mother had been right. *A Tiffany lamp glowed out there, somewhere, for her.*

Ella could fight. She *had* fought. And even if she failed here tonight, she would try again, and keep on trying. She'd never give up. If she couldn't dance, she would sing. If she couldn't sing, she would find something else. This was her answer, her way out. Because there had to be a Tiffany life for her, for anyone who refused to back down, who made her own luck happen. There had to be.

The breath she took next was not just a breath, not just air into her lungs: it was Uncle Clyde's exhale, warm against her cheek as he spun her in a turn; it was Miss Adeline's snort of approval when Ella alerted her to a looming policeman; it was Zukie's bark of amusement when one of the gambling women won their bet; it was Frannie's squeal when Ella baked her a chocolate birthday cake; it was her mother's laughter, rich and deep and echoing forever, on Christmas morning. It was all of them. But, more than any of them, it was Ella herself.

She reached down inside, imagined herself as Connee Boswell, imagined the Yonkers apartment around her, and her mother playing this song on the phonograph. At the same moment, simultaneously and contradictorily, she was in a black cell, in total darkness, with iridescent imaginary bubbles floating around her, up and up, to the ceiling.

No, there was no ceiling. The bubbles floated up, endlessly, forever. Like possibility. Like hope.

Ella let the melody that she had heard so many times flow through her, and from somewhere low, deep inside her, the words formed, and she began, again, to sing.

This time, she knew, the notes were absolutely perfect, pure, coming from that bottomless true place in herself that she'd found at the Training School. This was her voice. This was Ella Fitzgerald, and she let the audience, *her* audience, hear it and feel it.

The first row, perched to pounce, burst out in a thundering avalanche of applause, screaming cheers and praise.

She could do this.

She was no longer fighting this room. She was opening herself up and out, into it, rising like a breath on an updraft.

Her voice lifted into the next verse, floating over the tiers upon tiers of faces, all of them rooting for her, buoying her up. She felt like she was floating, and perhaps she was. The line of light bulbs at the base of the stage, each and every one of them handcrafted at Tiffany's, were far away now.

A woman somewhere above her shouted out, "That girl can sing!" and more clapping swarmed throughout the theater—above and below—and then the people were on their feet and their mouths were open as if they were singing, too. But they were cheering.

She finished the song, her voice pure and clear and filling the dark space of the auditorium with something more tangible than light: something vast and yearning and untouchable.

"Encore!" they shouted at her, stomping, screaming, and "Encore!" and "Bravo!"

She had done it. She'd forgotten the Executioner and the possibility of failure. These people loved her. They looked beyond the men's boots and the cast-off dress and the kinky hair and they saw something better, more true, more important. The last vestiges of fear fell away and it was Tempie there, in the audience; and Frannie; and Charles; and Zukie; and T-Bone; and Uncle Clyde; and a whole host of people who, somehow, had become family. All of these screaming, joyous people were her family.

The applause washed over her, and she grinned out into the light, and bowed. No more curtseying, no more yes-ma'aming. She bowed like a true performer.

It was time to leave the stage, she knew, but the audience pinned her there and she couldn't imagine walking away. Ralph Cooper was strolling over, microphone in hand, and he was looking out at the audience, and he was yelling, "Well, Apollo, what did you think about that!"

And they were yelling back, and stomping, and on their feet, and their joy and adoration ballooned around her, their roar a living thing that could bear her weight, could carry her upward as far and as high as she wanted to go: and she wanted to go everywhere with them.

Ella Fitzgerald had, finally, found her family.

Ella Fitzgerald was home.

Epilogue

New York City, CBS Studios, July 18, 1948

"Miss Fitzgerald?" Ella realized that someone had been repeat-ing her name several times. She shook her head and looked up to find the nervous house manager bending solicitously over her. "You okay? He's ready for you."

Ella stood and smoothed her black satin dress. She touched up her lipstick and blotted it with a napkin. "One breath at a time," she told herself, humming under her breath. "Her voice could bring / every hope of spring."

Adrenaline rushed in. She had never felt so alive.

The door of the greenroom opened into a short corridor whose far wall had been stacked with stage paraphernalia like lighting, props, and plates. The stage was to the left; to the right was a warren of makeup rooms, dressing rooms, offices, and all the other parts of the studio.

Eerily, though, the layout of the hallway—its depth and height, and the clutter of props on the far wall—made her think about that

restaurant in Hudson, New York, where she'd made her escape from
the Training School. In that restaurant, to the left lay freedom and
hope; to the right lurked the kitchen and endless drudgery. For a moment, as she glanced to the right, she fully expected to see half-
stacked plates of food on the floor, and the kitchen staff preparing
Christmas hot chocolate.

Instead, a cleaning woman pushed an enormous custodial broom
over the linoleum tiles.

Ella hesitated. The woman could have been her mother or Aunt
Virginia. But she was heavier-set and much older than Tempie had
ever been, with a head of thick curly white hair; and she had none of
Auntie's poise and height.

Their eyes met.

"This way, Miss Fitzgerald," the house manager was saying.

But instead of following him, Ella turned right, toward the
woman.

She thought briefly of the television set's empty stage, and gawky
Edward Sullivan awaiting her entrance, and the camera fixed on where
she should emerge through the curtains, and no one appearing.

But already she was moving in the other direction, toward the
older woman. She did not know why, nor what she would say to her.

Before she had a chance to speak, though, the cleaning woman
was saying, "Miss Ella Fitzgerald as I live and breathe."

"Yes, ma'am," Ella said, relieved she'd been recognized.

"You just as pretty as you want to be." The woman's voice was almost a whisper. Her shoes were worn but polished and her uniform
strained around her big frame. "I heard there was a colored girl going
to sing on Mr. Ed's show and I thought I could hear yah from here."

"You want to come in?" Ella said.

"Oh no, honey, don't want to bother you none. I can hear right fine from where I is."

"You sure?" Ella asked.

"Oh," the woman said, not quite answering the question, "they gon' fall in love with you."

A pause as Ella took that in. "Thank you," Ella said, leaning close, wrapping her hands around the old woman's, so that for a moment they both held the broom handle like a staff or a scepter—something regal, filled with dignity, worthy of respect. A faint smell, as if of sunshine and bleach, came from her.

"God bless you, child," the woman said. "I thought I'd never see the day they let a colored woman open her mouth to say something, no less sing."

"Thank you," Ella repeated. She cleared her throat. "Thank you for all the work you do."

The woman's mouth fell open slightly. She looked bewildered.

"Miss Fitzgerald, I really must insist." The nervous house manager was right behind them, and his voice was frantic.

The cleaning lady looked past Ella, at the man, and down the hall. She met Ella's eyes and pointed with her chin. "You go now. You go out and do us proud. What you doin' is for us all."

Perhaps it was the faint odor of bleach, perhaps it was what she'd been pondering tonight, but now Ella thought again about those bubbles in the laundry pot, the hallucinatory bubbles in the Dungeon; why some floated up and became air, and others stayed and boiled below. She had been in the fire for so many years—as had her mother, and her Auntie, and Frannie, and this woman standing before her; and somehow the fire had cleansed Ella and lifted her up into something more. Why Ella and not another? It did no good to wonder. All Ella could do was try to be worthy and always be grateful.

Now she nodded, pressed the woman's hands one more time, and followed the house manager's agitated strut down the hallway. She could feel the woman's eyes at her back. So many eyes, so many people behind her, all buoying her up, making these moments possible.

The corridor ended in a black curtain. The house manager pulled it back. Beyond, the stage lights gleamed.

She ducked her head, felt those crystal earrings dance reassuringly on her neck.

The sound set was too dark to see the audience, white or Black; the lights, so bright, left no room for shadows. And then Ed Sullivan's tall, beaky face was smiling at her. He met her at the curtain, reached out and clasped her hands with both of his, echoing the gesture that Ella had made to the cleaning woman moments before. She was more conscious of his hands than what he was saying, and she could never remember afterward how she responded, how she made the audience laugh, how they roared with approval.

And then she stepped forward, even farther into the light.

Ed Sullivan led her to the center of the stage, and released her hand.

Microphone at her lips, Ella Fitzgerald began, again, to sing.

Author's Note

I've always been fascinated by Ella Fitzgerald. She actually resembled my mother; when I saw her in the movies, singing "A Tisket a Tasket" to the passengers on a bus, for a moment I thought it was my young mom beaming up there on the screen. My mother had once wanted to sing and dance for World War II troops, but my grandfather didn't want her joining the USO. She passed her love of music on to me.

Ella had an approachability, a warmth that I immediately connected with, but growing up in Milwaukee, Wisconsin—which many people still consider to be the worst city in America for Black people—I thought that my life was nothing like hers. "Ella" is the first two syllables of the word "elegance"—of course the First Lady of Jazz wore pearls and evening gowns, scatted with Frank Sinatra and Louis Armstrong. She breathed different air from mine, in Milwaukee.

Besides, although I loved music, having a career in it felt impossible. I was a Black kid lost in the Midwest, the daughter of a nurse and a postal supervisor. Listening to Ella sing "Dream a Little Dream of Me" did nothing to help me achieve my own dreams. My father in particular was a naysayer. Whenever he caught me singing, he'd say sarcastically, "You don't want to sing. You just want to be in the lime-light."

But I didn't crave the limelight: I craved the way I felt when I was singing. I thought the most fabulous thing to do was to dress up, stand in front of an audience, lean into the microphone, and sing: the microphone amplifying the emotion in my voice. Singing took me out of Milwaukee into a universe crusted with diamonds and talent. Into a universe where people like Ella Fitzgerald lived.

So, when I first learned Ella Fitzgerald's origin story, it both shook and inspired me. I understood viscerally where she came from. She was, after all, like me: another Black child, wanting to perform, want-ing to pursue her dreams, confronted with a world that said that we shouldn't have dreams like this—that it was impossible for us to do what we loved most.

It wasn't just me fighting to sing, to do what I loved. It was also a fight to be who I wanted to be. My parents fought racism just to hold down their jobs. In 1963 I was on the freedom bus from Milwaukee to Washington, DC, for Dr. Martin Luther King's Poor People's March. On television, I watched the fates of Martin Luther King, Medgar Evers, and Malcolm X. Their fates showed me what happened when people speak out against being relegated to a downtrodden life. In America, being Black meant being less-than. Being Black meant you were in danger if you had the temerity to reach for more.

But sometimes—not always, but sometimes—true talent like Ella's can transcend racism. Can transcend the hopelessness and mistrust that can explode between people who look or speak differently. Ella's rise to fame was a spectacular long shot—and yet, more and more I realized that her story was familiar to me in the way it's familiar to all Black performers. Ralph Cooper, the emcee who discovered Ella at the Apollo's Amateur Night, said it best in his memoir: "Black artists, in the pursuit of their profession, unlike their white counterparts, were subjected to insults, deprivation, and unbelievable hardship. Their only companion, support, and confidant was their passionate dedication to their respective talents."

I hope this novel reveals, in some small way, the kind of "passionate dedication" that it takes to create an Ella Fitzgerald. She's gone now, so we can't know what it's like to be her—to know how she felt, what she really wanted, what it was like to overcome the incredible obstacles in her path. But we can imagine. We can show that achieving our dreams is not only possible but necessary. Our dreams are critical to our existence.

When I was nineteen, I walked off a New York City street, pulled my hair up into a chignon, donned a black-and-silver evening gown, and marched out onto the stage of Gil Noble's *Like It Is.* I took a deep breath, stared out at the audience, and sang, a cappella, Ella Fitzgerald's "Watch What Happens." I won the contest. I had no idea, then, that Ella Fitzgerald traveled a similar path, but Ella's story continues in all of us: as we all struggle, as we all strive for what we love.

Ella Fitzgerald is an inspiration to us all.

Acknowledgments

First and foremost, to the extraordinary team at Amistad and Harper-Collins, thank you. I am extremely proud to be one of your authors. To Executive Editor Patrik Bass, thank you for saying yes and for your tremendous belief in this novel. Publisher Judith Curr, thank you for your support. Francesca Walker, your diligence and attention to detail have made the publishing process a dream.

To my loving and supportive husband, Anthony Sinclair Mills, thank you.

Regina Brooks at the Serendipity Literary Agency, thank you for your years of belief in me and for your literary feedback. I'm forever grateful for your "weakness" for an author determined to write her heart out.

To all my friends and colleagues at the Harlem Writers Guild, thank you. To Rosa Guy, Grace Edwards, Ruby Dee, Ossie Davis, Louise Meriwether, Bill Banks, and Dr. Maya Angelou: thank you.

An enormous thank you to my father-in-law, Henry Sinclair Mills, who was one of the best-known numbers runners in Harlem in the 1950s, '60s, and '70s. He's passed away now, but I'm forever grateful to him for telling me how he operated—collecting numbers, handling cash, and maintaining his suave street-smart persona.

So many people have had faith in me over these years and I want to be sure to give them a shout-out. Thank you, Judy Sternlight, Malaika Adero, Terri Rossi, Deborah Kampmeier, Sylvia White, Minnette Coleman, Eartha Watts-Hicks, Marc Polite, Judy Andrews, Angela Dews, Jade Soares, The Artist Anubis, Kendall Glaspie, Andrea Broadwater, Gre Keltner, Betty Anne Jackson, Dr. Hasna Muhammad, John Robinson, Dr. Robert Woodbine, Laverne Kennedy, Cynthia Kitt, Yvette Taylor, Jacqui Murray, Sheila Doyle, Sandra Richardson, Jason Greer, Billy Richardson, Darcia Brown, Wanda Booker, Gary Gutman, Patti Skigen, Maureen Brown, Michael Dinwiddie, Naeemah Leonard, Glendora Toliver, Cora Toliver, Victor Toliver, Aaron Toliver, Wayne Toliver, Butch Barbella, Chazz Palminteri, Michael Weeden, Debra Belton, Andrea Parks, Jeff Feig, Michelle Feig, Ray Mcguire, Andrew Grosso, Anu Jayanti, Tom Fitzpatrick, Pradeep Kashyap, Gary Vincent, Toni Seawright, and Lonnette McKee.

And to the Harlem and New York City institutions that preserve memory and celebrate Black culture, you are a treasure and a blessing. None of us who enter your doors and learn in your halls can have adequate words to thank you enough for all that you do. To the Schomburg Center for Research in Black Culture (most especially to Director Joy Bivins, to Novella Ford, and to Khalilah Bates); to the Center for Black Literature (Executive Director Dr. Brenda Greene); to the City College of New York-CUNY (Dr. Vanessa K. Valdes); to the Apollo Theater (Director Michelle Ebanks, and Billy Mitchell, and Brad San Martin especially), where so many memories and careers have been made and treasured; to the New Federal Theatre (Founder/Director Woodie King Jr.); New Heritage Theatre (Executive Director Voza

Rivers); the Abyssinian Baptist Church (Reverend Dr. Calvin Butts III); the New York Society Library (Director Carolyn Waters, Sara Holliday, and Marialuisa Monda); and Dramatists Guild of America (Executive Director Ralph Sevush, and Tari Stratton): thank you all.

So many wonderful writers and researchers have written extraordinary works about Ella, and about the 1930s, that I can't possibly thank them all here. Beyond all the myriad online sites (YouTube is incredible for watching videos of the period, seeing how people danced and sang and laughed and lived!), I want to be sure to thank the following sources:

Historical Background

- Alexander, Ruth M. *The "Girl Problem": Female Sexual Delinquency in New York, 1900–1930.* Ithaca, NY: Cornell Univ. Press, 1995.

- Balliett, Whitney. *American Singers.* New York: Oxford Univ. Press, 1979.

- Cooper, Ralph, with Steve Dougherty. *Amateur Night at the Apollo: Ralph Cooper Presents Five Decades of Great Entertainment.* New York: HarperCollins, 1990.

- Cupit, Scott. Swing Dance: *Fashion, Music, Culture and Key Moves.* London: Jacqui Small, 2015.

- De Mille, Agnes. *The Book of Dance.* New York: Golden Press, 1963.

- Falzerando, Chet. *Chick Webb—Spinnin' the Webb: The Little Giant.* Anaheim, CA: Centerstream Publishing, 2014.

- Gioia, Ted. *How to Listen to Jazz*. New York: Basic Books, 2016.

- Harris, Lashawn. *Sex Workers, Psychics, and Numbers Runners: Black Women in New York City's Underground Economy*. Urbana: Univ. of Illinois Press, 2016.

- Harris, Middleton A., with Morris Levitt, Roger Furman, and Ernest Smith; foreword by Toni Morrison. *The Black Book*. New York: Random House, 1974; 2019.

- Hartley, Derek. *The Essential Guide to Tap Dance*. Marlborough, UK: Crowood Press, 2018.

- Lerner, Gerda, ed. *Black Women in White America: A Documentary History*. New York: Vintage Books, 1972.

- Lewis, David Levering. *When Harlem Was in Vogue*. New York: Knopf, 1981.

- Locke, Alain, ed. *The New Negro: An Interpretation*. New York: Albert and Charles Boni, 1925.

- Major, Clarence. *Juba to Jive: A Dictionary of African-American Slang*. New York: Penguin Books, 1994.

- Marberry, Craig, and Michael Cunningham; foreword by Gordon Parks. *Spirit of Harlem*. New York: Doubleday, 2003.

- Marshall, Paule. *Brown Girl, Brownstones*. New York: Random House, 1959.

- McKay, Claude. *Home to Harlem*. New York: Harper, 1928.

- Mellon, James, ed. *Bullwhip Days: The Slaves Remember.* New York: Weidenfeld & Nicolson, 1988.

- Meriwether, Louise. *Daddy Was a Number Runner.* Englewood Cliffs, NJ: Prentice-Hall, 1970.

- Morrison, Toni. *Jazz.* New York: Knopf, 1992.

- *New York State Training School for Girls at Hudson, N.Y.* Albany, NY: J. B. Lyon, 1904.

- Person-Kriegal, Lorraine, and Kimberly Chandler-Vaccaro. *Jazz Dance Today Essentials.* Oslo: Total Health Publications, 2014.

- Schomburg Center for Research in Black Culture; foreword by Maya Angelou. *The Black New Yorkers: The Schomburg Illustrated Chronology.* New York: Wiley, 1999.

Biographies of Ella Fitzgerald

- Mark, Geoffrey. *Ella: A Biography of the Legendary Ella Fitzgerald.* New York: Ultimate Symbol, 2018.

- Milan, Icei. *The Life of Ella Fitzgerald.* N.p.: White Star Kids, 2000.

- Nicholson, Stuart. *Ella Fitzgerald: The Complete Biography.* New York: Routledge, 2004.

- Stone, Tanya Lee. *Ella Fitzgerald: A Twentieth Century Life (Up Close).* New York: Viking, 2008.

Audiovisual, Visual, and Online Resources

- "Buying Power of $100 in 1932." in2013dollars.com. https://www.in2013dollars.com/us/inflation/1932#buying-power.

- Franklyn, Irwin, dir. *Harlem Is Heaven*. 1932; New York: https://www.youtube.com/watch?v=yrV4rmeMWYE.

- Miles, William, dir. *I Remember Harlem*. 1980; New York: https://www.youtube.com/watch?v=v14Hudwb7v8.

- "1933 Radio (Top 60 Song Playlist)." Playback.fm. https://playback.fm/year/1933.

- "Remember: The Bell Tower of Mt. Morris Park." Harlem + Bespoke, 2012. https://harlembespoke.blogspot.com/2012/04/remember-bell-tower-of-mt-morris-park.html.

- Woodhead, Leslie, dir. *Ella Fitzgerald: Just One of Those Things*. Eagle Rock Film Productions, 2019.

Finally—last but absolutely not least—the greatest thanks to Jeff Kleinman for being here every step of the way. None of this would have been possible without you, and I'm very aware of that. Thank you. You've made a huge impact in my life, and I'll always be grateful.

About the Author

Diane Richards is a singer, novelist, playwright, and producer, and she serves as the executive director of the Harlem Writers Guild.

From an early age, she's had twin loves: singing and writing. She's followed both of these passions all of her life. Born in Milwaukee, she was sixteen when she won Dr. Bop's Fox Singing Contest, the biggest Black Urban DJ's contest in Milwaukee. She worked at radio stations in Milwaukee and Chicago, and then moved to New York. There she sang everywhere—from the street to cabarets to Carnegie Hall. She studied with Howlett Smith, the legendary Broadway music director, and also had the privilege of singing backup for Whitney Houston.

In 2015, she was appointed executive director of the Harlem Writers Guild, the oldest, most prestigious African American Writers Guild in the world (founded in 1950). It launched and supported Dr. Maya Angelou's writing career, among many others. Other early and founding members include John Oliver Killens, Dr. John

Henrik Clarke, Rosa Guy, Terry McMillan, Ossie Davis, Ruby Dee, and Grace Edwards.

She lives in Harlem with her husband, Anthony Mills, a few blocks from the Apollo Theater, which launched Ella's career, and not too far from Ella Fitzgerald's Boulevard of Dreams.